The ELEMENTS of HITTING

The ELEMENTS
A NOVEL BY
MATTHEW F. JONES
of HITTING

HYPERION

NEW YORK

LIBRARY OF CONGRESS CATALOGING-IN-PUBLICATION DATA
Jones, Matthew F.
The elements of hitting / by Matthew F. Jones.—1st ed.
p.   cm.
ISBN 0-7868-6025-1
1. Fathers and sons—United States—Fiction.   2. Baseball players—
United States—Fiction.   3. Men—United States—Fiction.
I. Title.
PS3560.O52244E44   1994
813'.54—dc20

93-33658
CIP

DESIGNED BY HOLLY MCNEELY

FIRST EDITION

10   9   8   7   6   5   4   3   2   1

For Karen and Reuben

"It's what you learn
after you know it all
that counts."
—*Earl Weaver*

The ELEMENTS of HITTING

PROLOGUE

May 24, 1962

MISSING WOMAN'S BODY
PULLED FROM LAKE

By Herbert Lauper, *Staff Reporter*

A 38-year-old Caulfield woman who had been missing for three days has been found dead in a secluded inlet of Lake Owasco, police said.

Bing County coroner Wendell Ulrich said Susan Innis, of 92 Gardner Street, died of asphyxiation by drowning and had been dead a minimum of 48 hours when her body was recovered by two fishermen around 8 A.M. Friday.

The victim was last seen by her family at her home on the morning of May 21, shortly before she left for her job as a maid and housekeeper at the lakefront estate of nationally known philanthropist, entrepreneur, and movie producer Henry Truxton III.

County sheriff Carl Mabry said his office is handling the investigation and that foul play is not suspected.

Susan Olin Innis, born in Boston, is survived by her husband, Victor "Vic" Innis, well-known to high school baseball fans in the area for his pitching prominence in the early 1940s; a daughter, Kate; and a son, Walter. Her complete obituary will appear in Tuesday's edition of the Caulfield *Banner*.

Walter laid the twenty-two-year-old article on the kitchen table, next to the one about Henry Truxton III he had clipped earlier that week at the nursing home. He pictured the clothes his mother had been wearing on the day she disappeared—wrap-around print skirt, cream-colored blouse, bra and panties, lying in a dry, neat pile in the dory's bow.

He picked up the glass at his elbow and drank some water. In the living room, the television droned. A British narrator was touring a celebrity's house. Walter set the glass back onto the table. He pictured Henry Truxton dancing in his top hat and tails. He pictured him waving to a claque of admiring voters. He pictured the ink-colored blotches now marring his father's skin. A buzz started somewhere in his genitals. Another thing, Walter told himself, besides love and money, too long absent from his life—buzzing balls. But they were buzzing tonight. Maybe if he was rich, he thought. Maybe if Henry Truxton III were made to pay.

Walter folded the two articles carefully and inserted them into his wallet. He stood up from the table and walked to the wall phone. He dialed Maurie at home. "All right if I stop by the office tomorrow, Maurie?" he asked. "I got an idea I want to throw at you."

1984

Only in retrospect does a man discover what has been significant in his life. For me, I suppose, my very beginnings were an omen. From the word go, I made things difficult. I put my best foot forward, when it should have been my head. I was upside down. I was a breech baby.

Attempting to come into the world ass first, I am sure, made things quite painful for my mother. The delivery, I am told, was difficult, my mother's initial glimpse of me, traumatic. She feared I was defective— my face barren of all features, save for a gaping fissure that she mistook for a mouth.

The arrival was no picnic for me either. The doctor's forceps crumpled my buttocks. My head, when it arrived, was a deep shade of purple. It was only by virtue of my tender age that I have been spared more painful memories of the experience.

Nonetheless, its specter lingers in some dusty receptacle of my mind, I am certain. What else could cause me to have such dreams as I do? I awaken some mornings, even after all of these years, with my head at the foot of the bed, buried beneath the covers, my ass absorbing the light at the top, as if something there had caused me to turn tail and run.

My conscious memories start sometime later. They begin and end in the city of Caulfield, a city besieged by water—a lake, actually— spreading outward from the backside of town like a trail of blue exhaust. Trees line the perimeter of the lake and farther back, green rolling hills. From a photograph Caulfield beckons; it appears exquisite, delectable— a tart that awaits eating. One has to live within it before understanding the miracles that a photographer can achieve through the use of angles and timing.

Small for a city, Caulfield was just large enough to escape the designation of township. Its residents were hardworking folk, making livings for the most part off the tourist trade or in one of the pulp mills or creameries. When I was growing up, there were perhaps fifty thousand people within the city proper, of which my family comprised four—my parents, my sister, and myself.

My father was a salesman. He traveled throughout the tri-counties, selling a large variety of paper products. He sold mostly to restaurants, schools, and business supply stores. In addition, he had a couple of regular customers in the hotel business. For over twenty years he kept the same route. At dinner he would speak to us of the people he had encountered on his travels—people we had never met but had come to know through his monologues.

Jacques Bousquet, for example, owned a hotel on Owasco Lake. He was a Frenchman who purchased from my father two hundred rolls of lavender-pink toilet paper for his guests each month. Never white, or yellow, or blue. Always lavender pink. "Ze shade is so deef-er-ont," he told my father, "ze guests are cer-tan to re-mem-baire my 'otel above all others." Of course in the telling my father would add guttural embellishments, sweeping gestures of his arms, phlegm-spraying enunciations.

Another of his favorite characters was Ben Hooks. Ben was a lanky fellow with a walrus mustache and bright orange hair. He managed a restaurant in the town of Bruno, buying napkins, placemats, matchbooks, and toilet paper from my father. Ben was an amorous sort—a man, according to my father, who got more ass than a toilet seat. "Seems as if half the kids in Bruno are carrot tops," joked the Old Man. Each week a different waitress acted as Ben's purchasing agent, receiving the goods from my father and placing the following week's order. She was the favorite between the proprietor's sheets. Among the restaurant's clientele, a weekly pool was kept; odds were assessed and money placed on the name of the girl believed most likely to be the next to greet my father with an accounting sheet.

Perhaps I give this narrating aspect of my father's character more credit than it deserves. I don't wish to portray him as a dinnertime hero. The stories were not that frequent, the characters not overly diverse. Perhaps I recall the tales more fondly as a result of their infrequency. They were occasional treats, served up with a lavish dinner, garnished with laughter and speckled throughout with an abundance of warmth. Overall, my memories of the supper table—as well as those of my father himself—are somewhat more turbid.

Walter stayed in bed until he heard Marsha turn the stereo off. On weekends, he hated to rise before his wife had finished exercising. The soft sounds of Bach and Marsha's barely audible grunts were oddly reassuring. He imagined that through the tortured sounds of her exertions, she was demonstrating her wish to keep the lines of communication open between them.

Walter strained to interpret his wife's garbled messages as they floated up the stairway. Her grunts were somehow less guarded than her words. Walter often thought that had he and Marsha been aquatic animals—dolphins, perhaps, with their conversations nothing more than infrequent squeaks—their marriage would have been far more successful. Crunch time for him and Marsha had always been when one of them found it necessary to resort to words for anything beyond idle chatter.

The sound of the television news replaced the music of Bach. From the dour tones of the announcer's voice, his message was a grave one. Even on a weekend, bad news did not take a break.

Walter preferred to concentrate on the sounds soon coming from the kitchen—pots and pans gently clashing together, glasses tinkling. Despite whatever else had been lost, these were the sounds that had remained constant in their lives. Walter knew that when the day came that he could no longer discern these noises, he would be alone, he and Marsha total strangers.

Possibly there were no dirty dishes. She may simply have been washing clean ones over again. Dirt was not the point. Marsha had a need to remain occupied. She would search diligently for a task and, once found, engage herself in it wholeheartedly.

Painting their house, for example, had been Marsha's idea. The decision was arrived at soon after they were married, despite their agreeing just prior to the wedding when together they had picked the house out that one thing it did not need was a new coat of paint.

"I want us to start fresh," she had said.

So the red burgundy with gray trim that had been on the house less than three years was scraped off. A coat of primer was put on, followed by two layers of white enamel, all at a cost of eighteen hundred dollars. They were awash in white. The house shone like a great loaf of bleached bread amongst a neighborhood of rye.

It was simply a beginning. Marsha became possessed with a desire to paint things. She painted the fence surrounding their house—again, white; she painted the garage and the back porch with the same shade. Then she moved inside and started on the interior.

The hardwood floors were sanded and revarnished; the walls in the living room were painted a dusty blue, which, in combination with the light from the overhead chandelier and the freshly varnished floors, gave the room the appearance of a vast sun-drenched beach. The bathroom was next—pink, which, according to scientific research published in the *Ladies' Home Journal,* would lend to the room a soothing touch of effervescence. Marsha had even painted Walter, inadvertently of course. While attempting to reach the peak of an unpainted hall closet, Walter had moved his head directly into his wife's line of fire, emerging seconds later with a streak of white from the top of his head to the center of his heart.

Thus they had started their marriage eight years before in a freshly painted state—literally in Walter's case—and twenty-five hundred dollars in debt.

The money had not mattered at the time. There was to be plenty of that where they were headed. They were on their way up. Great plans were in the offing.

Marsha had informed Walter of these plans on their wedding night, while gazing upward at him from somewhere in the middle of their heart-shaped bed. Her eyes appeared large and cowlike; her lips gigantic and lush. About her whispered words was a booziness—a sloppy rolling of the tongue that imbued her message with a long-remembered quality, as if it were being delivered in the midst of a one-night rendezvous on the isle of Crete.

At that moment in their lives, she had informed him, they were like two young saplings in an expanding field of fruit trees. The world was their orchard. She said this with a straight face. In Walter's inebriated state, her breasts became a pair of luscious grapefruit, her ass an overripe melon.

One day, she continued almost without pause, the orchard would be theirs. There was but one road to this nirvana. Up. Always up, like disciples bearing baskets of fish to place at their savior's feet. They would not swerve from this road. They would not delay in pursuing its end. They certainly would not become waylaid in midjourney.

Walter had felt certain that Marsha would laugh at story's end, or at least smile wryly. She had done neither. His heart had fluttered. His erection had crumbled. He had closed his eyes, seeing in front of him then endless acres of dead and decaying fruit.

Sighing, Walter pulled back the covers of the bed, stood up, walked into the bathroom, and urinated.

My mother was ten years younger than my father. She was very pretty, everyone said. Her beauty was not the classic variety—that is, she was not tall and stately. Hers was a brooding, distant appeal that men found intriguing but also were frequently intimidated by. She was the sort of woman, I later came to understand, whom men might picture in their minds while blindly and obediently thrusting into their wives or pillows.

She was born and raised in Boston. She was nineteen years old before she ever set foot in Caulfield. A friend from high school who had married and settled in the town invited her up for a weekend. The following summer she quit her job as a legal receptionist and moved to Caulfield for the season. She had simply wanted a change, she told me later. In Boston she had felt a vague emptiness, a gnawing desire to see herself defined in someplace other than her hometown. That my father was a resident of Caulfield, she said, had no bearing on her decision to move.

"Malarky," claimed my father. "She maybe won't admit it, Walt—who knows, maybe she herself doesn't actually remember it—but you can bet your last dollar that your dear old mom spotted yours truly that first weekend. After that, well—it was just a matter of time 'fore she come up for good."

Although I'm not convinced that she ever bought into any particular dogma or cared much for the Scriptures in general, she was, in a certain way, religious. That is, religion held a place in her life. She was interested in historic figures—martyrs and heroes like the Virgin Mary and Jesus— and how they were perceived in their own time. She spoke to my sister and me of Jesus as if he were an interesting fellow who, many years before, had brought about some very significant changes. Some people, she said, claimed that he was the Son of God—others, only that he was a worldly saint. She didn't attempt to sway us in any particular direction. I seldom saw her pray. She always wore a gold cross about her neck as if she had been born with it.

For a time she took to brushing her long dark hair into a bun, covering it then with a plain-colored shawl like that which the Virgin Mary is often pictured as wearing. A large painting of Mary sat on our mantel, another hung from my parents' bedroom wall. When I was very young, I once came into their room and found my mother staring intently at the picture. "Mothers, Walter"—she sighed—"have never had an easy time of it."

My sister has since told me that she always thought of my mother as a serious woman. Humorless, she called her, lacking in mirth. "If her life was so miserable, for God's sake," she asked me, "then why in hell didn't she just pack up and leave?" What Kate didn't understand was that she had already left. She had left Boston to move to Caulfield.

Nor do I agree that she was without humor. It's true that I did not often hear her laugh. Her humor, unlike the Old Man's, was not there for the world to see, but it was there nonetheless. A subtle, secretive mirth that she attempted to contain. On occasion I would see it flickering at the corners of her mouth or catch sight of it struggling to escape through suddenly widened eyes. But I had to watch closely; I had to be attentive, or it would pass without notice.

CHAPTER 4

Breakfast was toast and eggs—runny, almost cold inside. Despite prefer-ring his eggs cooked hard, Walter said nothing. They had, once again, gone to sleep in roily silence the night before. Words, he knew, were what she was waiting for. Not just any words, but harsh or accusatory words. Words that could serve as opening jabs for her returning salvo. He smiled benignly across the table.

"You really must visit your father today," she said. "It's been almost a week."

"He doesn't even know when I'm there."

"He knows."

"He doesn't care whether I go or not."

"He cares."

"How do you know?"

"He's dying."

"Are you coming with me?"

"I'm going to Boston."

"What? When?"

"Today."

"What for?"

"To decide whether or not I still love you."

She stood up from the table, still dressed in her leotard. Turning away from Walter, toward the sink, she resembled a large cat. Her skin glistened. Her limbs moved in oily litheness. When, he wondered, had his wife developed such grace?

"To decide whether or not I want a divorce."

She disappeared, a large black shadow, through the doorway. The moment she was gone, Walter remembered her as being beautiful.

My mother found employment that first summer as a waitress. The restaurant where she worked was one of my father's regular customers. In consideration of a discount, the owner would provide the Old Man with a free lunch whenever he stopped in to make his deliveries. My father always ordered the same thing—linguini with clam sauce. For three-quarters of the summer, my mother brought him the dish, smiling without comment, ringing up NO CHARGE on the register, until, sometime around the middle of August, her curiosity had finally gotten the better of her.

"Isn't there something you would like," she had inquired, "besides linguini and clam sauce?"

"Of course," replied the Old Man.

"Then why," insisted my mother, "do you always order the same thing?"

"Because," said my father, smiling through a mouthful of pasta, "I knew that someday you would ask."

Through such persistence, according to the Old Man, he eventually wore my mother down. In the fall, she gave up her apartment in Boston and became a full-time resident of Caulfield. She married my father a year later, on her twentieth birthday.

At first, she had had many dreams for herself. In Boston, she had attended Katy Gibbs, dropping out six credits short of a degree in Secretarial Science in order to move to Caulfield. After marrying my father, she talked of enrolling in the local university, hoping to earn enough credits to eventually attend law school. Before the start of the next semester, she discovered that she was pregnant and abandoned forever her hopes of further education.

After giving birth to my sister, she opened a travel agency, a one-person operation that she attempted to run out of one corner of the living room. Six months after opening, it closed for lack of business.

Later she thought of starting her own advertising firm, but no one in Caulfield did much advertising other than in the local paper. She spoke of opportunities elsewhere. My father would laugh and say that Caulfield was his home.

There was a short period of time when she wished to become a novelist, arriving home one afternoon with several legal pads and a plethora of pens. Evenings, after the dishes had been cleared, she would sit at the dinner table, scribbling furiously upon the pads, quietly mouthing imagined dialogue. The novel, she said, would be a contemporary version of *The Frog Prince*. Several weeks after its onset, she suddenly abandoned the idea. While the rest of the family watched in silence, my mother tore up all that she had written, shredding each page into confetti sized bits of paper. "Of all the frogs I know," she told us, "none is capable of becoming a prince."

Eventually she took a job as a maid and housekeeper at a resort home on the lake. There were several of these homes, reclusive hideaways for the rich. They sat back from the water, hidden among the trees like great predators. From the public beach in town, the most exclusive of them could not be seen.

The one my mother worked at had been built in the early part of the century by Henry Truxton, a downstate millionaire whose fortune reportedly derived from the coal and steel industries. When he died, the place went to his son, Henry Truxton II, who was referred to in the local press as a business entrepreneur—the business, apparently, being to oversee the management of his father's millions. When Henry II passed away, his son, Henry Truxton III, my mother's employer, inherited the estate. Like his father, Henry Truxton III was referred to in the press as an entrepreneur. He was called other things as well, depending on the publications—humanitarian, socialist, hedonist, Marxist, international playboy, or various combinations of the above. Speculating about Henry Truxton III's various endeavors was one of Caulfield's favorite pastimes.

My mother worked at the estate, she said, because she enjoyed being on the water. It was peaceful. Most times no one was there to bother her. During the week she went out for a couple of hours each morning just to make sure that everything was in order and to feed the six dogs that Truxton kept on the place.

The Truxtons normally frequented the estate only on weekends. Sometimes just Henry and his wife would come or maybe Henry and a friend or perhaps just Henry by himself. My mother would go out in the late afternoon on Saturdays and Sundays to prepare the evening meal and to do whatever cleaning needed to be done. On other occasions the entire family might show up unannounced, bringing with them a wide assortment of guests. At such times, my mother was responsible for helping with the lavish parties that would ensue or with any other special events that the family might have planned.

In its gossip section, the Caulfield *Banner* would frequently print lists of those celebrities who had reportedly attended a Truxton bash. When asked by my sister or me to comment on the reports, my mother might confirm or deny what had been written, but would offer little by way of embellishment. As an employee, she explained, she had a duty not to divulge details of her employer's private affairs.

My father did not approve of my mother working. He especially did not approve of her working for Henry Truxton. It was a subject about which they often argued. "We need the extra income," my mother would say. "The kids need their mother at home," the Old Man would reply. My mother might accuse him then of being jealous or of trying to prevent her from having any life of her own. If she couldn't get out of the house for a few hours, my mother complained, she would go crazy. My father said it looked bad—his wife spending so much time away from her family, arriving home at all hours of the night. If the Old Man had been drinking, it might get worse.

Later in the morning, Marsha had removed her leotard and replaced it with a housecoat. It was actually a white robe, sprinkled with yellow flowers. Its hem rested just above Marsha's knees. She sat at the makeup table, facing the mirror, doing something with her eyes. The robe appeared old and somewhat tattered. Walter had seen her in it hundreds of times in the past. For the first time, he noticed that the flowers were not actually flowers but goldenrod, a sightly variety of weed. He found himself attempting to gaze up beneath her hem.

"My flight leaves at one," she said. "There's enough food in the house for three days; after that you will have to go shopping."

"Will that be necessary?"

"Only if you object to eating in restaurants."

"I meant," he said, finding his eyes drifting once again toward the hem of her housecoat, "will you be gone more than three days?"

"Would it matter to you if I was gone three years?"

"Of course."

She dabbed more determinedly at her eyes, her breasts bouncing jauntily beneath the housecoat. "I am talking, Walter, about a period of assessment."

"Assessment? Assessment of what?"

"Of us." She turned slightly in her chair, the robe coming apart at the top, one breast popping free from beneath the fabric. "Of whether or not there is a point to any of this."

"A point to any of what?" His eyes were on the point of her liberated breast. Its nipple, hard and erect, stood proud as a church steeple.

"For God's sake, Walter! Quit asking questions as if you are some adolescent schoolboy! This can't be that big of a surprise to you. We've been drifting apart for months . . . years, actually." In the midst of her gyrations, the opposite breast unearthed itself, appearing like a bird suddenly flushed from cover.

Why, wondered Walter, were so many things suddenly revealing themselves to him? His wife's left nipple, for example, when erect was slightly larger than the right one. It angled off haphazardly to one side, swaggering like a teen idol, pointing at Marsha's image in the mirror. At its center, he saw, the breast was actually a shade of brown and not the dark red he had always imagined. Why, now that she was finally leaving, was he seeing these things for the first time?

"Is it because you want a kid, Marsha? Is that it?"

"No, Walter. At one time I wanted a child more than anything. Now I only thank God that it never happened."

"I never told you to quit your job, Marsha. You have a college education, but decide you don't want to work and now you wonder why you're bored staying home all day long."

"I'm not bored—at least, not bored with staying home."

"I'm a car salesman, Marsha! I don't know how to do anything else, for Christ sake!"

"You don't love me, Walter. I don't want to live with a man who doesn't love me."

"Oh, Jesus. . . ."

"You reached some point, Walter—I don't know when it was, maybe way back when you were seventeen or eighteen—and you just stopped progressing. You don't want to get a real job, you don't want to have kids of your own. . . ."

"How much would I have to make a year, Marsha? How much! Before I would love you?"

"Is there anything that you do take seriously, Walter? Anything at all that you could commit yourself to?"

"Of course. . . ."

"Name it! Name one thing, Walter, that you consider worthy enough for your precious time and loyalty! One goddamn thing that isn't just another joke!"

"I don't know . . . something. . . ."

"Well, I know it's not me, Walter! And I know it's not your career or your family, which you never bothered to start!"

"Well, it sure as hell isn't playing the Calvin Chevrolet Cowboy, Marsha, on a goddamn white horse that shits whenever and wherever it feels like it, I'll tell you that!"

"I didn't ask you to tell me what it isn't, Walter. I asked you to tell me what it is!"

"Nothing, okay? There isn't one thing I take seriously! Are you happy?"

"I know it's upset you, seeing your father again. . . ."

"My old man's got nothing to do with it!"

"Fine. I'll stop guessing then. I thought you had a problem, Walter, but maybe I'm giving you too much credit. Maybe it's just you."

"All right, Marsha, you want a kid? We'll have a kid. . . ."

She was really quite beautiful. Walter was charged with emotion. His cock blew up like a carnival balloon. He stepped toward her, separating his own robe as he went. From behind, he clasped his hands upon her breasts. His prick, now free of the housecoat, collided with the back of her head.

"Walter! Have you heard one word that I have said?"

"Yes. Yes," he replied. "I heard every word." His hands wandered purposefully down, into the hidden portions of her robe.

"Then you are very confused. Or very sick," she said, pushing his hands away, getting up from the chair. Her robe was now totally open—everything exposed to Walter. It was all there in front of him and would soon be gone. He had never wanted her so badly.

"Just let me look," he pleaded.

"I think you need help, Walter."

"Yes! Yes!" he said, reaching for her hand, guiding it toward him. "Help me! Please?"

Pulling her hand back, she tied her robe and walked hurriedly by him toward the bathroom. Backing up, Walter's knees collided with the bed. He fell on his back into the sheets. The bathroom door slammed shut. He took his prick into his hand and yanked at it savagely, thinking longingly of his wife.

Walking into places, you could see him looking around sometimes, noticing who was giving my mother the once-over. If he spotted someone taking a good look, you could never tell how he might react. It had a desultory effect on him. One time he might smile and give her a pat on the ass, as if he were proud of her—like she was some kind of show dog, best in her class or some goddamn thing. Then he had this other side—a dark, stinking underbelly.

Sometimes you could almost see him wrestling with it—his mouth twisted into a weird wire-like shape, the vein in his neck, just below his right ear, all purple and ready to explode. And sometimes he would win. The thing would go away and he would be all right again. But sooner or later it would come back. And then it would get him—a white, hot flame as if he'd been goosed by the devil.

The first time I remember it happening, I was six years old. Some guy supposedly made googly eyes at my mother in Hurley's Bar and Grill. We were all there for supper on a Saturday—my parents, Kate, and me. A big night out, right? Everybody's dressed up. We're halfway through the meal, when the Old Man suddenly jumps up from his chair, dropping half of a hamburger into his lap. "You son of a bitch!" he yells out, pointing at this guy sitting two tables over who, as far as I can tell, is minding his own business, eating dinner with his own wife. Then he grabs hold of my mother's arm, drags her out of her chair, dishes and food landing everywhere. "I'm taking you home," he yells. "You're not going to make a fool of me in front of my own kids!"

He hauls her out of the place, crashing into tables as they go. Kate and I are alone at the table. We don't dare look around the restaurant. We don't dare look at each other. We want to crawl under the table, except the floor is covered with our dinner.

Finally Bill Hurley comes over and takes us into the kitchen. He sits us down at a little table, so that we can see the food being cooked and all. He brings us two fresh dinners—steak instead of hamburger. "On the house," he says. "When you're done, I'll give ya a ride home."

I didn't feel much like eating. I felt full. Fuller than I'd ever been, as if I would explode were I to eat another thing. But Kate, she was hungry enough. She ate her steak and half of mine. She starts smiling at one of the busboys, tells him he's kind of cute. She's twelve years old, I hear her say, though she's only eight. After a while, Bill takes us home.

Kate sits up front. She listens to the radio and talks to Bill. She wants to be a chef someday, she tells him. I sit in the backseat, hunched up close to the window. The headlights from approaching cars turn to shadowy monsters as they whiz by. The car is huge, cavernous. I don't say anything.

Bill stops the car in front of the house, puts it in park, leaves the engine running. "Your daddy's just blowing off steam," he says. "Don't worry none. He'll get over it." He pinches Kate's cheek, opens the door. She jumps out.

"Thanks, Mr. Hurley," she says.

I sit there, next to the door. The engine rumbles beneath me. The cold air blows through the front seat and hits me in the face. I don't want to get out of the car.

"Whatcha do? Fall asleep, boy? We're home," says Bill. He says it kindly, but he doesn't understand. I feel embarrassed, open the door, step out. "Thanks," I mumble. I see Kate walking down the sidewalk, away from the house. Hurley guns the engine. The car roars off down the street. I'm alone in front of my house.

Half a block away, Kate has stopped on the sidewalk. She's gazing back toward me. "Come on," she yells up the street. "They forgot all about us. I know a place where we can stay."

I look back at the house. It seems quiet enough. A light shines in the kitchen and one upstairs. Now, suddenly, I'm hungry. I wish I had eaten the steak. "I'm scared he might hurt Mommy," I say to Kate.

She has walked back up the sidewalk, and stood in front of me. She is taller than me, prettier, sharper features, better equipped for everything. "If he hurts her," she tells me, "then she's got it coming."

"No she don't," I say. "Why does she?"

"She tries to make him jealous. She's always flirtin' with other men."

"How do you know?"

"Daddy told me so." She smiled and pushed the hair from her eyes, appearing suddenly much older. "And I watch her."

"Where you gonna go?"

"Debbie Bristle's house."

"Well, I ain't going. I'm gonna go inside."

She shrugs her shoulders, starts to walk away. Over her shoulder, she says, "You'll wish you hadn't."

At the doorway, I hesitate, listen closely for telltale signs. There are none. I push open the door and walk inside. My father is sitting in the living room, drinking a beer, staring at the television set. He is watching the Three Stooges. Mo makes his fingers into a fork, pokes Curly in the eyes with them. Curly squeals and rubs his eyes. Mo pokes him again. Curly squeals and rubs again. Mo bops him on top of the head. My father laughs. I try to walk by him without being noticed.

He sees me, turns from the set, places his beer on the end table. "How'd ya get home?" He slurs his words. He is drunk.

"Mr. Hurley," I say.

"Bill's a good man," he says. "He knows what's what. Where's your sister?"

"She went to Debbie Bristle's house."

"Good. Good. That's good." He looks like he wants to say more, but his face gets all screwed up instead. He reaches for the beer, sloshes some on the table, puts the can to his lips. He turns back to the television set.

"Your mother left," he says. "She'll be back."

I run up the stairs, into my parents' bedroom. It's empty, sheets torn from the bed, clothing scattered everywhere. I check the rest of the rooms. She isn't there either. The Old Man was right. She's gone. In the bathroom, brushing my teeth for bed, I find drops of blood on the porcelain sink. In the wastebasket there are several wadded-up Kleenex—red, gruesome, all that remain of my mother.

While Marsha was still harbored in the bathroom, Walter dressed and made his way down to the kitchen. He scribbled a quick note and taped it to the refrigerator. "Went to visit my father. Enjoy your trip to B-Town. I anxiously await the results of your assessment."

Reading it back, he thought it sounded casual—good. And flip—not good. Well, it would have to do. She would, Walter hoped, consider the effects of a bruised ego.

He decided to walk the twelve blocks to the nursing home—partly because it was a beautiful day and partly because he was in no particular hurry to see his father. It was not, after all, as if he had an appointment to see him. After twenty years of not seeing him at all, a few minutes' delay in Walter's appearance at the Old Man's deathbed should not matter to either one of them.

It was early June. The sun was shining. Walter did not have to sell cars for two whole days and maybe, the way things were looking, ever again. For once, he did not have to hide from the weekend, shivering at the thought of Monday waiting at its end like a leering proctologist.

He turned his face upward, toward the sun, and smiled wryly. I will walk until I am hungry, he thought, and eat until I am full. Come Monday, I will sleep until my own thoughts wake me.

The path to his early retirement had been paved two days before. Appearing late as usual at the lot, rumpled and without benefit of caffeine, Walter had been met there by Old Buff and Puff Calvin himself. "There's plenty of young go-getters out there, Walter," Buff and Puff had told him, "who'd just love ta have a chance ta make a commission off a some of these inventories you're just setting on."

The inventories referred to were mostly seven- and eight-year-old junkers taken in on trade. Anyone who could manage to sell them and make a decent commission as well had a future as an illusionist. When the cars came in they were terminal—rust appearing like malignant lesions, gear boxes so seized up it would take an arm wrestler to move 'em—and still Calvin always gave them something. "Drive it into the garage and buff it, then put her out on the lot and puff it. She'll sell."

Ever since Buff and Puff had taken over from Calvin Senior almost two years before and moved Walter out to the lot, it was Walter who had been asked to perform the magic. He was the one who had to move the used inventory. It was he who had to pretend that the dead were healthy and then, after making a sale, pray to God that the clunkers at least made it out of the lot before breaking down.

Before Calvin Senior had retired, Walter had been in the showroom, selling the new cars. It hadn't been so bad then. Even if he did occasionally gouge someone on the price, they at least had the warranty and, hell, it wasn't the dealer's fault if something went wrong with a car fresh from the factory. "It just goes to show you, even the boys in Detroit mess up now and again. Tell ya what. I'll write 'em a letter myself, see if we can't get 'em to make it right for ya."

The used ones, Walter found out, were a whole different ball game. Something went wrong with one of them after thirty days and it was buyer beware. There was nobody in Detroit to point the finger at then. Only the salesman's nuts were in a sling—the same guy who, just a couple of weeks before, has promised that a car whose rear end has just fallen out will "run like a top. Just like new. If my manager wouldn't likely fire me for it, I'd give ya a year's warranty in writing. Tell you what, though, something goes wrong with her, you come see me."

Calvin Junior had tried to make the move sound like a step up for Walter, even though they both knew it was as far down as one could tumble in sales. "Lot a money to be made on the lot, Walt." The Puffer had smiled. "Out there, it's what the market will bear. And by God, you're right for it. You got that vulnerable look, like you couldn't cheat your worst enemy if it would save your life."

It was an unjust world. That's what really galled a man. Walter was close to forty and the unjustness of it pissed him off as much as it had when he was young enough not to know better. The only difference was, back then—when he didn't have any reason to know better— Walter had believed that what seemed unjust one day could just as easily turn around and become just the next. Only later did he discover how naive he had been. Injustice, like a crooked nose, marred some men forever.

The Puffer was a good ten years younger than Walter. Walter remembered when the little son of a bitch was washing cars on the back lot for Calvin Senior. Walter would hand the kid a couple of bucks once in a while and send him out for a hamburger. That was ten years ago, for Christ sake, Walter's first year at the place, and even then he had told everybody who would listen that the situation was only temporary. He did not plan, he had said, to spend the rest of his life selling cars.

Two years later, when he married Marsha, he had told her the same thing. "It's just till I got enough saved to start my own business." Jesus, what a sales job that had been, especially with Marsha's old lady. "Bad enough you marry one of them"—and by that she had meant a Gentile—"but a car salesman!" She had spit the words out like a bad clam. "What would your father think?"

The thing was, Walter was serious about getting out. Every day for ten years, he had gone in to work telling himself this would be it. Today would be his last day. He would clean out his desk, tell the Puffer to fuck himself, and then clear the hell out. And then what? At that point—when he started to think about options—was when his resolve would begin to falter. There was nothing he could think of to do besides sell cars, at least nothing that he might be any good at, let alone something that he might enjoy. Alternatives were as hard to come up with as good deals on Calvin's trade-in lot.

Anyway, he'd be out. He wouldn't spend the rest of his life like the Old Man had—tied to his job like it was a part of him, as if to just up and quit would have been akin to amputation. But Jesus. Walter had to give the Old Man his due. He had not stuck with much in his life perhaps, but for thirty years he'd stuck with the same job.

Walter had always hoped that one day the answer would come to him magically—like on one of those game shows where the answers just pop up from behind a board whenever someone pushes the right button. A card would suddenly appear, and on it would be written his destiny. From that point on, he would know what to do with his life. And then he would do it.

Only he had never pushed the right button and time was running out. He was still muddling along, like a blind man through a swamp.

Christ, did it matter whether he'd been dropped in this spot yesterday or two years ago? Well, fuck it, where else would you rather be? Who knows? What else would you rather be doing? Anything.

With such logic, he had cashed the job in. He had spent one night thinking about Calvin and his young go-getters. In the morning, almost as an afterthought—as if he weren't quite sure whether to get a cup of coffee or to step into the little twerp's office—he had done it. Sorry, Calvin, he had said, but I'm all done. Just like that? No notice? No nothing! Bet your ass, just like that. Pretend I told you a week ago Monday. There's your notice. I guess you know, Walter, that you'll get nothing back from your pension? And when it comes to a recommendation, my friend, I am not the one to see. I understand, Calvin. And, by the way, that two-tone Nova—the one with sawdust for rear fenders? Stan Wallace will be in to pick it up tomorrow. He paid two hundred dollars for it, twenty of which I kept for my commission. Two hundred dollars! Jesus Christ, Walter! I gave twice that for it. I was figurin' on getting a thousand, anyway. Sorry, Calvin. It's all the market would bear.

For a couple of hours Walter had felt great, on top of the goddamn world. Hopping into his coupe—all paid for as of last month—he had rolled back the sunroof, cranked up the radio. As he pulled out of the lot, two girls—young, tight, pretty, no more than eighteen—smiled and waved. Walter nodded his head, honked the horn, felt like Clint Eastwood. He drove over to the Shamrock Diner, ordered himself up three eggs over easy, a plate of homefries, a large stack of buttermilk pancakes, and coffee. "What's doing, Walt?" asked Sandy, when she brought him his coffee. "Where you heading on such a beautiful day?"

"Not sure yet, Sandy. Maybe California." He smiled. "Wanna come?"

But the feeling had not lasted. It began to fade, slowly, along with the day. By the time the sun had set, Walter was ready to go back and try his damndest to convince Calvin that the whole thing had been a joke. Instead, he stopped in at Maurie's office. Maurie congratulated Walter for his strength of character, then did his best to console his friend. They had gotten drunk. The rest of the evening was a web of faces and details.

Later that night, Walter had tried to tell Marsha about how he no longer had a job. The magnitude of his failure had overwhelmed him. He stumbled over his words, forgot what it was that he had hoped to say. His mind wandered. His cock stiffened. He aimed valiantly for a quick resolution and then watched helplessly as even that had failed. Marsha had left the next day, without knowing of his state of unemployment.

He would simply have to face facts. He did not have a job. For the time being, he did not have a wife. He had a Chevy Coupe—paid for; a house—not entirely paid for; moderate skills in the area of sales—dearly paid for, with ten years of his life and, it seemed, little else.

CHAPTER 9

Sales was what my father went into because a person has to make a living somehow and that seemed about as good a way as any—or at least no more objectionable. He drifted into sales in the same manner that a pianist who has lost his fingers drifts into another job. Steal a man's gift and what is left to him is a series of bland choices.

Baseball was his first, and only, chosen profession. His aspiration was to play in the major leagues.

In the days of his youth, the BLIPS—or radar gun—had not yet been invented. The speed of a man's fastball could be measured only by the human eye. Those batters who faced my father say that his "heater" traveled in excess of ninety miles per hour. "And it moved," Bill Hurley once told me. "The ball would start out around your waist somewheres, and by the time you got around to swinging at it, it'd be up around your chin."

The recollections of Bill Hurley, and other of my father's contemporaries, were the only evidence I had of my father's early pitching prowess. The Old Man himself seldom spoke of those days. It was as if, along with the gift, his memory of it had died as well.

"His speed fooled people, on account of his size. Your old man, Walt, was just a wisp of a thing." Bill might smile then, appearing almost apologetic for having spoken of my father in the past tense—a habit easily slipped into by those who once knew my father but no longer really did. "Come to think of it, I guess he ain't grown all that much, has he?

"They'd see this little skinny guy out there on the mound and even if they had heard about him, it was hard for 'em not to relax. Then Victor would go into that crazy wind-up he had—all arms and legs, like one of them Raggedy Ann dolls, flopping all over the place—and then, all of a sudden there would be the ball, coming at 'em like a goddamn BB. Then it would be in the catcher's mitt and there would be your old man out on the mound, smiling like a man with two peckers."

Bill Hurley first told me about my dad when I was seven or eight years old. I think he felt obligated, as if he had to tell me because the Old Man never had. Or maybe he knew there wasn't much else about my father that seemed very special. Here's something for the kid to hang his hat on, he was probably thinking. A morsel of good to sweeten the rest of it with. Only once he started the telling, I could see it was genuine, that it meant something to Bill as well—as if the simple recounting itself possessed value for him.

After that first time, I took to stopping in over at Hurley's Bar and Grill after school every once in a while. The place was usually pretty quiet at that time of day. Bill would let me sit up at the bar, drinking a cherry Coke and rolling pennies against the molding. He would tell me stories about my father—mostly baseball stories—and he would laugh or shake his head, like one does when he can't quite figure where the time went.

Unlike most folks, Bill never made fun of my father—leastwise, if he did, he was careful not to do so in front of me. I never heard him criticize the Old Man; only occasionally did I catch him lifting his eyes toward the ceiling and mumbling, "Damn shame, what happened to your old man, Walt." For a couple of years, I got into the habit of dropping in at Hurley's once or twice a week. There I got a glimpse of the Old Man at his peak. I learned of his dreams, saw him as if he were part of an old movie. I didn't stop going, I guess, until I realized that the stories—played over and over, like slides in a revolving projector—were destined always to end at the same point.

"You can't develop an arm like that," Bill told me one afternoon. "You gotta be born with it." He smiled then and shook his head in that way of his. "Sometimes I think being born with that arm, Walt, was the worst thing ever happened to your old man."

In high school, he set all kinds of county records, some of which still stand. In one nine-inning game he struck out twenty-four of the twenty-seven batters he faced. In the state playoffs that year, he pitched back-to-back perfect games.

During the season, his name appeared in the Caulfield *Banner* at least once a week. When I was ten years old, I found the clippings and several pictures hidden away in an old trunk in the attic. The snapshots were yellow and starting to crinkle around the edges. I dared not pick them up for fear they would disintegrate. I recognized the face all right—although it was younger and much smoother. The eyes were what threw me. They sparkled under the brim of his cap, laughed outward with a cockiness that looked eternal. They were eyes I did not recognize. Those that I had come to know—the eyes of my father—laughed and even danced on occasion, but they seldom sparkled; certainly never laughed and sparkled together as did those in the yellow photograph.

He was in tenth grade when major league scouts began coming to watch him play. In his senior year he was drafted by the Cincinnati Reds. The following summer most of the town gathered to send him off, anticipating greatness—envisioning, perhaps, Caulfield's first major leaguer. A picture from the trunk shows my father sitting near the back of the train as it pulls from the station, his head protruding through the open window, his right hand waving a Reds banner at the assembled crowd. Also present was the Caulfield High marching band, which, according to a clipping, played "The Star-Spangled Banner" and "Happy Days Are Here Again."

The Old Man was assigned to play for the Reds' Class A team in Charlotte, North Carolina. After nine starts, he had a record of seven wins, two losses, eighty-six strikeouts, and an earned run average of 1.09. In the middle of the season, he was promoted to Cincinnati's Double A team in Nashville. The sports page that day declared in large black print: INNIS, RISING LIKE A ROCKET TOWARD BIG LEAGUES.

He finished the season in Nashville, winning five more games, losing only two, striking out twice as many batters as he walked. Management was elated. Vic Innis, a spokesman said, would be invited to the Reds major league spring training camp that March. He returned home a hero. WELCOME HOME, VIC read the banner. Close to the top of the stack, this clipping was almost the last addition. Above the article was a picture of my father, getting off the train, kissing an unidentified female on the cheek. "What did you miss most about Caulfield?" a reporter had asked. "Home cooking," replied the Old Man, "and Yankee women."

There were only two clippings after that. The first one declared: INNIS HURTS ARM IN FREAK ACCIDENT. Below the headline, in small print, was: "Says He'll Be Ready for Upcoming Season."

But he never was. The clippings stopped, except for one dated two years later. It was from the back pages, in the "What's Happening" section. No bold print. Just two short paragraphs telling of how Victor Innis, the former baseball phenom, his career cut short by an injury, had enlisted in the marines.

What Bill Hurley called a "damn shame" had happened one night following a get-together down by the lake. Bill was there, along with several other people from my father's high school class. They had a few beers, according to Bill, and the talk had turned to the strength in my father's arm.

"There was a sailboat docked a good hundred yards offshore," said Bill. "Snake Barnett says he reckons that not even your old man can reach it. Your old man, Walt, was never one for backin' away from a challenge, 'specially if there was something riding on it, so he says to Snake to put some money where his mouth was, and Snake says he would wager five dollars that your old man couldn't plop a stone onto the deck of that boat in three tries."

As I listened, I tried to alter their appearances, to remove the excess years and to make them all younger men: my father and Bill and Snake Barnett, whom I knew only from seeing in church each Sunday where, wedged between his family, he sweated profusely from beneath his armpits and periodically cleared his throat. The years peeled easily from Snake and Bill. Relieved of excess poundage and given a little hair, I could picture them both lounging casually upon the wooden dock, swilling beer and sounding, almost, as they sounded then. My father was more of an enigma; some intangible, a subtle shading that I couldn't quite put my finger on, wouldn't leave him.

"Vic doesn't say anything, but finds himself three nice round stones, holding one in his hand and laying the other two at his feet. It was October, kind of chilly out, but your old man takes off his coat anyhow. He winds up, no warm-up nor nothing, and lets go with the first stone. It comes up about five feet short, but, more important, Vic lets out a little yelp. Standing right next to him like I was, I hear a tiny pop, not much really, like a kernel of corn going off in grease maybe, but I know enough to know it ain't good."

Bill stopped talking for a minute to tend to a customer at the other end of the bar. When he came back, he started in wiping the bar with a cloth even though he had just cleaned it up a few minutes before. He mixed another cherry Coke, poured it into my glass, then tossed in two cubes of ice.

"Your father didn't say nothing, just shook his arm a little like maybe it had fallen asleep, but there's Snake, that bastard, with a smile as big as his asshole and his hand straight out for his five spot. Your father looks at him and I know then there's no way of changin' his mind—though I tried. I take hold of his arm and say, 'Let him have the fiver, for Christ sake, Vic,' but he shakes my arm off and turns back to Snake. 'I got me two throws left,' he says, reaching down for one of the stones he's left layin' at his feet. He winds up and lets fly and this time there's no mistaking it. There's a rip like the sound of somebody's pants goin' at the crotch. Your old man grunts and then he commences to scream— a godawful sound it is too. When I look over, his arm is just hanging there from his shoulder like a limp noodle."

Taking another sip of beer, Bill started in with the cloth again, moving it back and forth along the bar without paying attention. Wiping the foam from his mustache with the back of his hand, he gazed absently at some point toward the end of the bar. "Your old man's throw come up no more than a foot short of where the boat was anchored," he continued in a loud voice, as if here, finally, was the most important part of the story. "Two days later, wearing a cast from the top of his shoulder to the bottom of his wrist, he hands that son of a bitch Snake every penny he's got coming."

A loud *thwaack!* echoed in his ears. He heard shouts, young and patternless. Walter was momentarily confused. He looked up and saw a wall—a short, green wall that was a center field fence. Without knowing it, he had walked into the middle of a Little League ball field.

A game had apparently just ended. The players, with their parents, were standing around in bunches. Two umpires, bulky and awkward in their chest protectors, walked side by side toward the parking lot. The scoreboard read: HOME 15. VISITORS 0.

Walter strolled rapidly through the crowd, back toward the street, certain he was sticking out like a sore thumb. This was practically his own neighborhood, yet the faces he saw were those of strangers. He was, he realized, a solitary figure on his own turf—a gruff and lonely bear foraging nuts during the daytime and retiring to his den at night.

He and Marsha had lived here close to eight years, yet he knew almost no one. He knew *of* people—like Bob Sturgeon, his next door neighbor, who spent literally hours on his hands and knees, tilling a tiny fenced-in garden that had, as far as Walter could tell, never produced a single living thing; and Bob Forrester, a sixty-two-year-old draftsman who, while jogging by Walter's house each night, would wave and break wind at the same time; and the couple across the street, the Warnkes, who enjoyed having sex with the lights on and the window shades wide open. He knew of these people—and many others—but he did not really know any of them. Nor, to be honest, had he ever really wanted to. People are of interest, he once told Marsha, only until you get to know them.

"Walter? Walter Innis?"

He wheeled quickly around. There, appraising him quizzically, was a hefty woman dressed in yellow and black sweats, the words COOLEY'S MEAT MARKET emblazoned across her chest. "Excuse me?" he said.

"It is you, isn't it?"

He was not at all sure that he wanted to acknowledge that it was he. But then, realizing that to deny who he was would in effect leave him no one else to be, he decided to confess. "Yes, it's me," he said.

"Walter?"

"Yes, it's Walter."

"Walter Innis?"

"Right."

"You don't recognize me?"

He did, but he wasn't sure from where. It must have been from a while back, because the memory was somewhat vague. It seemed as if a face he had once known had discreetly changed bodies. But he did know the face. It had once been very pretty. In fact, it still was beneath a pile of auburn curls.

"I do. . . . It's—"

"Jeannie. Jeannie Weatherrup."

"Jeannie. Jesus, Jeannie, you've—"

"Put on weight?"

"That's not what I meant. I'm so ashamed for not having known you right off." That was no lie. This was a girl—woman now—whom Walter had once made love to. Or at least attempted to make love to—if "making love" was the proper term. "Put the pork to" was the expression in vogue at the time. Even that, he recalled with a shudder of embarrassment, had not worked the way it was supposed to.

"I guess I didn't expect to see you ma—" Walter ran a hand back through his hair. "You are the manager, aren't you?"

"Oh, that." She giggled and brushed the hair from her eyes. In that one gesture, his recognition became complete. He saw her then, as if the forty pounds she had gained since high school had suddenly vanished. He wondered then why he had not recognized her immediately. "I'm just filling in temporarily. Until they can find a new manager."

"What happened to the old one?"

"He died . . . suddenly."

"Oh, well. I'm sorry to hear that. I hope it wasn't the misfortunes of the team that did it."

"No. It was a car accident that did it." She flicked at the hair again. "He was my husband."

Oh, shit. Some things never change. Walter was apparently pro-grammed for embarrassment with this woman once every twenty years. "Oh, Jeannie. I am sorry. I had no idea."

"It's all right. It happened almost a year ago. Right before the last game of the season. They had the whole winter to find a replacement, but no one seemed to want the job."

"How's the team doing?"

"We were the visitors today."

"I see. Well, there's always room for improvement."

"Today was improvement. It was the closest game we've had all year."

"The season is young."

"Oh, Walter." She giggled again. "You always were an optimist."

Now, thought Walter, she is paying me back for my gaffe about her husband. Or was he being overly sensitive? Even as a girl, he remem-bered, Jeannie had not been a vindictive person. Still, he couldn't help but recall that the phrase was nearly the same one she had whispered over twenty years earlier, as Walter had so ineptly taken aim at her virginity. "I think," she had breathily intoned at the time, "that you are being the supreme optimist if you think all of that hammering is going to get you anywhere."

"You must have a son then?" he asked, hoping the boy had not died in the same car accident as his father. Were that the case, Walter considered retracting his original admission; it was not he, he would tell Jeannie, but someone else who not only looked like him but coinciden-tally had the same name as well.

"Yes. He's our third baseman—Billy. He's petrified of the ball, I'm afraid, but I haven't the heart to bench him." She smiled. Her teeth, Walter noted, were in perfect order. A sign of good health. "And you? Your son, no doubt, went four for four against us?"

"No," said Walter. "I'm afraid not."

"Three for four?"

"No. He didn't play."

"Oh?" Now it was her turn to be embarrassed. "I hope he isn't injured."

"No. There isn't one."

"No son?"

"Right."

"Oh. I'm sorry. I just thought . . ."

"No. I was just passing by. I, uh, sort of wandered onto the field."

"A wife, though?"

"What?"

"You have a wife? I mean, I imagine you're married?"

"Yes. I have a wife and I am married, but—"

"But what?"

"Well, one can be married, and . . . well, not feel married, at times."

"You don't feel married, Walter?"

"Not recently."

"What does your wife feel?"

"I'm not sure. She's in Boston."

A young boy—small, frail, with a topping of blond hair—shuffled up to where Walter and Jeannie were talking. "Let's go, Mom. I'm hungry."

"Billy, this is Walter. Walter and I went to high school together several years ago."

"Yeah. That's great," said the kid, turning and heading toward the lot.

She started after him, before hesitating and turning back toward Walter. "Have you had breakfast yet?"

"No."

"I take Billy to the House of Pancakes every Saturday morning. Why don't you come with us?"

Her face, angled toward him and pointing slightly upward, had a fleshy fullness—an expansive terrain of gently rolling hills and barely perceptible valleys. It had been sharper, less full the last time Walter had seen her, yet he recalled her having cocked her head in much the same manner. "It's not that I don't want to do it," she had said, bent almost double beneath him on her parents' couch, "it's just that I don't think you have any idea, Walter, of how to do it."

"Why not?" he said. "I haven't eaten pancakes since I was a kid."

CHAPTER 11

One morning in early August, I awoke as usual and went to my bedroom window. The world outside had changed overnight; sometime between the hours of eight P.M. and six-thirty A.M., a renovation had occurred without my knowledge. A great white pole, the size of a ship's mast, stood in our front yard. Hanging from its very top, limp and barely moving in the still air, was the flag of the United States of America.

Rising from the kitchen, through the air vent in the bedroom floor, came the hushed yet frantic voices of my parents. The noise they made was ludicrous—like that made by bumbling hunters, crashing through the underbrush, believing that they might actually encounter game upon emerging on the other side. I'm awake, I wanted to shout. Why don't you speak normally?

"Where in God's creation," asked my mother, "did you get that thing?"

"Jim Crealy got a couple dozen of the flags special order from someplace in Washington, D.C. I put our name in a couple of weeks ago."

"Victor. . . ."

"The pole I got through Agway, in Bruxton City. I got a good deal on it. I wanted to surprise you. We put it in last night."

"We cannot afford a flagpole, Victor."

"We cannot," replied my father, "afford not to fly the flag. The country's crumbling. Americans have got to show their patriotism."

"So stand in the front yard," came my mother's even reply, "and sing the National Anthem. It would be cheaper."

"Do you think that's funny? Do you think this is a joke?"

"I hope it is, Victor."

We were not the only house in the neighborhood to fly a flag that summer. Flags waved up and down the city's streets, making those yards without them seem somehow empty. Our flag was certainly one of the largest. Yet, for all its size, my father was never able to get it to fly properly. The securing rings had been unevenly welded to the pole. Thereafter, no matter how the flag was attached to the rings it would always end up wrapped about the pole, clinging to the metal like a frightened child clinging to its mother's leg.

Around the time of the flag's appearance, my father developed a strange obsession not only with the flag but with a particular man as well. He would mention the man's name in conjunction with the flag or the flag in conjunction with the man, as if the two of them were flying side by side in our front yard. I was only nine years old and did not understand my father's obsession. I thought, perhaps, that the man had invented the flag.

This dual obsession, I discovered, was not unique to my father. Much of the rest of the country had become obsessed as well; obsessed, apparently, with the flag or the man or both. Parades were held almost weekly in Caulfield, flags waving throughout the ranks like matadors' capes. The man's name was mentioned often on the radio. One had only to pick up a newspaper to see his name in large black letters.

It was seen most often on the front page, in bold print, generally accompanied by a photograph of the man so that even the most uninformed readers would be certain to understand that the bold print referred to that man. The face in the photograph was broad and softly rippled, like desert sands, undone by constant winds. The mouth smiled, but not openly, as if the man's lips were being pinched from within. His eyes were narrowed specks of black that, even in a photograph, never lingered. The man was obsessed with colors—bright emblematic colors. Pink and red. White and blue.

One night, a week or so after the flag had first appeared, my father summoned us all to the kitchen. He had, on occasion, taken to parading about the house in his marine uniform. He wore it that night, as he got a beer from the refrigerator and sat down across from my mother at the kitchen table. Kate and I, pulling up the other two chairs, made it a full circle. Silently we waited for him to speak.

Instead, glancing first at his watch, he reached up to the shelf above the table and turned on the radio. It was the start of a broadcast, live from Washington, D.C. The speaker's voice was high-pitched—nasal in tone—and came into our kitchen with a sense of urgency. It told us that our great nation was being victimized by a conspiracy. We were, it cautioned, being infiltrated with Communists.

"Daddy, what's a Communist?"

"A bad person, son. A group of bad people who want to take over our country. Change our way of life."

"Change it how?"

"For the worse."

"Where are they from . . . Communists?"

"Russia, son."

"Is that another planet?"

"No. Just another country."

"What do they look like?"

"Like us."

"How will I know them, if I see them?"

"I'll tell you when you're older."

The voice on the radio, I learned, was the voice of the man in the newspaper—the man my father often spoke of, the one with the face like wind-blown desert sands. Much of what I heard frightened me. The man talked as if the Communist conspiracy were a sickness, a contagious disease running rampant within our borders. From what he said, I believed that those who caught it would become red, or perhaps pink if it was but a mild case.

"Is that how I'll recognize them, Daddy?"

"How, son?"

"Because they're pink."

My mother laughed. The Old Man silenced her with a glare. He stared at the radio, nodding occasionally, his face a mask of concentration. Rarely had I seen my father so serious. I felt pricks of fear at the back of my neck. A river of coldness ran through my stomach. Could communism be caught in Caulfield? In the future, I told myself, I would not drink from another's cup. I would be sure to wash my hands before eating.

"Victor," my mother said, "the children don't need to hear this. It won't do a thing other than to scare them needlessly."

"Maybe that's what the country needs," my father replied. "For more folks to be a little bit frightened."

"Well, I ain't scared," said Kate. "This McCarthy guy is just a bunch of hogwash, trying to stir up trouble and get some votes, is all."

"Who made you such an expert"—the Old Man chortled—"and at such a ripe old age?"

"Mr. Pinkerton, my social studies teacher, that's who," she retorted. "He told the whole class. He said values aren't about government, they're about people. 'Folks who are scared to find out about other folks' governments,' he said, 'must have something to hide themselves.'"

"Pinkerton—pinko," said the Old Man. "That's Commie talk. I don't want nobody teaching my kids that kind of anti-American garbage! Leastwise not while I'm paying school taxes to the United States government."

I remember several months later, when Mr. Pinkerton lost his job at the grade school. One day he just didn't show up for class. There was a new teacher in his place. I saw Mr. Pinkerton on the street one afternoon after that, passing out leaflets to folks walking by. He looked healthy enough, but I knew he was not. I crossed the street to avoid him. I was afraid of getting too close to him—of catching what he had, communism.

One afternoon, shortly following the broadcast, my father returned home from work early. He backed our Ford station wagon up to the garage and opened its back. He removed a pick and two shiny new shovels. He took them into the backyard. Soon I heard the furious sounds of his shoveling, the labored puffs of heavy exertion. Through the back window, it appeared that he was digging a grave. For whom? I wondered in panic. I ran outside to find out.

"I'm building a bomb shelter, son."

"What for?"

"For our protection."

"Protection from what? Is somebody going to drop bombs on us, Daddy?"

"I hope not, son."

"Well then, how come we need a bomb shelter?"

"Just in case, Walt," he said between shovelfuls of dirt. "I don't want my family to be unprotected." So it *was* a grave he was digging. One big enough for the whole family. Just in case the Communists dropped bombs upon us, we would all be buried together.

My mother, when she returned from work, was furious. She glanced once at the upheaval in the backyard and went quickly into the house. Running into her bedroom, she slammed the door shut behind her, not emerging again until just before dinner. The meal was silent, save for the clanking of glasses, the greedy slurping of food. Kate, at long last, broke the silence.

"Can I have my own room, Daddy?" she asked.

"What?"

"In the bomb shelter. If we gotta live underground, I want to have my own room."

"For God sake, Victor," interjected my mother, "is this what you want? For our children to believe that in the future we will exist as moles?"

She left the table then. Kate and I were left to stare into our plates or out the window, anywhere but into my father's face. There were tears streaming from his eyes, rolling down his cheeks, onto his plate. He wanted to do right, it seemed, and could not.

I knew better than to try to talk to my father then. He had removed himself from our presence—traveled to some unreachable sphere of his own making. The world was his enemy. He was its clown. We all laughed at the comedy that was his life.

He got up from the table, glancing frantically about the room as if he believed something of great value might be hidden within it, something that if not spotted that very moment might elude him forever. If something was there, he apparently did not find it. The chair he had been sitting in tipped over, startling him, causing him to run as if chased from the room. On the radio, a voice urged listeners to buy U.S. Savings Bonds.

Much later, after the rest of the house had gone to bed, he returned home. I heard the kitchen door open, my father's heavy footsteps on the floor, his incoherent mumblings as they drifted into my room through the open air vent. Please God, I prayed, let him not be drunk this evening. Let him drink tomorrow, or the next day, but not tonight.

I will help with the dishes for a week without being told. Never again will I steal penny candy from Mr. Barton's store. Please, God. Amen.

Lighter footsteps—those of my mother—came from another part of the house. They met in the kitchen.

"I'm gonna call Tom Brundage tomorrow," said my father. "I'm gonna have him and his boys come out and finish building the bomb shelter. We're gonna have the best goddamn bomb shelter in the city!"

"You're drunk, Victor."

"I had a couple of beers."

"You'll wake the kids."

"What will your high-and-mighty Henry Truxton have to say about that?"

"What in the world does Henry Truxton have to do with bomb shelters?"

"Not much, I reckon," spat the Old Man. "If it was up to him, the whole damn country'd be run over by Bull-shit-viks!"

"He's a socialist. Is that what you mean, Victor?"

"You think I don't read the newspapers? He's a Commie is what he is! They won't even produce his movies in Hollywood, for God's sake!"

"So that's what this is all about! Hen—I knew you didn't give a damn about McCarthy or communism, Victor! Until a couple of months ago you wouldn't even stand up for the National Anthem! Well, I won't quit!"

"My wife works for a goddamn Commie!"

"You ought to be glad, Victor! The day I leave that job is the day I take the kids and leave you!"

"In town they say I'm a pinko lover!"

"What do you care about pinkos? What else do they say, Victor? What else? Do they say I'm fucking him?"

The air vent was no longer necessary. Their voices rose throughout the house, probably most of the neighborhood as well. The pinpricks in my neck became sharp, probing needles. Deep in my stomach, at the very pit, my warmest parts turned cold.

"You're killing me!" he screamed. "Why don't you just shoot me?"

"That's something I won't do, Victor! I've done too much for you already!"

"You wouldn't even care!"

Following such buildups, their final, climactic battles seemed, at times, almost passive. The noises floating upward might even have been mistaken for the sounds of sexual passion. The pitting of one against another, accompanied by muffled slaps and punches, piercing screams and moans. The violence I learned of in my youth, like love, although preceded by much jabbering and promise, in the end came quickly. It was spit out in a final flurry of rage. And then it was over, the two combatants snapping apart like brittle taffy, limping off to separate lairs, lying finally in their own pathetic bundles of aftermath.

In the morning, I knew, the Old Man would bring flowers and maybe even breakfast in bed for my mother. He would walk on eggshells around her. Kate and I would be told that my mother was not feeling well, that she had walked, accidentally, into the bathroom door in the middle of the night. We would avert our eyes but remember the lie—repeat it to ourselves so that it would sound more real when we repeated it to others.

I stuck my head beneath my pillow and pressed inward with my hands. Have I asked for too much, God? After all, I am not forced to go to bed hungry; I am not in a wheelchair like Billy Brandt; nor do I have joints so stiff I cannot move them, spit rolling in a constant stream from the corners of my mouth because I have no means of controlling it. I understand, Lord. There is just too much else for you to take care of. You do not have time, God. And I am not even mad.

At two o'clock, pancakes lying like lead in his stomach, he was out on the streets again—a foot soldier, having been waylaid, now a bit late, on a much-dreaded mission of kindness.

The Old Man, if he noticed nothing else, would notice that Walter was late. His brain, vacuous in places, picked clean as if by a horde of maggots, could still discern time. Time to eat. Time for a bath. Time to roll over. Time to take a shit. Time for a visit from your only son, Old Man. He went from one time to the next time. It was all he had left. And he didn't, Walter knew, even have much of that.

Walking, it occurred to Walter, was something he should do more of. He enjoyed the pace. Slow. It gave one time to digest, not just pancakes, but what went with them. As he walked, Walter digested Jeannie Weatherrup with his pancakes, twenty years after.

She was plentiful, her body a great wave, having swelled with the passage of time. In that, there was no enigma. The woman ate like a horse. She had, with Walter, split a second plate of pancakes. Rolled up with cinammon and butter—their insides dripping from the back like oil through a broken gasket—she had devoured each in two gluttonous gulps. Afterward, she had wiped her mouth with the back of her hand and smiled. She had even belched—indiscreetly into her napkin, but with no attempt to conceal it. Ah, Walter thought, the years have not turned you brittle, Jeannie Weatherrup.

"So," she said, "did you ever get what you wanted, Walter?"

Was he reading too much into her smile? Did she actually believe that those misdirected probes of twenty years ago had signified his life to come? As if, had Walter scored that night—pushed himself right up to her belly button—he would have gone on to become President?

"I'm not sure I know what you mean, Jeannie."

"Jesus, Walter. It's no mystery. I just meant, are you happy? How are things going? All of that. You know, the things people always ask other people when they haven't seen them in a while."

"Oh. I see."

"You know, I really had a crush on you for a while."

"Yeah. Me too."

She glanced at the kid. He had eaten almost nothing. He was tying and untying the knots in his mitt. Walter felt he knew something of this boy, almost as if he had encountered him somewhere in his past. He was a troubled boy. He always would be.

"Billy, I want you to eat at least half of what's on your plate," she said.

"I'm not hungry." He didn't look up from the glove. "I'll eat later."

"Jesus, Billy," she breathed. "You sure know how to make it hard on a woman."

And then they had talked, Walter and Jeannie, as if the boy were not there. Eventually Billy got up and walked out to the car. He was there waiting for them when they emerged from the restaurant almost an hour later.

They had talked of many things. People they had known; places they had been; what they were doing now. Things that mattered little to either of them. Things that danced around other things; things that were of significance but that were concealed beneath these meaningless things. They laughed and enjoyed each other's company. They each drank four cups of coffee. She had gone to the ladies' room only once. Strong kidneys, Walter noted. Strong kidneys and good teeth. He had taken her phone number. They had agreed to meet again.

My mother was not a wordy person. Much about her was unstated. A stance, a certain look—are what I remember best. Displeasure appeared as a downward slant of the mouth; a narrowing of her eyes as if squeezed shut against the sun; a drop in the upper muscles of her back—around the shoulders—that became visible in the sudden plummet of her breasts.

Joy—the unabashed kind, like the blatant nakedness of a woman unexpectedly caught bathing in the woods—she doled out in stingy portions. I remember seeing it but a few times. Once, at the age of eight, after I had made it through "When the Caissons Go Rolling Along" without missing a note. It was my first and last piano recital and the only time I had managed the piece without error. My instructor, the widow Coska, teary-eyed and ponderous of breast, pulled me to her, threatening to suffocate me in those great piles of flesh. I suppose she felt vindicated— her hours of finger-bashing not wasted. When finally she let me up for air, I saw my mother standing there. Her eyes were tearless, but joy lit up her face and radiated outward like heat from an oven. When she hugged me, it was not the moist heat of Widow Coska that enveloped me, but the soft glow that warms from the inside out. I don't recall what words, if any, she said to me. Only that I had made her happy and wasn't it strange that it had been so simple.

There is, however, one conversation with my mother that stays with me. It occurred on a Sunday afternoon—following closely the appearance of the bomb shelter—and immediately following one of the Reverend Theodore Beemer's lengthier sermons. I even recall the subject on which the reverend spoke that day—"Judge Not, Lest Ye Be Judged." I recall my sister's snickering laughter; the unmuffled fart of James O'Dell, who looked then to blame it on his own sister; an ink notation in my songbook—"St. Peter was hung like a horse"; and my mother's dogged gaze toward the pulpit, her left cheek still glowing blue and black in the overhead lights.

The church we attended was made of red brick and had a clock as well as a great iron bell in its steeple. It was Presbyterian, I believe, although that really was of no relevance. Its selling point was that it happened to be the only church within reasonable walking distance of our house. My mother preferred not to drive and my father refused to take her to and from the Sunday service. A reasonable God, he argued, would have made house calls. It was not that he had anything against religion—nor God, for that matter. My father simply felt that neither God nor religion had shown much ability in bettering his or anyone else's life—and this after half a million years of trying—thus he was not about to expend time or funds in exploring their efforts further. It was, apparently, purely a decision of economics, the sort any salesman worth his salt would have made.

It was fall. The sidewalk was tattooed brown and gold with fallen leaves. I remember kicking purposefully through them, hoping to un-earth something of value, something missed by someone somewhere. Kate had run off ahead with two boys she knew from school. On the sidewalk in front of me, I saw her playfully tossing leaves at first one, then the other. She knew just how far she could go without angering them. Her laughter, like the gentle tinkling from a candelabrum, floated back toward my mother and me.

At my side, my mother walked with her head held high, gazing into the trees as if she expected to find some long-lost acquaintance perched there. She wore an ankle-length dress made of black cloth. It swished about her feet in gentle waves. On her head, sitting with the elegance of a great bird, was a dark hat, encircled with feathers. I recall that moment as being my first conscious dawning of my mother's beauty.

I took note then of how others greeted her. Mr. Lindsey, the butcher at the corner market, tipping his hat, almost shyly as one would greet a girl on a blind date: "Beautiful day, Mrs. Innis. Say hello to Victor for me." Martha Woodrow, from two houses down the block on our side of the street—she sold pies out of her home and ate up most of the profits, eventually blowing up to such dimensions that she could no longer leave the house without the aid of two solid oak canes. Beneath the brim of her hat, Mrs. Woodrow's face glistened like a wet rock; she nodded curtly at my mother, smiling in the same foolish manner one does while buying pornography and pretending not to. The infamous Snake Barnett—having found his niche in the life insurance business—flashing a smile much too wide for the occasion, chuckling slightly, firing off words in the manner of bullets: "Enjoy it while ya can, gonna be cold enough soon. How ya doin', little Walt? Tell Vic to get on over to the house—you too, Susy. Even better, why don't ya leave Vic home? Then you and I can really have some fun. Heh! Heh! Heh!"

To each, my mother nodded politely, offering up some pleasantry, smiling in the closed-lipped manner of a Buddha. She knew, I suddenly realized, all about her beauty and the varying effects it had upon others. Did no one else, I wondered, see the polished bruise beneath her left eye? What of the barely perceptible limp in her otherwise perfect gait?

"Mommy?"

"What is it, Walter?"

"Are Communists bad people?"

"Not really, honey. It's their ideas that people don't like."

"Do you like their ideas?"

"I don't really know that much about them."

"Does Daddy know much about them?"

"No. I don't think so."

"Then why does he hate them so much?"

"He hates them," she said, "because he needs something to hate."

She reached down then and took hold of my hand, squeezing it as if hoping to prevent me from asking further questions. A squeal of laughter came from in front of us. Kate, in her Sunday dress and half heels, was on the ground, one of her male companions sitting squarely atop her, pushing leaves down her front.

"Katy Innis! You get up from there this minute!"

The boy leaped up at the sound of my mother's voice and turned to face her. "I'm sorry, Mrs. Innis. I couldn't—"

"I know all about your coulds and could nots, young man. I don't want to hear another word. Now run along and you will be lucky if you don't receive a dry-cleaning bill for my daughter's outfit!"

The boy and his companion—heads down, hands jammed deep into their pockets—shuffled off in shamed silence. Kate sprang quickly to her feet and stood, carefully picking leaves from the front of her dress.

Matthew F. Jones ★ 50

"I'm ashamed of you, Kate," my mother said. "You shouldn't lead boys on like that. If you give them any excuse at all, they'll take advantage of it."

"We were just fooling," said Kate.

"Fooling leads to more fooling. I don't approve of roughhousing with boys, and you know it. You're grounded for two weeks."

"I'll tell Daddy!" said Kate. "He'll let me go out!"

"Your father will do as I say."

"Then I'll tell him about what everybody's been saying!"

"Been saying about what?"

"About you and Mr. Truxton, that's what! Then we'll see who's gonna be in trouble! That's why I jumped on that faggot Nelson Giles and why he started in jamming me with leaves!"

"You go home, young lady, right now! When you get there, go in your room and stay put until I get back! Do you understand?" But Kate had already run off, tears streaming from her eyes, the white lace from her Sunday hat trailing behind her.

There was that name again. Henry Truxton. I had never met the man, yet I was quickly nurturing a hate for him. His name evoked tears and even rage. My father had called him a Communist, as if it were the same thing as being a rapist. What strange power the man held over our family. I began to see him as the cause of much pain.

I recalled my mother's stories about the great mansion where she worked. Ceilings so high, there should be stars in them, she said; rooms as large as most people's houses; four separate fireplaces, each made of hand-laid bricks. She told us about the Hall of Fame located right inside of Henry Truxton's house. Baseball was a Truxton "passion," she said.

"Baseball ain't a passion," the Old Man snarled, "it's a sport."

"Well, to them it's a passion. The entire room is filled with memorabilia."

"Memorywhat?"

"Abilia," said my mother. Her eyes had grown to the size of saucers. Her voice rose in an excited tremor. She spoke about the place as if it were her childhood home. "The entire room is filled with baseball things."

"What kind of things?"

"You know, bats, balls, gloves, pictures, that sort of thing. I don't really know their significance, just that I'm impressed with anyone who takes such good care of things.''

"No sense saving things once they're wore out," said my father. "If ya can't field with a glove, what good is it?"

"It means something to the collector, Victor. Henry, er, Mr. Truxton, showed me a glove that used to belong to Willie Mays.''

"Mays just up and gave it to him, huh?"

"Apparently. The Truxtons are very influential people, Victor. The things they collect are not relics from the minor leagues."

My mother carefully adjusted her hat, as if her shouting might have caused it to go awry. She breathed deeply and blew her nose gently into her open handkerchief. It was a beautiful nose—slanting gently out from beneath her eyes, coming to a smooth apex, punctuating the rest of her face like the period at the end of a sentence. "If eyes are the windows to a woman's soul," the Old Man once said, "then her nose is the front gate. It oughtn't to be completely closed, but it better not be wide open either."

My mother reached down for my hand again, squeezing it gently. Her palm was moist through her dress gloves. I felt the fingers, strong and durable as oak. We walked again—me, looking down, kicking through the leaves, my mother staring off once more into the trees.

Benji Merwin was in front of his house raking leaves, stacking them into small piles. Several of the piles sat on his lawn like colorful anthills. Benji moved from one to the other, raking a few leaves into each, apparently unsure what to do with them. Benji was thirty-two years old, with the mind and emotions of a six-year-old. Some of the kids in town pointed at him and called him a retard. Others waved and said hello. Benji smiled and waved to all of them, unconcerned with their motives or unable to tell the difference. He seemed always happy. He had the advantage of being six years old his entire life.

Two houses farther on, Mitchell Finch had his head beneath the raised hood of his Corvair. His wife, Myrtle, sat behind the wheel. "All right, Myrtle, easy now," said Mitch. "Give it some gas." A roar came from the engine block. Blue and black smoke shot from the rear of the car. Mitchell appeared from beneath the hood—glasses askew, face black, hands clasped tightly over his ears. "Jesus, Myrtle! I said easy, for God sake! Ya trying to kill me?" Across the street, Bob Allen roared, his laughter coming in great gasps. As we turned the corner onto Elm Street, their voices faded away like the chattering of angry squirrels.

"In a small town—or anywhere for that matter, Walter—people often say things—things that may not even be true—just because they've heard someone else say them." I glanced up at my mother. If she hadn't spoken my name I would have believed she was talking to herself. Her eyes were still in the trees. "I guess it's because they get bored or they haven't got anything of their own to talk about."

She looked at me then to see if I was listening. I had no idea what she was talking about. Was it something Mitchell Finch or his wife had said?

"Yes, ma'am," I said.

"Have you heard these things?"

"What things?"

"The kinds of things that people say because they don't have anything of their own to talk about."

"Well . . . one time Billy Brundage told me that he was adopted and that his real father was Joe DiMaggio."

"Why do you suppose he told you that?"

"On account of his father really ran off to California when Billy was only two years old, so Billy just started pretending that Joey D. was his father. When folks would ask him, 'Where's your father at, Billy?'— Billy would say, 'He's in New York, playing center field.' I reckon he said it so much that now even he believes it."

"Do you believe it?"

"That Joey D. is Billy's father?"

"Yes."

"No. But sometimes I wish it was true. It'd be nice for Billy. Everybody ought to have a father."

"Why don't you believe it?"

"Just because . . . I mean, if he was his father, why wouldn't he come and visit Billy sometimes, or send him presents on his birthday and stuff?"

"So Billy made it up and you were smart enough to know why he did?"

"I reckon."

"Do you like Billy less because of the lie?"

"No. Billy's a good guy."

We came to the intersection of Elm and Townsend Street and turned left onto Townsend, moving parallel then to Elm Street Park. There was no more than two feet of water in the park swimming pool. What there was was brown and speckled with leaves.

A basketball bouncing off the paved court next to the pool reverberated like a series of brisk shots in the autumn air. A half-dozen teenage boys, dressed in long pants and high-top sneakers, were playing a game of half-court, three on three. On the grass behind the basket, a boy and a girl sat with their arms around one another, quietly watching the game. They wore identical orange and black CAULFIELD HIGH varsity jackets and had a single scarf wrapped securely about their shoulders. At the other end of the court, a young, lanky kid—clumsy in the way of a yearling colt—shot baskets, acting as if he were trying to ignore the older boys.

"Walter, I think you are a very knowledgeable boy." My mother smiled—not her usual tight-lipped smile, but an open-mouthed, dress-white, do-your-shoes, thank-you sir, left-right-see-you-in-a-while kind of smile. "I believe the truth will never elude you for long."

"Elude?"

"Hide. I don't believe the truth will ever stay hidden from you for long."

"Oh."

"What I mean is, some people will look right at the truth and never know it—or only see part of it, because the whole of it might be something they don't want to believe. But other people—and I think you are one of these—will see the truth even if it's surrounded by lies. Do you understand what I mean?"

"Sort of."

"You will, someday. And when you do, you might not be happy about it. You might even wish, for a time, that you were one of those people who never knows the truth. But that will change, and one day you will be glad that the truth did not elude you, because when you know the truth about things there is nothing left to hurt you."

"What will be left?"

"Understanding and—God willing—love."

We were on Gardner Street now, in sight of our house. My father's

Ford, shiny as an otter's back, sat out front. The hammock on the porch swung gently back and forth as if someone had just climbed out of it. The Old Man was out back, raking the lawn with a large wooden rake he had bought the day before. An open cooler sat beneath the shade of the porch awning.

Tiny pricks of apprehension covered my body, crawling over it like a troop of ants. Why would I remember this walk forever? And yet I knew I would. A tiny voice, barely acknowledged, told me to speak. Ask the great questions, it said, while she is in a mood to talk. What of the bruises upon her face? What of the sounds of violence in the night? What of Henry Truxton and his museum of memorabilia? Anything at all, the voice said. Latch onto a word. Soon the spell will be broken and you will be alone with your questions. The Old Man hesitated in his raking. Soon he would see us.

"Love?"

"What did you say, Walter?"

"Do you love Daddy?"

The Old Man saw us and waved. "Hello!" he shouted, and started toward the sidewalk to greet us.

"We both love you very much," whispered my mother. "He, nearly as much as I."

CHAPTER 14

How is it, Old Man, that you have managed to live so long? Those who should know say that your liver has rebelled—shriveled up, become fibrous and ornery like a mistreated wife—an analogy, I admit, with ironic qualities. Your heart, they say, beats timorously, skipping sporadically like a flat stone across the water. Everywhere, it seems, they have found clogged channels and dead ends. And yet you endure.

Surely living for you is but an act of will. But why bother? What here—in this world—could you hold in such esteem? If there is something worth that much, and you have seen it, please tell me what it is. As my father, it is your duty to inform me of such things.

Or is dying what you really fear? After skirting so close to the edge, Old Man, have you taken a peek around death's corner? Does evil retribution lurk there? Flat out—no more disguises—is it the Devil that you have seen? Does it appear that he may not be a drinking man?

"How is he?" Walter asked the nurse on duty. Gray-haired, lean of build, she appeared androgynous. She would, thought Walter, keep the boys from getting overly excited.

"The same," she responded, smiling as if status quo was a victory of sorts. "Sick and tired of being in bed all day, I should think."

"There's not much we can do about that, is there?"

"I suppose not."

"Is he eating all right?"

"Like a bird. But he asks for enough food to feed an army."

"Is he getting everything else that he needs?"

"What else does he need, Mr. Innis?"

"That's what I am asking you, for Christ sake. Whatever else he needs—and I'm not sure what it might be—I just want to make sure he is getting it."

"I see." She turned and started off down the hallway. "You don't know what he needs," she said, "but you want me to give it to him."

Christ, thought Walter, the kind of people they hire to work in these places. But then, what could one expect from a county-run facility?

He stepped into the room. Light filtered through the slats of the open shades, creating half-broken ribbons on the Old Man's bed. A fan whirred in one corner. Everything smelled of antiseptic. His father was staring out the window. Walter was never sure what to call the Old Man after twenty-two years of not calling him anything.

"Hello," he said.

"Hey, Joey, my boy, all the way from St. Louis you come! I knew you'd make it back to see me. How about that, Mr. Innis? How about that!"

Jesus. Walter had not even noticed that the Old Man had a new roommate. Almost a week ago, the man who had been sharing the room with his father had died during the night—simply blinked off. Afterward the bed had been empty, freshly made up—its top unruffled and flat as an airstrip. Now it was filled once again. Its new occupant had apparently mistaken Walter for his own son.

"I'm afraid you've made a mistake," Walter said. "I've come—"

What stopped him from going on? Was it the photograph on top of the man's nightstand? A picture of a handsome kid dressed in a uniform, leaning casually against an army tank. The picture was in black and white, not from this decade. The boy's hair was combed into a ducktail behind his neck.

Eyes—glassy, clouded by cataracts—sought Walter out. They begged to be lied to. Walter's own father had not turned from the window. Either he had not heard Walter or he did not care to. The Old Man's nightstand, save for a glass of water, was empty. Walter turned back to the roommate.

"Of course I came to visit you," he said. "Didn't I say I would?"

"But how did you get here?"

"By plane. The morning flight to Syracuse, a commuter from there."

"But it's so expensive."

"You're my father, aren't you?"

"Yes. Yes I am," said the man. "But to come so far . . . to see me. . . . You're a good son."

"And you're a good father. I think of you often."

"How are your boys . . . their names? I forget."

"Jonathan and Rodney. They're fine. They send their love. They would have come to visit you, but their mother didn't want them to miss summer camp."

"She still runs your life, then?" The man blinked constantly, his eyes had filled. "She was always a cold woman. I warned you not to marry her. But you were always weak."

"Yes," said Walter. "You were right."

"Of course I was right! But you knew it all! You thought you had the world by the nuts!" As he spoke, the man grew irate. Phlegm flew from his mouth. His hand, knotted and blue with veins, clutched the sheets of his bed. Walter feared the man would have a seizure.

"Yes. Yes, Father," he said placatingly, anything to make the old fool calm down. Christ, if he died they would probably charge Walter with manslaughter. "You were always right. She was no good! I threw her out. The boys and I live alone."

"Blasphemy!" railed the man. "What kind of a Catholic are you? You would leave your own sons motherless!" The man was gasping for air. His face had taken on a bluish tint. Screaming, Walter ran from the room.

"Nurse! Nurse! Jesus Christ, somebody call the nurse!"

The android came around the corner, moving at a rapid pace. "What is it, Mr. Innis? My God, you'll wake up the whole facility."

"It's, it's, Mr. . . . Jesus, I don't even know his name . . . next to my old man. I think he's having a heart attack!"

"Mr. Johnson? Well, let's go have a look."

The man lay calmly in his bed. He gazed up toward the ceiling, eyes slightly calmer now, less clouded. He breathed at a steady rate, a smile playing at the corners of his mouth.

"Mr. Johnson," said the nurse. "Are you all right?"

"Yes. Yes. I'm fine, Nurse Hunchhammer. I had a strange dream, is all. My son, Joey, from St. Louis came to visit me. Such a weak boy. . . . I hope he turned out well." He closed his eyes and appeared to sleep, a smile still lingering.

The bomb shelter was never completed. For close to a year, its beginnings remained as an ugly scar in our backyard. On that first night, my father had staked out an outline, twelve feet in width and length, before he began shoveling. He had removed approximately six inches of soil from the surface before he quit digging forever. What remained was a recessed area of dirt taking up close to a quarter of the backyard.

With the arrival of winter, the indentation filled with water and froze solid. Kate and I, after carefully shoveling off the snow, attempted to fashion a skating rink from it. The shelter's dimensions, though, proved to be too confining even for my short legs. No sooner would we build up the speed needed to stop the wobbling in our knees when it would become necessary to slow up once again to avoid colliding with the frozen borders of the pond.

"Can you imagine living in this thing!" complained Kate. "Talk about stir crazy. We woulda knocked ourselves out running into the goddamned walls!"

In the spring, once the snow had thawed, the area became a black quagmire of mud. Soon it was a haven for the peepers and frogs of the neighborhood, croaking a constant cacophony. In the midst of this plethora of peeps and chirps, I slept fitfully, dreaming I was in the steamy jungles of Africa.

"Maybe we could raise pigs," suggested Kate, in reference to their supposed preference for slop.

The problem was that there was a local ordinance against raising barnyard animals within city limits. At any rate, none of us liked pork.

"How about a garden?" asked my mother.

Although the idea was somewhat appealing—"Just think," Kate said, "it would be like having our own supermarket, right in the backyard"— it too had certain drawbacks. A garden would have required both careful planning and constant attention, neither of which the Innis family had shown much inclination for. If family history was any indicator, then our garden would soon have been hopelessly clogged with weeds and other superfluous plants, its untended borders offering easy access for scavengers. Any vegetables stubborn enough to survive despite such conditions would surely have been picked too early or left hanging on the vine long past their prime.

My father offered no suggestions at all. The entire subject seemed to irritate him. Whenever the problem was broached, he would respond with a tight-lipped frown. "I'm thinking on it," he might say when pressed for a possible solution. "Just give me some time, is all." Such a response seemed to suggest that he had great plans for the area. As the months went by, though, he steadfastly refused to fill and reseed what had been dug up, acting as if in doing so he might be burying far more than the simple remains of a bomb shelter.

His crusade against communism had ceased as quickly as it had begun. Although the flag still flew, the name McCarthy had suddenly lost its appeal. The evening broadcasts, as well as my father's anti-Communist tirades, were replaced by a station that played chamber music. When Mr. Pinkerton was unceremoniously drummed from his job at school, my father shook his head and sighed. "Poor son of a bitch," he said, "has got a wife and two kids to feed."

Never again did I see him dressed in his marine uniform. I came across it one day in the attic, neatly folded and carefully placed in the trunk that held the rest of my father's belongings. It was on top of his baseball clippings and the pictures of my mother and him on their wedding day. His past, I realized, was neatly stacked within that trunk. I could have reached lower, beneath the clippings, and seen my father as a boy. But something stopped me—fear, maybe, of liking too much the child I might find.

Some nights he would take his beer out to the back porch and sit, staring at the hole in our backyard as if it were a phenomenon of nature—a crater perhaps, caused by a dying meteorite. He might fall into a boozy silence, traces of a smile flickering periodically near the corners of his mouth. After downing another couple of beers, he might start to whistle low and melodically.

"Victor," my mother said one night, "we really must do something. I dreamt the other night that my pillow turned into a clump of frog's eggs."

"I'm thinking on it," replied the Old Man. "Just give me some time, is all."

"What's to think about? The thing is inching up on us each day."

"Admit it, Susan," he said, a smile flickering like candle flames from both sides of his mouth. "It sort of grows on you after a while."

"If you don't do something soon, Victor, it will grow over us!"

"You have your job with Henry Truxton," said my father, calmly opening another can of beer, "and I have my swamp."

On a day in late June nearly a year after my father's initial excavation, a dump truck appeared in our driveway. In the truck's bed was a dark mound of top soil. The Old Man, just home from work and still dressed in his salesman's suit, hurried out to greet the driver. He stood behind the vehicle, directing truck and driver into the backyard.

Before coming to a stop, the truck backed to the very edge of what was left of our lawn. There was a hissing of air. The truck's front wheels jumped slightly. Its back raised up, slowly depositing its load directly into the middle of what once was to have been our bomb shelter. My father paid the driver, laughed heartily, and waved as the truck drove off.

"Come on, Walt," he said, shucking his suit coat, "let's get you onto the business end of a shovel."

That afternoon and the following day we spent filling in and leveling out the area. In a small pile near the back edge of the yard, we deposited the unused dirt. When we were finished, my father walked back toward the house, stopping about twenty feet from it. He took off his shirt and dropped it onto the ground. After reaching into his back pocket, he removed a tape measure.

"Come hold onto this, Walt," he commanded.

He handed me the end of the tape. I stood just above his shirt, gripping the thing in my hand. My father turned then and started walking in the other direction, letting tape out as he went. Almost in the middle of the fresh soil, he stopped and drove his foot into the ground. Then he reached down, picked up a shovel, and stuck it in where his foot had been. "Sixty feet six inches," he said. "Perfect."

"Perfect for what?" I asked.

"A pitching mound," he answered. "What else?"

"But there isn't enough room for a diamond, or even the base paths."

"Who needs a diamond or bases?" he bellowed. "You're standing on home plate and I'm standing on the mound. From me to you. It's a two-man game."

"But what about a batter?"

"To learn how to pitch, you don't need a batter. If you want somebody to stand over the plate, just to know where the strike zone is, we'll get your mother or sister to stand in."

The leftover dirt was used to fashion the mound. The Old Man padded and groomed it. He even got out his level, checking the mound from all sides to make sure it was even and properly angled. The coup de grâce was a one-inch, regulation-size pitching rubber, carefully inserted into the hill at just the right distance from home plate. "I stole that from a ballpark in Danville, Virginia," he said. "It was right after my first shutout. I got an outfielder from the Danville squad—fellow name of Perkins, a northener like me—to help."

He cut out a diamond from a piece of wood, painted it white, and stamped it into the ground where his shirt had been. Then we drove down to Barton's hardware store together and bought a coil of chicken wire. After tying two strands of the wire together, my father nailed it onto three posts and then hammered the posts into the ground behind the diamond, creating a backstop between home plate and the rear of the house. "This way," the Old Man said, chuckling, "your mother won't have to worry about a wild pitch ending up in one of her casseroles."

When at last we were finished, he stepped back and took a good look at our work. He climbed up onto the mound, his right arm hanging loosely by his side, the fingers flexing, moving up and down like a spider's legs. "What I wouldn't give," he said, smiling slightly, peering in at the plate as if he could see a batter standing there, "for the chance to fire a high hard one right up beneath some cocksure son of a bitch's chin."

CHAPTER 16

The nurse pulled the curtain surrounding Mr. Johnson's bed. The old man disappeared behind the white fabric. Walter imagined he heard quiet laughter coming from within the enclosure. He turned to confront the nurse.

"He was excited. . . . I thought he might be having a heart attack."

"Why should he be excited?"

"I guess he thought I was his son," said Walter.

"You don't look a thing like Mr. Johnson's son," she replied curtly. "He's taller than you and has more hair. Didn't you see the picture?"

"But . . . his cataracts. I thought—"

"G.I. Joe," she barked, nodding toward the picture, "died nearly thirty years ago."

"But he seemed so convinced. . . ."

"Hmmph!" breathed his accuser, as she turned to walk from the room. "I guess it's true what they say. There really is a sucker born every minute."

Walter was left alone to confront his father. The Old Man had not yet turned from the window. Had he heard nothing? Or did he simply not care? On those rare occasions when he had talked with his step-mother—the last time being when she had unceremoniously dumped her husband at Convalescent, announcing that she was relinquishing all responsibility for his care—Walter had been told that the Old Man spoke in proud and glowing terms of his only son.

Yet whenever Walter came to the nursing home, the Old Man seemed unable to recognize him. And when he did acknowledge his son's presence, he had nothing significant to say. Victor, it seemed, was interested only in the basics—enough food and water, a smooth-as-silk bowel movement, an afternoon ball game on the tube, or perhaps a rerun of *Rawhide*. At least, Walter thought, his father was being consistent in his old age. What else, besides enough to eat and drink and a few simple pleasures, after all, had ever concerned him?

Above all else, Walter longed to hear one word of explanation from Victor before the Old Man died. Even a simple ejaculation of grief or regret might suffice. If not for that slight hope, he would not bother to visit at all.

He studied the back of his father's head. The white hair had thinned slightly; traces of blue veins covered the top of his skull like a series of interwoven highways. A scar, distended and pale, was at its apex. Walter remembered the night that the Old Man had gotten the scar. He had arrived home drunk, after a night at Hurley's. He hadn't liked his wife's lipstick or her hair or her goddamn dress, or something about her appearance had angered him—it was too alluring, too cheap, just not right. An argument had ensued. From his room, huddled beneath the covers of his bed, Walter had heard his mother scream. There had been a series of slaps and muffled groans. God, thought Walter, let them kill each other so that I can sleep. Then he begged forgiveness for having prayed for such a terrible thing. A loud crash—like broken glass—came from the kitchen, followed by a scream, drenched in pain as terrible as Walter had ever heard. The Old Man has killed her, he thought.

He leaped from his bed and charged down the stairs. There, kneeling on the linoleum floor in the kitchen, was his father. Blood spurted from a gash on the top of his head. He clutched the sides of his skull with both hands, as if trying to push something out through its top. A broken bottle of Jack Daniels lay next to him on the floor. He had clubbed himself with it.

"God take the devil! God take the devil!" mumbled the Old Man, over and over as if trying to purge his soul through some voodoo ritual. Blood oozed through his fingers and ran down his arms. His eyes, bulging and clouded, were like those of a pickled pig. "God take the devil! God take the devil!" And there was Walter's mother, kneeling next to his father, kissing his bloodied head, trying to stop the bleeding with her hands. Blood from her own wounds merged with her husband's. Her hair, stringy and damp, covered her face. The two of them held tight to each other as if they were lovers. The terrible, ugly truth, of course, was that they were.

. . .

At long last, the Old Man rolled away from the window. His eyes open, gazing in scattered disarray about the room, rested finally upon his son. The Old Man took in a shallow breath, then slowly released it, the air escaping in a series of pathetic squeaks and groans. "His lungs are as bad off as his liver," the doctor had told Walter. "They're so plugged up that any air he manages to suck in is hard-pressed to find sufficient room in which to move."

"Time to eat yet?" he asked.

"I don't think so," said Walter. "The nurse said you just had lunch."

"Ain't no rule against seconds, is there? I always told my boy, grab seconds whenever ya get the chance. They'll see ya through the hungry times." The words had tired him. He rolled his head up toward the ceiling and closed his eyes.

He had a scar on his right index finger as well—a callus really, from throwing knuckleballs. The skin there was so thick, or at least it used to be, that if you tapped on it, it would make a hollow sound as if the finger were made of wood.

Despite his early admonitions about the knuckler—telling Walter that it was a pitch used only by old men and cripples—the Old Man had once tried to teach his son how to throw it. But Walter had no more success in mastering the pitch than he had in mastering the other aspects of the game. The ball would flutter for him but not dance. The final illusion—the elusive dip that would avoid contact—had never revealed itself to him. It was a brand of magic that the Old Man possessed, the secret of which even he did not understand.

"He just doesn't know how to watch other people doing things," Walter's mother had once told him regarding the Old Man's drunken antics while watching his son's Little League games. "He wants so badly for you to succeed, but he knows he can't swing the bat for you. He can't pick up a grounder to your left."

Immediately following her funeral, the two of them—father and son—had walked directly from the cemetery to Hurley's Bar and Grill and gotten drunk together.

It was a Saturday afternoon and the place was nearly empty, most of the regulars having stayed away out of respect for Susan Innis. Even Bill Hurley had not beaten Walter and his father back from the cemetery.

Walter and the Old Man had sat at a booth near the back, drinking several boilermakers without speaking. "This isn't such a hard thing to do," Walter remembered thinking. "There's nothing at all magical about this."

The Old Man spoke first. "I never liked her working out there. You knew that, right?"

Walter had frowned.

"I was against it. A goddamned accident—what else could it have been?"

Walter had drained his beer, saying nothing. He knew what else, but he couldn't bring himself to tell the Old Man. Even though he had wanted to—wanted to humble the son of a bitch, bring him to his knees, bleed everything out of him just as he had bled all the good from Walter's mother. But he couldn't do it. More for the sake of his mother than anything else. Or was it more for his own sake? he wondered.

"From the day I first set eyes on your mother, Walt, I never thought about another woman. Sometimes I wished I could. It woulda made things a hell of a lot easier on her."

"I don't have the slightest fucking idea of what that means."

"You think I was a rotten bastard, Walt?"

"Me, you're asking? You want to know what I think?"

"I'm asking."

"One day you'll either burn in hell, is what I think, or you won't."

"What is it you think I should have done differently?"

"All of a sudden you want my opinion? Why? It's a thing I don't understand!"

The Old Man had gazed down into his beer, a boozy, pied-eyed look upon his face. Whatever strange demons tormented him would not leave upon his wife's death. Walter figured that the Old Man had loved her, had always loved her; in his eyes, that made the whole relationship even more pathetic.

"Goddamned foolishness." Looking up, Victor had forced his lips into a tight line. "Rowing out there and back in all kinds of weather. I was against it." He stood up suddenly, as if the conversation were over. After reaching for his coat, he shrugged his arms into the sleeves.

Half drunk, Walter had reached out and grabbed hold of one of his father's pant legs. Gripping it between his fingers, he had twisted the material as if trying to squeeze something from it. What he wanted was a word, a gesture, an explanation, anything. Maybe, even at that late date, a shoulder to cry on.

But the Old Man had pulled away, spinning free of Walter and then stopping several feet from him. He stood staring down at his son, offering nothing, shaking his head forlornly. "God, we'll miss her," he said, frowning ironically. "Won't we, boy?"

He had not stopped pitching, even after the injury. It's just that the arm was never the same. It had lost its pop. The muscle he had torn was located in his shoulder and was called the rotator cuff. Even today full recovery from such an injury is rare. Back then it meant a quick trip home and a job in the old man's business—if you were lucky enough to have an old man with a business, that is. If not, maybe something where your name might come in handy. Something like sales. And if the arm comes back even halfway? Why not have a few laughs—maybe even drum up a little business along the way? There's always a league, ain't there?

He had played in the county league until he was past forty. Only he had quickly learned that he couldn't blow it by anybody anymore—not even those weekend leadbellies, stuffed like lumpy socks into their stretch uniforms, dreaming all the while of pinstripes—so he had come up with a new pitch. A knuckleball. He hadn't had to practice it much. Like the heater he used to possess, he had come by it naturally.

The thing about the knuckler was that you didn't have to throw it hard to be successful. If you threw it too hard, in fact, it wouldn't dance at all and then it was just a big, helpless balloon waiting to be burst. But if you held the ball correctly and then threw it with a nice easy motion, it would flutter for you. And if you did it just right, the ball would do a jig right there in midair—a quick drop and a do-si-do—or maybe even a promenade—and that's all she rode. The batter might swing over it or under it or maybe just nick it, grounding the ball weakly to the infield or lifting it without purpose, like a dying quail, to nowheresville.

I used to go and watch him play on weekends during the summer. We all did—my mother, Kate, and me—until it was too painful to continue. Until, in order to spare us all, he had made us stop coming.

He had been one of the better pitchers in the league, dancing the knuckler by opposing batters, laughing all the while. But his pitching was no longer why folks came to see him play. Most who watched were not aware that his high school records still stood, that he once was the man of heat. The sprinkling of spectators sought only momentary diversions from the workday week, much beer, and maybe a few laughs. The Old Man, more often than not, provided the latter while heartily indulging in the former.

For years he was the crown prince of the county leagues. One game he had worn his hat backward and pitched from his knees. The batters on the other team were laughing so hard that they couldn't get their bats off their shoulders. He struck out the side without once getting to his feet. On another occasion, unbeknownst to anyone, the Old Man had rigged his belt so that halfway through his delivery it came undone completely, his pants dropping clear to his ankles; escaping at the same instant—fluttering skyward like a lazy pop fly—was the white pigeon he had carefully secreted there.

And always, of course, there was the alcohol. On occasion, he would drink so much between innings that he could barely make it to the mound. Bobbing and weaving—the crowd roaring its delight—the Old Man would take his position on the hill. Once there, he'd peer intently in at the plate, seeing one, two, maybe three batters at times. But always he seemed able to dance the knuckler by 'em.

"Do you enjoy being the town clown?" my mother had asked him after the last game that we were permitted to watch.

"I'm not a clown," my father had replied. "I'm a pitcher."

"No, Victor, you are not a pitcher. You used to be a pitcher. Now you are simply a clown and, what's worse, you are generally a drunk and disgusting clown."

"It's just for fun. It's how I relax."

"Why don't you just give the game up, Victor? Why torture yourself?"

"No."

"Neither the kids nor I will come to another game."

"Yes. That would be best." He sighed.

I was six years old then. I have not seen him pitch a game since. Most Saturday mornings during the summer, he would leave the house carrying his glove and uniform in a sailor's bag slung over his shoulder. When he returned late in the afternoon, glassy-eyed and smelling of beer, he would stumble through the house to his room, slamming the door loudly after entering. He would sleep then until supper. He never spoke of the games. He never talked about baseball at all. Then, that summer when I was ten, my father built a pitching mound from what was once to have been a bomb shelter.

"Forget about the knuckler," he told me. "It's a junk pitch."

"But that's the pitch you use."

"Forget about it. It's for old men and cripples. It won't take you anywhere. Now, get up on the mound and lob a couple to me." Crouching down behind the plate, he fit his hand into the catcher's mitt.

"Jesus!" he bellowed. "You throw like a girl! Come over the top, Walter. Over the top, just like you're pulling on a rope."

He showed me how to stand, toeing the rubber, coming forward on the windup so that all of my weight landed on my left foot. "The power comes from your legs," he said. "Not your arm. Keep the arm loose, like a whip—always loose."

I saw my mother walk through the back door of our house onto the porch. Dressed in a long summer dress, one hand shading her eyes from the sun, she watched as we played. The light caught her hair, bouncing off in splinters of dark gold. She turned away, pulling dry laundry from the line, dropping it carefully into the basket at her feet. The Old Man, his back to her, never noticed her at all.

"That's enough for now," he hollered, standing up and striding out toward the mound.

"But I've only been throwing for half an hour."

"Tomorrow morning it will feel like half a day. If your arm's not in shape, the worst thing you can do is throw too much. Tell you what, get a bat and I'll lob some balls at you—see if you've got any kind of an eye for it. Just keep 'em on the ground is all, so you don't break any windows."

An hour or so later, sitting beneath the willow tree at the edge of our yard, beads of sweat dropped from my father's brow. The willow's branches dipped and swayed rakishly above us in the warm breeze. The Old Man's arms hung loosely between his knees. He chewed on a piece of grass, absently moving it from one side of his mouth to the other. I felt the exhilaration of something learned, the simple joy that comes with the sudden knowledge of one's father.

"Walt?"

"Yes?"

"I gotta tell ya . . . I mean, an arm is something that God gives ya. Either you're born with it or you're not. You know what I'm saying?"

"Yes." I knew exactly what he was saying. Bill Hurley had told me the same thing when I was eight years old.

"Well, I don't know why some folks are born with a pitching arm and some aren't. It just is, that's all." He spit the grass out and reached quickly for another piece. "But if you don't have one, there's no sense pretending you do."

"And I don't?"

"Does it bother you?"

"No." How could he know the relief I felt? I did not have what Bill Hurley had called my father's curse. Not having the arm, I would not have the dreams. Not having the dreams . . .

"Does that mean we can't play any more?" I asked.

"No, son. It doesn't mean that at all. I just thought I should tell you . . . now, is all." He smiled up at me with his eyes. "You got a pretty natural stroke with the bat, I noticed. With practice you could become a damn good country hitter. Anyway for Caulfield. And if you can hit my knuckler, you can hit most anybody in the county."

"Then you'll pitch to me?"

"As often as I can."

Even then I don't think he understood. It didn't matter that I didn't have the arm. It didn't matter if I never learned how to hit against anyone but him. It was the longest conversation I had ever had with my father—leastwise about anything that mattered. And he had promised to play with me as often as he could.

Nurse Hunchhammer appeared in the room once again. Equipped with a washcloth, dry towel, and bucket of suds, she looked as if she might be preparing to mop the floor. Instead, with a disapproving glance toward Walter, she disappeared behind the fabric surrounding Jacob Johnson's bed. With a brisk flourish, she whisked the curtain shut.

"Will you peel yourself," she trilled, banging her bucket on the floor, "or shall I peel you?"

"Go away," railed the man from St. Louis. "When I get dirty, I'll wash myself."

"If I leave it to you, Mr. Johnson, it's not likely to get done, now is it?"

"So? I'll stink and be glad of it—and who is it that will care?"

"Now, Jacob," replied Nurse Hunchhammer, in a voice generally reserved for young children or housepets, "we've been through all of this before, haven't we? You tell me that you don't want to get cleaned up and then I tell you that it is one of our rules that you must and that it is my job to see that you do. So, please, let's not make it difficult on each other, shall we?"

"Rules? Where in the rules does it say that you can play with my pecker?"

Walter heard the splashing of water, the gentle slapping of skin. A trail of bread crumbs ends in this room, he thought. The clock winds down and, in the process, somehow backs up. Great men lie on their backs and endure sponge baths; robust souls are fed formula through a straw. Nurse Hunchhammer, all hormone and starch, is here to prepare us for the grave.

He glanced back at the Old Man, lying faceup in his bed. The face was weathered, lined, as if it had finally been moved inside after too many years in the cold. The nose was bent to the left, the result of being broken three times. Once by a line shot back up the middle—if the Old Man had not gotten his glove up to deflect it, he might have been killed; once when he had been drunk and walked into a telephone pole—that time, recalled Walter, the Old Man had not even realized the extent of the damage until he had awakened the next morning in a pool of blood; and once, before Walter had been born, in a manner never explained to him. If lives, thought Walter, were measured through the nose, then his father had lived a full and unyielding one.

He had missed his dead wife for only a year and a half. Then he had married Rita Glenberry, from two houses down the block on the corner of Broad Street and Newton. Walter remembered Rita as a plump, pleasant woman, whose sturdy hips had given birth to half a dozen children. One night shortly after the birth of their last child, her husband, Henry, had disappeared, just dropped from sight, as if God had suddenly snapped his fingers and caused him to vanish. A strong rumor had placed Henry in New Jersey, living the good life, shacked up with a gypsy palmist and shipping out, when he needed the cash, as a merchant seaman.

What could the Old Man have seen in Rita Glenberry, for Christ sake? She certainly did not compare to Walter's mother. Even when Walter was a child, Rita's massive breasts had been the butt of countless neighborhood jokes. "Where is the deepest valley in the Northeast?" Answer: "On the corner of Broad and Newton, in between Rita Glenberry's tits."

His sister had written Walter about the marriage. "You mustn't be upset with Father," she had said in her letter. "I think it was the only way he could start to get over Mother's death. . . . Besides, he's lonely like the rest of us."

They had lived together in Rita's house less than a year before she started summoning the police, seeking orders of protection against her husband. The Old Man would get drunk and slap her around. She would call the police and file a complaint. By the time the police got around to hauling her husband into court, he would have sobered up and Rita would have forgiven him.

The cycle continued for six years, until Victor had finally moved back down the street. He evicted the tenants he had allowed into the place and took up residence as a bachelor. He and Rita continued to see each other during the week, sharing meals and sleeping together when it was mutually convenient. The complaints to the police stopped.

Nurse Hunchhammer appeared at Walter's side, a fresh bucket of suds hanging at the end of one arm. Brushing by Walter as if he were invisible, she stopped at the head of the Old Man's bed.

"Are we ready for our bath?" she inquired, pulling the curtain shut, trapping Walter inside with her and the Old Man.

"Jesus," said Walter. "Can't you wait until he's not sleeping?"

"He's not sleeping," she said smoothly. "Are you, Victor?"

The Old Man's eyes rolled open, something like a smile flickering across his face. "Ain't sleeping," he said, "just restin'. Lots easier restin' . . . when my eyes are closed."

"Did you know you have a visitor?"

"Somebody . . . here earlier." The Old Man coughed. "Said I couldn't eat."

"Did he say who he was?"

"Nope, didn't say. Reckon it was my boy though."

Standing back from the bed, Walter caught Nurse Hunchhammer's eye. He shook his head from side to side. If the Old Man wished not to acknowledge his presence, that was okay with him. Maybe his father was pissed off because Walter had not been in for a while—or perhaps the Old Man's booze-ravaged brain really had lost the ability to recognize his own flesh and blood.

She frowned and pulled back the sheet covering Victor. His body was sallow, yellow; the frame lanky as ever, but far less sturdy than Walter remembered. Dark blotches, the color of spilled ink, appeared sporadically upon the Old Man's skin. He closed his eyes, without glancing to his right, without once taking apparent notice of his son.

Beneath his backless gown, the Old Man was naked. Pulling the gown to one side, Nurse Hunchhammer soaped him from head to toe, then commenced to go at him with her sponge, paying extra attention to the areas beneath his arms and about his genitals. The Old Man's cock and balls, noticed Walter, were lifeless—lying like a bag of discarded fruit to one side of his body. After lifting them gently, Nurse Hunchhammer wiped the organs with her sponge, then lay them carefully back onto the Old Man's leg. Victor's breathing, slow and sporadic, never altered. The aged cock did not flutter. A tear came to Walter's eye. My father, he thought, is dying.

A road meandered through the dock side of town, into the country, down the length of the lake, and out to the isolated point where the Truxton estate lay. My mother could have taken the road out, but she didn't have a car of her own, and even if she did it wouldn't have made any difference. She craved the exercise, she said. Besides, it would have been a waste of gas to drive the twenty miles there and back when the estate was no more than a mile from the edge of town.

Each morning after Kate and I had left for school, my mother would walk from the house down to the city docks, carrying a goosedown pillow beneath one arm, her lunch neatly tucked into a brown paper bag in the other. From the docks, in a small skiff she had purchased with her own savings, she would row out to the Truxton place, the pillow delicately placed between her buttocks and the hard wooden seat of the boat.

In the afternoon, after paddling back to shore, she would tie the skiff to the side of Sam Porter's marina and stow the long wooden oars beneath the elevated floor of Porter's bait shop. Only when the lake was frozen would her routine vary. Then she would walk out across the lake, bundled up in a caribou fur she had brought with her from Boston.

On weekend nights and on those rare weekdays when the Truxtons entertained guests, she sometimes didn't return home until after dark. Occasionally she wouldn't get back until two or three o'clock in the morning—but that didn't happen often and even then she would take the skiff.

The subject would come up between them sporadically. Long periods would pass in relative tranquility, when the name Henry Truxton III was rarely mentioned. Then, out of the blue, my father would come across the name in the newspaper or perhaps hear it mentioned somewhere he happened to be. As a child, I did not understand that what came after that had little to do with Henry Truxton III.

"Says here—you listening, Susan?—that 'Caulfield's colorful entre-preneur or resident hedonist, as some would prefer to call him, had another boring dinner party over the weekend. Among Henry Truxton's notable guests—Sir Edmund Raymond, noted author Benjamin Brundage, actress Caroline Dumarr, and one Theodore (Ted) Williams.'"

He looked up from the paper, waiting for my mother's reaction. She was busily engaged in peeling carrots into a half-made salad. The peeler moved frantically in her hand, back and forth, as in the final strokes of masturbation. She did not gaze up when my father spoke.

"What is a hedonist, Susan?"

"A pleasure seeker." It was Kate, standing in the doorway, who answered him. "One who pursues a life of pleasure."

"How come you know so much?"

"I looked it up in the dictionary, that's how come."

My father, just home from work, sat at the kitchen table. Unknotted, his tie hung loosely from its collar. He leaned casually back in his chair, his feet propped up on the edge of the table, the newspaper open in his lap.

"Kate, get me a beer from the fridge, will ya?" Removing his feet from the table, he leaned forward in his chair. "Susan. Did you know that a hedonist was a pleasure seeker?"

The carrot was an orange stub in my mother's hand. Still the peeler whipped back and forth. "I am aware of what the word means," she said. "Yes."

"Course you are." The Old Man cracked open his beer, poured down a long slug. "You had nearly two years of college, after all. Only an uneducated slob like myself would not know what a hedonist is. But I am more than happy to be educated. So, tell me, Susan—if I had popped in at Mr. Henry Truxton's last night, would I have seen some hedonism?"

"I don't know what you mean, Victor."

"I mean"—taking another swallow of beer, he pushed the chair casually backward with his toes—"were the guests involving themselves in hedonism?"

"One does not involve oneself in hedonism, Victor. One pursues it like one pursues a dream or an ideal. The word is a noun—as the word 'ass' is a noun. One can be either an ass or a hedonist, but one cannot involve oneself in either one." My mother put the peeler down at long last and reached quickly for a tomato. After squeezing it once for firmness, she set about slicing it into the salad.

"Were they—for Christ sake—pursuing it then?"

"Pursuing what?"

"Hedonism!"

"I wouldn't know. I was in the kitchen most of the night. Doing my job." Slicing—as opposed to peeling—was slow and deliberate, a gentle motion almost, a loving but careful prelim to the main event.

My father crushed the now-empty beer can between the fingers of one hand. He tossed the can casually—like a knuckleball—in the direction of the wastebasket. It fluttered in midair and missed, coming up short, clattering noisily onto the floor of the kitchen. "Honey," he said to my sister, "toss me another one."

"Daddy," I asked, "can we go out and hit some balls?" I was crouched in my favorite spot—the alcove between the kitchen and the back porch. From there, I was a step lower than everybody else and several feet closer to the back door.

"Not tonight, kid." He opened the fresh can of beer, blowing foam from its top. "Your old man is tired."

"But you were tired last night," I said. "And you promised that tonight we could play."

"Play with him, Victor. We've got a half hour until dinner."

"I said I'm tired, goddamn it!" He brought the chair back down onto all four feet and glared up at my mother. "I work all day! I'm not some . . . some . . . hedonist, damn it! I haven't got time to be one . . . unlike my wife. If I'm too tired to play ball, that's why!"

I went outside then, stopping only to get my glove and a baseball out of the porch closet. I began throwing the ball against the cement molding at the base of our garage, trying to field the ball as it bounced unpredictably off the cracked foundation. A grounder fielded cleanly was worth two points; a pop fly, three. Playing against myself, the score didn't really matter, but I kept it just the same.

It had been nearly two months since my father and I had built the pitching mound. The Old Man had been teaching me how to hit—low line drives mostly, so that they wouldn't carry out of the yard. "You'll never have the strength to be a power hitter," he had told me, "so you might just as well learn how to drive the ball up the alleys."

He had taught me how to wait until the last possible moment—until the ball was right on top of the plate—before striding forward and flicking at it with my wrists. Wrestling with a tree trunk for emphasis, he had showed me the futility of trying to make a ball go where it wasn't meant to go. "The key to hitting," he explained, "is seeing the ball all the way from the pitcher's hand to the plate and then driving it into whatever field it's destined for. Hit it where it's pitched. In other words, don't argue with it. Punish it." He gave me a hard rubber ball to carry with me. "Squeeze that whenever you haven't got anything better to do. Before long, your forearms will be hard as lead pipes."

Next summer, he informed me, I would join a Little League team. "By then," he said, "you will be able to hit the ball to all fields. Folks will say 'Who's that kid?' and you'll tell 'em 'I'm Walter Innis, Vic Innis's boy.'"

"But what if I never learn to hit to all fields?"

"You will," he said. "I'll make sure that you do."

It mattered little to me whether I played in a league or not; or, for that matter, if I ever mastered the finer techniques of batsmanship. What mattered was the sudden flurry of time spent with my father, and the smile—rare and precious as the perfect diamond—that would cross his face whenever I managed to stroke one "just right."

What I had learned of my father before then had come mostly through Bill Hurley's stories and from the yellowed relics concealed within our attic. Beyond that, only the Old Man's occasional anecdotes, which he spewed forth from the dinner table more in the manner of a public bard than a father to his family. Finally, of course, there were the nocturnal noises that floated upward through the kitchen vent—hushed voices and muffled violence, rattling the house like invisible ghosts.

Suddenly then, from the precise distance of sixty feet six inches, I looked for much more than just the dancing knuckler. There came too, in the Old Man's easy, overhanded delivery, the gradual unfolding of my father; there, beneath each crease, carefully hidden like a pearl within its shell, was a father's love. Or perhaps it was simply warmth—as close to love as the Old Man could manage.

Love or warmth—I would not quibble—it provided me with my only ammunition against the often cruel barbs of my classmates. "My dad says your old man is a drunk," I often heard. "One time he seen your old man so pissed at a ball game that he passed out behind the bleachers." They said other things as well, things that I began to hear more of as I grew older—dark, foreboding things that accumulated within my head like particles of dust. Things about my mother and Henry Truxton III, about what she really did out there on the edge of the lake and what a drunken fool the Old Man was for not knowing about it.

I had never answered them before. I had not known how. I did not answer them even afterward, but at least now I had a picture of the Old Man that was all my own. Not a yellow photograph in a trunk, or a picture pulled from someone else's recollection, but a real-life, state-of-the-art likeness of the Old Man.

There he was, coming straight over the top with the knuckler, and there I was, standing at the plate, poised to swing. Or perhaps the two of us were lounging beneath the willow tree in the backyard, him smiling, gesticulating with his hands, showing me how to snap with my wrists at the ball. You are wrong, I would say to those who teased me—not aloud, but in my mind where the pictures were. You don't know my father. He's not a drunk. He pitches overhand to me, from a mound we built together. Soon you'll see what a hitter I've become—what my father has taught me. Could a drunken fool manage such things?

My sister appeared behind the fence surrounding our driveway, her face a mesh of tiny lines through the wire. She wore a white cotton dress. Her hair was pulled together behind her ears, falling in a knotted braid down her back. She smiled, twisting the braid carefully between the fingers of one hand.

"You want me to play with you?" she asked.

"Nah." I threw the ball so that it bounced off the fence. The wire mesh trembled, Kate's face turning into waves. "You don't know how to pitch."

"So, we'll just play catch. I'll get Daddy's glove." She turned then and ran toward the house, the hem of her dress flying up like a rabbit's tail.

Loud voices came from the house. A door slammed. My father appeared on the back porch, jacket and hat in hand. He hurried toward the driveway and got into the station wagon. Without waiting for it to warm up, he jammed the wagon into reverse, causing it to lurch and stagger like a fighter on weak knees. Once in the street, he put the car into park and pressed on the accelerator, sending a jet of blue smoke out the back. A swirl of dust rose from the road. A second later, the Old Man got the wagon into drive and disappeared down the street, never once looking back.

"Don't get that dress dirty, young lady." My mother's voice trailed after Kate into the backyard. "And don't be late for dinner. . . . fifteen minutes, for whoever's here to eat it."

Hurrying across the yard, my sister had the Old Man's glove on her hand. Her arm hung at her side, the mitt at its end, like a great claw. As she ran, her braid beat rhythmically against her back.

"Ready to play?" she asked.

"I don't feel like it," I said. Slamming the ball into my glove, I started toward the house.

Kate stepped in front of me. She was much bigger than I. From a physical standpoint, she was much like my mother. She possessed the same dark features and penetrating eyes, yet something about her appearance lacked clarity—as if, because of her youth, her beauty had not yet been brought into proper focus. "What about me?" she asked. "I went into the house and got a glove so we could play."

"So, play by yourself."

"If you're counting on him coming back to play with you," she said, "you might as well forget about it! He'd rather get drunk."

"That ain't true! He's gonna teach me how to hit. Next year, I'm gonna play in a league."

"Huh!" She laughed. "Next year, that mound'll be nothing but another pile of dog shit . . . and he'll probably make us clean it up!"

Out in the lake, at its very tip, where Truxton's acres jutted out into the water like a broken thumb, there was a baseball diamond of major league proportions. At least, such a place appeared to me in a dream that night;

a manicured field of green and brown, surrounded on all sides by a great steel fence. Peering in from the mound was Henry Truxton III, his uniform creased pin stripes, his cap pulled low over his eyes. At the plate stood my mother. She was smiling in her closed-mouth way, shouldering a bat, readying herself for the pitch. The rest of the stadium was empty. Outside the fence, leaning against the locked gate, was the Old Man. He appeared haggard and alone, like a fan without admission.

"He'll sleep now," said Nurse Hunchhammer, tidying up the sheets, tucking them in around the Old Man as if they were all that held him together. She moved like a cyclone about the room—picking up this, discarding that, pulling a curtain about the Old Man's bed, pouring the remains of his bath carefully down the sink. Would it kill her, wondered Walter, to leave *Sports Illustrated* open upon the nightstand? Or a ruffled sheet hanging from the end of the mattress? What strange hormone possessed her? Why must her world be so neat?

"There's no point in you waiting around." She smiled like a Gestapo interrogator. "He'll sleep right up until dinner."

"I thought I might just sit here a few minutes longer."

"What on earth for? He doesn't even know you're here and he won't wake up for hours."

"I don't have anything else to do."

"You don't have anything else to do?" She sounded incredulous, as if Walter had just confessed to a murder. "Well, isn't that nice."

"I mean," said Walter, wondering why he was bothering to explain and for whose benefit, "at the moment."

"Hmmph! Well, I have plenty to do." She eyed Walter, as if contemplating sweeping him up with the rest of the room's debris. "At the moment."

"Well, don't let me stop you."

"Don't get insolent with me. It's tough enough as it is, working in this place. I don't need some welfare bum getting insolent with me."

"Who says I'm on welfare?"

"Who says you're not?"

"Well, I'm not."

"Do you work?"

"No. Not at the moment, anyhow."

"And you're not on welfare?"

"That's right."

"And you're certainly not rich—by that, I mean independently wealthy—or you wouldn't have stuck your old man in a place like this." She scratched her head, poked absently at her nose with a finger. "Can mean only one of two things."

"What's that?"

"You're a schemer or you're a writer. There's only two types of people that can get away without working, welfare, or a rich uncle. Schemers and writers. Which are you?"

"Well . . . I'm not a writer."

"So. You're a schemer. I thought so."

"Why did you think so?"

"Cause you don't act like a writer. Writers like to read, and the only thing I ever see you reading is the sports page. Besides, my first husband was a schemer and you've got the same look about you that he had."

"What kind of a look was that?"

"Dazed. Like by mistake, he got dropped into this world when he was supposed to have been dropped somewheres else."

"Where else?"

"I don't know where else. And neither did he. That's how come he was a schemer. He was always scheming on ways to get where he thought he was supposed to be, instead of working to stay where he was."

"Where did he end up?"

"Selling chicken in Delray Beach, Florida. It was his grandest scheme—barbecue chicken four months of the year, to the vacationers. Girls in bikinis, sand and sun the rest of the time. He cleaned out my bank account to do it."

"I'm sorry to hear that."

"Don't be. He did us both a favor. We've seen each other since, even had some laughs together, but I keep him a good distance from my pocketbook, I'll tell ya. He never did lose that dazed look." Nurse Hunchhammer's smile softened, just slightly. She dropped her arms to her sides and started toward the door, stopping first by Jacob Johnson's bedstand. She picked up the evening newspaper from where it lay neatly folded upon the stand and turned back toward Walter.

"The truth is, I've got a weakness for schemers. Always have. They make the world seem like a much bigger place than it actually is." She tossed the newspaper toward Walter and looked quickly around the room. "I guess that's why I work here. Most of them that end up here are schemers. Schemers that ran out of schemes."

As she opened the door to go, she said back over her shoulder, "Long as you don't get Mr. Johnson excited again and you don't fool with things I've already straightened up, you can sit there and scheme all afternoon far as I'm concerned."

A schemer. The word had a bad connotation. Walter thought immediately of island paradises sold through the mail; of young hustlers going through the obituary pages, carefully circling names of sole survivors. Was a schemer really no different from a hustler? Nurse Hunchhammer seemed to think so. To hear her tell it, a schemer was simply an honest soul with vision.

Sitting on the bookshelf between Walter's father and Jacob Johnson was an *American Heritage Dictionary*. The book certainly would belong to Mr. Johnson. The Old Man, recalled Walter, never had need of a dictionary. Were he to encounter a word he did not understand, he would simply bluff his way through, perhaps even substitute another in its place.

After pulling the dictionary from the shelf, Walter leafed through the pages until he spotted "hustler." In slang, it meant one "making money by questionable means." A disreputable character without question. A slimeball. The broker of island paradises and false love. A man acting not from vision, but from simple opportunity.

A "schemer," on the other hand, was quite different. He who schemes or plots does so "through a careful and systematic program of action." The schemer schemes in the hopes of obtaining some "visionary plan" or "object." Nothing underhanded or disreputable about that. Taken to extremes, a schemer might indeed be a visionary. One could be called much worse, thought Walter, than a schemer.

Bolstered by this bit of knowledge and heartened by the possibility that he might at last have found his calling, Walter sat back to contemplate the possibilities. He looked at his father and wondered what scheme might lessen the Old Man's suffering. Why did he care? The Old Man had done nothing to lessen his son's—or anyone else's, for that matter.

Walter sighed and turned away from the bed. He glanced at the newspaper that Nurse Hunchhammer had tossed at him.

On the front page of the Caulfield *Banner* was a face from Walter's past. Somewhat older than Walter remembered and perhaps a bit fuller, it shone nonetheless with the timeless glow of success. Unwrinkled, apparently untouched by the years, this was the face of a man of stature, well connected, with a bent toward white tuxedos and subservient women. The picture was of a candidate for the state Senate.

Beneath the picture was an article. The article purported to be one of human interest. It told why Caulfield's richest and most reclusive property owner had, at the age of fifty-nine, suddenly decided to enter politics. He was bored, said Henry Truxton III, and felt he had a contribution to make. A lifetime Democrat, he aspired to win that party's nomination.

. . . Truxton, the grandson of the steel and oil magnate by the same name, was once blacklisted in Hollywood. It was at a time when he was becoming well known as a motion picture producer and virtually ended that aspect of his career. "That era, of McCarthyism and blacklisting," Truxton related, "was one of the saddest moments in this nation's history. As Americans, we must never forget it, but we should also remember—and be proud of the fact—that our nation weathered those times and came through them more unified than ever."

Truxton is proud of his own stance during the time following the Korean War, when Senator Joe McCarthy and his committee on Un-American Activities helped bring the nation to a state of near panic over the spread of communism and what journalists termed the Red Scare. "I had friends who were or at one time had been members of the Communist Party. A lot of people were looking for answers following the Depression, and they jumped into and out of the Party that quickly. I myself was never a member nor interested in becoming one. I knew somehow that this country would survive and prosper through the system of government envisioned by the framers of the Constitution. But, I will say this, I believe—and I won't apologize for my beliefs—that one must stand by one's friends. That is what my parents taught me and that is what I have attempted to teach my own children. And for that I was blacklisted. It hurt me financially at the time, and in other ways as well. But I found out who my real friends were and what it actually means to be an American. . . .

Noises coming from behind Jacob Johnson's curtain interrupted Walter's reading. The rustling of sheets, the clattering of an object hitting the floor, the old codger's muttered swearing as his arm groped blindly beneath the curtain for whatever had dropped.

"Hey, kid," he said from behind the curtain, "you still out there?"

"Yeah. I'm still here," said Walter, quietly so as not to awaken the Old Man.

"Come on over here and pick up my pipe, will ya? I'd get it myself, 'cept then I'd have to get out of bed, and whenever I get out of bed I feel like I have to take a piss. So I walk all the way into the bathroom, only then I can't go, and I end up standing there holding my dick for twenty minutes, trying to make the damn thing work. And I'll tell ya, kid, there's nothing sadder than holding onto an eighty-year-old dick that don't work. So all in all I'd rather just lay here."

"Why should I believe you?"

"About what? The dick or the pipe?"

"Any of it. After the stunt you pulled, I don't know if I'd help you even if you were crippled and couldn't get out of bed."

"You talking about what happened before? When you first came into the room? That was just for laughs. I get bored, that's all. Nothing personal, kid. I tried the same thing on Hunchhammer, only she didn't fall for it. That's how come she knew what was what."

"I thought you were dying. I thought I had killed you."

"When I die, it'll be of my own accord." Mr. Johnson pulled back the curtain and looked out at Walter. "I didn't know you were such a serious sort or I wouldn't have played the prank. For that I am truly sorry."

He propped himself up on his pillow and reached over to pick up a pair of glasses from the nightstand. After putting the glasses on, he peered closely at Walter. "If I had been wearing my peepers, I'd have spotted you right off as the serious sort. You got those deep-set eyes. The kind of eyes that draw the world in—sucks it right back into your head and holds it there like tobacco smoke."

Mr. Johnson shook his head, smiled in a crooked sort of way. "I guess maybe you might be serious enough to think that you could kill somebody without laying a hand on 'em—as if a person couldn't have managed to die without you. The young," he said, "sure do think they're something powerful."

Walter walked over to Mr. Johnson's bed. Bending down, he picked up the pipe from where it lay on the floor. It was one of those S-shaped pipes, with a big bowl at the bottom and a wide open stem to draw the smoke through. Absently Walter tossed it onto the bed and turned away. Mr. Johnson's hand on his arm stopped him.

"Give an old fool a break, kid? My eyes stick out of my head like onion bulbs," he said, tapping the glass in his spectacles. "They're like goddamned mirrors. They haven't sucked anything in for years. So let's not stay mad, huh?"

Walter liked this man and knew it was no use pretending that he didn't. He suddenly envied Mr. Johnson, hoped in another forty years he would learn as much as he—that, someday, his eyes too might expand outward. The muscles in Walter's arm relaxed, the steady throbbing behind his eyes lessened.

"Nurse Hunchhammer know you've got that pipe?"

"Sure. She just doesn't know where. She comes flying in here, sniffing Bull Durham or Raleigh Light, and she's fit to be tied. 'There are rules, Mr. Johnson,' she says, and then she starts to tear the place apart, looking for the pipe, but she hasn't found it yet and she isn't likely to." Glancing quickly at the door and then back at Walter, Mr. Johnson lowered his voice.

"Can you keep a secret, kid?" Then chuckling. "Forget I asked. With those eyes, I'd trust you with my nymphomaniac wife on a virgin island."

He reached over to the bedstand and removed the picture of the boy standing next to a tank. The picture was in a hollow box frame with room for three more to surround it. Working quickly, Jacob removed the back of the frame, reached inside, and pulled out a pouch of tobacco and a tamp. "The pipe comes apart," he said. "The two pieces fit inside like they was made for it."

"Is that your real son?"

"Yep. Died in Korea, for God knows what reason." He filled the bowl and began tapping the tobacco down into it. "He had the same deep-set eyes as you. Was a real serious boy. That's how come I trust him with my pipe."

He spit out a couple of pieces of tobacco, then reached back inside the picture frame and produced a lighter and lit the pipe. A cloud of white smoke instantly filled the room. Waving at the smoke with a frail arm, Jacob sent it toward the open window on the other side of the room.

"The older one gets," he said between puffs, "the less serious the world should become. You see, there are fewer and fewer things within it that can scare you." He coughed, his chest shaking like the branches of a dying tree hit by the wind.

"Take smoking. To a fella your age, its possible consequences are a serious concern. To me, such talk has lost its sting. I read the latest health statistics before or after the comic strips and with no more regard." He drew on the pipe again, this time with less vigor, and let the smoke ease slowly from one side of his mouth. "I suppose," he said, "when nothing at all appears serious, one will die."

He took one more draw from the pipe. Then, holding the smoke in, he turned the bowl over and tapped the remaining tobacco into the wastebasket. As he blew the smoke out, he sputtered again. "I am still serious enough"—he smiled and, Walter saw, looking into Jacob's eyes, much life remaining there—"to allow myself only half a bowl."

"In that case," said Walter, "may your next full bowl be several years in the future."

"Hah! You do have a sense of humor after all. Now, if you will be so kind as to return my sports page, I will tell you something about your own father."

"What about my father?"

"First, the sports page," said Jacob as he put the pipe back into its hiding place and placed his son's picture back on the nightstand.

Walter walked to the other side of the room and removed the sports section from the rest of the paper. Back at Jacob's bedside, he handed it to the old man. "I'm halfway through an article in the front section," he said. "I'll give it back to you before I leave."

"I don't care anything about the front section. There's nothing there that I can take seriouly." Jacob spread the paper out in front of him on the bed.

"So?"

"About your father?"

"Yes."

"I don't know him well," said Jacob, looking up from the paper. "He doesn't talk much except at night, and then not to me."

"Who does he talk to?"

"God, I think."

"He prays?"

"No. I don't think it's praying, really. It's more like talking. He talks to God like I've been talking to you."

"My father is not religious . . . or, at least, he never was. He wouldn't even drive my mother to church."

"I didn't say he was religious. I said he talks to God. I tell you this because you're his son and I like you and I don't believe he would tell you himself. With all due respect, he doesn't seem to talk to you at all."

"Do you hear what he says?"

"Occasionally. I'm not an eavesdropper, but I have trouble sleeping at night."

"So?"

"That's it. That's what I wanted to tell you. He talks at night and it's not babbling, but serious talk about you and your sister, Kate, and sometimes about your mother. He talks about other things. Your father is a very serious man. It is unusual—and sad to see—in a man so close to death."

"My father is not serious."

"Nor is he religious? Go finish your article," said Jacob. "I want to read the sports."

Mr. Johnson turned on the light above his bed and pulled the curtain shut. Returning to his own chair, Walter listened instinctively for the Old Man's tortured breathing. Then he picked up the front section of the paper and started reading where he had left off.

"The freedoms contained within our Constitution are what separate us from so many of the oppressed nations within the world. Those freedoms must be strictly construed," said the man who many claim is the richest in the state. "One, for example, may be offended by pornography—as I myself certainly am—but that does not mean that we, as a nation, have the right to tell others, who wish to do so, that they do not have the privilege to view such materials in the privacy of their own homes. It also means, in my opinion, that we—as a nation—have the absolute right to regulate its public sale and to zealously protect our children from being exposed to such filth."

During the 1950s and 1960s the Truxton estate was the site of countless bashes and celebrity get-togethers. During this period Truxton gained his reputation as a womanizer and international playboy. He was even accused of plying young women with promises of stardom and celebrity introductions. The estate was a well-known haven for celebrities and sports figures of the time.

Truxton plays down most of these stories as exaggerations and outright lies. "The press loves to create mythical characters out of tiny grains of truth. It's what sells. For the record," he said, "I have been happily married for 29 years. Other than a couple of minor indiscretions during my youth—which I now regret and don't feel compelled to reveal to the press—I have always been a loyal husband and father." The much-venerated philanthropist then smiled, wrapping his arm about the shoulder of his wife, Beth Anne. "I believe in the traditional values. Without the backbone provided by a solid home and family, I would hate to think where I might be today."

Later that night, lying in bed, I heard my father's return. Even with my head buried beneath my pillow, I could not escape the raised voices, the muffled slaps, my mother, first screaming, then whimpering in the manner of a child suddenly stripped of all privileges.

Finally, as a prelude to silence, came the sound of the front door slamming on its hinges and, a moment later, the roar of the station wagon pulling from the driveway. My mother, I was certain, would not be around in the morning.

For the first time, the idiocy of their behavior did not escape me. For what had they done but change places? After half an hour of combat, he had taken her spot in the marital bed, while she had escaped in the family wagon, its engine still warm from the Old Man's recent toot.

I did not rush down the stairs after her. I did not cry. I did not beseech God for a quick and peaceful resolution to this latest battle. I was thankful only for the silence—given, it seemed, like a trophy at the end of a grueling race. The station wagon, I knew, would be at the bus station in the morning for my father to pick up. And my mother would return home whether she wanted to or not. Where else, after all, would she go? Everywhere else, apparently, there was nothing. Here, at least, there was something. Possessing the strength of an undertow and the lure of a narcotic, whatever it was would not allow my mother to drift too far or to stay away too long.

Four days later she telephoned to say that she was coming home. She spoke only to my sister, keeping her message brief. She did not say where she was calling from—Kate was able to detect only the sound of dogs in the background and someone with a foreign accent screaming for an order of fish—nor did she mention where she had been. She would be home that evening, she said, in time for dinner.

The Old Man rushed down to Hurley's and put in a special order. "It's take-out, Bill," he explained, "and I need it ready by five o'clock."

When my mother walked through the front door at five-thirty that evening, she was greeted by a banner hanging from the stairway. My father had purchased the white backing from which it was made and had supervised as my sister and I performed the necessary cutting and pasting. WELCOME HOME MOM, it said.

She stepped gingerly into the room, as if not certain she had found the right party. One side of her face, still swollen and black, glistened grotesquely in the overhead light. Her lower lip, distended, yet comic, was incapable of forming a straight line. Thus misshapen, she appeared frozen in either constant pain or pleasure.

For dinner there was a rump of lamb, cooked to order by Bill Hurley himself. The dish was garnished with applesauce and browned potatoes. As an appetizer there were popovers with boysenberry jam. My father had spent almost forty dollars for the feast to be elegantly spread upon an imitation silk tablecloth. The dishes were my mother's best china.

Beaming like a proud father, the Old Man led her into the dining room on his arm. The room was lit by candlelight. The three of us— my father, my sister, and I—wore cone-shaped hats atop our heads, purchased especially for the occasion. Around each hat's base, "Happy Birthday" was printed in a multicolored band—the best the Old Man could do, he explained, on such short notice. The peak of each hat was a Styrofoam bauble.

My mother, I realized, would never be quite so beautiful as she once had been. The face would reshape itself; the hideous lips would heal. But something else—a warm spot, maybe, in her eyes—had somehow vanished. In a picture one would not notice. This was not a gaping loss, not some black hole in her countenance, but a subtle transformation, deftly disguised but not hidden.

Both of my parents drank heavily of the wine. There was much laughter. The discussion turned to times past, remembered fondly. It became a joyous occasion. At long last, my father leaned over and kissed my mother sloppily on the lips. "I missed you so," he said. "Another day without you and I would have died."

Her eyes moved constantly—from the half-devoured lamb, to the banner hanging from the stairs, to each of our faces—coming to rest, finally, on my father. "You're such a romantic, Victor." The words were slightly slurred. My mother, I could tell, was drunk.

And, oh yes, we sang "My Bonnie lies over the ocean, my Bonnie lies over the sea"—each of us taking a verse, all coming in together on the chorus. We sang loudly, as if to drown out something.

I recall this scene as being a significant moment in my life. I see the whole thing through some hideous veil, as if all of our faces—not just my mother's—had been distorted. And I recall, at about that time, a persistent rumbling beginning somewhere in the pit of my stomach—hardly noticeable yet, but seeming capable of acquiring greater momentum.

I did not dwell upon the possible motives behind my mother's return. That she may have done so for the benefit of my sister and me did not occur to me. That her coming home may have been the result of some deeper emotion was beyond my immediate understanding. I saw only the significant benefits to be gained from port wine, a rump of lamb, and slavering bits of nostalgia.

Getting up from the table, my father broke a wineglass. He swore under his breath, apologized out loud to my mother for breaking such a valuable piece of china. She laughed breathily, waving it away as if it could be replaced easily.

Stumbling into the kitchen, the Old Man got another bottle of port, then returned to the living room and slung my mother over his shoulder. Her dress flying up over her knees, she laughed heartily as the Old Man carted her and the bottle up the stairs. "Bring back my Bonnie to me," he sang as he went.

Even before they had made the turn at the top of the stairs, my mother's hands were groping at the front of the Old Man's trousers, clumsily manipulating the snap that secured them. Hanging in tangled disarray, her hair all but concealed her once-magnificent face.

After carefully wrapping what was left of the lamb, my sister and I placed it in the refrigerator. The leftovers would make sandwiches for a week. Then we did the dishes. Kate washed. I dried.

Her hands were a flurry of action—wiping, sudsing, rinsing, and tossing each dish into the rack, barely hesitating to wipe an occasional soap sud from her face. Although she was only two years older than I, the difference, to me, seemed far greater. Kate seemed always to have a handle on things, in a way that I never did. The trick, I think, was that she was adaptable, always prepared to shrug off the old and take on the new. Why, I wondered, was she never frightened? What inner knowledge did she possess that gave her such confidence?

My mother's laughter—the confused, foolish sound of chattering birds—floated down the stairway. Then came the deep, trembling baritone of the Old Man. The sounds merged and hovered in the house like the contrasting music at an opera. With a disgusted look toward the stairway, Kate walked quickly over to the record player. After placing a record on the turntable, she turned up the volume.

"Jesus Christ!" she said, returning to the kitchen. "It's like a goddamned zoo in here!"

"I wish Daddy wouldn't drink," I said.

"That ain't drinking up there, Wally," said Kate. "That ain't got nothing to do with drinking."

"Still, I wish that he didn't."

"Trouble with you, is that you wish too much! He fucking drinks and all of your wishing ain't gonna change it." She plunged a hand into the sink, groping blindly in the dirty dishwater. Soon her hand reappeared holding the sponge, gripping it tightly. "I could wish this was gold!" she said, shaking the sponge inches from my face. "Every day I could look at it and wish it was a solid brick of gold and do you know how much good it would do me? None! Not one goddamned bit of good! Because this ain't gold, Wally! It ain't nothing but a goddamned kitchen sponge and all of my wishing ain't gonna change that!"

I wiped water and bits of lamb from my face. Picking up a plate from the rack, I gazed with interest at its still-damp surface. I saw my face— placid, I thought, amazingly calm to belong to me—and that of my sister, staring intently over my shoulder. I could see that she was not really upset with me, only concerned. Greatly concerned with her vision of the world, this analogy of the sponge. And there was love there. Love for me, her younger brother who wished for gold.

"Even so," I told her. "I wish he wouldn't."

She reached out suddenly and hugged me. Still wet from the dishwater, her hands left cool prints upon my back. She pulled me in close to her body—for a moment I felt her breasts, hard and unyielding as rock— then just as suddenly she pushed me away again.

"Poor Wally," she said, staring at me from arm's length. "You're just a wishful thinker."

Therein was the steel lining of Kate's character. There was no wishing within her. Only the hardness of reality. She saw what was what and did not wish for more. The world would not change; only fools would wish for such a thing. At a young age she discovered these things. She stopped wishing and began to look for ways to gain from the wishes of others.

A group of older boys from the neighborhood used to follow my sister around like hounds that have picked up a scent. Occasionally, when my mother worked late, one of them would accompany Kate home from school. Now and then, one would follow her into the living room. From the other side of the closed door, I sometimes stood and listened. These boys let their wishes control them. And Kate knew it. "I don't want nothin' but to touch 'em, Katy," I heard one of them plead. "Won't nobody know. I'll give ya a quarter."

Silence followed, save for the boy's labored breathing. At long last came my sister's steady, confident reply. "They're worth a dollar," she said, "and I don't much care who knows, long's they're willing to pay the price."

That day in the kitchen, following my mother's return, Kate had been thirteen. I was eleven. After we finished the dishes, the two of us sat in the living room playing cards. War at first, then double solitaire and finally spades. Every time we heard a noise from upstairs, Kate would turn the record player up and place her hands over her ears.

"I hope he doesn't do that to Mommy again," I said after a while.

"There you go wishing again."

"I said hope, not wish."

"Wishing, hoping, it's the same thing, Wally." She sighed. "Besides, she only got what was coming to her."

"What do you mean by that?"

"I mean, dummy, that anybody who sees a storm coming and don't do nothing to get out of the way deserves what they get."

She trumped me with an ace, taking my king of spades. She smiled as she raked in the cards. "How many times I told ya to hold onto your high cards till you can't get trumped?"

"I always hope," I said sheepishly, "that the ace won't come up."

"You know what I think?"

"What?"

"I think that they wouldn't fight so much if it weren't for us."

"What do you mean?"

"They fight 'cause of us."

"Who said?"

"Ma." She looked up from her hand. "That's who said."

"What did she say?"

"I heard her talking to the Old Man. She said if it weren't for us, they wouldn't have any problems at all, 'cause she wouldn't be here. She said we were like an anchor 'round her neck."

"I don't believe she said that."

"She did."

"What did Daddy say?"

"He laughed and then he said he guessed it was a good thing we was born after all."

CHAPTER 22

Maurie's office, like its occupant, was large and disheveled, lacking in the usual proprieties of the profession. A law degree from St. John's, under glass, partially covered by what looked to be New Year's streamers, hung crookedly from one wall. A mysterious photograph of a dilapidated building in the heart of New York's Bowery hung on another; above the entrance to the building sat several pigeons; on the way out, covering his head, peeking slyly from beneath his tattered hat, was a man who might have been Maurie.

His desk had once belonged to Walter and before that to Walter's father and grandfather. Victor had never had need of it, nor had his father. Wanting to end the dormancy, Walter had given the desk to Maurie on his friend's graduation from law school. A large oak desk, it was the only object of substance in the room.

Open files and papers lay about on the desk's top like discarded Christmas wrappings. On various chairs throughout the room, piles of law books teetered like the rotting pillars of Rome.

Maurie himself sat behind the desk in a brown, springless chair. His feet, propped up, were placed among the scattered files. Both of his hands were occupied with the business of eating—a sesame bagel, made fat with a thick layer of cream cheese and lox. "So," he told Walter. "I got a call from your wife."

"Oh?" Walter looked at the desk that had once belonged to his father. The Old Man, he supposed, would be pleased that it was finally serving a purpose. "When?"

"A couple of days ago. I'm afraid I may have gotten you into a bit of hot water. I didn't realize that she was unaware of your present state of unemployment. It just sort of slipped out."

"How did she take it?"

"She said something about filing for a divorce and hung up." Maurie shoved the rest of the bagel into his mouth, chewed vigorously for several seconds, then swallowed. "Under the circumstances, I feel obliged to offer you free legal representation."

"Thanks."

"If she files, do you want to contest it?"

"I'm not sure. I'll have to think about it, I guess."

Maurie stood up from the desk, then moved over to the cabinet. After opening it, he took out two glasses and a bottle of Chivas Regal, filled both glasses, and placed the fuller one in front of Walter. "What have you been up to? I've been trying to reach you all week."

"Scheming."

"What?"

"You asked me what I've been up to. Scheming. I've been scheming. Sitting in the Old Man's room and scheming."

"How is Victor?"

"He's dying, Maurie. The man in with him says he talks to God."

"Your old man, talking to God? I don't believe it."

"That's what he says, this fellow—Jacob is his name. He says at night the Old Man talks to God about me and Kate and sometimes about my mother. But he never talks at all when I'm there."

"It's better when they go quickly—like my old man. Ate a good dinner, had a glass of wine, then, in the middle of the *Carson* show, slipped off quiet as a mouse fart."

"I don't think my father wants to die just yet. I think he could, if he wanted to, but he doesn't want to. He thinks maybe he can straighten everything out with God now, before he dies."

"That doesn't sound like your old man. I can't picture Victor asking forgiveness, so's he'll have a better shot at heaven."

"It's not forgiveness he's asking for. He's pissed off, Jacob says. Genuinely pissed off, about ending up in such a miserable state."

"Who's he pissed off at?"

"God, I guess. At least that's what Jacob says. According to him, the Old Man has gotten serious in his old age."

"Serious. What do you mean serious? Serious about what?"

"The things he was never serious about before, when it mattered— like me and Kate. It's a sad way to die, says Jacob. Serious."

"Who the hell is this Jacob, for God's sake? A rabbi or what?"

"He's a retired sheetmetal worker from St. Louis. His sister lived in Caulfield. When she died, he ended up in the home."

"A sheetmetal worker is talking to you about God and death?"

"Sheetmetal workers die the same as rabbis, Maurie."

"Meshuggener, Walter! You have gone meshuga! What else does the Old Man speak of at night?"

"Baseball."

"What? He still dreams of the major leagues?"

"No. The one thing he thanks God for—over and over again, says Jacob—is for the injury to his arm. If he hadn't been injured, he never would have been in Caulfield that summer he met my mother. Katy and I never would have been born."

"Jesus, Walter. Do you think he has any idea . . . ?"

"About my mother you mean, and Henry Truxton? He knew if he wanted to. It was there for him to see. But I don't think he ever cared to see it, therefore he never did. So he will die thinking she was a saint and be happy, at least, with that. You and I, my friend, will live knowing she was something less."

Walter raised his glass then and tipped it at Maurie, before swallowing its contents in one gulp. There was a lull in the conversation—one of those pregnant lulls that takes the place of words; a silence that can say much more than any words could, a silence that creates a moment of reflection. A moment when two people both look distractedly at the floor to be sure they are able to locate their feet, or perhaps one will gaze into his glass, a sudden curiosity with its contents occurring to him. Then one will clear his throat or perhaps get up to refill his glass and the silence will be broken. When they speak again, it will be of something quite apart.

"Walter, what are your plans? Do you know what you're going to be doing?"

"Doing when?"

"Jesus. Now—in the future, for Christ sake."

"I've got a date with Jeannie Weatherrup this weekend. She's going to make me dinner."

"You mean 'Periscope Up Weatherrup?' The girl with cement between her legs?"

"Cement for you maybe. I have reason to believe that area may have softened over the years."

"I wouldn't know. It's been at least ten years since I've seen her. But I understand she got into the deli business since her husband died. Kosher. Can you imagine that? Jeannie Weatherrup and her gigantic Gentile tits peddling kosher lamb to the Jews?"

"She coaches her son's Little League team. That's where I ran into her, at the ball field."

"And now you're hoping to give her the high hard one?"

"She's a nice girl, Maurie. I wasn't good enough for her in high school. She knew it. Maybe things have changed. Maybe all I want is a good dinner."

"Things have not changed that much, my friend. Anyway, what about Marsha? It's not really over, is it?"

"From what you say, it is."

"She was just blowing off steam. That's the way women are, Walter. Promise her something—a kid, more money, more sex. She'll come back."

"Maybe."

"Or don't do anything at all and maybe she won't."

"Who knows? I haven't exactly done much to make her happy, Maurie. The thought has crossed my mind that I may not be capable of it. When I should be thinking about her, I find myself thinking about other things."

"Your future, I hope, beyond Jeannie Weatherrup and whatever may transpire there?"

"Yes. My future."

"Good. Have you thought more about my suggestions?"

Maurie had encouraged Walter to apply for a city housing inspector's job—"It's strictly no-show, with plenty of perks for an enterprising sort"—or for a bailiff's position at the county courthouse—"Civil service, Walter. Means you can't get canned. And the best part? There's juice money to be had right there in the halls of justice. Every judge or lawyer I ever met bets football or plays the ponies. What better place to run a book?"

"I rejected them both," said Walter, "as being too risky, too degrading, too much like work, or too damn much like selling cars. I can't think about another job right now."

"That makes two things you aren't thinking about. What the hell are you thinking about—this idea you said you wanted to throw at me?"

Walter took the article on Henry Truxton III from his shirt pocket, unfolded it, and carefully placed it on the desk in front of Maurie. "Have you seen this?"

Lowering his feet from the desk, Maurie brought his chair down. He pushed his glasses on and began to read. When he was done, he looked up again, slowly shaking his head from side to side. After shoving the article back across the desk, he picked up a pencil from the desktop and pierced the tangled nest of hair atop his head with it.

"Sure I've seen it. Who hasn't?" The pencil stuck out like antennae from opposite sides of his head. "He announced his candidacy a couple of weeks ago. So what?"

"Yesterday afternoon, Maurie, I'm sitting in the nursing home by the Old Man's bed and the nurse calls me a schemer, then she flips me the newspaper and there—on the front page—was the article on Truxton. Otherwise, I wouldn't have known."

"You would have known sooner or later, Walter." Maurie moved the pencil back and forth through his hair.

"Maybe, but that's not the point. It's the way I found out, Maurie. It means something."

"What the hell are you talking about? Means what?"

"An opportunity to balance the books, I guess. A chance to make an entry on our side of the ledger for a change."

"What kind of an entry?"

"I don't know why I even care, Maurie, that's the strange part, but I guess I must or I wouldn't be going into that home every day thinking about it."

"Thinking about what?"

"If there is a way for the Old Man to die at peace—or at least with a little dignity, or maybe only in a less serious state of mind—then, all in all, Maurie, I think I would feel better about things."

"What things?"

"All things."

"Is it your Old Man's peace of mind, Walter, or your own that you're concerned about?"

"I'm hoping that one might be derived from the other."

"Forget it, Walter. Whatever it is, forget it. . . ."

"The three of us—you, me, and Henry Truxton—can make it happen, Maurie."

"Jesus Christ! Marsha was right! She said you were weirded out and she's right on the money. I don't blame her for going to Boston. That isn't far enough!"

He jerked the pencil from his head, its splintered point catching on several hair strands as it came free. Maurie cursed and threw the pencil against the wall. He picked up his glass and finished the Chivas in one swallow. Talk of God and death always unnerved Maurie, began a fluttering somewhere in his stomach. He preferred not to linger on such subjects. Nothing was gained by such talk. The latter was a certainty— a barrier, lingering like a great wall at the end of a darkened runway. You can't bribe it and you can't hustle it. What the hell good did it do to think about it?

"I think I've worked out a scheme, Maurie. If I'm right there's a dignified death in it for the Old Man and money for us."

"Money?" Maurie placed the empty glass next to the picture of his wife. "How much money?"

"Lots of money to us," said Walter. "Not so much to Henry Truxton."

At some point, I figured the whole thing out; that is, I got a handle on what I assumed the rest of the world must have known all along. Maybe I was twelve or thirteen at the time. I can't really be sure because I didn't experience a sudden revelation, or wake up after a dream one morning feeling smarter. Mine was a slow dawning, like fog gradually lifting from a lake to reveal in the end sparkling blue clarity. So clear and unmuddled that one wonders why he did not notice it before.

Ass hard to a pew, bedecked from head to foot in unemotional black, my mother prayed for what? When she opened her mouth in pious song, who did she imagine might listen?

Kate, with her steel lining and breasts for hire, had been right all along. Wishes were valueless, worth less than pennies in a man's pocket. So it was that I began to see the same things I had always seen, only in a different light, the entire picture framed with a sardonic glow.

As the plate passed amongst the parishioners, I wondered, was it for love or opportunity that they had gathered together? If for love, then why did they avert their eyes and beseech one another? What was it that they, as a congregation, were hoping to purchase with their aggregate wealth? Whatever it was—this great reward—would it be divvied up tit for tat, or would each of us get a piece regardless of his or her contribution?

Caught removing coins from the collection platter, I was reprimanded by the Reverend Beemer, then blessed. I drew a mustache and large ears on the image of St. Mark in my Sunday school primer and was expelled from class. Once again I was reprimanded by Theodore Beemer and blessed. My mother, when she found out, took a belt to my backside. The Old Man, in response to the news, shrugged his shoulders and laughed.

I met Maurie Winthrop around that time. He was new in my grade, yet not new to Caulfield. His parents, although not rich, were upper middle class, and thus rich in my eyes. They had, at first, shipped Maurie to a private school somewhere downstate. In time, he had been expelled for conduct unbecoming to an eight-year-old. He had been enrolled in two other institutions with similar results. The tuition increased with each dismissal until, finally, Maurie had priced himself beyond his parents' means. "Maybe," said his father, lacking both conviction and funds, "public school is what's needed to straighten you out."

He had appeared one day—shaggy and disheveled—in my homeroom class. Even then, his glasses were thick as windowpanes; his hair, frayed at the ends, sat atop his head like a trashed rug. Snickers abounded. Someone had announced, "It's Dr. Frankenstein." Mrs. Bartlett, my homeroom teacher, said, "Class, this is Maurie Winthrop. Let's make him feel welcome." Maurie had taken a seat in the back, broken wind— the sound reverberating about the room like an unmuffled engine—and promptly announced, "Jesus, it's early for geese, isn't it?"

I liked him from the start but was wary of telling him so. He didn't seem to want to make friends. Not that he disliked people or that they disliked him, it was simply that he appeared to have more fun by himself—engaging others only as accomplices in pranks or to get information. No one—not even the most feared bullies in school—seemed to bother Maurie. It was as if the aura of weirdness surrounding him served also to protect him; as if, were he to be engaged physically, he might give off some strange, infecting odor.

One afternoon in the spring, following school, I was accosted by Stanley Ball and Cleeve Seward, the most mismatched pair of brutes then roaming the junior high school corridors. They caught me out behind the school, as I cut across the playground. The attack was neither original nor unexpected. The playground, shielded from the street by the school itself, was a favored haven of bullies and perverts. It was also the most direct route to my house.

Coming at me from two sides, they hemmed me in at the shoulders, walking close and wrapping their arms about me as if we were all fast friends. I knew what was to come next. I had dealt with it before. Let them do what they want, I prayed, but quickly so that no one would see my humiliation.

"How's Prickless Innis?" asked Stanley who, despite being in my grade, was two years older than I. That year was the third straight he had spent in eighth grade. It was a stumbling block he would never overcome. In another year he would be sixteen and old enough to quit. That, however, would not be soon enough to save me from what had become one of his favorite pastimes. "Been getting much, Prickless?"

"Much what?"

"Poon-tang. That's what."

"No."

"You're keeping your eyes open, though. Right, Prickless?"

"Right."

"You know what else you gotta watch out for?"

"No."

"Pearl Harbor sneak attacks, that's what."

Instinctively I dropped both hands to the area beneath my belt, but not soon enough. Stanley's hand was already there, his fingers already latched securely about my genitals. My balls felt no larger than a baby's rattle in his hand and just as breakable. Stanley held onto them until he knew that I knew just how small and fragile they really were and then he squeezed.

First my vision went gray, then I felt the pain; then it began to billow upward in thick clouds of nausea filling my stomach. When Stanley finally let go, I fell to the ground, clutching at my private parts, praying that they were still there and close to their normal size.

Stanley appeared both unmoved by my pain and genuinely disappointed that I had been such an easy victim. "Ain't nobody to blame but yourself, Prickless. How many times have I tol' you to watch out for them damn Nip attacks? How many times have I tol' him, Cleeve?"

"You tell him all the time, Stanley. Just 'bout every time ya see him, I reckon," answered Cleeve, who unlike his friend was not, and never would be, in the eighth grade. Cleeve had been placed in what was called the Special Education Class when he was ten years old. He was given certain tasks, such as running the movie projector and bringing around afternoon milk to the lower grades. He was from a farm family and rumored to be the son of his sister. Stanley was his God. Cleeve's loyalty was without bounds. Whatever Stanley asked, Cleeve did without question.

"Let me give ya a hand, Prickless."

Extending his arm downward, Stanley smiled, showing dead teeth and deteriorating gums. Were I to take the hand to pull myself up, Stanley, of course, would loosen his grip and, once again, I would find myself on my ass in the middle of the playground. On the other hand, to refuse the offer would only show Stanley up and make him even madder than he already was. It might even cause him to unleash the hair-trigger wrath of Cleeve Seward.

Seeing no way out of the situation on my own, I sought God's help. Perhaps, I prayed, He might cause a bolt of lightning to strike the son of a bitch dead? Even a well-aimed clump of pigeon shit would suffice.

Alas, the sky was clear. Not a bird or cloud in sight. After leaping unaided to my feet, I took two steps backward. Stanley's smile faded. He dropped his arm to his side, moving forward.

"You're gonna help me out, Prickless."

"How can I do that?"

As he walked toward me, I continued to back away until I felt pressure at the backs of my knees. Taking one more step, I felt my knees buckle, then collapse, landing me once more upon my back.

Having managed to sneak in behind me, Cleeve had lowered himself onto all fours, setting himself up as a barrier, a trick he and Stanley had obviously practiced to perfection. Rolling about on the ground, Cleeve gripped his stomach, belching laughter. Standing above him, Stanley shook his head in mock bewilderment.

"You better watch where you're goin', Prickless," he said. "You're likely to make old Cleeve mad, walkin' on him like that."

Cleeve Seward, still on all fours, gazed upward, growling through yellow teeth, his eyes flat and barren as a stretch of desert.

Stanley frowned. "Tell me about your sister, Innis."

"What about her?"

"How's she doin'?"

"All right, I guess."

Back on my feet, I began to gauge the distance to the main road, the most likely point of safety. I could outrun Stanley, I was sure. But Cleeve was an athlete—a farmboy, quick and strong from hard work. And dangerous—not through meanness but just plain stupidity, like a hound that runs till it drops only because it doesn't know any better. If Cleeve caught me, Stanley wasn't likely to call him off right away.

"You talk to her much?"

"Some."

"Who's she gettin' it on with?"

"I don't know."

"I hear she likes to get it on for 'bout anybody can afford it." He chuckled, air hissing sporadically through the gaps in his teeth. "What I'm asking for ain't that much really. It's what anybody would do for a friend. You're my friend, ain't you, Prickless?"

Cleeve was close enough for me to take a swipe at. If I hit him just right, enough to put him on the ground, I might manage to escape. By the time he recovered, I would be halfway to the road. And what about tomorrow? And the next day? Well, I would just have to chance it. . . .

"What's up, guys?" Maurie Winthrop appeared suddenly from around the corner of the school. Without even hesitating, he came up to the three of us and stopped. He was casual as you please, all loosey goosey and full of good cheer, like a golfer whose shot has gone awry and landed in someone else's fairway. "Stanley! Cleeve! Say, when we all gonna get together and go over those algebra problems?"

Stanley Ball bared his teeth. "What d'you want, Fuzz Ball?"

"I hear you're looking for a date."

"A what?"

"I couldn't help but overhear your conversation with Innis here." Maurie flashed a lopsided smile that made his mouth look as if a hotdog had lodged within it. He reached up with one hand, pushed his glasses up from the end of his nose, then widened his eyes. "Stan, this is your lucky day."

"Get lost, Kike head, 'fore I turn Cleeve loose on ya!"

"Okay." Maurie smiled. "Okay!" He put his hands up in a conciliatory gesture. "You're not interested, I understand! Only say it, please?"

"Huh?

"Say you're not interested—no way, nohow—in getting into Kate Innis's pants, and I'm gone!"

"S'posin' I was." Stanley guffawed. "How's a little pecker like you gonna help?"

"It wouldn't be the first time."

Their words buzzed about me like the drone from a cluster of bees. What nonsense. Negotiating over my sister as if she were for sale, Maurie Winthrop stepping forward and acting as her agent. Kate, I was sure, barely knew who he was. Attention, at least, had been momentarily diverted. I sensed an avenue of escape yet hesitated in taking it. Something strange was happening. Maurie actually had Stanley Ball listening to him—shaking his head and gesticulating in the manner of one bargaining over the price of fish.

"Course, something like that doesn't come cheap," said Maurie, his glasses sliding like a seal toward the end of his nose. He stopped the descent with one finger, then poked deliberately at his hair with the other hand. "She's a pretty girl. Knows just what she's worth too. She doesn't do nothing for free."

"You sayin' I gotta pay!"

"Why else would she let a slob like you near her?"

Stanley Ball had Maurie by the collar, hoisted onto his tiptoes, his free hand cocked into a fist before Maurie could say another word. Once started, however, Maurie's words fell in a patternless torrent and betrayed, amazingly, not a trace of panic.

"Course the money's not for me or Innis! Our normal commission? Forget that, Stan! This is a freebie, from one friend to another! But Kate, she's not in it for love, you know what I mean?"

He stopped and looked up, his eyes huge and distorted through the glass, his lips, incredibly, still forming that crazy, lopsided grin. After releasing Maurie's collar, Stanley dropped his hands back to his sides. "How much?" he growled.

"Twenty," said Maurie. "Per customer."

"He ain't gonna be there," said Stanley, nodding at Cleeve. "What'll it get me?"

"Everything, Stan. The whole enchilada!"

"When? I can't have twenty bucks till tomorrow."

"Tomorrow's perfect, Stan. Couldn't be better! I'll set it up in the morning."

He had, and Kate never knew.

After Stanley had paid in full, Maurie had explained to him about how Kate would be waiting for him that evening at the Winthrop house. His folks were away, said Maurie. The door on the back porch would be unlocked, just push it open and step inside. The second room on the right is where Kate would be. Around ten o'clock, Maurie told him. Oh, and Stan, better wear a ski mask . . . it turns her on.

At the appointed hour, Stanley entered the unlit house through the back porch and tiptoed silently down the hallway until he reached the second room on the right. After carefully adjusting his ski mask, he opened the door and stepped inside.

A scream rose from the bed. Two heads popped up simultaneously from their pillows. Mrs. Winthrop reached to secure her nightie about her breasts. Mr. Winthrop reached for the loaded Mauser he kept beneath his bed. He blew a hole in the wall, inches above Stanley Ball's head.

Stanley rolled through the doorway, a millisecond before Mr. Winthrop's second shot whizzed past his ear, on its way into the corridor wall. The intruder thrashed about in the living room—crashing into several pieces of furniture and breaking two legs on Mrs. Winthrop's baby grand—before managing to escape. He made it two blocks before the police ran him down. They cuffed him, threw him into the back of the cruiser, brought him down to the station house, and booked him on felony level burglary.

Although only fifteen, the defendant had a long juvenile record. The judge did not believe that Stanley felt any remorse—"I don't want to hear any more of your cockamamie bull about paying a thirteen-year-old twenty dollars, so's you could break into his house in the middle of the night wearing a ski mask"—and gave him two years in reform school.

Cleeve Seward was unable to corroborate any of Stanley's story. Without Stanley around, he became a gentle soul. Almost friendly. He could be seen at times during recess, on his hands and knees, carrying preschoolers around on his back and whinnying like a horse.

Her deceased husband had been Cooley, of Cooley's Meat Market. While on his way to the team's season finale—the company van loaded to capacity with Wiener schnitzel and Ballpark Franks in readiness for an impromptu barbecue to follow the game—he had been blindsided by another vehicle. The driver of the other car—a man named Goldman—was the owner of a kosher deli on the east side of the city. He was en route to a bar mitzvah when the mishap occurred. Cooley had been killed instantly. Goldman had walked away unscathed.

Jeannie, at first, searched for some grain of reason in her husband's death, some small message to be gained from such an ironic coming together. She began going to temple, thought briefly of converting. She went to see a rabbi, told him of her husband's death. "I know Max Goldman," the rabbi had told her. "He is not a good Jew. He seldom goes to temple and often drinks more than he should. He has one DWI that I know of."

This information sent Jeannie into a month-long depression. Life and death, she surmised, were nothing but a series of garbled and meaningless coincidences. What kind of a God would not grant a woman the chance to say goodbye to her husband? Who could live in a world where a man's life was of less value than a hundred pounds of nonkosher Wiener schnitzel? Her solace was food. She stayed in the house, vowing to eat herself to death.

After several months, still very much alive, she had gained thirty pounds. Her clothes no longer fit. She had no money to buy new ones. The meat market was in disarray. Her son—staying with her in-laws—had drawn into himself, refusing on several occasions to even attend school.

It was then that Jeannie decided the choice was not hers to make. She would get on with it—ask no special favors, but not jump in front of cars either.

She found she possessed a certain business acumen. Much more so, she discovered, than had her late husband. After taking over management of the meat market, she soon had it back on its feet. In time she added a kosher deli, entering into direct competition with Max Goldman. She brought in her own Jewish butcher—a man well liked in his synagogue. She undercut Goldman's prices, offering her meats at just above whole-sale. The old man began to sweat. He consumed even greater amounts of alcohol. He was arrested and charged once again with driving while intoxicated. This time his license was suspended indefinitely. He could no longer make his deliveries. With creditors hounding his every move, he soon filed for bankruptcy.

Walter was impressed with the story. In his eyes, Jeannie's excess weight took on new possibilities. She carried it, he thought, with great aplomb. Her breasts, although large and ponderous, appeared firmly entrenched within their foundations. As for her ass, it seemed to him a great bowl of hidden delights.

"Would you listen to me ramble on," Jeannie said at long last and Walter was more than content to do so. He had forgotten what a soothing effect words could have, how simple undulations in tempo could slacken a man's reserve. "So, tell me. What has Walter Innis been up to for the last twenty years?"

"There really isn't much to tell," said Walter. Before dinner, they had shared a bottle of wine. Now, the meal over, they were halfway through a second. A warm veil of alcohol spread gently over the room. He felt strangely confident. He would go with what worked—the truth or something close to it.

"What about your wife?" she asked. "You've hardly mentioned her."

"We're separated."

"For how long?"

"A long time."

"I don't particularly want to get involved with a married man, Wal-ter," she said, "although at my age, a woman often doesn't have a choice."

"Of course."

"You don't want to talk about it. I understand. We're only having dinner, right?"

"Right."

Marsha had been gone eleven days. It was the evening of the twelfth, and still she had not called. Two nights after her departure, Walter had awakened in the middle of the night, sweating profusely, his mind lingering upon the image of a Hindu woman wrapped, from head to foot, in a white sari. The woman might have been Marsha, but she wore a veil, and Walter, at any rate, suddenly could not recall what his wife's face looked like.

In a panic, he had switched on the light and taken Marsha's picture from the bureau. Staring at the photograph, he willed himself to have an erection, then began to masturbate. Before he could finish, he had turned limp and fallen asleep. In the morning, he found the picture, lying facedown in the sheets.

"The first time I saw you on television," Jeannie said with a smile, "I didn't recognize you."

"Back when we knew each other, I didn't often wear cowboy hats," said Walter, "and I almost never lassoed cars."

In the ad, he sat on a horse, swinging a looped rope above his head. "We've rounded up the best used cars in the area, pardner. Come on down and break one in." The slogan had been Calvin Junior's idea. He thought it might appeal to rural types—"Tobacco spitters, Walter, woodchucks who buy used cars because they can't afford new ones and then spend all of their money on hemie engines and dual-tread tires."

"You look kinda cute in that outfit," said Jeannie, "sort of like a young Slim Pickens, I think."

"It was designed to fit Calvin Junior, then two weeks before they were to shoot the ad he went to Waikiki and gained twenty pounds. The rest of the salesmen were at least as big as Calvin, so that only left me. With a little alteration, the pants fit fine."

"When I told Billy that I went to high school with the Calvin Chevrolet Cowboy, he was quite impressed."

"At the age of thirty-nine, I'm wearing spurs and lassoing cars. It's more than I ever dreamed of."

"But you've quit?"

"Right."

Fat and serene beneath the wine's glow, Jeannie wiggled into one corner of the couch. Only a large puffy pillow separated them. The living room, comfortably dark, filled with homey furniture, had the feeling of a deeply rooted den.

"After that night at my parents', Walter, I had hoped you would at least call. I mean, I never said we couldn't try again, did I?"

"There didn't appear to be much point to it," said Walter. "Besides, my confidence had been dealt a severe blow."

"How do you think I felt? I was the one, after all, left lying with her pants about her ankles."

"Do you really think it's wise to rehash such a mutually painful experience?"

"No. I apologize. It wasn't as though we were even involved seriously. A girl just wonders about such things, is all."

"If not for the fact that I left town shortly after that, I certainly would have called."

"That was right around the time your mother died, wasn't it?"

"Right."

Next to him on the couch, she was slowly rolling a joint between her fingers. She has plans for me, thought Walter. But first, she will ply me with her drugs.

"I always wondered . . . about Susan, your mother, I mean. . . ."

"Wondered?"

"Yes. I mean, it was tragic. I never understood how it happened . . . and, well, right after that came graduation and then you just sort of disappeared. The next time I heard your name again, you were getting married." She lit the joint. The acrid, sweet smell of its smoke whirled about Walter's head, settling finally in his nostrils.

"It must have affected you terribly." She held the joint out toward him, a burning stick, as if she would singe him. He took it from her, sucked on it deeply, closed his eyes. There, smiling benignly, was Susan. His mother. Long-haired, brown-eyed Susan. Lazy Susan, all she want to do is lay all day, play all night. My Lazy Susan, you're all right. . . .

"Forget I asked," said Jeannie. "Sometimes I'm too nosy for my own good." She had moved nearer to Walter, was studying him closely.

"I don't mind you asking," said Walter. "It's just that it's something I haven't thought about in a while. I've tried to put it out of my mind."

. . .

The smoke took effect. Walter was floating above the water of Owasco Lake—across a desert of blue glaze, toward a place barely visible from the soiled shores of Caulfield. With him, floating just ahead and to his right, was Maurie. They had a grand view of the world. The sun was hot on their backs. The water below barely rippled, but blinked constantly up at them, pulsating in the sun's reflected brilliance like a broad avenue of neon. They were floating among the birds of the lake, dipping, twisting, pirouetting above the water's surface without purpose. Below fish could be seen swimming, unhurriedly, looking as easily obtainable as if they were under glass.

"I actually saw a bird and a fish together," he heard himself say, or perhaps it was only someone who sounded much like him.

"What?"

"I don't mean a bird diving into the water and coming up with a fish. That in itself is rare enough. No. What I mean is that I somehow saw the bird and the fish as one—moving parallel together, although the bird was a good fifty feet higher than the fish." The glass in his hand had mysteriously refilled itself. He took a long swallow of wine and laid his head back against the couch. Behind his neck he felt the soft, plump arm of Jeannie. Opening his eyes, Walter gazed into her round face. "And then the bird—it was an osprey, I think—just dropped from the sky. Like a rock, it hit the water. And all the while, I could still see the fish, even saw it gaze upward and try to dive at the last second. But it was too late. The bird hit the water. I saw its claws take hold of the fish. And then the two of them rose together from the water, one of them probably already dead."

"I don't think you should have any more smoke," Jeannie murmured, although she said it kindly and Walter could see that she wanted him to have more, much more.

"Maurie saw it too."

"Maurie? You mean Maurie Winthrop? God, to think of him as a lawyer. The trouble you two got into. Makes me laugh every time I read his name in the paper now."

Walter let his head rest softly upon her shoulder. It was a great pillow. Fat—so unjustly maligned by most—certainly had its place. Her softness pleased him. He imagined himself with twin handfuls of her ass, kneading it between his fingers.

"So when did you pair of hellions see this phenomenon of nature?"

"The day my mother died."

They had, he remembered, beached the sailboat a couple of hundred yards down from the Truxton place—behind a stand of pines, out of sight from any passing boats.

"I thought you were in school the day they found her."

"But not on the day she died," Walter said without shifting his head. "The day she died—really died—was that day that Maurie and I went sailing, in a boat we stole from Sam Porter's dock."

"Walter . . . I don't know what you're saying. But we can talk about something else if you'd like."

He downed his wine and took the fresh joint Jeannie passed him. He sucked in the smoke and held it until he thought his lungs would burst before blowing it out. He smiled at Jeannie, loved her for letting him do this thing in his own ramshackle, unhurried way. "I've never told anyone."

"I understand."

"I'm not sure I ever will."

"Okay."

"Sometimes I'd really like to."

"All right."

He closed his eyes once again and felt Jeannie's arm, like a safety belt, wrap securely about his shoulders. For what reason, he wondered, had the world suddenly turned meatless? Why this aversion to fat? What was it about thin women that had once appealed to him? There was no mystery to them; no warmth contained in those stark, fleshless bones. It was Maurie Winthrop who was always bragging about the fat—"Fat, Walter, in a thin world, is what makes life worth living. Live off the fat, my friend, and you're living the best you can"—and now, suddenly, Walter understood why.

For here was a package worth unwrapping; a great envelope of treasures, to be opened slowly and savored one piece at a time. Within each crease, hidden beauty must surely abound. Walter felt his head slip down the length of Jeannie's shoulder—bouncing gently off each breast—before coming to rest within her lap. Here was an oasis, as spongy and yielding as a patch of moss, yet with the tenacity of long-suffering wood. He turned his head facedown, buried himself between her legs. If I scream, he thought, no one will hear me. The sound will be absorbed—gobbled up by these stanchions of flesh. He breathed deeply. . . .

CHAPTER 25

The way I saw it, my debt to Maurie Winthrop would be an ongoing one. He had risked much in coming to my aid, seeking nothing in return. At the very least, I owed him loyalty and friendship, both of which I happily surrendered.

Stanley Ball, my tormentor for years, was out twenty dollars and effectively removed from my life forever. He had been cowed and victimized in a way he could never explain, let alone understand. Cleeve Seward, rendered impotent by the loss of his mentor, was a mere ghost of his sadistic past. A simpleton—derailed by fate—now willing to pull up grass with his teeth in order to please those who had adopted him.

Profits came to me in a more subtle manner as well. I cast my eyes about, like a rodent crawling out from beneath a rock, and sniffed timidly at the brisk air. Touched by the whiff of sudden possibilities, I breathed more deeply and found the air to be rich with potential.

No longer did I toss fitfully at night, like one who lives above a volcano, one ear always alert for the first signs of the next explosion. Alone in my bed, with every shade pulled tight, a rag beneath the door to expunge all light, I fell instantly into a deep sleep. The night opened like a book, an epic of countless chapters, each one containing its own unique descriptions and distorted images, worlds newly discovered and thus eminently superior to the one I knew.

Often the images were of people, many of whom I nearly recognized, but not quite. Those of my parents—blown up and clownish, like circus balloons—appeared too flimsy to touch, as if, were I to do so, they would disappear altogether. It saddened me to see them in such a state, and then it filled me with pity and finally with disdain. Next to their flimsiness, the rest of the world was strong and durable.

Another of the images—a garish fellow, thick through the shoulders and with bright dancing eyes—smiled brazenly, as if he knew me. Indeed, over time, he did begin to appear familiar. He would show up at the strangest of times, always tipping his hat and winking like a salesman who has bilked everyone in the room except for the one he's winking at, and no one can tell who that is. On one occasion, moving with a certain cockiness that seemed out of place, he appeared without his hat in my mother's kitchen. I saw then that he was quite muscular and that his face blazed with some undefined anger. He made an exaggerated wink in my direction, as if to say "Now do you know who I am?"

CHAPTER 26

"Walter? Jesus, Walter, wake up will ya?" Jeannie Weatherrup peered down at Walter from what seemed like a great height. Actually, it was only the distance from her neck to her lap, the latter being where Walter's head rested. One of his hands hung haphazardly off of the couch; the other was out of sight somewhere beneath Jeannie Weatherrup's great and plentiful ass. His fingers were numb. His mind was foggy—a collage of horrific images.

"No wonder your wife left you," said Jeannie. "She was probably afraid you would kill her while she slept and, given the way you thrash around, I can see why!"

"Christ . . . I'm sorry, Jeannie. I guess I fell asleep." He gazed up, glad to find a smile upon her face. "I had this dream. . . ."

"Want to tell me about it?"

"No. I mean, I can't really remember it now."

"Well, Walter, as much as we sometimes don't want them to, things do change, don't they?"

"Say again?"

"There was a time when you wouldn't have fallen asleep before your plate was empty."

"Huh?"

"I was warming up to it," she said. "I could have been convinced."

"Oh."

"I couldn't be now, so don't make the effort."

He felt a stiffening beneath his head, in the region of her thighs, as if she wanted him to understand that the area was closed for the night. He removed his hand. His fingers tingled. His thoughts reeled, trying desperately to find solid ground.

"Before you so rudely fell asleep, you started to tell me about your mother's accident."

"Oh . . . well, there really isn't much to say. Coroner just figured her rowboat somehow got tipped over, and Mother never did learn how to swim. The Old Man always told her she ought to carry a life preserver, but she wouldn't listen. Said she could always grab onto the side of the boat if something happened."

"That's why she really died before she actually died?"

"What?"

"Forget it. I'm no nosy broad. You don't want to talk about it, fine." Her tone had changed for the worse. She shifted her weight, causing Walter's head to fall abruptly between the crevasse of her knees. "You never were very good at finishing things you started."

"Oh, Jesus," he breathed. "Must a man's failures follow him forever?"

"You know, your problem was that you gave up too easily."

"I recall making quite a valiant effort before you finally informed me that it was fruitless."

"But you never came back."

"I was nursing a bruised ego." He glanced carefully upward, making certain that she didn't possess any visible weapon. "Besides, I always suspected you of foul play—setting me up to fail and then blaming me for it."

"What do you mean?"

"Muscle control. Some girl I saw in L.A., at a strip joint, was a master at it." It was true. The girl had clamped up so tight, you couldn't have thrown a dart into her.

"Muscle control? Huh! You just didn't know where to aim that thing of yours, was all! If I wanted to clamp up, you'd have known it, believe me." She brought her knees together. They closed tightly upon Walter's head, holding it just long enough for him to understand that they were still friends. "You want to spend the night?"

"Tonight?"

"No. Next week sometime. Of course tonight." She smiled and it was genuine. Ran her fingers down his face. "Sometimes I get lonely."

"What about the kid?"

"His grandparents aren't bringing him home until late tomorrow."

"Sometimes I get lonely too."

"Walter?"

"Yeah?"

"I don't want to do nothing. I mean in a sexual way. Okay?"

"Okay. I'll sleep on the couch."

"No. I want you to sleep with me, but not in me. You know what I mean?"

"Sure. You want me to respect you in the morning."

"At least I want to make sure you'll be here in the morning."

At first he had tried to isolate himself on one side of the bed. He had believed, number one, that that was what she had wanted, and, number two, that thus positioned, there would be less temptation on both their parts to break their vow of celibacy. The bed, though, would not cooperate. It was a water bed, of the unbaffled variety. Keeping one's distance was all but impossible.

No sooner would Walter get his mind off of his cock and what not to do with it than a mountainous tremor of water would move beneath him. A wave of lesser magnitude would ensue and then Jeannie's arm, or one of her breasts, would flop softly across Walter's chest. An erection would follow. His mind would reel—focusing, finally, upon a Kareem Abdul Jabbar hook shot or a throw to the plate by Roberto Clemente. His cock might finally acquiesce and then he would be hit with another wave.

At his request, they had rearranged themselves. They lay back to back, delicately balanced within the bed's center. The problem then became one of precision. If their shoulder blades and rear cheeks were not touching, equilibrium would be lost, causing the two of them to roll simultaneously toward one side of the bed or the other.

Grazing cheeks, at least in Walter's mind, created the same problems all over again. Could one sleep with his ass touching Mount Everest? Could any man—Roberto Clemente not excluded—keep his mind on the game under such circumstances? Walter gave up trying. His erection could cut glass. Slowly, so as not to rustle the sheets, he reached down to address it. He gripped it gently in one hand, moving it back and forth ever so slowly. Even that was enough to start a small barrage of waves. Maybe, he hoped, she will think I'm having another bad dream.

Masturbation, like skiing, is not something to be done slowly. As in all sports, momentum is a key ingredient to success. A certain rhythm is picked up over time; with rhythm comes a desire for speed. Walter threw caution to the wind. Recklessly he began whipping his hand up and down, hoping for an early conclusion to his misery.

"Walter? Are you still awake?" Groggily Jeannie rolled toward him, sleep gathered in tan crusts at the corners of her eyes. Her breath was a forest of scents. Her nightie, of impenetrable wool, was bunched about her waist like a burlap sack.

"I . . . couldn't sleep." Casually—ever so slowly—he slid his hand away from his cock, attempting to place the former on neutral ground, hoping eventually to reach a believable spot in the area of his head. "Just restless, I guess."

Her eyes went down to his hand, to his hastily removed underwear, to his dying erection, lying then like a wounded animal atop one thigh.

"You poor dear," she said. "Here, let me."

Her hands were warm cushions, so much softer than Walter's own. She seemed practiced in the art—slowing for a moment, speeding up when necessary. Even whispering things—dirty, verboten things—in his ear. That had been the final straw. He had exploded in her hand, feeling much relieved, yelping in some strange guttural language.

She wrapped herself securely about him, everything seeming to fit just so. She was large, weighing nearly as much as Walter. His head sank neatly between her breasts. His hands were warm and snug beneath the burlap. He felt safe from the world for the first time since he could remember. He decided, for the moment at least, that he was in love.

Several weeks following the downfall of Stanley Ball, Maurie approached me in the school corridor. We had not talked since that day, although whenever I caught his eye, Maurie would smile in the same distorted manner—his lips curling upward, his eyebrows moving in a sudden flurry of spasmodic jerks.

Chuckling, he pressed a ten-dollar bill into the palm of my hand. "Your share of Mr. Stanley Ball's estate," he said. "I figured I'd wait till things cooled off before I gave it to you."

"I didn't do nothing for it," I said. "You're the one. You ought to keep all of it."

"You did plenty. Take it and when ya decide to spend it, think of that goofy son of a bitch dodging bullets in his ski mask."

I put a hand to my mouth, trying to stifle a sudden fit of laughter. Another image, of Stanley—docile as a cat in his prison cell—leaped briefly from the shadows. I wanted to howl with delight. We—Maurie Winthrop and myself—had brought this about. Don't mess with us, world. We're two bad-ass boys just looking for a place to land. Jesus! God! What a feeling, to have some power in this world.

"Was you scared?" I asked.

"Of what?"

"Of Stanley Ball. And Cleeve. I mean, I was scared. I was so scared, I thought I might wet my pants. Weren't you scared? You musta been scared."

"Of what? Getting beat up? That don't scare me. What scares me is letting somebody know they scare me. Sometimes I wished somebody would beat me up, just to show 'em they don't scare me."

"What do ya mean?"

"Nothing. Why, you scared?"

"Yeah. I reckon."

"Of what? Getting beat up?"

"Everything, mostly. Yeah, I guess most everything scares me." The words just kind of slipped out. I hoped Maurie would ignore them, pocket them like spare change, maybe even forget he had heard them.

"I'll tell you what, Walter." It was the first time he had called me by my name. He pronounced it in two crisp syllables, giving the word a firm, snappish sound that appealed to me. "Don't ever tell nobody else that."

"What?"

"That you're scared. Long as we're friends—and even after—don't ever tell nobody else that you're scared."

"How come?"

"Cause then they know. And once they know—whoever it is—they got ya. If you don't say it, it ain't so. You understand?"

"Yeah. I think I do. We ain't scared."

"You promise?"

"Yeah. I promise. We ain't scared of nothing."

I reached into my locker, pulled out my glove and cap. I stuck the cap on my head and shoved the mitt beneath one arm. That afternoon, I would tell the coach that I would not be coming to practice. I was quitting the team. Maybe it would bother my father when he found out. Maybe it wouldn't. I hoped it would, but I somehow knew that it would not.

I hadn't turned out to be as good of a hitter as the Old Man had predicted. I had a tendency to pop the ball up when I hit it, sending long fly balls to the outfield that were ultimately caught, instead of driving the ball up the alleys. I was only batting two-fifty for the junior high team. The Old Man's interest in pitching to me had all but disappeared. Who needed him showing up at a game now and then, drunk and riling the umpires, making me want to dig a hole in the field and bury myself? He was a drunk like everyone said, and he was weak—fragile as a circus balloon. And he was scared—and everyone knew it. Maybe he would slap me around when I told him about quitting. Maybe he wouldn't. Who cared? I wasn't afraid of him, or anything else.

"How 'bout your folks?" I asked.

"Huh?"

"They figure you had anything to do with the break-in?"

"As long as it don't cost 'em nothing, they don't give a damn."

"How about what Stanley Ball told the judge? About the twenty dollars and all?"

"See no evil, hear no evil. That's my folks. The wall and the baby grand were insured."

"The day after it happened, I heard your old man talking on the radio. He said he wouldn't a cared if he had shot Stanley Ball."

"Yeah. They made a hero out of him. Got his picture on the front page of the newspaper, holding onto his Mauser, looking like J. Edgar Hoover himself."

"I can't believe he came up firing. Jesus, what if . . . ?"

"The old lady got so nerved up, she's been popping tranquilizers like they was penny candy ever since it happened." Maurie chuckled, pushed at his glasses. "Course it doesn't take blowing a hole in the wall to cause that. She hears even a dog fart and she'll start to shake. How 'bout your folks?"

"Huh?"

"They suspect anything?"

"Nah. The Old Man kinda frowned, is all, and shook his head when he heard about it, and I don't even know if my mom knew what happened. She doesn't pay much attention to the news, only listens to chamber music, is all."

I slammed my locker shut and turned to face him. I had never had a best friend before. Nobody who really knew how scared I was—of everything—and didn't care; who instead of laughing at my fears convinced me that they weren't real, that they only became real when you talked about them. As I thought about it, I realized I had never really had a friend at all. I turned and started down the hallway, Maurie falling in step next to me.

"You play ball?" he asked, nodding at the glove in my hand.

"Nah," I said. "Not anymore."

At the end of the corridor, just in front of the glass doors to the outside, sat a trash can. After pushing the doors open with one hand, I flipped the mitt into the can with the other. I stepped outside and didn't look back.

That night Maurie and I walked over to the east side of the city, where the upper crust of Caulfield lived. We waited until it was dark before sneaking into the rear driveway of a big stone house at the top of Burton Street. The driveway led to a garage, its door unlocked and ajar. We eased it open and stepped inside. Two bikes were leaning against the rear wall—a Raleigh three-speed and a Schwinn cruiser.

A fluttering commenced somewhere in my chest. Sweat popped up on my forehead, rolling down into my eyes, dropping onto my tongue, filling my mouth with its taste. I glanced at Maurie, who was looking at me. "We ain't scared of nothing," I whispered.

Together we walked over to the bikes and wheeled them from the garage. It was easy—amazingly easy. We rode them right through that fancy neighborhood with its circular drives and manicured lawns, laughing out loud as we went. It felt even greater, I believed, than the *thwack* of a solid line drive.

We rode them all the way over to the west side of town. Maurie knew an older boy there who gave us ten dollars apiece for the bikes. He would paint them, he said, and resell them for twice that, maybe even to someone in the very neighborhood from which they had been stolen. "Who knows," he told us, "you might bring me these same two beauties again next week."

In the morning, there were more pancakes. Walter, wearing a red cotton robe two sizes too large, sat at the kitchen table as Jeannie prepared them. She made the batter thick, dropping it in a series of puddles on the griddle's surface. As the puddles firmed, she slipped a spatula under each cake, flipped it casually with her wrist, and let it fall gently back onto the grill.

"You know what I don't understand," she said with her back to Walter. "I don't understand why a big kid like you has never had any of his own."

"Any what?"

"Kids."

"What, I'm over the hill? Jesus, woman, I'm still on the sunny side of forty, you know."

He watched her backside—large but not forbidding, more like a mountain smooth with foliage than one ragged with rocks. If it was a mountain, he thought, it would be ideal for children to hike upon—its rounded peaks easily accessible, its gentle valleys, even the great canyon at its center, in no way treacherous.

"Don't joke," she said. "A person does not hang out at Little League ball parks unless he's a pervert, a parent, or desirous of becoming one. You're not a parent and I can't believe you're a pervert. So? Were you never desirous?"

"Of many things." He smiled. "But never of children."

"I don't believe you. For the sake of argument though, why not?"

"I guess I didn't want them to be disappointed."

"Of what, for God sake?"

"Of life . . . and people, the way they sometimes are."

"My God, Walter, you think they break like eggs? They don't you know. You can drop 'em, bop 'em, and disappoint 'em a thousand times and they won't break. Did you break?"

"No. I didn't break."

"You bounced though, huh? A time or two?"

"Sure, I bounced."

"If you didn't bounce, Walter, you would never learn that you wouldn't break." She removed the cakes from the griddle, piled them into stacks on two separate plates, dropped a large pat of butter onto each stack. "My son, Billy, I'm waiting for him to bounce. I hope it will be soon." She slid the slightly smaller stack in front of Walter and kept the other.

"He isn't a third baseman, you know?"

"What?"

"Billy. Third base is not his best position."

"How would you know? You haven't even seen him play."

"You said he's afraid of the ball. He tries first to get out of the way, second to knock the ball down. In baseball, the hardest-hit balls go to the third baseman. Of all the positions on the field, it requires the most courage."

"So?"

"Billy should be somewhere where he has a longer time to watch the ball as it comes off the bat, so that he has a chance to get ready for it. Once he picks a couple of grounders up cleanly, his confidence will grow. I imagine he'll even become a better hitter."

"By becoming a better fielder, he'll become a better hitter?"

"Hitting is mostly confidence. If a kid believes he's a hitter, he'll become a hitter." Walter sipped at his coffee, fumbled with the folds of fabric at his waist. Jeannie's husband had been a large man. His robe fit Walter loosely, like a monk's habit. Walter felt a sudden urge to give benediction. "It's a principle with more than one application."

"Are we still speaking of my son's fielding deficiencies, or have we moved onto your own?"

"I have no problem fielding a ball, once it's been hit to me."

"From what I have seen, Walter Innis, you're not bad with a bat in your hand either." Jeannie smothered her pancakes in maple syrup before delving into them. She came up with a forkful, shoving it into her mouth in one easy motion. Walter felt her foot move against the inside of his leg, coming to rest finally in the lap of his robe, just beneath his crotch.

Her eyes were on the ceiling. She finished chewing before speaking again.

"So, what position do you think he should play?"

"Second base. In the outfield he might get bored. The other infield positions he probably isn't ready for."

"Okay. Second base it is, then. If his average doesn't go up fifty points by the end of the season, your theory—along with all of its applications—goes out the window."

They ate then, silently and somewhat in unison, their forks moving and clicking in a strange cadence. They smiled and dribbled things down their chins and, with their napkins or the backs of their sleeves, wiped off what had spilled. Jeannie's mouth puffed outward and became beautiful when full, in sharp contrast, thought Walter, to the tightness that overtook his wife's mouth as she ate, as if, suddenly, the air had been expunged from her cheeks. Walter had always marveled at the physical changes that occurred in Marsha while she ate. Once he had hugged her from behind as she chewed upon a drumstick and felt her whole body become taut. Even her ass was like igneous rock.

Jeannie's foot moved slowly along the inside of his leg, her toes nibbling gently at the hairs that grew there. Peaceful with pancakes, coffee, and Jeannie Weatherrup's toes beneath his robe, Walter shut his eyes and thought of the women he had known. He thought of his mother and of his wife and of Jeannie Weatherrup and of a dozen or so others whose lives had, to some degree, impacted his. In one way or another each had gotten beneath the hem of his robe; each had dawdled there, upon his most unprotected parts—dancing gently, lingering as if to stay—and each, but Jeannie, had now gone. What now, he wondered, was left of them? A collage of pictures—some dirty, some kind—a reservoir of memories, siphoning off day by day like rainwater off a roof.

"I don't know where I would be without him," said Jeannie. "If not for him, the need to care for him, after Cooley died I would have just said the hell with it, would have sat here and eaten linguini until I burst."

"Who?"

"Billy. You wouldn't understand because you have never had a child of your own. For the last year I needed him more than he needed me.

His being alive—a human, physical presence—meant I needed to be alive as well. Do you know what I'm saying?"

"Not exactly."

"I can't love a spirit, Walter. Only a presence."

"You are saying memories are a waste of time?"

"Not a waste of time, Walter, just superfluous. I don't keep any pictures of Cooley in the bedroom. The two in the den are only so that Billy won't feel like a fatherless child."

He felt her toes range farther up beneath his hem, their destiny only inches away. Spirits. Walter supposed that is what people became once they became memories. Whether they were alive or dead, in the rememberer's mind, people were nothing more than spirits. And then he thought of the flesh-and-blood Marsha—her brisk, muscular way of fucking, her tongue flicking every which way like a broken speedometer's needle—and how during eight years of making love, he had never seen her come with her eyes open; it struck him now as being symptomatic somehow of their failed marriage.

"He's unhappy, yet I'm not sure what to do about it."

"What do you think would make him happy?"

"To bat three hundred. Maybe to go through a game without making an error."

"And if he's not capable of it?"

"To understand that it doesn't matter."

Her foot struck pay dirt. Her toes nestled softly into his crotch, played like blades of grass upon his scrotum. Walter shifted slightly in his chair, gave thanks for her husband's large girth, felt the fabric of his robe go up like a pup tent. Across from him, Jeannie's mouth opened slightly. Her lips, clinging together in spots, glowed in a veneer of maple syrup.

"I am not much of a coach, Walter. I'm more of a cheerleader, better suited for throwing pom poms than teaching hook slides."

"Says who? I mean, you didn't exactly ask for the job."

"No one else wanted it. It was mine by default, like when a politician dies and his wife is automatically appointed to succeed him."

"From what I've seen, you're doing all that could be expected."

"We haven't come within ten runs of a victory, Walter. Three of our games have been called off after four innings, something called the mercy rule."

"With all due respect to your husband and his players, Jeannie, it doesn't sound as though you inherited an abundance of talent."

"Last year's team had a few good players, but after Cooley died most of them changed teams. Their fathers didn't want them to be coached by a woman. Most of my players weren't capable of making another roster."

"I see."

"I don't seem able to motivate them. I mean, they look at me and can see that I never played much ball."

"Lots of great coaches were not great players."

"After a week of practices, I still didn't know what a walk was. I thought it was slang for 'get lost.' You know, like 'take a walk'?"

"It is a confusing phrase."

"Walter?"

"Yes?"

"You've got some free time, right?"

"I guess. I mean, I'm working on something with Maurie at the moment . . . but, I suppose. . . ." Her toes were long, more like fingers. They moved farther up, wrapped themselves about Walter's cock as if it were an olive branch. Clinging in prehensile fashion, her foot swayed gently.

"Why don't you coach the Meat Market?"

"Me? I've never coached. I don't think I would be much good at it."

"Don't be ridiculous. You know about things like reflexes and how to handle a bat. The players would at least listen when you told them something, instead of giggling."

"I've never spent much time with kids."

"Billy took a shine to you. I could tell."

"He didn't say two words to me."

"He's like that with every man I've been out with since Bob died. It doesn't mean anything. He just sees most men as a threat to his father, that's all."

"How many have there been?"

"What?"

"Men?"

"Not enough and far too many. Will you?"

Jesus. What the hell, thought Walter. I'll never last this way. Might as well get a leg up. May the spirits rest in peace. He lifted his own foot from the floor, managed to get it into Jeannie's chair, between her thighs. Her hand grasped it, showed him where she wanted it. He tested the water with his toes, threw caution to the wind, dove in foot first.

"All right, if you'd like. I'll coach the team . . . help Billy all I can. . . ."

Jeannie's eyes were wide open, head back, her robe agape. Walter saw the proceeds gained from years of pancakes, loved her all the more for it, wished to invest in her deeply.

"The pay . . . Walter. Oh, Walter . . . the pay."

"What?"

"You want to know about the pay?"

"What pay?"

"It's good . . . Walter! So good!"

There were dogs residing there. Snarling, merciless hounds. According to rumor, a would-be burglar was roaming about minus one testicle and a solid piece of his scrotum; his bloodied trousers had been found with tooth marks in the crotch, the missing items still in them. Another miscreant, wrongly believing that the dogs could be bribed, was run up a tree for his mistake; when the police arrived, he was found cowering on a branch, clinging to a half-devoured box of puppy chow.

Such were the stories. They served their purpose for the most part. In all their years of residence, the Truxtons had never reported a successful break-in to the Caulfield City Police Department.

Yet my mother fed the dogs each day. She even petted and played with them. They were friendly, she claimed—genial, fun-loving pups that had never so much as nipped at her heels. But then she possessed the secret to their emotions—and, through her, so did I.

A simple piece of cloth was what it took to quell the beasts. Little more than a rag permeated with some strange odor. Who knew what? A drug? A chemical of some sort? To me, it smelled of urine. It was part of the family lore, perhaps. Henry Truxton I, upon obtaining his first million, had ceremoniously relieved himself upon the rag. For every million thereafter, the reigning Truxton had done likewise. A whiff of this, perhaps, was the one thing the dogs had been trained to fear. Returning from her duties each day, my mother hung the rag on a small hook beneath the kitchen sink. I knew just where it was—above the plunger, right next to my mother's can of Ajax.

The inlet where we had landed stuck out into the lake like an injured finger. The entire strip, except for the area immediately surrounding the estate, was covered with trees and foliage. The Truxtons owned it all. No one else lived within a mile of the place. The residence itself was located at the very tip of the finger. Next to it was a smaller house for guests, a garage, and a building that looked like a converted barn. The dogs ran loose in a paddock that circled the big house. It would be impossible to enter the dwelling without first encountering them.

Approaching the rear of the estate, Maurie and I heard the immediate snarling of the beasts. Crouched behind a tree, we scouted out the terrain ahead.

In front of us were more trees, an acre of lawn, then the paddock. With the sacred cloth, we assured each other, the rest would be easy. We even had keys to the front door; I had slipped the originals from my mother's purse, spent a dollar to have them copied and, undetected, returned her set that same evening. Still, we sat there for several minutes before moving closer.

My mind was a mesh of jumbled wires. Pumped up, I was excited as I was when Maurie and I had slipped through the screen door of Priscilla Greer's summer house and stolen her pet parrot. Bird and cage wrapped carefully in Maurie's overcoat, we had made our way over to the high school, jimmied the lock on one of the first-floor windows, and left the bird hanging from the overhead lamp in Principal Grayson's office. I would have given anything I then owned to be there when the old fart had opened his office door to a chorus of "Aye! Aye! Captain! Hit the deck and give me twenty!" Word had it that Grayson—the retired admiral—had fallen to the floor and fired off a quick ten before recalling that there were no captains in the navy.

Somewhere in the back of my mind there dwelled a meanness as well—a skulking, surly presence that I had never come to grips with but had felt on other occasions, when I was about to do something illegal and almost wished I would be caught and confronted so that I could let the meanness out on the poor son of a bitch who had caught me.

Then there was something else—fear, of course, but beyond that— a prickling of apprehension, as if I had known all along that I would someday be there in the bushes behind the Truxton place. As if I had been led there, and the decision had in no way been mine to make. As if, upon opening the door to the house and stepping inside, I expected a bolt of clarity to strike me suddenly. In one flash—a moment's dawn-

ing, as when the sky clears and the unblemished sun shines through—
I imagined the tangled wires in my head might miraculously untangle
and there would be the plain and simple truth.

Maurie, on the other hand, was there because he was my partner and
best friend and because he knew that I would never be able to manage
alone this crazy, half-baked scheme that I had somehow dreamed up.
Even so, Maurie had originally refused to go along. The hounds had
him worried. "These two here," he had explained, touching his denims
to indicate the two he had meant, "I'd just as soon hold onto for a
while." Only upon hearing of the sacred cloth had he changed his mind.
Cloth or no cloth, I was certain that he would have found a way around
the beasts. Maurie, it seemed to me, was like the only man with an
umbrella in the midst of an unexpected storm; dry and unruffled, he
laughed while everyone else got wet. I couldn't figure out how he did
it. The two of us went to the same places, did the same things; yet for
Maurie all seemed to go so smoothly, while I, on every venture, had to
grit my teeth and pretend for the moment that I was the cocksure
stranger who occasionally appeared in my dreams.

At times, I was convinced that Maurie had made a deal—with either
God or the devil, whoever had offered the best terms. Nothing in life
seemed capable of shoving him off course; or perhaps it was just that he
possessed a unique ability to roll with the punches, to follow whatever
new course he found himself on. Although he was bumbling and actually
not competent at much of anything, these characteristics only lent
credence to his easygoing demeanor.

When the two of us had been caught stealing bicycles on the east side,
it was I who had been arrested and summoned to Juvenile Court. Maurie
had given the arresting officer some cock-and-bull story about his mother
being crippled as a result of her years in a concentration camp and about
his father, recently fired from his job, being too proud to apply for public
assistance. "Here, kid," the cop had said, reaching into his pocket.
"Take this fiver and buy your folks a decent piece of meat for dinner."
Unbelievable! And I had gotten six months' probation and a severe
beating from the Old Man.

I looked at Maurie and smiled. Far from being resentful of his unfettered personality, I was grateful for it. I felt safer in Maurie's presence.

On a walk through a minefield, Maurie would skip and I, if I could manage it, would grab onto his coattails.

Maurie wiggled his eyebrows. Clenching his fist, he punched it once at the sky. Then, adjusting his glasses, he sprang to his feet and started at a brisk walk toward the front of the house. "We ain't scared of nothing," I mouthed, jumping up and hurrying after him.

Walter wondered how he had ever had time to hold down a full-time job. Little League practice was four times a week, in the evenings from five to six-thirty. On Saturday and some Sundays there were games. There had been two so far with Walter at the helm. Two losses, but one had been relatively close—ten to two—and Walter thought he had found a pitcher. A big, lazy kid named Wally Seymour, but with a live arm and a natural motion. Jeannie had been playing him in right field where he had neither sufficient speed nor ambition to run down fly balls.

Billy Palumbo had been inserted at second base, where he was still tentative, but less so. He had managed a hit in one of the games, causing his mother to leap excitedly to her feet, in the process dropping a soda onto the back of the man seated in front of her. Walter spent time after practice hitting grounders to Billy, showing him how to charge the ball, how to get his body in front of it while still managing to get his glove down. Afterward, on occasion, they went out for Cokes and wieners. The kid still didn't say much but he'd laughed when Walter showed him his batting style, using his wiener as a prop.

Each afternoon, Walter spent a couple of hours at the nursing home. Usually he just sat there, near the Old Man's bed or on the other side next to Jacob Johnson. He spent the time talking to Mr. Johnson and occasionally to Nurse Hunchhammer when she felt like it. The rest of the time he read the newspaper and schemed. The thing was, he didn't know why he was there. The Old Man hardly spoke, and when he did it wasn't as if he recognized his son or even cared whether or not Walter was there. He would ask Walter to get him a glass of water or to hand him something to read or to call Nurse Hunchhammer. But then Walter was not anxious to talk to him. He didn't love his father, wasn't sure he even liked him. If the Old Man had been walking around healthy, Walter was certain that he would not have bothered to look him up.

But he was there for some reason, so Walter sat and hoped that the reason would come to him, as an expectant father sits and hopes for a healthy child.

Then there was the business with Maurie. The two of them had sat for hours in Maurie's office going over the plan in detail, discussing the risks, the possibilities of detection, the potential profits to be had. Maurie had even checked the applicable statute of limitations to make certain that he and Walter could not still be prosecuted for a burglary twenty-two years old. They had talked about the repercussions, what would have to be unearthed and whether Walter could face up to it. In the end, it had been Walter who had wanted to go ahead with the plan, for the same vague reasons he went to see his father each day.

For Maurie the reasons were more precise. Although he had been against the idea at the start, he had agreed to go along in order to placate Walter and because he was intrigued by the possibility of such a big score. But he would not proceed further, he had told Walter, unless he were put in charge of the details. He had a friend, he said, who had agreed to act as a middleman. Maurie had spoken to Walter that morning and told him that the middleman, having made initial contact, was ready to meet with them.

Walter had not thought much about Marsha or his marriage, or about whether he still had one. He presumed he did since he had not been summoned into court, been ordered to vacate the house, or had his assets attached—all of which, Maurie had assured him, he might expect once Marsha decided to act. Thus, after having had no direct word from his wife for four weeks, her phone call on the evening of the twenty-eighth day came as a surprise to him.

He was at the kitchen table, scrutinizing Cooley's roster, trying to put names with positions, deciding at that moment who to bat in the leadoff position, when the telephone rang.

"I'm calling from Boston, Walter, on my mother's telephone, so we can't talk long."

"I'm honored to hear from you, Marsha. I was wondering if we were still married."

"Don't be a kvetch, Walter. Have you got a job yet?"

"Yes. I'm coaching a baseball team. Cooley's Meat Market."

"Coaching?"

"We had our second game on Saturday. The team is oh and seven, but they're not as bad as that. A lot of people were playing out of position before I took over. I've got a pitcher with real potential and a couple of kids who could turn out to be decent hitters."

"Kids?"

"Nine through twelve, D level Little League. Their coach retired in midseason."

"You're coaching a Little League team, Walter?"

"Yes."

"Are you doing something of a more prosperous nature as well?"

"Well . . . I've got a business deal going with Maurie."

"What kind of a business deal?"

"Commodities. We've got them. Somebody else is buying them."

"I hope it's legal, but if Maurie is involved, I'm certain that it isn't. Have you looked for a job?"

"What kind of a job?"

"Any kind of a job. For God's sake, Walter, you do plan on working again, don't you?"

"I am working, Marsha. I told you that."

"Walter, in my address book you will find the number of Dr. Ira Bernstein. He does wonders through psychoanalysis. In three sessions, he cured my fear of public toilets. He can do the same for you."

"I don't have a fear of public toilets, Marsha. Of course, it might be different if I had to sit on one."

"Please call him, Walter. He's a genius at getting to the roots of a crisis. Bun Welsh thought she hated men, until Dr. Bernstein told her it was a simple case of penis envy."

"I'm sure she was relieved."

"You haven't changed, have you, Walter? It's all still a joke to you . . . life, commitments, responsibilities."

"Only parts of it, Marsha. Like Bun Welsh with a case of penis envy."

"God knows I've tried, Walter."

"I'll ask him when I see him."

"Walter, I wanted to tell you so that it wouldn't come as a surprise. I closed out our joint checking account this morning."

"You mean closed out, as in cleaned out?"

"Boston is an expensive city, Walter."

"Even when you're living with your mother?"

"There are other expenses. I've had to buy a whole new wardrobe. The styles here are quite different than in Caulfield."

"I wouldn't want you to be out of style, Marsha. It sounds as if you plan on staying for a while."

"Didn't Maurie tell you?"

"He mentioned something said in anger. Something about a divorce."

"You should be getting served with the papers soon. I met with Mother's lawyer last week to have them drawn up."

"Drawn up?"

"Drafted, Walter. Prepared. That should not come as a surprise to you."

"No. Of course not . . . it's just so decisive. A divorce. I thought maybe we could talk about it first."

"Talk, Walter? We haven't talked in five years. What would we talk about, for heaven's sake?"

"Changes, I suppose. Whatever people talk about when they don't see eye to eye."

"Eye to eye? Even in the best of times we didn't see eye to eye, Walter. How is one supposed to see eye to eye with a man whose only aspirations are to coach a Little League baseball team?"

"You're upset. . . ."

"Yes."

"I'm sorry."

"At least we didn't have children, Walter. We should at least be thankful that we didn't have children. I've been doing a lot of reading since I left, Walter. Children of divorced parents often don't fare well. I'm so thankful we didn't have children. I mean, we might have remained together just for the children's sake."

"Yes. They're lucky we didn't have them."

"Are you home most of the day? For service, I mean?"

"You might find me at the ball field . . . or at the nursing home."

"How is your father?"

"Serious. And close to death. He doesn't have much time, I'm afraid."

"I'm sorry, Walter. But it isn't like the two of you were at all close."

"No. It isn't like that at all. Good-bye, Marsha."

"Good-bye, Walter."

. . .

The papers arrived the next day. The process server, not finding Walter home, tried the next address given to him: the Caulfield County Convalescent Home.

He had a beard and wore army fatigues. On one sleeve was a patch identifying him—or the coat's previous owner—as a member of the National Rifle Association. On the other, a slightly larger emblem proclaimed TAKE MY WIFE, BUT DON'T DRINK MY BEER.

"You Walter Innis?" he asked.

"Yes."

"Than today's yer lucky day, Jack," he said, thrusting the papers onto Walter's lap, chuckling through eroded, soon-to-be-dead teeth. "She's decided ta dump ya."

"I thought your job was to deliver 'em, not read 'em."

"No hard feelings, Jack. If she's anything like my old lady, yer lucky to be rid of her." He left, exuding an odor of onion dip and stale beer, already reaching with one hand into his tattered coat for the next envelope, with the other swiping a packet of Ritz crackers off Jacob Johnson's nightstand.

A fan rotated on a shelf above Jacob Johnson's bed. Angled downward, it covered the room in slow, sweeping circles. With each pass of the fan, the papers in Walter's lap fluttered and went limp. Sneaking through the blinds, a beam of sunlight rested languidly at his feet. Within its core, bits of dust spun; two flies humped in flight.

Walter folded the papers down the center, forming a triangle, creating a hat. He placed it on his head and waited for the pass of the fan. When the air came, the hat fell from Walter's head, floating slowly down through the corridor of light, to land finally at his feet. He reached down, picked up the hat, placed it carefully back onto his head and waited for the wind to hit it again.

Then he stood up and walked over to the Old Man's bed. His father had his back to him, sleeping or pretending to. Through it all—the booze, the fights, the internal grip of death—the Old Man had kept his hair. It was dappled gray, matted and still thick, collecting like the discharge from a volcano at the nape of his neck.

Walter's head was empty of words, although there was much that he wished to say. What specifically? Get at it, boy. What do you care if this old man dies or not? Serious or laughing, he'll still be a corpse. I wish I could serve him with papers, thought Walter, the way she served me— be done with it then, once and for all. You plead your case, Old Man, and I'll plead mine. We'll let the judge decide where the equities should lie.

Hah! So that's it? You have been pleading your case, Old Man, during the dark of the night, with no one but God and Jacob Johnson as witnesses. Is it God you think will judge you? Or Jacob Johnson? Perhaps you believe that they are one and the same? That this sheetmetal worker from St. Louis is, perchance, a special envoy from Heaven? In that case, we will do battle by proxy. The winner will be allowed, once and for all, to take a giant step out of the past.

How does it feel, Old Man, to know that when you die, your son will not shed a tear? Balance is all that I'm after. You've kept a tally sheet of my sins and I of yours. But the ultimate sin is neither of ours. We didn't kill her, Old Man. She died of her own accord because she couldn't face you or me. She said I would know what the truth was when I saw it, but I have seen it—stark naked and stripped of all pretensions—and I still do not know what I have seen. Have no idea, in fact. Hoped that before you died, you might give me a clue. I see now that that was foolish of me. You, in fact, have no more idea than I. Or do you?

I see, by your silence, that answers from you will not come free of charge. After everything, do you still believe it is I who should be the repentant one? That there is something due you? Perhaps only for the small favor of bringing me into this world? Or do you think it was I who abandoned you? That I took it all too seriously—those petty slaps and broken bones? Pissed-in pants and whispered jokes? Well, all right, maybe I owe you this one thing. And you shall have it. Die laughing, old man, and head straight for hell or anyplace else that you can talk your way into.

The dogs—six of them altogether—flocked about the rag like disciples to the Holy Shroud. As I dangled the cloth through the holes of the fence, each in turn breathed deeply of its mysterious essence. The snarling hounds became compliant housepets. Two of them lay on their backs at the entrance to the compound—feet pedaling madly in the air, as if waiting to have their stomachs scratched. The rest walked away, sniffling with unaffected boredom.

The first duplicate key slid smoothly into the heavy iron lock at the front of the compound. After pushing the gate open, Maurie and I stepped carefully over the pedaling hounds and made for the front doorway. We tiptoed, afraid that too much noise might cause the dogs to react. Neither of us spoke. The dogs seemed bored, hardly alive. The second key worked as smoothly as the first. After pulling back the dead bolt, I pushed the heavy door inward.

We stepped into a large hall, its top rounded and fractured by skylights. Beams of light came in at angles, crisscrossing before reaching the floor. Some of the windows were stained glass, in blue, purple, and pink. This is not a room, I silently marveled, but a hollowed-out mountain meant to look like a room. The oval ceiling, where the light breathed through, might have been a thousand miles away. I remembered my visit one summer to Howe Caverns, and the feeling I had experienced as I stood in the center of the earth. You scream in here, brother, and you'll be hearing your voice forever. Jesus, it was big. My entire house—and probably Maurie's too—would have fit with room to spare into the front hall.

Maurie and I looked at each other and giggled like kindergartners. We were giddy. We couldn't contain ourselves, were in danger of spilling out our success in peals of laughter. And why not? Who would hear us? Two seventeen-year-olds, we had maneuvered our way into the heart of a fortress. Maurie's smile broke first. Then mine. Our laughter gushed forth in waves of hysteria, bouncing off the walls and back to us. Going out and back again. We held onto each other and laughed for several minutes. Then we stopped.

When the echoes ceased, it was still again. I looked around at the walls, the ceiling, the floors. The place was like a museum—paintings of half-naked women everywhere; a chandelier hanging from the center of the ceiling, glass crystal dripping like ice from it; a great oak table, set as if for company. This then, I thought, was what my mother had meant by another world. I could feel my pulse. In my temple, just below my skin, I could actually hear it—a sputtering, monotonous sound, like an engine idling in low gear. I had a vision of the veins in my temple popping and spurting blood onto the hardwood floor beneath me, and of my mother, dressed in her black maid's outfit, kneeling down to wipe it up.

"Oi vey. . . ."

Maurie was admiring the walls, the ceiling, the open-air look. Face turned upward, his glasses fired off shards of light. The stained glass gave his features a dark, distorted look. In the great room, he appeared small. He was standing in front of a large, wooden mantel. On top of the mantel were dozens of miniature figurines. Tiny people, animals, a variety of automobiles—each one made of sterling silver or cut glass. Behind the mantel, halfway up the wall, a face gazed down. A stern, forbidding presence in a gold frame. Confident, barely smiling. A man with square shoulders. Eyes, licorice black. Perfect complexion. Close-cut beard. *Mano a mano* with the world. This was him, then. The collector. The one my mother worked for. The one my father despised.

"Be careful not to break nothing," I breathed. Staring at the picture, I kept hearing my blood pumping from my heart to my brain and back out again. It made a swishing sound in my ears. Maurie picked something up from the mantel, a curio of some kind. Turning it over in his hands, he examined it from every angle. Sideways, forward and back. It was made of glass. A thick body, with protusions in the middle. It might have been an angel or a bird landing on water. Maurie rolled it back and forth in his hand as if it were an egg. Looking over at me, he shrugged his shoulders. "Here, catch," he said, faking as if to toss the thing.

"Jesus!" I hissed. Throwing my hands up, I prepared, if necessary, to hit the floor in order to catch it. If it broke, my mother would have to sweep it up. She would have to explain to Henry Truxton III how it had broken in the first place. The plan—my plan, which had been agreed to by Maurie in advance—was to touch, not harm; to look without leaving a trace. Chuckling, Maurie placed the curio onto the shelf where he had found it. "What," he said, laughing and raising his eyebrows at me, "I'm an asshole?"

I let out a lungful of air. My heart dropped back to where it belonged. One tiny curio out of a collection of hundreds was all; a glass bird or an angel; nothing for the man in the picture to replace; more than enough though, were it to break, to cost my mother her job. I turned away from the picture and walked slowly across the room. I stopped next to the great oak table. It was set for sixteen people—seven on each side, one on either end. Each setting had six pieces of silverware. Three forks, a steak knife, a butter knife, a spoon.

"Why would ya need three forks?" I asked Maurie.

"Huh?"

The table was dirt brown. I was standing at its head. "I can see having different knives," I said, "but why would ya need three forks?"

Maurie was examining another one of the curios. Something boxy, with wheels—an early-model car, perhaps, or a locomotive. "One for dinner," he said. "One for salad. One in case ya drop one of the first two."

"You know, right?"

The dishes—two plates, two bowls, a teacup—were made of white china. A wineglass sat to the right; to the left, one for water. The napkin was rolled up inside of a gold ring. There were four pitchers on the table; six or seven casserole dishes; a silver tray for condiments. The centerpiece was a brass horse and rider. The chairs were armless, stiff backed. I sat down in the one closest to me. Looking down, I saw my reflection in the china. I reached up and combed my hair; fixed my collar; buttoned the top two buttons of my shirt. Glancing up at the man in the picture, I cleared my throat. I held my head high. Chin up.

Chest out. Lips tight together. I picked up one of the forks. The blood buzzed in my ears. My eyes began to water. Moving my arm forward, I gently tapped the fork against the side of my wineglass. It made a soft, tinkling sound. Like a bell. A bell used to summon cows or servants. I didn't stop tapping until I had Maurie's attention.

"Let's find the glove," I said.

CHAPTER 32

"So," said Maurie, "she has taken the bull by the balls."

He leaned back on his bar stool, sipping at his whiskey, smiling in the manner of a victorious matador. Of course, thought Walter, levity flows freely from he who is not the bull. When it's not your own balls that have been taken, it's easy to smile.

"You must not take it personally, Walter, when she begins to squeeze. You must understand that squeezing under such circumstances is the human thing to do."

"I should not take it personally if my wife attempts to castrate me?"

"She will, Walter. She surely will. And, above all, you must *not* take it personally. It will not be personal to her. There will come a time, in fact, when she will even forget that the balls she's holding are yours."

"Who else's might they be?"

"Anyone's, Walter. Absolutely anyone's at all. The important thing for her is the grip."

They were at a bar called Ruston's, drinking boilermakers, facing each other across plateful of empty clam shells and linguini, conversing in the animated manner of half-bombed buffoons who believe they are intellectuals. They said such things as "women are like clams, but harder to eat," and imagined they were being profound. They dropped depth charges into their beers and said "Salut." They peeled bills from their wallets and handed them out as if they were leaflets to a massage parlor.

"Maurie," said Walter, holding his index finger at the side of his nose, jerking his head as if it were on a turret, "why do you suppose it's such a frightening prospect to lose one's cock?"

It had recently occurred to Walter that the male genitalia were not well protected. He was acutely aware, suddenly, of how easily they might be snatched or damaged. Bereft of armor, virtually defenseless, they were made to hang from a most vulnerable spot—the approximate level of a raised knee. Life, at such a level, was fraught with danger.

Many dogs, for example—and some of them ferocious—went through life eye to eye with a man's penis.

"Because," Maurie answered, after pondering the question for a time, "after that he would no longer have one."

"And?"

"A man without a cock, Walter, is weaponless."

"How so?"

"You see, Walter, discussions are conducted with words and often gestures"—here he hesitated, swallowed a glassful of whiskey, picked up an empty clam shell from the table, examined it carefully, then flung it carelessly over his shoulder, seeming not to notice as it landed with a clatter on the next table—"but, when all is said and done, it is the great cock that ends the debate."

"The cock, then, is the final arbiter?"

"A judge by any other name."

The phrase pleased Walter, seemed to him to state much that was usually unstated. He saw his eminence outfitted in black judicial robes, tilted stiffly forward from the judge's great bench, his head—bereft of hair—glowing in the overhead lights of the courtroom. There was a point to it, after all, and it had nothing to do with that which he had been taught. It was beautiful in its clarity. He looked up and smiled at his friend, Maurie, basking with him in the glow of shared knowledge. He raised his glass. "To the cock," he said.

Maurie was informed about the cock, of course, as he was informed about all else. The breadth of his knowledge never ceased to amaze Walter. Why should one man know so much and another so little? In regards to divorce, for example. Maurie had been through two of them, yet, in the midst of his third, he appeared unscathed. It was, supposed Walter, a matter of instincts. Maurie saw the punches coming—anticipated them, in fact, before his adversary had consciously planned on throwing them. He had bobbed and weaved when he had to and—most important—he had never believed too seriously in love.

That, of course, had been Walter's mistake. Not the fact that he believed in love—one could hardly go wrong there—but that he believed in it too seriously. As if it were a commodity in great supply and one had only to ask in order to have copious amounts of it heaped upon oneself. Walter had been disappointed to learn that love was, in fact, in rather short supply and that the acquiring of it could exact a substantial price. Even after making the initial investment, one could never be sure that one had the real thing—that one had not, in actuality, been sold a bill of goods.

Walter rummaged through the debris on the tabletop, carefully picked up a shell, examined it as Maurie had done, then flung it over his shoulder in the same haphazard manner. The shell landed with a splash, a direct hit in someone's bowl of French onion soup—the day's special with salad bar for four-fifty. Dripping bits of onion, oozing long gobs of cheese, the shell came back, landing squarely in Walter's lap. "You're gettin' the bill," a voice growled, "and a hell of a lot more than that if it happens again!"

"How do you do it?" Walter implored, feeling the warm tentacles of booze reaching outward, touching and numbing him everywhere like an injection of gas. "Why is it so easy for you?"

"It's simple, Walter." Across the table from Walter, Maurie's head loomed like a great piñata, his mouth leering red and white in the glare of neon. "I always pick an empty table." He threw another shell over his shoulder, listened for the clatter on the tabletop, indicated with his hand the empty booth.

"I'm not talking about shells, goddammit!"

"A man shouldn't throw things without first being sure of what he's throwing at."

"Fuck the shells!"

"All right, fuck the shells, Walter. We have business to attend to. The man I told you about will be here soon. Under the circumstances, I suggest you let me do the talking. You seem to have other things on your mind."

"You will handle my divorce?"

"Of course."

"I don't want to hear any of the details . . . don't even want to see her again if it can be avoided."

"It probably can be, but I'm sure you'll change your mind."

"What do you mean by that?"

"You are at heart, Walter, a chronologist, which means you will insist upon a logical sequence of events. It is not logical to end a marriage over the telephone."

"Bullshit. Our marriage was over years ago, days after the honeymoon, in fact."

"In repose, Walter, it is not unusual to point to the beginning of a thing and insist that it was actually the end."

"She herself, Maurie, said we hadn't talked in five years."

"Perhaps. But to an emotional chemist such as yourself, the end result alone is never satisfactory."

"This result satisfies me just fine."

"Nonetheless, you will insist upon putting it on a scale, weighing it all out, until in your own mind you have reached some kind of balance."

"What's so wrong with a little balance?"

"There is no such thing, Walter. You're trying to stand up straight in a tilted world."

"Jesus! You're a hell of a bargain, Maurie. A man hires you, he gets not only a lawyer, but a psychiatrist and a philosopher to boot!"

"You want to know what I think you should do?"

"What?"

"Stay tilted. Lay the house on Marsha as a property settlement. Move into Jeannie Weatherrup's house and sell Wiener schnitzel and Ballpark Franks until you're old enough to retire."

"What makes you so smart, Maurie?"

Maurie smiled, the skin at the edge of his eyes shooting upward, waves of wrinkles forming on his forehead. He reached for a clam, the biggest and blackest of the bunch. He threw it upward and back, over his shoulder, waiting until it landed with a deep thud on the still-empty tabletop. "And here," he said then, pointing in the direction of the doorway and the heavyset man walking through it, "comes our retirement pension."

CHAPTER 33

To see, perhaps even touch it—that was the goal. Maybe though, I would try it on, slip my fingers into the exact slots where Willie Mays had slipped his; pound my fist into the glove's well-oiled pocket; pretend to circle under a high arcing pop fly. I might, if there were room enough and a ball available, even prevail upon Maurie to toss me a few grounders, which, I hoped, I would manage to field flawlessly off the hardwood floor. But that would be all. There would be no hitting fungoes, no playing catch.

"Where do you 'spose he keeps it?" asked Maurie.

"It's on the first floor," I told him. Placing the fork back onto the table, I pushed my chair back and stood up. "I know that much."

The two of us started down the hallway—a large, orbicular-shaped corridor at the back of the foyer—Maurie on one side, I on the other.

Although I had quit playing, I had retained a fondness for the game. I kept up on things. The teams. The players—what they were batting, their averages from either side of the plate. In bed at night, I listened to whatever my old Electrolux could pick up—the Yanks, the Mets, the Red Sox, so long as it was a game. It helped to block out the other sounds. And to give me a focus. A picture of grown men in uniforms, running, sliding, spitting, arguing; a world I had touched but never entered. A game. Occasionally I was sorry I had quit. I felt the burden of unused potential; talent siphoning off instead of boiling over.

"Are you saying she's actually seen it?" Maurie opened a door leading into the kitchen. It was the first kitchen I had ever seen made of marble. Everything but the stove and the refrigerator were glossy white. Maurie pulled his head out of the room, squinting. "Your mother, I mean?"

"Huh?"

"If she's seen it, that's one thing," said Maurie. "If she's just heard about it, that's another."

Across the hall, I had discovered a bathroom with two sinks. It was the size of my bedroom at home. The toilet had a pull chain. The walls were stenciled with an orgy scene. Roman warriors—eating, drinking, fucking. I backed out, carefully shutting the door behind me. "She's seen it," I said. "She's been in the room where he keeps it."

If I had worked at it, wouldn't I have eventually learned how to hit a breaking ball as well as a fast ball? Mightn't I have one day developed enough strength and bat speed to drive an outside pitch into the right-field bleachers? The wondering was the thing; wondering in place of knowing. My foot speed was good, yet I had never learned how to steal a base. I had the hands to be a shortstop. Also the range. I might have developed the arm. Worse than not playing though was the thought of playing again and of my father knowing about it. It would have been like giving in . . . or giving up . . . or . . . or . . . I didn't know what it would have been like exactly, nor why the thought of it bothered me so much. I only knew that it did.

We opened the doors to several more rooms—a bedroom, a sitting room of some kind, another bathroom, a library that looked interesting but the books were roped off. Like rats sniffing out cheese, we glanced into each room we came to, moving on quickly when we didn't find what we were looking for. I was sure that I would know the room when I saw it. It would be hidden near the heart of the house. Was it, though, only for the glove that I had come? Or did I hope to find something else? Some clue to the years of turmoil between my parents? A reason for the muffled slaps and groans? Henry Truxton III. When I heard the name, I thought of my mother's job, my father's bitterness, and the game of baseball.

"This is it," I said, stopping suddenly in front of a large wooden door, stained dark.

"Huh?"

"Right here."

Off to the right, under a stairway, the door was secured by an iron latch. In here, I realized, was where Henry Truxton III secreted his most prized possessions. Behind this door beat the heart of the iron man— the emotion of an empire, tucked carefully beneath a stairwell, as if somehow less vulnerable there.

The bolt moved easily upward, away from its casing. Turning the knob, I pushed gently against the door, feeling the heavy wood move inward.

The room was pitch black. It smelled of old cigars and sweat. After groping about with my hand, I found a switch and flicked it upward. The room was illuminated with a soft yellow glow.

The man's name was Walling—Edward T. Walling. Maurie had represented him most recently in a price-fixing scheme involving city garbage collectors. Walling had been one of those who had been indicted but not convicted, for which he was eternally grateful to Maurie. Since then he had been involved in various endeavors—"public relations, you know, and some general contractin'." He and Maurie had developed what Maurie referred to as a symbiotic relationship.

Ed Walling, Walter could not help thinking, was shaped like a garbage can himself, cylindrical and seemingly neckless. His head resembled a poorly designed pot, as if worked on by someone with palsy. The face was marred throughout by chinks where the artist's chisel had apparently dug too deeply. Two hollow depressions—appearing as finger marks shoved prematurely into a drying creation—served as eyes. In the middle of this disaster, Edward Walling's nose appeared as an outward explosion of red clay.

He had nodded only slightly at Walter before sitting down next to him in the booth, Walling's substantial girth pushing Walter up against the wall. Walling, clearly, was one of those people who did not trust strangers. He spoke mostly to Maurie and then only in a gravelly whisper, requiring Walter to put a hand to his ear in order to hear. In the midst of such an ugly face, the man's teeth shone white and perfect. He flashed them often, as if proud of this, his one good feature.

"I take it," said Maurie, "that negotiations with our friend have been opened?"

"I mailed the envelope like you said, Mr. Winthrop. No return address."

"Did you look inside?"

"What for, look inside? I was paid to do a job. That's what I done."

"And?"

"Two days ago, I got a reply at the box number you give me."

"Anybody see you pick it up?"

"I had my kid go to the box while I kep' an eye out. There weren't nobody else in the place."

"You're sure?"

"Positive." His teeth, through leathery lips, flashed like a row of sabers. "I'm a professional, Mr. Winthrop."

"Right. Where is it?"

"What?"

"The reply."

"Right here, in my pocket."

"It better not be open, Ed. If it's open, I'm going to be very upset."

"It ain't open," said Walling, the teeth flashing again, "and there weren't no need for ya to ask."

"All right, Ed. I'm sorry. This business has made us all a bit touchy, I'm afraid. What I want you to do is to slide the envelope over to me, across the table. I'm going to read it and then I'm going to let Mr. Innis read it and then we're going to burn it in that ashtray next to your arm."

C H A P T E R
★ 35 ★

The shrine was much larger than I had expected. It appeared to extend the entire length of the stairway. At the end closest to me was a dual row of felt-covered benches. Above and behind the benches, enclosed on three sides by a wooden box, was a movie projector, its glass eye protruding like a snake's head from the front of the box.

"Jesus," said Maurie with a whistle, "it's a movie theater. He's got a goddamn movie theater in his house!"

At the other end of the room hung the screen, a white oasis occupying most of the back wall. Along both sides of the room, running from one end to the other, were display cases enclosed in glass. Lining the shelves of the cases were balls, bats, bases, photographs, uniforms, and mitts. An entire history of the game, within one man's house.

"Son of a bitch," breathed Maurie, "it's another Hall of Fame. . . ."

Looking about, I felt vaguely self-conscious, as if I were being secretly observed. An eerie presence inhabited the room. Gremlins of things past. Spirits of those once present and perhaps still living, if even in another dimension. Ghosts.

"Look at the size of this ball, would ya?" Maurie had kneeled down and was peering into one of the glass cases. "It's as big as a grapefruit, for Christ sake."

"That's what a ball was," I said. "Up till the turn of the century."

"Take a strong man to hit one of those out!"

My mother, no fan herself, had talked endlessly of this place. Of Henry Truxton's "collection." Of his passion for the game. So much so that my father would put his hands over his ears or simply stand up from the table and walk away whenever she brought it up. Her always mentioning it, as well as the Old Man's reaction, was what had piqued my curiosity. That's why I had come. I realized it now. Henry Truxton and his singular fascination was the one common thread running through my parents' lives.

"Get a load of this." Maurie sputtered. Nose pressed to the glass, he was staring at a photograph. The picture was egg-shaped, framed in gold. "It's Truxton with the Mick."

"How can you tell?"

"He's the one in the painting, isn't he?"

"The Mick, though. How can you tell it's the Mick?"

"Ah, Jesus. . . ."

"That's Bob Feller." I laughed, pointing to another picture behind the glass. "I know that for sure."

"The guy with the big schnoz, ya mean?"

"Bill Hurley said he's the best pitcher this century."

"That mighta been true up until Koufax come along."

" 'To my good friend, Henry Truxton,' it says."

"You 'spose he really knows him?"

"How else would he get him to sign his picture that way—'less he knows him?"

Standing back from the glass, we stared intently at the contents inside, the purpose of our mission momentarily forgotten. We were gawkers at a museum. Fans at a shrine. The thought of touching anything within the cabinets seemed sacrilegious, as if this were a holy place of some kind—a tabernacle perhaps, where one spoke in hushed whispers. I dared not even smudge the glass of the cabinets.

"Well, I'll be damned." Maurie whistled. "Here it is! The glove! Mays's glove from the fifty-four Series. . . ."

I kneeled down next to him, peering intently into the cabinet. The glove was carefully oiled, obviously well used at one time. Beneath the mitt, a brass plaque served as a label: "Mays—'54. 'The Catch' off Vic Wertz." I remembered the Old Man's cynical reaction on first hearing of the mitt. "I suppose Mays just up and give it to him," he had said with a sneer at my mother. "Is that it?" I had a sudden desire to appropriate the glove. To take it home with me. To hang it on the hook in the Old Man's closet so that he'd be sure to see it when he got up in the morning.

"How would you know," Maurie asked, "if it's really the right mitt or not? He could've stuck anybody's glove in there and labeled it that way."

"Why would he?"

"Why wouldn't he?"

"It's the one all right," I said. "He don't believe in fakes."

"It must have cost him a fortune."

I shrugged. It looked like a glove. Any one of thousands. A little better kept, perhaps, but no different. There was nothing magical about it. It had five fingers, a pocket, just like the one I had owned and tossed into the trash four years before. I was wary of touching it though. Willie Mays had worn it.

"I'll betcha he's got films of the World Series," Maurie said, making his way over to the projector. "Maybe even interviews with the players."

"Could be," I said. I was studying a team picture of the '61 Yankees. 'To a great fan, Henry Truxton. Thanks, Yogi,' it said. Among the memorabilia were hundreds of photographs, many of which Truxton was in—smiling, holding a bat, his arm around the shoulders of one superstar or another. Ballplayers, past and present, all had good things to say about him. "My true friend," "a fan's fan," "a great American." There was no shortage of accolades. I wondered if Henry Truxton had ever played the game himself. Although he was fit enough, he didn't look much like an athlete. Holding a bat, he appeared awkward, disengaged—as if he were worried more about how he looked to the photographer than about getting a base hit.

"Hey," said Maurie, "there's film in here!" He stood at the end of the room, on the top bench, peering into the box that held the projector.

"Film of what?"

"How the hell do I know?"

Leaning to his right, Maurie pulled the wooden door shut. A moment later, he switched off the lights.

"What if somebody shows up?" I asked. I was alarmed at suddenly being in the dark. I couldn't see a thing, not even my hand in front of me. Behind me, I heard Maurie fumbling with the projector. I heard a snap, like a button going on, then a gentle hum. When he spoke, Maurie's words sounded as if they were coming from beyond the walls.

"They would care, right?"

"Huh?"

"Like it's okay to break into the man's house," Maurie said, chuckling, "so long as you don't mess with the man's projector?"

I reached out with my hands for the padded bench. Finding it, I sat down on the bottom row of seats. The darkness was complete, every shard of light miraculously sucked from the room. The smell of sweat and cigars became more pronounced. I felt as if a cocoon had suddenly grown around me. My skin itched, first a spot in the middle of my back, then a place farther down where I couldn't reach.

"Hurry up, Maurie," I said. "In the dark, this place gives me the creeps."

My words were lost in the sound of the projector. It clattered and whirred, like an engine in cold weather, before finally turning over. The screen turned bright white, then dark; numbers counted backward from ten and there, all of a sudden, was Henry Truxton III dressed in a white tuxedo, black suspenders, and a top hat. He removed the hat—a felt bowler with a ribbon around it—as he bowed to the camera.

"What the hell?" scoffed Maurie. I stared at the screen and reached farther down, groping for the itch.

"You 'spose he's on his way to the Series?"

There was no sound accompanying the film. Henry Truxton cocked his ear. He turned toward the front hall as if he had heard a bell. I heard Maurie chuckling. "Christ." He moaned. And a moment later: "Get on with it. . . ." Truxton strode toward the door, stepping like a deer through high grass. When he got there, he stopped. His lips moved as if he were holding a conversation with someone on the other side. "Open it, for Christ sake," hissed Maurie. I recognized the room. It was the large foyer, into which Maurie and I had first entered. Behind Truxton was the oak table. On the far side of the door was the paddock and six panting dogs. Truxton smiled and pulled open the door. Into the room walked a woman so beautiful, I didn't recognize her at first.

"What the . . . ?"

"Shhhh!" I hissed.

Combed back from her temples, her hair was an elegant crown atop her head. Intricate strands of it trickled down next to her ears. The style narrowed her face, revealing its delicate contours, unearthing the tapered bones in her neck. Her cheeks were touched with rouge. She was wearing a dress I had never seen before. Long and black, it moved as she moved. A silk scarf circled her neck. My mother never wore such things. So far as I knew, she didn't care to. They were too expensive for one thing, much more than my father could afford.

She nodded her head, inclining it just slightly to one side of her neck. Her lips came together, forming a perfect crease. This was a smile, but not a smile that I had ever seen on my mother's face. It made me feel embarrassed, vaguely excited.

Reaching out, Truxton took her hand in his. After bringing it up to his lips, he kissed her fingers softly, bending from the waist in order to do so. This time my mother's smile was radiant, like a thousand lights coming on at once. As she stepped easily through the doorway, she planted a kiss upon Henry Truxton's cheek. I was transfixed. I stared open-mouthed at the screen. Behind me, Maurie had grown silent. I heard his feet or hands bounce nervously up and down on the bench.

The couple moved gracefully to the center of the room. And then they were dancing, spinning and moving about the room with the grace of two swans. Other couples appeared on the screen—athletic young men in tuxedoes, elegant women in evening attire, all dancing to imagined music. But it was Henry Truxton III and my mother who were the most graceful and beautiful of all. Truxton, trim and debonair, stepped toward my mother and then away, letting her drift out to arm's length, holding on by just his fingertips before pulling her easily back to him.

My mother seemed to glide across the floor. Accompanying her movements, I imagined that I heard the gentle rise and fall of whatever music was playing. Up on her toes, she spun about with absolute ease— although I had never known her to dance. Certainly she had never done so with the Old Man, he who believed that all men who did such things suffered from some sexual disorientation. She was a natural, I guessed, and she seemed so alive while doing it. I found myself smiling, thinking that there—at the center of such beauty and grace—was where my mother truly belonged. Instead, she had been miscast as a salesman's wife. As I watched, I realized with a mixture of sadness, longing, and despair that my mother believed this as well.

The film blinked, as if spliced. In the half second before it came on again, I heard Maurie swallow as if trying to unplug his ears. He started to speak, then cleared his throat instead. Staring into the darkness, I only had time to wonder at the poor quality of the film. There were no titles. No credits. Unusual, I thought, especially when Henry Truxton was said to be a big-shot movie producer. Then again, perhaps what we were seeing was only a screen test.

Henry Truxton suddenly reappeared dressed only in bedroom slippers and long-sleeved pajamas, nervously pacing back and forth in front of a large canopy bed. Behind him, his tuxedo lay rumpled on a chair. He glanced angrily at his watch. He ran his fingers back through his hair. He put one hand to his mouth and appeared to shout.

"Oh, for Christ sake," breathed Maurie. "What now!"

My mother strode easily through the bedroom door. After untying her scarf, she tossed it onto the bureau. Truxton was incensed. He grabbed her arm. He pointed angrily at his watch. Pulling away, my mother sat down on the edge of the bed. She reached up, pulled off her stockings, then dropped them casually onto the floor. She tossed her purse aside, then released her hair, letting it fall down around her shoulders. Frowning, pretending to pout, she waved an accusing finger at Truxton.

"Jesus, what . . . ?"

Henry Truxton was suddenly contrite. Putting his hands together, he fell down upon his knees in front of my mother. Gazing up at the ceiling, my Mother feigned indifference. She reclined backward upon the bed, causing her ballgown to rise above her waist, revealing much more than I cared to see. A pair of crotchless underwear. An extraneous chemise. In the middle of the rug, Henry Truxton looked as if he would cry. Biting his lip, he fumbled pathetically for the string that held together his pajamas, causing them to drop to the floor in one motion. In front of him the legs slowly opened: my mother's legs. . . .

"Shut it off!"

Crawling forward, Truxton bent forward from the waist. My mother's hands reached down and wrapped securely about the entrepreneur's thin, tensing buttocks. . . .

"Jeez' Chris'," Maurie mumbled, as the screen, finally and too late, went blank. "Walt—I . . . damn—I—I couldn't find the right button."

This time I was thankful for the darkness. I welcomed the cocoon. My vague itch, like so much else, had left me.

CHAPTER 36

Ed Walling had ordered a double scotch. When it arrived, he tasted it with the tip of his tongue, then ran his tongue in a series of complete circles over his perfect teeth. He smacked his lips, nodded his head toward Maurie, and downed the scotch in one gulp.

"Is there somethin' more you want with me, Mr. Winthrop?"

Maurie had just finished reading the contents of the envelope Walling had shoved across the table at him. It didn't appear to be much—a sheet of paper with writing on one side. He folded it carefully, put it back in the envelope, and looked across the table at Ed Walling.

"Why, Ed? You're not in a rush, are you? Hang around, have another drink or two. I want Mr. Innis to read what you've brought. Then we can discuss our next move."

"I don't want to read that," said Walter. "Whatever it is."

"Why not?"

"I'm the schemer, Maurie. You're the doer. Just tell me whether he's interested."

"He's interested—in the complete package at our price."

"What the fuck is that—complete package, at our price? Jesus, Maurie, this isn't the CIA! We're talking about dirty pictures here!" Walter turned and nodded into the pot that was Ed Walling's face. "Involving the person you sent that envelope to."

"A shakedown?"

"Yeah, yeah! That's it, Ed! A shakedown! He thinks we've got the pictures, and he wants 'em back. For a price, Maurie says he can have 'em. I say all the money in the world won't buy back what was in those pictures. What do you say, Ed?"

"Jesus, Walter," hissed Maurie, "why not let the whole bar in on it?"

"Don't tempt me, Maurie. That's just what I'd like to do. I'd like to take a poll and see who gives a shit."

"I don't need this," said Walling, reaching hurriedly for his coat. "I'm on parole."

Walter grabbed him by the arm. "Sit down, Ed. We'll fill you in on some things."

"I don't want to know nothin'. The more I know, the worse it is for me when you guys get caught."

"Caught? What are you saying, caught? This is politics, Ed. Pure and simple. Maurie and I don't make dime one. We're simply a couple of civic-minded citizens, making certain of the public's right to know about the people they vote for. You vote, don't you, Ed?"

"I got a felony rap. Gov'ment won't let me register no more."

"Jesus. You'd think it was enough that a man spent time behind bars."

"I voted once. When I was eighteen—for Truman, I think. Though I couldn't swear to it now. He was the one with the wire rims who took long walks with his wife?"

"And carried a big stick while doing it," Walter said emphatically. "Lotta folks wouldn't have remembered that, Ed."

"I believe in the flag, and I ain't afraid to admit it."

"What do you think about Communists, Ed?"

"No manners. I can't respect people without manners. I was around thirty when Khrushchev took his shoe off and banged it on the table somewheres."

"U.N., Ed."

"Me and nobody. I read it in the newspapers."

"It was at the U.N.—United Nations—where Khrushchev banged his shoe on the table."

"Whatever. I ain't thought much of 'em since. You don't see the president banging things on the table, do you?"

"Guy you sent that envelope to is a Communist."

"What are you sayin'?"

"His name is Henry Truxton III and he's running for the state Senate."

"Jesus Christ." Maurie was holding his head, massaging it at the temples as if it were a lemon, his eyes searching through the field of devoured clams. "I hate it when you get like this."

"It's true," said Walter, signaling for another round of drinks, seeing Ed Walling as a true patriot. "My father knew about it years ago and tried to tell the public, but no one would listen. Even my mother was taken in by the guy. When she found out what he was really up to, he had her killed."

"What?"

"Jesus, Walter!"

"The thing is this, Ed. My father was a flag waver like you. He had one flying in our front yard, right outside my bedroom window. He wanted to show the town what he stood for, that he wasn't gonna let no Commie like Henry Truxton take nothin' from him."

"Yeah?" Walling, his face sweating—its surface appearing like a puddle-stained road—was trying desperately to disengage. "What's it got to do with me?"

"The public has got to be made to understand about this guy. Maurie and I infiltrated his place years ago, found documents with names of people who were Communists—some of 'em famous, folks you would probably recognize, from all over the United States."

"Russians?"

"Hell, yes! Russians. But not so's you'd know it to look at 'em. Some of 'em were ball players—major leaguers—right here in the U.S. of A. Truxton is Russia's main man over here. If they ever get him into the Senate, Ed, who knows where it might end. The presidency could be next!"

"I'm leaving now, Walter." Maurie, struggling to his feet, was having trouble with his balance. "If you are arrested and the police ask me any questions, I am going to tell them that you have just recently lost your job, that your wife has left you, that, in the best of times, your sanity has been questioned."

Walling too was attempting to rise, teeth flashing in bewilderment, his misshapen nose shining like a lit bulb. He looked uncertainly from one face to the other, emitting a strange whistling noise as he breathed.

Their waitress arrived with the drinks. She surveyed the booth and its occupants, deposited the drinks on the table, and stood back, waiting to be paid. Walter, one hand on Ed Walling's sleeve, reached with the other into his pocket and pulled out a wad of bills. He flung it toward the waitress, taking no notice as it slid to the floor.

"You see, Ed." Now the words were coming harder, getting caught somehow in his throat. He saw everything as if through a wall of water.

"This guy, Truxton—hurts people." The wall broke, the water now running down Walter's face. He talked louder, in order to be heard through the rushing sound of it.

"He has no manners . . . would bang a shoe . . . or anything . . . right on his tabletop."

CHAPTER 37

He came out of sleep slowly. His skin, the sheets, even his pillow were wet with perspiration. An odor pervaded the room—the thick, mossy smell of lingering ill health. He thrashed out violently with his arm and found, to his relief, that he was alone. Lying back on the bed, he felt the pulse in his neck, rapping insistently like an angry neighbor at the front door. Each rap sent the pain in his skull in circles.

He searched through the painful chaos of his mind and was unable to come up with a passable excuse to move, and so stopped trying. He lingered in the afterbirth of a dream, certain that an idea had been born, yet just as uncertain of what it might mean. Somewhere a church bell was ringing.

He saw his mother in church attire—the long pleated dress, the hat elegant atop her head, the scarf tied neatly about her neck. Next to her, Walter sat with his sister. Kate raised her eyebrows, smiled coyly at Bennie Woodson. Across the aisle, Bennie turned red and reached with one hand to be certain nothing was hanging from his nose. Bennie's father, like Bennie but larger and with less hair, gazed into his folded hands, his lips moving in silent prayer. Mrs. Woodson, fragile and twiglike, perched next to her husband, her eyes closed tight as caskets.

On the other side, George Bolton, so large his stomach was creased by the pew in front, sat in the midst of the Bolton clan, seven altogether, three on each side of George. The two littlest girls sat farthest from him, at opposite ends of the pew. From there they went up in size, like steps to a pyramid. Together they had the loudest voice in the congregation and, according to most, the tightest pockets whenever the collection plate made its rounds.

The Reverend Beemer, his bald head refracting the overhead light like a prism, raised his arms in supplication. His eyes did not burn with fire but glowed with a more subtle message. They sought out those even in the farthest reaches of the church—the very last row of pews—where nonmembers and those lacking proper attire sat tightly bunched. Organ music moved like a soothing wind through the congregation. The Reverend Beemer's voice, lifted by the music, wafted gently through his flock. Amen was sung in unison. All were at peace. Love filled every heart.

The music stopped. A time change for bingo was announced from the pulpit. The back doors were thrown open. The flock flowed into the aisles, careering and bumping into one another in a mad rush to get back to the world. Somewhere—much closer to Walter's ear—another bell was ringing.

He fumbled to get free of the sheets, remembered that the telephone was on the nightstand to his right, and made a stab at it with his hand. He managed to knock the phone to the floor, the receiver skittering across the hardwood, his sister Kate's voice making insistent demands. "Walter? Is that you? Jesus! Hello? Operator? I've been cut off. I want credit for the call. Do you hear me?"

Walter reached out, watching his hand pass from shadow into sunlight. He picked up the phone.

"Kate?" His voice sounded throaty, as if the words were being squeezed through a rusty gasket.

"Walter? Is that you? Jesus, you sound half dead!"

"Can you call back in half an hour?"

"What? Jesus Christ, Walter! It's long distance, you know?"

"Reverse the charges if you want. I can't talk now."

"What, you and Marsha doing the tango?"

"Thirty minutes, Kate."

In the kitchen, he made a pot of coffee, poured some into a large soup mug, then took it and the Sunday paper out to the back porch. Positioning himself on the chaise lounge so that the sun's rays fell directly upon his shoulders, he gulped down half the coffee and opened the paper.

With the light at his back, the front-page headline seemed to gloat: "Truxton Gains Backing of Democratic Party." Underneath, in smaller print, adjacent to a picture of the beaming candidate himself, were the words "Looks like a shoo-in for the nomination."

Without reading further, Walter flipped the entire front section casually to the floor. Ignoring everything else, he turned to the Sunday sports.

The feature article spotlighted local stars from the past—what they had once been, where they were now. A boxer named Antoine Brundage—a state Golden Gloves champion in the early 1950s who had turned pro, had two fights, was knocked into oblivion during the second and retired—now ran a guard dog school in Dundeen. "Best thing ever happened was me gettin' powdered like I did," he declared. "If'n it hadn't been so bad—if'n I'd just lost, 'stead of gettin' murdered, I probably woulda kep' right on fightin' till the inside of my head was Cream a' Wheat." Guard dogs, he said, were a lot like fighters. "The best of 'em is nasty, mean, and too dumb to hurt."

There was a high school wrestling champion from Caulfield who was now a dairy farmer. He had tried college, flunked out after one semester, and joined the pro wrestling circuit. A hundred pounds above his former weight, his hair teased and springing from his scalp in green-colored sprouts, he performed for three years under the pseudonym "The Malaysian Mauler." "Weren't nothing special 'bout Malaysia," he claimed. "Promoter give me the name. Probably 'cause it was far 'nough away, that weren't nobody from there likely to catch my meets." He injured his back when a body slam went awry, sued for compensation, lost and came back to Caulfield to work on his father's farm. As for his failure to get a degree, he had no regrets. "Cows," he said, "don't give a hoot whether I'm educated or whether I ain't."

Wayne "Dancin'" DuFries was an All-American halfback in the mid-'60s for Dundee High. In college he had never made the first team, but did manage to earn a degree in business administration. He lived downstate, owned the largest fuel oil business in the area, was president of the local school board, a member of the NCAA rules committee, and the most well liked man in town. "I never forgot that my success on the field might end at any moment. I learned early to put God and family above all else." He was pissed that he had never been given an opportunity to start in college and was now considering a run for mayor.

The last was a piece on Victor Innis. "Without a doubt," the article said, "the best pitcher this area has ever produced, until a tragic arm injury ended his career before it could really get started." The reporter claimed to have interviewed Victor at the nursing home for close to two hours. He found a "jovial" man without a "trace of the bitterness that one might expect to find in one who had suffered such a setback." Sure, he would have liked to have pitched in the major leagues—to see how well he night have fared against the best hitters in all of baseball—but he did not dwell upon it. He had found satisfaction in other areas, namely his family. "I have two wonderful children," he said. "They learned well—probably from their mother—that the things that matter most are what can be held onto . . . the rest should not be taken too seriously." He was particularly proud of his son, Walter, who visits his father each day at the home and has followed him into a career in sales. "And," the Old Man said, beaming, "he has recently gone into coaching."

CHAPTER 38

Afterward—once the screen had gone blank and the lights had come up—I was aware of no particular feeling; not anger, not melancholy, not despair. Numbness, maybe. The projector had snapped off, Maurie had cleared his throat for the umpteenth time, and I stood up to go. I stopped only to remove the film. While I was holding it in my hand, something told me that I ought to do more, so I shredded it—ripped it up into tiny pieces and stuffed the pieces into my pants pocket. And then I stole the glove. Not because I wanted it, but because I didn't want Henry Truxton to have it. I didn't think he ought to have it. Not any longer. I loaded the glove with stones. On the way back across the lake, I dropped it and the shredded pieces of film overboard.

It was not hard for me to imagine the sequence of events afterward. Arriving at the estate to find his archives invaded, his showpiece mitt stolen, a film classic missing, Henry Truxton III would have been outraged, in a mood for vengeance. He would have confronted the only possible suspect. His own maid and occasional perversion; the one person, aside from members of the Truxton family, with both a key to the house and the wherewithal for calming the dogs.

My mother would have known who the burglar was. Who besides the Old Man and I knew about the sacred cloth and the strange power it had over the hounds? One look at the inside of the Truxton archives would have confirmed her worst fears about what had been found. Then what thoughts might fill a mother's mind? The shortest route from Armageddon? The lake must have appeared as a noble way out. If only there had been another film in the reel. If only the projector had been broken. If only Maurie and I had left as we had come, discreetly, without having touched or taken a thing. If only my mother had—as she had so often admonished me to do—taken a moment to think. If only . . .

When the phone rang for the second time, Walter carefully placed the newspaper on the floor next to the chaise lounge, swallowed the last of his coffee, and got up to answer it. As he walked through the living room, he made a mental note to himself that the room needed cleaning. Newspapers and several unmatched socks lay strewn about; dust balls the size of desert weeds clung to the white rug; a pair of Walter's underwear trailed like tinsel from a lampshade. The stereo was as Marsha had left it—Bach on the turntable, the record's empty jacket teetering precariously from the edge of the coffee table.

The room, he realized, had been more hers than his. Since Marsha's departure Walter had used it only as a walkway from the kitchen to the back porch, or as a depository for dirty laundry and dated newspapers. In fact, it seemed, most areas of the house had been more hers than his. Of the nine rooms, Walter could have made do with three—kitchen, bathroom, and bedroom, plus the basement, where he spent time each day pounding his gloved fists into a bag he had fashioned from discarded clothes, rope, and a pup tent he and Marsha had once purchased with hopes of becoming campers.

The tent had made its debut in a state park outside of Middlebury, Vermont. Walter and Marsha had awakened during the night, cold and wet, the tent, unearthed from its stakes, covering them like a great shroud. A mad dash for the car had ensued, the tent being hastily wadded into a wet, black thing that forever stained the cloth seats of a Calvin loaner. The excursion, they agreed, had been an unfortunate series of events, but no reason to deter them from future outings. But something had.

If he was not unemployed, if money was more readily available, he would have hired someone to come in and clean the house. The kitchen was fast becoming an embarrassment, beyond anything Walter felt equipped to handle. Whenever he cooked a hamburger, the grease lodged beneath the armor of the stove, hardening there like cement. Walter had gone at the area with a hairbrush, scrubbing until his arm ached, until he felt something pop just above his elbow. Finally he had surrendered for good, letting the stuff pile up—until now nothing short of a chisel would remove it.

Before broiling chicken wings smothered in barbecue sauce, he had neglected to place the wings in a pan, feeling that tin foil would do. The sauce had run over, baking onto the sides and bottom of the broiler, causing the inside of the oven to now resemble the shaft of a coal mine. When opened, an odor akin to rotting refuse emerged. Walter had thus given up using the oven altogether, limiting his dinners now to things that could be boiled in water or zapped in a microwave.

He might, he believed, have had a better chance at self-sufficiency had he been abandoned in the Adirondack Mountains instead of in his own house. In the woods, at least, a person did not have to worry about setting off smoke alarms while cooking dinner, toilets overflowing, washing machines malfunctioning—Walter had watched in horror one day as his own machine started hopping about with its load, jumping up and down as if suddenly possessed by the devil. Finally it had pulled free from its hose, dying in a final gasp of agony, spilling its ravaged contents onto the cellar floor.

In the wilderness, a man might starve or freeze to death or maybe be eaten by a wild animal, but at least he need not lie down each night in the same spot. In the woods, each day is a regeneration. At daybreak, a man kicks aside his bed of pine needles, buries his own filth, and makes off for unseen vicinities. There is not the cyclic ennui that comes from the day-to-day existence in one's own squalor. One need not witness the static ineptitude of one's own life and then, in a cruel twist of irony, be made to wallow in it. So, take off, Walter Innis! Pack your belongings and drive west, stop in Yellowstone, sleep with your head on a boulder, your feet in a stream. Ah! But who is to feed me there? Who is to rub me with her foot? Who is to say "Walter, darling, what's not to love?"

Tripping over the garbage can, spilling its contents onto the kitchen floor, he reached for the phone and caught it on the fifth ring.

"Tough night?" asked Kate.

"Maurie and I had a few drinks."

"A few drinks, Walter? It's almost one o'clock. You're still in bed?"

"What's the harm? It's a day of rest, isn't it?" They hadn't talked in over a month, since shortly after Marsha had flown to Boston. That was forever ago. Whatever Walter was back then, he was not now. Kate would know nothing of his unemployment or of his pending divorce. She certainly would not know that her only brother was a blackmailer. She was his sister and he loved her, and still he had not told her.

"Yes. It's a day of rest. How's Marsha?"

"Fine. She's in Boston. At her mother's, I gather."

"Still? She's in Boston still?"

"Yes. She's still there, talking to a lawyer, sending out fliers by courier. She's convinced that she's finally discovered a way to make money."

"Really? In advertising?"

"Sort of. It's a scheme her and this lawyer have concocted. Sponge economics. The idea is to find one man—preferably of means—and then to squeeze him for whatever he's worth. The only problem is, the guy they picked is meansless—or meaningless—depending upon your enunciation."

"What are you saying, Walter?"

"In theory, it's beautiful. In practice, it will be a profitless disaster for all concerned."

"Stop speaking in riddles, Walter. Is she divorcing you or what?"

"Unfortunately, for her, I am the only one eligible for that honor."

For several moments, Walter heard nothing but a series of clicks on the line. They were tapped out as if in a code—a cadence, filling the void in intervals of threes. *Tap. Tap. Tap.* Silence. *Tap. Tap. Tap.* Walter knew exactly what the sounds were. Kate, since she was a child, had a habit of tapping when she was agitated or deep in thought. She would pick up a pencil, or use her finger, and tap in a series of threes until the taps became thoughts and the thoughts became words. She was tapping now, probably with a pencil, on the mouthpiece of the telephone.

Walter had not meant to tell her about him and Marsha. It had simply slipped out, as if he had no control, the announcement would come out whenever it felt like it. This lack of command over his own utterances was something that was occurring with more and more frequency. On the previous evening, for example, he had begun to ramble in incoherent fashion to Ed Walling. Walter would have to be more careful. A man who could not keep a lid on could not possibly hope to succeed as a schemer.

"Walter?" The tapping had stopped. Kate's voice was now that of the child psychologist she had become and Walter was—as it seemed he had been forever—the child. "What else aren't you telling me?"

"Isn't getting divorced enough?"

"You and Marsha have been pointed in that direction for a long while. You're only upset that she made the move before you got around to it. No. There's something else. You are a lot of things, Walter Innis, but not usually a cynic with your big sister."

"There's nothing else. In fact, life is rather good at the moment. I just finished reading a newspaper article about our father in which he was quite complimentary to both of his children."

"What? What newspaper?"

"The local. I'll cut it out and send it down to you. I think you'll find it interesting."

"How is he? Have you been to visit him lately?"

"Yes. His health is not good. But his spirits are. He speaks often of you and me, when we were kids, growing up. All the fun times we had."

The tapping began once again. Walter gazed out the kitchen window, saw children in shorts and T-shirts playing across the street. Swaying back and forth in an arc, a lawn sprinkler sprayed water in a gentle pattern on the grass. The children danced timidly outside the drops, afraid to go further. Afraid, thought Walter, to get unabashedly wet.

"Walter. I think I am going to come up and visit."

"When?"

"This weekend. Maybe next."

"It's not really a good time, Kate. I've been very busy, what with work and all, plus Maurie and I are involved in a business venture. And I'm coaching a Little League team."

"You don't sound right, Walter. I'm worried about you."

"No need, sis. Everything is fine."

"How's work?"

"Excellent. Couldn't be better. What with new car prices being sky high, everybody is buying used these days. Good for me. Bad for Detroit."

"I hate to see you waste yourself selling cars, Walter. You could do better. Why don't you move to New York?"

"I tried that. Remember? Took me twelve years to find my way home."

"Maybe that was a mistake . . . moving back to Caulfield."

"Thomas Wolfe, for one, would agree with you."

"That's what I mean, Walter. You've got a mind. You read things."

"Only when sales are slow. I memorize the titles of all the classics, maybe skim the first and last chapters."

Across the street, a bigger kid, maybe ten, wearing nothing but a pair of cutoffs, plunged into the center of the spray. He laughed as the water hit him full in the face. He reached down with one hand and picked up the nozzle. Holding it out like a gun, he began chasing the other kids with it. Their squeals reached Walter through the window. The children scattered, screaming.

"Father understands why I can't visit more often, doesn't he?"

"Of course. You're busy. You have your own life."

"I wish I could send money, move him into a better nursing home, but there just doesn't seem to be any. I don't know where it goes."

"He understands. How's Bernard?"

"It's Bar-nard and he moved out two weeks ago. I knew from the start that he had a male lover. I believed I could change him, that his bisexuality was adult onset, the result of gay stereotyping. He's a hairdresser, you know? I suppose I overestimated my abilities as a therapist."

"Well . . ."

"There is a man though. His name is Maurice. Sexually speaking, we are absolutely compatible—which, at my age, counts for a lot—but intellectually he's a complete zero. He's a hockey player—Larsen. Maurice Larsen. Ever hear of him? Probably not. They just brought him up from the minors at the beginning of the season. Anyway, I asked him what he thought of Chekhov, and he said 'a goood skater'—he's Canadian, you know, draws his ohs out like that—'but not much of a stick.' Can you believe it? He thought Chekhov was a right winger for the Islanders. Anyway, like I said, the sex is good."

He wanted to stop her, to say "You are my sister whom I love more than anyone in the world. Remember when we could talk and it didn't matter about what?" But he didn't stop her. He let her go on about her life, about things that to Walter were as strange as the characters in a Vonnegut novel, but to her were not. Most times it didn't matter—people grow up and apart and maybe they see each other at funerals or weddings and, what the hell, over spiked punch it's just like old times and "by gosh by golly, you haven't changed a bit"—but, every once in a while, like now, it did matter. Right there, in broad daylight, a chasm opens up before your eyes and you see your sister drop into it. You make a stab for her with your hand, but it's too late, she's gone—dropped off like a dying quail. Then all of a sudden there she is again—only it isn't her. It's someone else, a nice person who looks like her and talks like her but is not her, because you don't know the first thing about this person and she doesn't know the first thing about you. You talk, but you don't talk. You dance just outside the drops, afraid to get unabashedly wet.

". . . and I'm writing another book: *Pubescent Anger—Adult Stress*. It should be done by Christmas. Then it's just a matter of getting my editor to accept it. God knows I could use the money."

"Do you think they loved each other?"

"What? Who?"

"Mother and Father."

"Yes. I suppose. In their own perverse way."

"What about us? Do you think they loved us?"

"Like any parents. Why are you asking me these things, Walter? You've never mentioned them before. Something is wrong, isn't it?" Her voice started to rise in the way that it did when they were younger, when Kate suddenly became angry over something and she wasn't sure why. "Is he dead? That's it, isn't it? Father's dead and this is your wheedling way of telling me about it. Goddamn you, Walter!"

"Kate. That's not it. I've just been thinking about the two of them lately—had them on my mind for some reason, that's all."

"Quit using weasel words, Walter! If he's dead, he's dead! I'll come up and arrange for the funeral and we'll bury him next to Mother, I suppose."

"He's not dead."

"You're certain?"

"Positive. I told you, he's in good spirits."

"Well then, why are you talking about him?"

"Must he be dead before we talk about him?"

"Goddamn it, Walter! If you've something to say, why don't you just come out and say it?"

"I was just wondering, that's all."

"Wondering what?"

"Why it is, that—lately—they've been on my mind so much . . . particularly the Old Man. The thing is, I'm not certain that I care at all what happens to him, but. . . . these thoughts won't go away. I keep thinking that, after all these years, maybe I missed something good in him. And I just wondered if it was ever like that for you."

"I'm not cold, Walter. I know you're trying to say that I'm a cold bitch, but I'm not—"

"No."

"They were my parents and as that, they were no more than adequate. He was a boozer. She was a martyr who wanted the world to know it. I never felt too special . . . but then, I don't suppose I had any right to. So, yeah, I think about them both once in a while and when he dies I'll come up for the funeral and on that day I suppose I'll think about them both a little more than usual and then I'll get on with my own life. So why, for the love of God, can't you do the same thing? Do you think you are something special, Walter Innis? Is that it?"

Then came the tapping again. Walter supposed it was up to him to say something, to put an end to it, but he wasn't certain of what to say. He wanted to say Yes, it had always been his hope that he was something special and that he believed Kate was something pretty special as well. But then he supposed that the former would have sounded a little foolish at the moment. He was thirty-nine years old, without a job, without a wife, and with a father who talked to a newspaper reporter before he would talk to his own son. His father was nothing special, but he was the only one that Walter had, and as the life slipped slowly out of the Old Man, Walter felt no closer to knowing him than he ever had. He felt, somehow, that if he did not know his father, he would never know himself. So, you see, it had nothing to do with love really. It was simply a matter of self-preservation.

"I just wish you would stop trying to figure everything out, Walter, as if thinking about it long enough will somehow cause it all to make sense."

"It's the schemer's curse," said Walter, "to believe that every rhyme has a riddle."

"What?"

"Nothing. I've got a ball game to coach. I love you, Kate."

"And I you, Walter. So, why do our conversations always end like this? After an argument?"

"Better after than during."

"Think about me coming up soon?"

"Sure. Bring Maurice. We'll put skates on, go down to the rink, do something physical together."

"Bye, Walter."

"Bye, Kate."

CHAPTER 40

At the nursing home, Doris Hunchhammer had burst unannounced into room 212 and encountered Jacob Johnson, pipe lodged between his teeth, surrounded in billowy puffs of smoke like a Hindu holy man. Panicked, and without defense, Jacob had opened his mouth to speak, causing the pipe to drop like a stone. The fiery instrument landed upon the sheets, starting a small blaze, singeing the skin upon his leg. Yelping in pain, throwing his left hand out in what was a reflex response, Jacob knocked the nightstand and its contents to the floor.

The commotion brought Victor Innis to an upright position—the first time, unaided, in weeks—his normally pallid countenance now red with anger. The Old Man's hand emerged from beneath the sheets, swiping blindly at air, dueling with some unseen enemy. One swipe sent the stand adjacent to his bed tumbling to the floor; another unhinged a tube of glucose from his other arm. A bedpan, waiting to be emptied, spun like a dervish across the linoleum and through the open doorway, crashing finally into someone's breakfast tray.

Defiant and not at all contrite, the Old Man reached behind him then and retrieved his pillow. After hurling it across the room, he watched as it dipped and swayed with the magic of his fabled knuckler. The pillow caught Nurse Hunchhammer full in the chest. "See what you have done?" the Old Man raged. "And all because of a goddamned pipe!" He coughed once, turned blue, and fell back upon the mattress.

Dazed but recovering quickly, Nurse Hunchhammer found Victor's pillow against her breast. The fire still smoldered. With what, she claimed, were only laudable motives, she raised the pillow high above her head and brought it down forcefully on the center portion of Jacob Johnson's bed. And, in case once was not enough, she did it again. Only an orderly, rushing to the scene of the commotion, prevented a third assault from occurring.

In the aftermath, there was chaos. A contingent of medical personnel filled the room. Hooked to a machine, Victor had his chest pounded upon, his head tilted back, his lungs rejuvenated by the breath of strangers. At long last, a slight fluttering ensued, a blip no louder than high-flying geese appeared on the screen. Although his heart was coaxed into continuing awhile longer, Victor remained unconscious.

Jacob Johnson, lamenting like a supplicant at the Wailing Wall, was treated for a minor burn to his leg. Salve was applied, the wound carefully wrapped in an aerated bandage. Fearing damage as a result of Nurse Hunchhammer's overly zealous attempts to put out his fire, he insisted too that his testicles be examined. He claimed that it had been her intent to castrate him. Glancing up at the crucial moment, Jacob had seen his attacker's eyes and they were, he insisted, "big as silver dollars!"

Given the size of the fire, there was some debate as to whether or not Nurse Hunchhammer's actions had been necessary. Upon examination, the sheet had a hole no larger than a penny. Jacob Johnson's pipe, when found, was but half full of Bull Durham. Stress, Doris Hunchhammer claimed, had created a brief hallucination. In the moment of her panic, Jacob's bed appeared like a flaming rotisserie, he like a leg of lamb. She was contrite, appearing genuinely concerned for her patients' well-being. As they were treated, she stood with her head against the wall, still dazed, mumbling incoherently about the propriety of rules.

Jacob's testicles were examined by a female practitioner behind drawn curtains. Those in attendance heard first a yelp of surprise—whether from the practitioner or Jacob Johnson was a matter of debate—followed then by the soothing voice of the examiner. "It may stay up for a few days," she said. "The blow seems to have caused a plethora of blood to have amassed in the area." When the curtains opened, both doctor and patient were smiling. Later Jacob would tell Walter, "Ten years since I had an erection," hesitating, shaking his head as if in utter amazement, "and it took a blow by Doris Hunchhammer to do it."

It had all happened on Saturday night, while Walter was getting drunk with Maurie Winthrop and Ed Walling. The nursing home had tried to reach Walter that evening. They tried again the next morning as Walter, no doubt, dreamed of God and the Reverend Beemer. Office personnel had eventually given up, assuming Walter had gone away for the weekend. It wasn't until late Sunday afternoon when Walter showed up for a visit with the Old Man that he heard the news. Before he could start down the hallway toward his father's room, he was intercepted by Mr. Jules Pembleton, the home's assistant director.

Pembleton, a short man, trim and snappish, smelling vaguely of mint juleps, possessed the perpetual smile of a majordomo. He linked his arm through Walter's, sauntering off with him toward his office as he explained what had occurred, using crisp, delicate gestures to emphasize, raising his voice where appropriate. By the time he and Walter had reached the office, most of the story was out.

The Assistant Director's desk was a half circle of mahogany, covered by clear glass, polished to a glossy luster. Smiling warmly toward Walter, Pembleton seated himself behind it, nimbly placing his cheeks atop a faldstool. Facing him, Walter sat in a spongy, off-white lounger, his ass only inches from the parquet floor. Across the way, a picture of Pembleton, in chaps, hung on the wall. He was mounting a Thoroughbred. At his waist, a tiny whip dangled by a thread.

"The doctors have called it an infarction," said Jules Pembleton.

"A heart attack?"

"Quite. He may also have had a small stroke."

"And he's in a coma?"

"Temporarily, at least."

"What you're saying, Mr. Pembleton, is that he might never wake up."

Pembleton pinched his lower lip, creating a set of minute buttocks. "My Lord, let's not be so bleak, Mr. Innis! Anything's possible, of course. But why look on the down side?"

"What's the up side?"

"Why, he could come out of it at any moment. The doctors just can't say."

"Really?"

"Sure 'nough. He might be his old self soon's tomorrow!"

"Discounting the effects of a heart attack and a stroke, you mean? Not to mention the cirrhosis of the liver and emphysema he already had?"

"We mustn't hope for miracles, I suppose." Pembleton released his lip, gave a jaunty wave of his hand. "Still, as my dear mother used to say, a bushel of faith is worth a peck of medicine!"

"Your mother, I'll wager, was never a patient in County Convalescent."

"Bless her soul, she went in one fell swoop." He wrinkled his nose, as if suddenly he had gotten a whiff of something foul. "Why, Mr. Innis, I'm afraid I don't get your meaning."

"It's tough to keep the faith, Jules, when one hears of nurses setting fire to patients."

"That's not exactly—"

"Not to mention assaulting them with pillows."

"Let's not forget," said Jules Pembleton, priggishly shifting his ass, "who threw the first pillow."

"He awoke in the midst of a free-for-all. There was, for God's sake, a bonfire on the next bed!"

"We will never know," countered the assistant director, "exactly what caused Victor to act as he did."

And that, Walter knew, was the truth. Maybe his father had felt the big one coming and simply wished to expire with a bang; or had God, at long last, supplied the Old Man with the answer he had craved for so long? Perhaps, in tossing his pillow at the unsuspecting Nurse Hunchhammer, Victor had sought nothing more than a cheap laugh. Whatever the reason, it was now certain that Victor Innis would do anything to avoid explanations.

The man's life, thought his son, had been one impulsive act heaped upon another—all emanating, somehow, from his right arm. The limb, oft injured, remained limber. With two ill-fated heaves, a life had been irreparably altered. With the first pitch that had gone awry, the Old Man had sidestepped his future; with the last, he had slithered out from beneath his past. And who was it that was left to explain his motives? Certainly not Victor himself. The Old Man danced his knuckler and passed into oblivion—questions floating like goosedown in the wake.

"Your father has been with us for close to a year, Mr. Innis."

"Is that some kind of a record?"

"Patients don't generally arrive here in the best of health."

"And on the off chance that they do, apparently you and your staff will make certain that they don't leave that way."

"What I am saying, sir, is that we offer little by way of recovery."

Pembleton swallowed firmly, his Adam's apple trembling. With the index finger of his left hand, he began to caress it gently. "Our chief concern is to provide a comfortable conversion."

"Conversion? Conversion to what?"

"Most of our patients pass on within a year of their arrival. So, it seems, may your father."

"Pass on?"

"Die, Mr. Innis." With barely a flutter, the assistant director's hand moved from his Adam's apple to his fountain pen. "Speaking frankly, given Victor's health, it is somewhat surprising that he has endured as long as he has. The severity of those physical ailments, I am certain, is what led you to decide upon Convalescent in the first place."

"The decision was not mine to make. Until his arrival here, I hadn't spoken to him in over twenty years."

"I see." Pembleton's delicate fingers moved slowly along the shaft of his pen. "It was his decision then?"

"His wife made the decision to admit him. She then relinquished all responsibility."

"Legally?"

"Personally. On the telephone."

The call had come while Walter and Marsha were in the midst of dinner. They were once again discussing the orchard—what a drought it had encountered, whether or not it would endure. Walter had been thankful for the phone's ring. At the sound of its jangle, Marsha's mouth was puckering in preparation for the bit about the ascending road.

Marsha had been on the verge of hanging up, believing that she was the victim of a prank call or that Rita Glenberry had reached the wrong Walter Innis. But Walter, recognizing the name—conjuring up memories of jugs the size of tropical fruit—had snatched the receiver from his wife's hand. In all the years Rita had been married to his father, Walter had spoken to her only once—on a chance meeting during one of Walter's infrequent forays into the old neighborhood. He had, of course, followed the saga of the Old Man's marriage in the local police blotter.

"I'm calling about your father, Walter."

"What's the problem?"

"All of his sins have caught up with him. He hasn't left the house in weeks. He lays all day on the couch, watches TV, eats frozen dinners, falls asleep with his head in the leftovers. The next day I come in and clean up. I'm too old, Walter."

"What are you saying, Rita?"

"I've gotten a place for him in Convalescent. County expense. I thought I should tell you. You might want to visit him."

"You would know what's best, Rita. From what I hear, you've been good to him."

"He drunk up most of his money. There's only the house, and I figure I earned that."

"You won't get an argument from me, and I can't imagine that Kate has any interest in the place. Rent it out till he dies. After that, as far as I'm concerned, you can sell it."

"Walter?"

"What is it, Rita?"

"I'm only dropping him there."

"What do you mean?"

"I ain't gonna visit. I don't want to see him like he is now. When he was strong enough to beat me up, I couldn't get full of him. Now . . . it's different. He's a tired old man. I still gotta live. You understand?"

"Sure, Rita."

"Take care of him, Walter. Visit him once in a while. He's your old man."

That quickly, Walter had regained a father. Not knowing why, he had gone to see him the first time. Swearing he would not, he returned for a second visit and had kept going for close to four months, his visits increasing to once daily, and still he was not sure the Old Man recognized him or even remembered him. After a while he realized that the Old Man had no other visitors. On three occasions, Kate had accompanied him to the home. Although the Old Man's eyes were clearly open and he must have seen her, she had stood just inside the doorway at first, staring at her father from a distance. Finally Kate had walked over to his bed, bent down, and planted a kiss on his yellow forehead. "I've seen you looking better, Poppa," she said, and he laughed. The Old Man actually laughed, exhibiting teeth like a row of decaying fence posts.

He had asked his daughter crazy things out of context—who she would go to the prom with, what she would do when she graduated, whether she had been to visit her aunt Erma—and Kate had not missed a beat, supplying out-of-context answers to out-of-context questions. They had laughed some more, appeared to have a good time. Kate peppered the Old Man with kisses. At the end of each visit, she promised to come back soon. In the hallway, after the last one, she had whispered to Walter, "I'm researching a new book, Walter. I don't foresee getting back to Caulfield for several months. If he dies suddenly, give me a call. I'll catch a plane."

Always ready with a kiss, Kate never lingered long enough to feel its effect. In three visits, she had spoken more to the Old Man than Walter had in twenty years. Walter could not bring himself to place his lips upon the skin that felt like rotting bark. He could not come up with answers to out-of-context questions, although none were ever asked of him. When it came to his son, the Old Man remained uniquely contextual. Silence, like an unruffled banket, lay between them. They sat, a pair of stone Buddhas, staring into the sun.

"This is highly irregular," said Jules Pembleton, clearly agitated, his fingers moving roughly along the shaft of his pen. "Our admission sheet does not indicate a living spouse."

"I've told you, they're separated. She no longer feels responsible."

"What about legal responsibility? In the event of death or . . . other-wise?"

"That would be me, I suppose. Or my sister."

"A small formality then, if you please, Mr. Innis." With his free hand, the one not choking his fountain pen, Pembleton shoved two sets of papers across the desk. Pointing at the bottom line of each sheet, he flashed a waxy smile. "Sign here, please."

"May I ask what I am signing?"

"It's a simple waiver of legal responsibility, quite common in these cases." Pembleton's voice cracked delicately on the high notes. In his right hand, the fountain pen seemed ready to spurt. "You are simply agreeing that the home and its employees are in no way responsible for your father's present physical state."

"I would be waiving my right to sue?"

"I can assure you," Pembleton continued quickly, his voice popping now on every other syllable, "that the employee involved will be terminated."

"I will sign," said Walter, "only if Nurse Hunchhammer is neither fired nor reassigned. That is, I want her to remain as my father's nurse."

"If that is what you wish, I am sure it can be arranged." Palm up, his hand indicated the legal forms.

"And . . ."

"Yes?"

"That his present roommate—Mr. Johnson—not be assigned a new room, that he and my father be permitted to continue rooming together until one or the other requests a change."

"We thought, naturally, that you would wish Victor to be given a private room."

"No."

"Agreed."

Walter reached into his pocket for his own pen. After snapping the point out, he quickly signed both sheets. Across from him, Jules Pembleton released a stifled moan as the fountain pen in his hand erupted, spitting gobs of blue ink onto the front of his pastel shirt.

CHAPTER 41

Nurse Hunchhammer's shot to Jacob's groin turned the retired sheet-metal worker into an instant celebrity. His cock, in its swollen splendor, became the talk of the nursing home. All manner of personnel wandered in to get a look at it. Nurses, doctors, janitors came at all hours of the day, gazing openly upon the statuesque prick, leaving with the dazed look of those who have seen the pyramids.

Mr. Johnson was a gracious hero, smiling and nodding patiently to all who entered. To some—generally those of the female persuasion—he politely unveiled the treasure, its great head surfacing above the sheets like the back of a whale. The rest saw only its outline, a great pole at the center of a raised awning, and could only imagine what it was that could raise bedclothes to such heights.

But his elation was short-lived. Within a few days Jacob had grown tired of the attention. His erection was constant, like a steel girder in his pants. It never went down. When pissing, he had to stand several feet back from the bowl, prick held like a cigar between the index and third fingers of his right hand. His hope was that by operating the engorged member in the manner of a derrick, he might at least come close to his target. Starting was slow, requiring mental concentration and a small amount of manual persuasion with the off hand. All too often, the stream appeared without warning, shooting upward in a powerful arc, once even catching Jacob beneath the chin.

Sleeping was difficult as well. A wrong turn and the prick might be severely sprained. Jacob had always been a stomach sleeper, a position that now was anatomically dangerous. Given the unpredictable nature of sleep, even dozing on his back did not guarantee safety. One night, in the midst of a dream, Jacob had flailed with his arm at some imaginary foe, hitting his prick instead, which seemed never to rest, but stood throughout the night like a medieval sentinel. Getting up later to go to the bathroom, stumbling about in the half-lit room, he had walked into a wall, prick first.

It was Nurse Hunchhammer who had responded to his agonized cry. She had stayed with him throughout the night, applying hot packs to the affected area, touching him gently with her androgynous fingers. Be it shared guilt or mutual admiration for Jacob's constant erection, they had grown close. The friction between them had vanished. They commiserated together over Victor's plight and took turns standing vigil over his bed, searching for any sign that he might be emerging from his coma. Behind Jacob's drawn curtain, they whispered conspiratorially, giggling like schoolchildren and prodding the immense cock. Upon emerging from behind the curtain, face flushed, blood showing in the veins of her legs, Nurse Hunchhammer might appear disoriented.

But their games were not physical. There was no rustling of sheets, no surface breathing, no wafting noises of slippery lust. Ah! But did they talk dirty to one another? Of course, Jacob confided to Walter, and in the most perverse manner. Opposite one another on the bed, Jacob's cock between them like a vertical Ouija Board, they conjured up bizarre physical feats. What they would do to one another. How it would feel. Something might happen for Nurse Hunchhammer. Somewhere in that body like a plywood plank, a small envelope eased open like a slow-blooming rose. And that, claimed Jacob, was what caused her face to flush. But that was all. And that was enough.

Walking into room 212, one might find Jacob Johnson sitting up in bed, enjoying a pipeful of Raleigh Bold, his erection protruding like a unicorn's horn from his layered lap. The door might be wide open. Nurse Hunchhammer might be puttering about, sloshing Victor with a wet cloth, peering brazenly into his bedpan in hopes of spying something solid there. Yes. The rule had been broken or at least rewritten. Jacob was allowed to smoke—and with the door wide open—but only if he blew the smoke upward, away from Victor Innis and toward the air vent above his bed.

There was, about the room, an ironic vitality—a lilting upheaval, like that felt by those newly versed in mortality. Life, it had been seen, was as precarious as pipe smoke, death as near as the rising wind. Eyes close, as if in momentary anger, and do not open. A man after cursing, has his mouth shut forever. Seeing these things causes some to react strangely. It may make a man feel his pecker rise. It may cause a woman's face to flush.

"She's a fine woman," Jacob intimated to Walter, "and I believe she cares for more than just my prick. Of course, I suppose I won't be absolutely certain of that until the damn thing deflates. But isn't it great—at my age—to be in the position of wondering?"

Walter wished to give Victor credit for something and this seemed a fine thing, an outstanding thing, in fact. He imagined that his father had hoped for it all along, had perhaps even planned to the last detail when to unleash his last and greatest pitch. A man's life might still have value if, when looking back, one feat stands far enough above the rest. Who did not remember Don Larsen? A mediocre pitcher throughout his career, until that one game—the great game—that had made him immortal. When people spoke of him, they spoke of that one game; all that came before it was conveniently forgotten. And so, Walter hoped, it might be for his father. His last conscious act—the finest feat of a checkered career—was what, in years to come, Walter hoped he would remember.

Seeing Victor in his coma, Walter wondered at first if the Old Man was actually asleep. In the past, his father had slept or had pretended to sleep through many of his son's visits. Might this be his final game of possum? Was deep sleep, perhaps, the Old Man's greatest deception? Then, looking closer, Walter saw that this was not a feigned sleep. There was no effort in the Old Man's repose. His eyelids were not squeezed shut as before, but lay placidly unruffled over his eyes. The skin about his face and forehead, no longer wrinkled, was smooth as unbroken water. His mouth was mostly shut, the lips turned gently outward in what Walter hoped was a smile.

The nurses turned him regularly, as if his bed was a burner and his skin might be singed. He rolled over easily, pliant and unresisting in their hands. While he slept, he was fed through tubes. He filled the bedpans, sometimes on his own, sometimes only after he was induced to do so. He did not talk. Perhaps he dreamed. Above him, a monitor beeped and fell silent. He appeared peaceful. He would die soon. He might wake up first or he might not. It did not really matter.

"He stopped talking to God," Jacob told Walter.

"When?"

"Two nights before he went under. The day it happened, I didn't hear him say a word to anyone, except to swear at the orderly who came to pick up his dinner tray. 'I know now,' he told the orderly, 'what dog shit tastes like. Dog shit without salt.' "

"At home—when I was growing up—he would salt everything. Even peanuts and presalted popcorn. After taking them from the bag—before putting them into his mouth—he would salt them again. He loved salt."

"Here they wouldn't give it to him. It always angered him. A couple of times, I gave him my salt. I didn't guess a little of it would hurt him, any more than a pipeful of tobacco would hurt me. And," Jacob continued, "your father didn't like the desserts he was given."

"What was wrong with the desserts?"

"Fruit. They used to give him strained fruit—for his bowels—and so he wouldn't get too much sugar. 'Fruit is not a dessert,' he would say. 'Ice cream, cherry pie, chocolate layer cake, those are desserts. But not fruit. Fruit is something you give a young child to take to school.' It was funny the things he didn't like. Once he threw a peach cobbler against the wall."

"I had the idea he never talked much."

"He didn't. Except when he didn't like something, like fruit for dessert, then he would talk plenty, and it might not be all that pleasant to listen to."

"Did you like him, Jacob?"

"I liked him all right, didn't know him that well. Like I said, he didn't talk much about things that mattered, except at night, when nobody but God was supposed to hear."

"Why do you suppose he stopped talking to God?"

"Who knows? Maybe he found out what he wanted to know. Or he ran out of things to say. Or maybe he thought nobody was listening."

"Well, he talked to somebody, all right," said Walter, pulling the folded article from the Caulfield *Banner* out of his pocket and handing it to Jacob. "And somebody listened."

"I guess—now that I think about it—there was a reporter here, week or so ago."

"He made the same mistake I did, didn't he? You suckered him, like you suckered me."

"Not exactly . . . no. He came in asking for Mr. Innis. Your father was sleeping."

"But you didn't tell him that."

"He wanted a story. He didn't seem to care who gave it to him."

"I don't know how you pulled it off, Jacob, but I know my father wouldn't say anything to any newspaper reporter, especially about his own family."

"Are you mad?"

"Should I be?"

"No. I only said what your father would have said, if he were a different kind of man." Jacob gazed at the Old Man, smiled slightly, reached absently for his erection, and began to tap lightly upon it through the sheet. "Almost a week now, and still it's like steel."

"Is it terribly painful?"

"It hurts, all right, but that's not the worst of it. Having a prick like this is like carrying around a weapon that won't fire." He pulled back the sheet then and showed the thing to Walter. It looked swollen, painful, the head glistening like a halogen headlight. "All that dirty talk with Doris Hunchhammer has given me blue balls."

He covered it gently, as one would a flower to protect it from the frost, being careful not to lay the sheet too heavily upon it. Sitting daintily in his bed, his veined hands folded securely about his prick as if it were an urn containing holy ashes, Jacob shone in a mystical aura. Were he to drape his head, thought Walter, the former sheetmetal worker from St. Louis might be taken for a Franciscan friar.

"I keep thinking," Jacob said, "about the amount of blood it takes to cause an erection, let alone to keep a prick blown up for six days."

"What better use would you have for it? The blood, I mean."

"I worry that the blood from my brain may have drained to my prick. My memory is not what it was before the erection. There are things I can't recall, like what I may have said to that reporter who was here."

"It's not important," said Walter. "I enjoyed the article. I'll send it to my sister, who will probably refer to it in her next book." Walter smiled at Jacob, for he truly enjoyed this jovial holy man with his swollen prick. His heart, at least, had not been drained of blood. It was in the right place. Knowing that Jacob Johnson would continue as his father's roommate—

even while the Old Man was unconscious—made Walter feel he had done all he could for him.

"I do remember one thing, if it helps," said Jacob. "When we were through talking, the reporter—a young fellow with breath that would kill a horse—pulled back the curtain surrounding my bed. I saw your father then. He had been listening to our conversation. He was looking straight at me and he was smiling. When I smiled back, he laughed, the only time I had ever heard him do so. He gripped his fist in a victory salute. He didn't appear at all serious."

"You are a good man, Mr. Johnson."

"From what you know of me."

"It's enough."

"From what I know of Victor, he too was a good man."

"You don't know enough, then."

"Ah. Not as serious as you were, perhaps, but still serious enough, Walter. And now I must rest. My prick is throbbing, and Doris Hunch-hammer will be here in less than an hour."

CHAPTER 42

In mid-August, when a baseball season is three-quarters through, teams are not generally seeking first victories. Players and fans talk of pennant drives, of regrouping for the stretch run, of games out and games in, of what might have been or what might still be, but certainly not of what never could be: a winless season.

The talk first starts around the beginning of June—simple supposition, idle chatter, like broken wind, emanating from unspecific bleacher points. "You know, they ain't come within five runs of a win. You don't suppose . . . ?"

"Don't be a jackass! This is baseball, not football, for Christ sake! Why, they'd hafta go oh and twenty."

"You're right. Don't know what I was thinking. Ain't nobody that bad."

Around mid-July it starts to heat up. The talk is no longer aimless. It is pointed and usually right at the coach because the players, after all, are only kids and in this country, goddamn it, kids shouldn't have to shoulder that kind of responsibility. But, Jesus, they are bad, aren't they?

"Why, that first baseman's got no more coordination than an eel. And that little munchkin? The catcher? If he was my kid I'd show him how to buckle his pants up 'fore anything else."

"Have a look out in left field, why don't yuh. Ya ever seen a kid so light in his loafers?"

"Why, that's Bob Walke's kid. You sayin' Walke's kid's a fag?"

"I'm saying he could be a fag if somebody don't teach him how to throw a ball overhand!"

"Hell, that's just coaching that's what that is."

"Ain't that what I said?"

"Well, least they got rid a' Cooley Palumbo's widow. She didn't know a curve ball from a puff ball."

"Those weren't puff balls 'neath her shirt, I'll tell ya."

"Ain't that the truth! It'd take more than a little rosin and slippery elm to get a proper grip on that pair."

"What they wouldn't do to a man's fungo bat!"

"Puff balls or footballs, she still couldn't coach."

"Yeah? Well, I say, so what? If you gotta watch your kid lose twice a week, you might as well have something worthwhile to look at. This Innis guy ain't nothing to look at and he can't coach to boot."

"That's no lie! He's got my kid walking around squeezing a rubber ball, for Christ sake!"

"So? Whyn't you coach, ya got such a gripe?"

"Who's got the time? Some of us have to work for a living."

"You saying the man doesn't have a job?"

"Sure he's got a job! Shags flies and pounds his fungo while the rest of us punch a time clock!"

"From what I hear, he hasn't worked since his wife up and left him."

"Well, I'll tell ya what he used to do. He used to sell cars for Calvin Chevrolet, on Erie Street. Jim Denton bought a Caprice off of him a couple of years back—used, seventy-five, with air and an eight cylinder."

"By God he's right, men! Put him on a horse and Innis is the Calvin Chevrolet Cowboy!"

"Three weeks after he buys it, the transmission drops out right in my driveway. Denton hauls the thing back to Calvin's—I mean actually hauls it on the ass end of his neighbor's dump truck—and what do yuh suppose they told him? No warranty on used cars, that's what. Give ya two hundred, though, toward anything on the lot!"

"No shit! And now the guy's coaching my kid?"

"You got it, mister."

By the time mid-August rolls around there aren't a lot of secrets left. The present coach is sleeping with the ex-coach and the present coach, unlike the ex-coach, doesn't even have a kid on the team or a kid at all for that matter.

"Do you 'spose he's one of those pre-verts who likes little boys?"

"Fat chance. It's women he likes, widowed ones with large puff balls and kids of their own. From what I hear, only reason he agreed to coach in the first place was so's he could get into Jeannie Palumbo's pants."

"I won't begrudge the man for layin' a little pipe. I just wish he could coach is all."

"Well, he must know a little something about the game. My kid's average has gone up fifty points since Innis took over."

"Okay, maybe they ain't losing as bad as they was. But they're still losing!"

"Listen, I can't complain too much. At least my kid has quit running the other way whenever he sees a ball coming at him!"

"I tell ya, my kid can't wait to go to practice."

"Can you imagine that? And on a team that's oh and forever? And how about bringing Wally Seymour in to pitch?"

"That was a good move, all right. Kid's got a cannon for an arm."

"Sure, but they still ain't won a game, have they?"

No. The Meat Market had not won a game. They were, to be precise, 0 and 19, with six games remaining. But Walter saw victory on the horizon, perhaps arriving sooner than the first southward-flying geese. Wally Seymour had an arm. The kid came over the top, all sloppy and unhinged like a collapsing puppet, somehow letting the ball go in the midst of all that confusion. It would next appear around the plate as a blur of white. The problem was no one ever knew exactly where around the plate it might appear. Sometimes the ball passed in front of the batter, sometimes behind, sometimes it thudded thickly into an unmoving ten-year-old's fragile chest. Wally led the league in strikeouts, walks, and evoking tears from hit batsmen. He usually lasted three or four innings before unraveling completely, sending balls into the dirt, into the stands, and, on one occasion, through the opposing coach's windshield. But the talent was there and Walter had worked hard on helping Wally to harness it.

Rusty Tillman, whom Walter was trying to make into a first baseman, had shown potential for hitting the long ball. The problem was that Rusty didn't believe it. He was a stocky kid, a carrot top with more spots on his face than a pepperoni pizza. Perhaps as a result of his complexion, he was self-conscious. A simple hello would evoke spasms of giggles and turn Rusty's face the color of his hair, causing him to hide it then in the crook of his elbow. When he connected with a ball, which he did often in practice, he would shrug his shoulders, turn red, and forget to run the bases. The only time he had connected in a game, he took off for first base with his head down, stopping when he got there. As the ball rolled to the fence, Rusty stood on the first base bag, giggling, hiding his face in his elbow. But he was showing progress. Now he could carry on partial conversations without giggling, even swaggered on occasion after hitting a practice blast. If he could only learn how to hit when it counted.

The best hitter on Jeannie's team had been a kid named Bobby Burns. He was big for his age, mean, with eyes like a ferret's. He liked to sneak up behind other kids, shove a bat lengthwise between his victim's legs, then jerk it upward like a flywheel. Bobby had no interest in improving the way he played baseball. He only liked to disrupt practice with his flywheel gag and others, all of which seemed to involve painful contact with another boy's genitals. Walter did not like genital gags. He did not like boys with genital fixations. He suspected that Bobby Burns might be the illegitimate child of Stanley Ball. Walter thought of offering Bobby a date with his sister Kate. Instead, he gave Burns a warning; the next time Bobby made other than accidental contact with another boy's genitals, he was off the team. When it happened—as it was destined to—and Walter found out about it, he made good on his threat. The mood at practice improved. The other boys, no longer in fear of losing their own balls, concentrated more upon the one they were attempting to hit. Burns was steamed. He promised, in the near future, to castrate Walter.

Billy Palumbo could not at first understand what his mother found appealing about Walter. To Billy, Walter seemed an odd sort, possibly even touched in the head, like the man who came to tune the Palumbo piano and talked constantly to himself. Walter did not talk to himself, but he did exhibit a number of strange mannerisms—for example, rolling his head around in an owlish manner, as if hoping to swivel it in a complete circle, and thereby surprise anyone standing behind him. Then there was the way he occasionally approached Billy's mother—from the rear, his hands clasped neatly behind his back, his legs bent slightly at the knees; he would lean his head then on her shoulder, rubbing up against her, purring all the while like a cat in search of warm milk. Billy's mother did not seem to think this behavior odd. She seemed to understand it completely. But then, Billy's mother, at times, also seemed touched.

They were touched by each other. Maybe that was it, as corny as it sounded. Of course, when Billy thought about it, most adults were pretty corny. Who else would go to such lengths to pretend a thing wasn't happening when it actually was? Like sex, for example. At least that part of it was over. Billy no longer had to go to his grandparents' house whenever his mother and Walter decided to spend the night together. Walter might stay over, be up in the morning before Billy, padding around the kitchen in a pair of slippers as big as duck's feet, sniffing about the cabinets, fiddling with the television set, hiding himself beneath an opened newspaper. He might emerge suddenly from beneath the paper, pat Billy's mother on the ass, then shake his hand, as if it had been pulled from a fire. He might crawl across the living room floor, the hem of his bathrobe at the level of his buttucks, to where Billy's mother sat drinking her coffee. He might roll onto his back, kicking his feet into the air, not stopping until Jeannie Weatherrup reached down to scratch his white, hungry belly.

Walter loved to be scratched, hugged, patted, stroked, and slobbered over, as if he were some lost puppy freshly plucked from a roadside dumpster. Even Spatula—Billy's half Lab, half cocker spaniel—did not at first know what to make of Walter. The dog would peer cautiously through one eye as Walter gyrated about, perplexed perhaps by the canine attributes of one so visibly human.

Eventually, a beam of possibility illuminated the dog's head. He was not without resources. He saw a new playmate, one most generous with attention and with the hands and height necessary to reach where Spatula could not—into those closed cabinets with their endless supply of treats. If a man could act doggish, could not a dog act mannish?

Hopping nimbly from his prone position on the couch, Spatula approached carefully the splayed person in the midst of the living room rug. From amiable acquaintances, the dog and Walter soon became friends. They might be found tugging at opposite ends of a single sock, backpedaling together to the sounds of Brahms or lying quietly at times, heads resting upon each other's stomachs, legs curled inward at their sides. And Walter, as always, was grateful. Spatula ate like a king.

Billy too had approached Walter carefully, waiting to see what might happen when Walter grew tired of his mother. Billy remembered the first man that his mother had brought home following his father's death. At dinner, the man had laughed and made jokes, complimenting Billy's mother on the meal, mussing Billy's head, promising to take him to a Yankee game that summer. After dinner, while Billy's mother was in the bathroom, the man had taken a five-dollar bill from his wallet. Bending down toward Billy, his breath a mixture of linguini and scotch, the man had stuffed the bill into Billy's shirt pocket. "Here, kid," he breathed, "get lost for a couple hours, will ya?"

Later, from his bedroom, Billy had heard the stifled moans, the piggish squeals that he knew were his mother's—an eerie cadence of sounds, floating up the stairway like the dying grunts from a slaughterhouse— then the front door opening, and the man's voice, loud and crisp in the night air, "I'll give ya a call." Through his bedroom window, Billy had seen the man hunch into his coat and knot his tie as if late for work. A few minutes later, Billy heard only his mother, sobbing into her pillow. The man had not come back. There had been one other and then Walter.

When his father had died, Billy had been angry with him at first. Why hadn't he been more careful? He was always harping at Billy and his mother for not using their seat belts and then he had not fastened his own. Had he but looked both ways before driving into that fateful intersection, would he maybe have spotted the other truck in time? Jesus! If he loved Billy, he would have done something to avoid his own death. On more than one occasion, after Billy had had a bad dream, his father had promised him that he would never go away. But he had. And how could you forgive a man for that?

After a while Billy's anger had subsided and then it disappeared altogether. He realized, without anyone telling him, that what had happened was not his father's fault, that dying was something his father had had no control over. Billy's anger then became fear, the prickly variety of fear that accompanies the unknown. People—even the strong ones, the ones who acted like they would last forever—unraveled each day, like strings from a cheap suit, and there wasn't a thing any of them could do about it. Life was a charade—an elaborate hoax—with death lurking like a whoopee cushion beneath each seat. When Billy had mentioned this to his mother—or something like it—she had looked at him, shocked, as if he had discovered some adult secret. Her face paled, her expression revealed the usually well-hidden grief. It was then that Billy realized his mother's pain exceeded even his own. For her sake, as much as for his own, he had decided to keep what he knew to himself. Possessing the secrets of an adult, he feared he had become one.

In time, he cried only at night. Even then—facedown in his pillow so that his mother couldn't hear his sobs—he had felt ashamed. When he had awakened one night from a dream, unable to recall what his father had looked like, Billy had feared for a moment that his father had never even existed, that he had only existed in Billy's imagination. Then he had heard his father's voice, as if he had been in the room with Billy, saying nothing in particular, but sounding just the way that Billy remembered him. The voice was reassuring, but only to a point. It was all right to be afraid and it was all right to miss the father you had loved. But how, at the age of ten, did one go back to being a child?

And there, suddenly, was Walter—potbellied and slightly balding, possessing the guise of adulthood, without the weaponry. Unafraid to finger a naked wiener as if it were a bat, undeterred by a mouthful of dog hairs, Walter's delight in such things rose up as if from the bottom of a barrel. At first Walter had made Billy's mother laugh, deep-throated gasping sounds that to Billy were as warm and comforting as a summer rain. But Billy did not trust laughter alone. He thought of the man who had breathed linguini and scotch and waited for Walter suddenly to not appear.

But he had kept appearing and Billy's mother not only laughed, but she began to giggle and twitter as well. Billy knew what giggling and twittering meant, and he was happy for his mother but still somewhat afraid. Then Walter began to speak to Billy about baseball, first as a coach and then as a friend. But never as a father. It was as if Walter knew that a father was irreplaceable—one to a customer, like a heart.

They never spoke about Billy's father or about being afraid, but Billy began to feel that Walter knew much about both. It was in his eyes— with their deep, dark centers. Seeing them and knowing that Walter could laugh despite them made Billy less frightened. Then it made him want to laugh. And then it made him want to learn how to hit a baseball.

Walter taught Billy how to keep his eye on the ball, even while it was still in the pitcher's hand. He showed him how to wait until the last possible moment before stepping out of his hitter's crouch, then to swing with his wrists and hips, taking the ball where it seemed destined to go. He gave Billy a hard rubber ball and told him to carry it with him wherever he went. "Keep the ball in your pocket," he said, "and squeeze it whenever you've got nothing better to do."

It was long, hard work, learning how to hit, for Billy was not a natural hitter. Only through practice and repetition would he improve. Each afternoon, he worked on the things Walter had shown him. Each night, he lay in his bed, gazing up at the ceiling, squeezing the hard rubber ball and dreaming of the major leagues.

In time, the baseball appeared bigger to Billy. Or was it simply that it was moving slower as it approached the plate? Neither explanation made sense. A hardball was a hardball, and the pitchers he faced today were the same ones he had faced earlier in the season. Perhaps Billy's eyesight had suddenly improved.

Whatever the reason, as Billy stood ready to hit, the ball began to appear more like a ball and less like a white blur. Swinging only at what he could see, Billy began to make more frequent contact. He was a great, powerful cat leaping from a tree, landing with a solid thud on the back of a lethargic lamb. The *thwack!* made him smile, laugh giddily on the inside, look proudly toward his coach. Standing on the bag, Billy tipped his cap toward where his mother sat in the stands, spat casually onto the ground, and eyed the pitcher with the level gaze of a predator. Somewhere the whoopee cushion lurked, but today the sun shone and he—Billy Palumbo—was a ball player.

CHAPTER 43

A day without a date—or so it seems, because it's summer and what man, after all, cares what day it is when the sun softly warms his naked feet, his head pinched gently between the velvet vice of a large woman's legs?

The sway is easy, the wind but a whisper. The man's feet tingle as if being breathed upon, his head rolls like a buoy being tossed by a wave. He basks in plentitude, his guts warm and sated.

Sluggish whirrings from a window fan, a giddy disarray of chattering songbirds, the tumultuous rumblings from the large woman's lap blend discreetly in his ears. And she is humming, a sad but peaceful song that Walter remembers from grade school choir and even now recalls the words to. "Down in the valley, the valley so low, hang your head over, hear the wind blow . . ." At this refrain, bending forward and blowing loudly into the ear of Melanie Sisting, causing her to cry out—startled, groping with her hand to clear her ear of imagined spittle—Walter had been caught and banned forever from singing into that or any other ear. But the words, like some ancient curse, had remained with him.

After love, women sing and men sleep; girls dance and adolescent boys step into their pants.

Walter was not asleep, only resting. Melanie Sisting's was but one face among many, appearing like shadowy fingers in his thoughts, lingering without dallying, touching without feeling. There was, however, only one woman's hand in his hair, sketching a map with her fingers, appearing most intrigued with occipital imperfections, sampling the dewy dampness that had gathered there.

Were Walter to open his eyes, he would see her face, large and glabrous, like the flank of a horse, her secrets drained and glistening upon her cheeks and forehead in a lover's sweat. She would be smiling, revealing a full array of teeth, uncapped and without gaps; her eyes, like her mouth, open and large.

In white BVDs and aerated football jersey—RED adorning one breast, RAMS splashed brazenly across the other—she still looked the part of the coach. He, in flowered boxers and a woman's robe, might have been a member of the band.

Days without dates, or perhaps countless days lumped into one general date—as in "one summer, a few years back" or "the year I counted, like Blanche DuBois, upon the kindness of strangers"—Walter wished might last forever. But for dates—those blanks filled in by historians and overachievers—what then would cause him to shift his pillowed head? To think nervously of his ever-dwindling pocket change?

If days were not dated, a man might forget that he had no job, that his cash assets were four thousand and shrinking, that his wife's lawyer had proposed a divorce settlement whereby he—the ungrateful ex-husband—would sign over everything to her—the equally ungrateful ex-wife—who would then promise not to ask for more.

"What kind of an offer is that?" Walter had wondered upon hearing it. "Has she also agreed not to laugh, Maurie, when she sees me naked on the street?"

"It's not as bad as it sounds," Maurie had assured him, managing not to smile, gripping his teeth firmly instead upon the stem of his pipe.

"I hope not," said Walter, unconsciously feeling for his wallet, fearing it may have been lifted osmotically while he spoke, "because it sounds very bad to me. It sounds as though I may soon be living in a tent on Caulfield Mountain."

"The car you would keep."

"I can drive to the mountain then, come into town once a week, scavenge through garbage cans looking for provisions—perhaps, in the midst of winter, even sleep on the backseat."

"The car is paid for, Walter. It's worth at least four grand."

"Does it come with a free tank of gas? If not, it will remain parked next to the tent, fuelless with no prospects of becoming otherwise."

"You're overreacting, Walter."

"She is the one with a college education, Maurie. She learned how to sell things, like bread—even how to make whole loaves of it smile and take on human qualities. She could get a job anywhere, while my talents are limited to lassoing cars."

"But she did not work during the course of the marriage."

"And I am not working now."

"You were the family's only breadwinner."

"And so, it seems, will I continue to be."

"It is, after all, only an offer."

"What about our offer, Maurie? Please tell me that we have one."

"Legally, she is in a much stronger position than you, Walter." Maurie drained his glass, waved absently at the envelope full of papers that had arrived that day from Boston. The envelope had been torn open, the papers quickly scanned, before being deposited on one corner of the desk. "You, after all, are the adulterer."

"She left me, for God's sake! She cleaned out our checking account and moved in with Boston's version of Moshe Dayan!"

"The legal phrase is abandonment, Walter, and, next to adultery, it's a pimple on an elephant's ass."

"Whose side are you on, for Christ sake?"

"Yours, of course. I'm simply telling you what we're up against, Walter. I warned you that she would squeeze and that you must not take it personally."

"I remember also tossing a clam shell over my shoulder and being threatened with bodily harm."

"According to her complaint, Marsha went to her mother's for a long weekend, heard through a reliable source that you were diddling another woman, and tearfully decided to commence the instant proceeding." Maurie moved one hand through his hair, picked determinedly with his index finger at a spot toward the back of his head, and smiled. "The papers, in fact, are quite artfully drawn."

"What reliable source, Maurie? How can she know of things occurring here while she is in Boston?"

"You haven't exactly been discreet, Walter. Marsha has several friends in town, at least one of whom, apparently, has access to a zoom lens."

"What are you saying? That I have been photographed?"

"You and Jeannie Weatherrup, aka Palumbo. It's all there." Maurie's head twitched slightly, indicating the half-hidden mound of legalese at the edge of his desk. "Nothing too juicy. Any judge, though, would get the gist, I'm afraid."

"Jesus Christ, Maurie! Is such a thing legal? Taking snapshots through a bedroom window?"

"Only if the shades are open, Walter. Of course it's legal. It even has a name. It's called pretrial preparation."

"And what about our preparation, Maurie? Where are our pictures? How do we know whose knob she has been polishing?"

"You will recall, Walter, that I've been operating on a rather thin budget. Investigations cost money."

"So do divorces, Maurie. What are we to do?"

"Draft an answer to her complaint, search for the polished knob, throw in several shovelfuls of dirt, perhaps even obtain our own candids."

"To what end, Maurie?"

"To win, Walter. To win."

"What happened to equitable distribution? An amicable parting of the ways?"

"It gave way to justice, Walter. When she squeezes, you must squeeze back."

"And what about fairness? Will that concern the judge?"

"Fairness has been reduced to a formula. For her, it's whatever she can get. For you, it's whatever you can keep. That's justice, Walter. Ain't it grand?"

If not grand, at least eminently clear. Power could be seen through an aperture; money was funneled through a long-angled lens. The photographer with the best camera would be king. Marsha had Walter on film, as Walter once had Henry Truxton III on film. Walter felt slimy, pictured himself slithering from the room, holed up forever above some barrio porn shop with a carton of eight-by-ten glossies.

And what of Walter's own lawyer? Did proof of his opponent's shady tactics fill him with rage? Did he sputter indignantly to Walter about fairness and ethics? Quite the contrary. Maurie simply leered, unable to conceal a certain respect for his adversary, ready himself to roll up his trousers and wade into the slime.

"Give her what she wants," Walter had said, while getting to his feet, happily aware that they, at least, were still his own and would carry him easily where he wanted to go.

"What?"

"Agree to whatever she is asking for. Draw up the papers, let me know when they're done, and I'll sign them."

"Jesus, Walter! I was just giving you the down side. We've got a long way to go before we agree to anything!"

"Not me, Maurie."

"She'll want a deed to the house, everything in the joint savings accounts!"

"Give them to her. All I want is the car, the four thousand that's in my name, and the negatives of those pictures her lawyer sent you."

As he had walked out the door, Walter had been acutely aware of the coins jingling in his pants pocket, of the afternoon sun coming through the slats over Maurie's office window, cutting his friend in two—leaving him half in shadows, half in screaming light. In Walter's rear pocket was his wallet; inside it, snugly tucked between several credit cards and assorted small bills, was a picture of Marsha, smiling at the camera, her tiny mouth forming a funnel. He had turned left at the bottom of the stairs, heading down Maple Street, first to see the Old Man and then to see Jeannie Weatherrup, to lay his head in her large and generous lap. And for the past three days, with time out for food, baseball practice, and to lend a hand at the Meat Market, he had done just that.

"Has it been as good as I promised, Walter?"

He opened his eyes, still out of sync, half expecting to gaze upward into the pickled countenance of his wife—her funnelled mouth, narrowed to a pinprick, emitting tiny bubbles in the manner of an aquarium guppy. Seeing instead the ample, wet lips of Jeannie Weatherrup, Walter smiled, felt a flutter at his groin, and thanked God for large appetites. He wished only to lie in Jeannie's lap forever—or until he could find a more comfortable spot or at least until the end of the baseball season, whichever came first. He would roll up wheatcakes the size of Frisbees and feed them to her. He would sink slowly into the expanding gulf between her thighs until, like a dinosaur sucked into a tar bog, he simply disappeared.

"The pay, Walter? Has it been satisfactory?"

"Huh?"

"For coaching the Meat Market?"

"Oh, yes. It's been more than generous." Reaching down, Walter placed a hand on the fleshy part of one thigh, rolled his head upward, and smiled. "Particularly in light of the on-field results."

"Wins and losses don't concern me. You've done a wonderful job with the team, particularly with Billy. To see Billy with a cocksure smile—any kind of a smile really, but a cocksure one! I never thought baseball, or anything, would ever be that much fun for him again." She leaned forward, breasts bobbing at the letters, and dropped a kiss onto his forehead.

"He bounced, that's all. You said he would and he did."

"You would make a wonderful father, you know?"

"I only taught him how to hit. If he's happy, it's because he wants to be. Or, perhaps, it's something he learned from watching his mother."

"It's true. I'm happier lately than I've been in years, the last several with Cooley included."

"I didn't know."

"Nothing original. We just stopped talking, that's all . . . and laughing. We didn't do much of that either."

"That sounds worse than not talking."

"It is, in ways. And not loving, that's even worse." She held her hand to her mouth, emitting a silent hiccup, then dropped the hand back to Walter's head. Gazing up, Walter heard himself swallow.

"Loving?"

"What would you call it, Walter?"

"Call what?"

"This?"

"I hadn't thought to call it anything . . . except nice."

A grumbling—deep-throated and vague, like a string of grunts floating through a gym window—began somewhere within Jeannie Weatherrup's stomach. These were not, Walter knew, idle, harmless sounds; they heralded something, as surely as upward-turned leaves herald a storm. Gazing at his bare feet, soaking up sun on the windowsill, he felt suddenly awash in his own impotence.

"Don't misunderstand, Walter, I can do without it—love, that is. And I will too, before I'll have it doled out to me in limited portions— left to the mercy of some short-order cook. It's feast or famine for me. I'm not interested in snitching somebody else's scraps."

"I'm not sure—"

"Women outnumber men almost two to one, Walter. I read it in *Good Housekeeping*. Men keep getting killed in wars, have weak hearts, bad prostates, don't have the mental toughness of females."

"Well . . ."

"Seventy-five percent of what's left are sexually misidentified or outright pikers."

"I think—"

"And when you're my age, with a child to boot, it's even worse. A woman learns to be tough—and direct. She can't afford to be any other way. She might only meet one or two good men in a lifetime."

"But—"

"And when she does she wants to be sure she's not wasting her time."

"Jeannie . . ."

"Walter . . . ?"

"Then you would have been as generous had I not agreed to coach Billy's team?"

"Please don't joke, Walter. Usually I like it when you joke, but sometimes your jokes aren't like jokes."

"I won't joke again," he said, "unless it's a real joke."

"Things I'd like to know, Walter, I don't dare ask. Why is that?"

"Perhaps you're afraid you won't like the answers."

"Why must you always make things so complex? They really aren't, you know? Not every question has two meanings. Some people are happy, believe it or not, genuinely happy, working eight hours a day with their weekends free, going home to their families, eating meat when they can afford it. . . ." She spoke with her hands, legs jiggling, slapping gently against Walter's ears, causing a strange vibrant hum in the inner sanctum. "Some people actually don't give a shit, Walter, whether they were raised by God or the devil, whether what seemed like love was actually hate or vice versa—just don't give a shit!"

"Jeannie . . ." But her legs had not stopped jiggling. The noise in his head vibrated as if a pitch pipe had been shoved through one ear.

"Why not crawl into bed with your old man and die with him? Then he'd really know what a failure he has been as a father! That's what you're trying to prove, isn't it? Men! Must you all be such sentimental jerks? So busy mooning over what's been or what may be that you can't even see what the fuck is!"

"I don't understand. . . . Jeannie, why are you so upset? Jesus Christ, isn't a man entitled to one bad joke?"

"First you marry some bitch with steel in her tits, let her half drain the life out of you, then watch her walk out and figure you deserve that too. Or were you waiting for the day that she would melt? Christ, Walter, why don't you stop trying to balance the books!" She dropped onto her back, Walter's head popping free, the hum in his ears turning to a silent quake. "You haven't changed one bit since high school! You're still hammering away at empty spaces, hoping one day—by some blind miracle—you'll slip into one! I should never have asked you to breakfast."

"Jeannie, what is it that you wanted to know?"

"Know?"

"The things you did not dare ask."

"What things?"

She was supine on the mattress, her briefs a knotted wedge between her buttocks, a pillow pressed to her face, her chest and stomach heaving. Walter supposed she was crying. Half of him wanted to reach down, hold her, confess that yes, he was lost, rudderless, a bad risk, but he was in the process of trying to turn things around so could they maybe put this conversation off for a while? His other half wanted desperately to put on his pants and run. "How would I know? You haven't asked them."

"Oh, Walter." Her voice passed through the pillow like a dog's bark through a storm. "Can you see yourself preparing Wiener schnitzel?"

"What?"

"How about kosher ham or brisket?"

"Christ, I can barely make a hamburger!" Then, sensing the desperation in her words: "I suppose—you know, someday—I might learn."

"Walter, I need to know, it's terribly important." Jeannie's face, briefly free of the pillow, shone red and wet as a rain soaked slicker, her mouth, open and large, so wide it seemed capable of swallowing the pillow. "Are you just another piker in man's clothes?"

CHAPTER 44

I was not allowed to see my mother's body immediately after it was brought to shore, but was told by others that most of her face and skin had been eaten away by the freshwater crabs inhabiting the lake.

I fixated on the clothes she had been wearing, hoping, perhaps, that they might contradict my final memory of her or at least help to erase the vision I had retained of her reclining in an evening dress belonging to Henry Truxton III. Joe Dorsey, the undertaker, refused to give the garments to me, claiming they were in no condition to be saved. When I insisted, he sent me to see the sheriff, who handed me a wrap-around plaid skirt, cream-colored blouse, bra and panties, all neatly folded and without apparent damage.

"But they're not even wet!" I raged. "Why aren't they wet?"

"They were in the boat," said the sheriff evenly, without emotion, his tone, no doubt, for dealing with distraught relatives. "Folded—like they are now—stashed in the bow beneath her handbag."

"Then that means—"

"It doesn't mean a thing, young man," he interrupted, firm but careful not to offend. "At that hour, where they found her—she might have decided to go for a swim and developed a cramp or—"

"My mother would not go skinny-dipping! She was religious, very conservative!"

"She chose a secluded spot, son. A place, almost certainly, where she would not have been seen."

The sheriff, beneath his nonchalance, was a thoughtful man. He did not tell my father in what state of undress my mother had been found. The Old Man, having slipped comfortably into his own conclusions—any other possibilities apparently not in accord with his viewpoints on death and marriage—did not ask. But for me, any lingering hopes of a tragic accident disappeared with the sheriff's presentation. Frugal right to the end, my mother, I surmised, had hoped that some poor soul— maybe even her own daughter—might make use of the carefully folded garments after her death.

CHAPTER 45

On the lake's surface, the sun hit in a barrage of yellow, exploding into brightness, too much for the eye to bear. There—amid that light—a man might drown in arm-waving agony and not be seen. If someone was there now, thought Walter, I couldn't save him. But then, most of us die in broad daylight, and with a gallery of onlookers to boot. So why are we so shocked at the thought of it? A person dying and no one raising a hand to help? What, after all, could anyone do?

Light thrown back by the water ricocheted outward in clear, fractured lines. A sailboat moved easily over the surface, its prow churning up layers of orange and white, leaving in its wake bubbles of blue. The shrill sound of gulls—circling above, gazing with sharp-eyed interest into the water—reached Walter where he stood above the lake, almost as high as the birds, gazing downward, not into the water but at the sharp, black rocks at its edge. Five miles out of Caulfield, off the main road, he stood atop a hill overlooking the water. Save for three or four Scotch pines huddled together like bag ladies against the wind, the hill lacked trees, shrubs, vegetation of any kind.

He was on the very edge of a rock, inches from the cliff, what Maurie would have referred to as the tip of the penis. As far as a person could go with a bluff; another step and there would be no more doubts, no more sloughful ambiguities. The moment of soaring, some said, would be worth the pain of landing. Then—during those few seconds of unimpeded flight—dark would become light, doubt would become certainty. Others believed that a person actually died before hitting the ground, heart in throat—as if, at the last moment, the heart attempted to spring free from a dying soul.

To die thus—throwing oneself over the edge, braced as it were against momentary indecision—was one thing; to die as Walter's mother had done was quite another—breathing one final breath and then, through force of will, fighting the urge to take another. Such a choice necessitated

more than a moment's taste for the mission; it required malice afore-
thought on the doer's part and sheer determination to see the death
through.

While on vacation in the Adirondacks, Walter had once held himself
under the surface of a motel swimming pool. It had been off season in
the mountains, and he and Marsha had had the place to themselves.
Leaving Walter poolside with a pitcher of Tom Collinses, Marsha had
gone shopping for a pair of designer long johns. The crystalline, unbroken look of the water had drawn him. What fun, he had thought, to be
peacefully suspended there, undisturbed by even a ripple. It would be,
Walter told himself, an experiment born of malaise, unencumbered by
lurking thoughts of self-destruction. Once situated at the bottom—ears
cleared through a gentle blow of the nose, arms outward and head down
to prevent floating to the top—Walter had been seized, though, by an
overriding compulsion to stay exactly where he was until he died or he
didn't.

Pain was the predominant sensation, vague at first, then becoming
sharper as if a blade were being pushed outward from the center of his
chest. Within this large pain were circles of smaller pain, infiltrating
every tissue in his body, screaming in tiny, frightened voices. He felt his
mind go numb, his body slacken. The pain almost disappeared. He
gazed upward, through the filtered blue water, and saw a face gazing
downward—a face with a beard and a sardonic smile, glassy blue eyes
that were already dead.

So this was the face of death? The antlered head of a moose, hung in
effigy above a pool bar? Enraged at such desecration, Walter thought to
inquire at the front desk about the animal's pedigree. What kind of
relatives would permit such a thing? He thought of Marsha, in her
zippered long johns, coming back to find her husband hanging on the
wall opposite the moose. He tried to laugh then and found he could
not. His lungs seemed depleted, nearly drained of life. Frantically he
pushed for the top, remembering a million things he wished to do when
he got there, first and foremost to breathe.

Once safely on the deck, his lungs filled with the bitter sweetness of
life, Walter had understood that a planned death was not in his makeup.
He could not stand by witnessing in silence the single-file surrender of
each piece of his life. The temptation to pull back a piece or two, to

turn them over in his still-vital mind, would be too great. A little tinkering might alter his entire outlook, cause him then to change his mind. Not for him the slow turning of the screw. If voluntarily abandoned, his life would not stand a lengthy review, a piecemeal critique. The resolve to die, if acted upon at all, should be done so unequivocally.

Throwing oneself headlong over a cliff, for example, left little room for equivocation. For those with a resolve to die, it had much to recommend it. What could be more economical? No parts or assembly, no wasted movements, one step forward was all that was required. There was, also, the small margin of error involved. Horror stories were heard, of course—those who had bounced and somehow survived, in physical disarray, left then to contemplate how next to proceed. But such tales were rare, and what method, after all, was totally without flaws? And if a person sought ambiguity in death, an obscurity of intent, what better method than the cliffside header? Feet adorned in polished Bostonians, he inches closer to the edge, seeking to improve his view of the rock dwelling hibiscus . . . and what? He feels the gravel suddenly slip out from beneath him? Or did he perhaps have an enemy?

Surefooted, with only idle thoughts of an imminent leap, Walter pondered the stoical gray boulders below. Glimmering wet, frothy, licked clean periodically by the docile lapping of the lake, they waited like the caged lions of Rome. Would such predators care how their victims arrived? A step or a leap, a push or a shove, were mere semantics to those waiting. Thousands had stood where Walter now stood—some had jumped, probably a few had been pushed, but to the rocks it did not matter which. If a person was looking for clues, these heartless boulders were not the ones to ask. Still, when Maurie had called with the news of Ed Walling's death, Walter felt that he must come here— to stand, as Ed Walling had stood, looking out at life and death from the outermost tip of the penis.

"A windsurfer found him on the rocks below Sperry's Point," Maurie had said, sounding no different from when he had told Walter of Marsha's planned embezzlement of their marital assets. "The police think he may have been there a week or more."

"Do they know who killed him?"

"Not who, Walter. How. He came down upon the rocks from a substantial height, suffering a crushed skull—countless internal injuries."

"So?"

"Sperry's Point, Walter. It's quite a drop."

"What leads do they have?"

"They're calling it suicide. Ed had a Cutlass, a real junker. It was found about a mile away, parked on a dirt road across from the point. The locals say it had been there a few days, maybe even a week. They figured it for a breakdown." He breathed into the phone as if waiting for Walter to reply. When he didn't, Maurie continued. "The car was locked. The keys were in Ed's pocket when they found him. On the front seat were some personal papers. A picture of his wife—"

"What wife?"

"Myrtle. She just got out of the slam a month ago—check forgery. She stopped home long enough to pick up her belongings and to ask Ed to sign over their combined life savings to the Christ Is Our Lord Baptist Church. Ed declined. Myrtle took off with the preacher, a shyster who used to offer guidance to the ladies in lockup. Probably sold snake oil too. Anyway, the police figure Ed was pretty upset about it."

"Bullshit."

"I am telling you what the police are saying, Walter."

"Why are they saying it?"

"Oh, come on! You said it yourself, this isn't the CIA, for God sake!"

"That doesn't answer my question, Maurie."

"How would I know why they're saying it?"

"How do you know anything? The death hasn't even been in the papers yet."

"Ed was my client. I have friends in the department. One of them gave me a call."

"Did it ever occur to you, Maurie, that we may have caused Walling's death?"

"No one causes another person's death, Walter. It's a matter of choice, even if it's a seemingly insignificant choice such as sticking to a high-cholesterol diet or going to work for the wrong employer."

"Have you forgotten that we were in Ruston's a few weeks back, engaging in political high jinks with the deceased, directing our rancor toward a local candidate for the state Senate, even talking candidly about shakedowns?"

"I had forgotten that, Walter." Maurie's voice, slightly lower, had not lost its bounce. His tongue landed on each word with the assurance of a pianist's honed touch. "I strongly suggest that you do the same."

"What?"

"Let's talk about this at my office, Walter."

"Do you think we're in danger, Maurie?"

"I don't know what you mean—danger. What danger?"

"Jesus, Maurie. . . ."

"Don't try and come this afternoon, Walter. I'm going to be tied up with clients all day."

"When?"

"In a few days, maybe. After the funeral."

From where he stood—the highest point in the county, according to the cement marker at his feet—Walter could just make out the tip of the finger that contained the Truxton estate. In the calm waters just to the other side of the finger, among the pussywillows and chlorophyl, was the spot where his mother's body had been found. It was a pretty spot, protected from the winds of the lake. Barely a wrinkle creased its placid surface. Beneath the surface, pike and pickerel thrived, snapping turtles hunted for slower fish, and the tiny freshwater crabs paddled easily about. To the left, the lake got narrower as it approached Caulfield, blunting into a dull point as it hit the town beach. On the other side of the city, clearly visible from Sperry's Point, was a small hill, part of Mountain View Cemetery, where Walter's mother was buried. Just beyond that hill, if Walter could have seen that far, was the Caulfield Convalescent Home where his father lay dying.

Had he possessed binoculars, Walter could have picked out his own house, a white dot in a field of rye on the northeast side of town. Empty of people, the house would be filled with belongings, Marsha's belongings mostly, soon to be packed into boxes, hung carefully in movable closets. When the belongings were gone, the house would be empty, save for what few items Walter would be left. Those too would have to be moved. To where? A storage bin? A one-bedroom flat in a building full of screaming children and barking dogs? Perhaps Maurie could find space in his cellar, leaving Walter free to take up temporary residence in a furnished motel room. And when the house was sold, what would be left of him and Marsha? Precisely nothing, except for the sickly aftertaste of medicine.

Dismayed by the thought of it—ten years of marriage disappearing without a trace, dropping into a void like one of those planes flying into the Bermuda Triangle—Walter searched for a single pleasant memory. He knew there had been several, but as he tried to recall just one, he could not. Nothing came to him, save for the nauseating aftertaste. In time, he supposed that more subtle memories would surface—a whiff of some unique bedroom smell, the lily whiteness appearing beneath normally clothed body parts. But such memories, were they to come at all, would come later, eventually to be boxed and stored, piled up somewhere with so many others. And what good were they if he had then to search through so much to find them? If he could not then touch or feel them? And again, Walter wondered, what was left?

He thought of Jeannie Weatherrup sobbing into her pillow, while he, envying her ability to cry so easily, had walked from her room in a mute stupor, unable even to give her an honest assessment of his own character. Imagining her and Billy without him at the dinner table, he was sick with loneliness. And shame. How could he tell them that they were too much of a good thing—too warm, too honest, too full of love— and that was why he had left? Live off the fat of the land, Maurie had always told him, but the truth was, thought Walter, the fat—those warm, stolen interludes and pleasant excesses that as a child he had learned would last only until the next explosion—had always petrified him.

When a man lives long enough, such a point is bound to arrive— when he climbs to the top of a hill and looks out at the scattered pieces of his life, dead and dying beneath him, like fallout from some emotional explosion, the whole valley lying heavy under a pale, carcinogenic glow. Ah! But not so quickly, thought Walter, not so quickly should I have reached the prick's tip! This backward acuity has its place only in old age or imminent death. Amongst that rubble, there must be a few salvageable pieces. If I am not here to jump, I must be here to reconnoiter.

And what of Ed Walling? Stone beasts nipping savagely at his feet, did he take a peek backward? If only for a final glimpse of his wife, adorned in holy garb and receiving a shyster's benediction? Walter wished he could recall more about Walling—one should know something of those he sends out to die—but all that he could recall were perfect teeth in a face full of errors, eyes conditioned to wariness, the man's unique way of tracing political history. Still, one draws composite sketches, jumps to immediate conclusions.

Ed Walling, thought Walter, was not a man for backward glances. He was not one to take his own life lightly, jailhouse preachers and shysters be damned. In all likelihood, even had he been so inclined, Walling would not have had much time for restrospection as he stood where Walter now stood. Walling would not have walked gently into the jaws of the lion. No. He would have required prodding, Walter thought fearfully, and not gentle, persuasive prodding.

CHAPTER 46

"Walter?"

"Yes?"

"It's Jeannie Weatherrup." The crackling of the line altered her voice somehow, causing it to ricochet, to whiz like a misfired bullet through his ear.

"Either you have been wearing a disguise, Jeannie, or else you have stopped coming to your son's ball games."

"I talked it over with Billy. We—that is, I—thought it might be best if I stayed away for a while."

"A large woman with pimples has taken your seat in the bleachers. She drinks beer and belches whenever the other team scores."

"Have you missed me?"

"I was all set to ask her to leave and then someone told me she was Rusty Tillman's mother."

"So?"

"Who likes fat women that belch, even if they are your first baseman's mother? I was afraid that you had been sick."

"Sick? No, I haven't been sick, Walter. Lonely, yes. Angry, maybe. But not sick. And you? Have you been well?"

"I suppose."

"I haven't heard from you in almost two weeks. Billy says you haven't asked after me. He says you seem okay, but you know kids, okay to them may be terminal illness."

"I've been busy—a friend died."

"Your father?"

"No. A friend. I don't think you knew him."

"Well . . . I'm sorry."

"They found him in the lake, below Sperry's Point. Smashed to death on the rocks."

"I *am* sorry. I don't know what to say. . . ."

"It's a beautiful view up there. The whole valley unfolds like a topographic map. At the very top, there's a grass-covered knoll, a tremendous spot to eat sandwiches, throw bread crumbs into the water, watch the gulls swoop down and pick them up. You wouldn't want to go up there with kids, though. It's a bit windy for kids. Kids aren't good in the wind. They tend to think they can fly."

"Was he a close friend?"

"More of Maurie's than of mine. But it was ironic where he chose to die."

"Chose, Walter?"

"He was a very dedicated man—family, profession—they meant everything to him. In terms of dedication, he was much like my parents, I think. When a person is that dedicated, what happens to him is always a matter of choice, don't you think?"

"I'm not sure, Walter. Did your friend commit suicide?"

"Doubtful—but, you know, suicide, that's a slippery slope—I've never been able to get a handle on it what it means, exactly. Sudden death, with a degree of choice, involving, I think—as I say, a person's, among other things, being dedicated . . ."

Disseminator of pain, concealer of emotions, buried cable of lies, that allows a man to sit in tattered bathrobe, at a table fingerpainted in yolk and seedless jam, in mindless chatter talking to no one. Talk. Talk. Talk. Small holes to lie through. Even smaller ones to hear from. Through this we will touch each other? Through this hand-held device we will see?

"I promised myself I wouldn't call, Walter, but then I was hoping you would call me. I had no right—"

"You had every right."

"—to assume you felt the way I did. I pushed when I shouldn't have pushed. It's just that suddenly I saw myself as another lonely fat broad with a kid, a grateful widow who cooks a good meal and can still do the bump and grind."

"You're not fat, Jeannie. You're only big boned."

"If it was just me I wouldn't mind bumping and grinding only when it was convenient, Walter—but it's not just me I have to think of."

"How's Billy? He doesn't seem interested in talking to me. I asked him to stay after practice, to work on his hitting, and he said he had homework to do. It's August, for God sake. How could he have home-work?"

"He doesn't understand. He's used to his coach eating breakfast with him."

"I was hoping this wouldn't happen, Jeannie. I offered to buy him a wiener. He told me that they're unhealthy, that he's thinking of becoming a vegetarian."

"He'll get over it, Walter. He thinks the world of you. It's just that's he's confused."

"But have you explained things to him? Have you told him that I'm not abandoning him? That we're still friends?"

"As long as you're sure. If you tell me that you're sure, then I'll explain it to him and he'll be all right."

"Sure?"

"About us, Walter, you and I: that we're only friends from now on, or else that we're something more than friends, but only something acceptable by a ten-year-old's standards—and by mine."

"I'm not sure. How can I be sure of something as black and white as that?"

"Being sure is not such an outrageous thing, Walter. Not everyone spends their life in no-man's land."

"My wife has only been gone three months. Our divorce isn't even final."

"I'm not asking for instantaneous marriage, Walter."

"What are you asking?"

"For you to be sure. So that Billy and I can be sure."

"Then I shouldn't come over for the weekend?"

"Not without several suitcases. I can't have you running in and out of my bedroom, Walter. It's too confusing for Billy . . . and for me."

"There's a game this Saturday. Will you be there?"

"I didn't call to pressure you, Walter. I really didn't. I am vulnerable in certain areas—men who have not quite grown up, mutts who aren't quite housebroken. I have a weakness for not-quite things."

"It's the last game of the season."

"I've told Billy we should get rid of Spatula. He keeps digging up my tulips, pissing on the rug."

"In order to win, everybody will have to have their head in the game. Mental errors cost more ball games than physical ones."

"And just yesterday I discovered a turd beneath my bed."

"I don't want Billy's mind to be occupied with things other than baseball."

"I'll talk to him, Walter. He wants to win as much as you do. Nobody likes to lose every game, you know?"

Walter replaced the phone in its cradle, a faint hum all that was left of their words. Then even that faded and Walter heard only the sporadic sounds of midmorning, the sharp, intermittent bark of Bob Warnke's setter, the less pronounced yapping of its churlish sidekick—a toy poodle, in teased coiffure and ribbons, tiny balls flouncing as it pranced— the inanities of arguing songbirds, a roar from Bob Knighton's Pontiac as it answered Mrs. Knighton's lead-footed call. And somewhere, a baby crying. The men were gone, all those not too old or infirm, off pursuing the day's ration of bacon. Many of the women too had taken up the cause. The neighborhood was left to dogs, ladies with babies, and the aged infirm. And schemers, like Walter, who carried their trades with them and were anomalies among men.

It was not self-pity he felt, or even twinges of perceived guilt. He had taken a shot, made his best effort to balance the family books. Looking back, it appeared to have been predestined for Walter to have lost to Henry Truxton, as had his parents before him. Viewed logically, then, it was a simple matter of genes, this latest mismanaged scheme only part of Walter's heredity. The nobility of revenge—at first so clear in his schemer's logic—became hopelessly scrambled with the death of Ed Walling.

Walter now realized that Henry Truxton did not have the power to destroy what had been noble about his parents. The good he had not touched. Truxton had played only upon the bad—the evil underpinnings in man, those shaded areas that respond only to the devil's incantations. The man was an incubus, landing on Walter's mother as she slept, ravaging her as she dreamed. But that had not killed her. What had killed Susan Innis was waking from the dream, feeling the hot breath of the incubus still upon her. Being noble, she died.

The noble, Walter realized, might disguise itself as the ignoble, and the ignoble simply did not care. To harm an incubus, Walter had decided, one need become one. To hurt Henry Truxton one must match him dirty picture for dirty picture; death for death; soul for soul. What then would be left after revenge? Who then would care?

And what of Ed Walling? His life had surely been worth as much to someone as the life of Susan Innis had been worth to Walter. And now he was dead and Walter's mother was no less dead than she had been, but Henry Truxton was still alive and running for the state Senate. And Victor Innis was in a deep sleep and no longer gave a shit one way or the other about any of it—if, in fact, he ever had. And Walter was scared, scared that whoever had taken Ed Walling's life would not want to stop there, but would cast his eyes about in search of the starry-eyed schemer who had put Ed in motion and who had been naive enough to believe that in so doing he could infuse some kind of balance into his life.

Walter poured himself another cup of coffee, sloshing some onto the kitchen table. He dabbed at the wet spot with a bathrobe sleeve. Across the street, a man in a United Parcel uniform rang the front doorbell of Bob Warnke's house. Mrs. Warnke appeared in the doorway. Her eyes circled the neighborhood, moving with smooth, practiced precision.

The phone rang at Walter's elbow. As he reached to pick it up, Mrs. Warnke backed into her house, followed quickly by the UPS man. The door shut quickly behind them.

"Walter? Why didn't you tell me that Father was in a coma? It's been close to a month and still you don't tell me? I have to hear the news from a stranger?"

"I didn't think it mattered to you."

"What's that mean?"

"It's not like you visit him. . . . I didn't think you would care that he's one step closer to death. I thought if I called when he died, it would be soon enough."

"Because I don't visit him doesn't mean I'm not interested. It doesn't mean I don't want to be told of changes in his condition."

"What does it mean?"

"It means I'm not interested enough to alter my schedule in order to see him, talk to him, care for him. Who the hell are you to decide what I should and should not be told of my father's health?"

"He's no different than he has been, really. Just sleeping a little deeper, not waking up as often."

"Not waking up at all from what I understand."

"How did you find out?"

"Some man from the hospital called me. He had a strange name: Ghouls or Fools, something or other. . . ."

"Pembleton. What did he want?"

"For me to sign some paper absolving the hospital of all responsibility for Father's condition. He said it was standard in these situations. He said you had signed one. What situations is he talking about, Walter?"

"The Old Man went into a coma after another patient dropped his pipe."

"What?"

"A nurse tried to extinguish the pipe with a pillow. Father came to the defense of the pipe or the pipe-smoker—I'm not sure which. Anyway, the excitement was too much for him."

"So?"

"So, patients are not supposed to be smoking pipes and nurses are not supposed to be extinguishing them with pillows. Pembleton wants to make sure that the hospital doesn't get sued over it."

"I'm not sure I understand."

"To you—or me—a pipe means nothing. To Jacob Johnson it means everything. Each time he lights it, he recalls that he's alive. He then smokes half a bowl so that he'll feel alive awhile longer. Father understood that. Doris Hunchhammer did not, until after she damn near castrated Mr. Johnson. Of course you don't understand any of it. Nor did Jules Pembleton. How could either of you understand? You know nothing of the people involved. You flounce in and out of their lives, dropping kisses and mint julep sticks, not wanting to hear specifics until someone dies or damn near dies."

From the window, Walter could see the UPS truck. It was three houses down, beneath the shade of an oak tree. Bob Warnke's setter had just finished pissing on the truck's right front tire.

"Shall I sign the papers when he mails them?"

"Why not? There's nothing to be gained from a lawsuit."

The tapping began on the other end of the line. Kate's thoughtful, analyzing tap. Walter was sorry now that he had not told her. But what was there to tell really? Their father lies on his back breathing but not speaking? Living but not alive to his children? Where was the change in that?

"Marsha telephoned the other day, Walter."

"Who?"

"Marsha. Your wife? Soon to be ex, from what I gather."

"I didn't realize the two of you were that close."

"She's worried about you, Walter."

"Worried? Why should she be worried? She has a collection of eight-by-ten glossies that prove, beyond a reasonable doubt, that I'm having the time of my life in her absence."

"She's tried to phone, she says, and can't get through."

"I can always tell when it's her, the phone whines like a wood saw running hot. When I hear that ring—the wood saw—I don't answer."

"She seems to think you're having some kind of breakdown."

"What did you tell her?"

"That you're fine. That my brother can take care of himself. That she should take a swim in the Charles River with a lead fucking suit before she calls me again."

"I'm not contesting the divorce, Kate. I gave her the house . . . and everything."

"Come visit, Walter. New York can take your mind off of anything. First, we'll get you laid—some real hot number with a master's in muscle control maybe, or else an import from Nebraska with lulus the size of hay bales—then, if you want, something more meaningful, like an Oriental exchange student majoring in transcendental meditation, with a minor in the seven levels of love. What do you say?"

"At one time I loved her, Kate. I really did."

"But not as much as you thought you did, Walter. You loved having her. Seeing her. Thinking about her. But not her, at least not much."

"What's the difference?"

"One's an idea, the other's a person."

"What makes you so fucking smart? Even when we were kids, you were smart. You saw the whole thing, all the time, while I could only see little snips, could never figure out how all the snips fit together. Every once in a while, I grabbed hold of one of the snips, held onto the goddamned thing like it was gold, until finally it would just dissolve.

Then another snip. But never the whole thing. Why is that, Kate? Why is it that you could always see the whole fucking thing?"

"I never saw anything more than you, Walter. I maybe just expected less out of what there was. I didn't expect much out of the Old Man, for example, so I never hated him like you did."

"Jesus . . . Kate. A family should mean something. . . ."

"What do you want it to mean, Walter?"

"Something."

"Name it."

"Good. Something good."

"By whose definition? If we go by yours I'm afraid nothing will be good enough."

He started laughing then. A snort through the nose at first, followed by an expulsion of hilarity. His eyes filled with water. Oh, yes. She could still make him laugh. And cry. Kate was his family, and he loved her.

"Kate? Will you come up and see me? I have to be out of the house soon, so I'm not sure where I'll be living, but wherever it is, I'll find room for you."

"I thought you were coming to New York?"

"I don't think I could handle seven levels of love just now . . . but later, I promise."

"So, when do you want me to come?"

"Soon. Maybe in a couple of weeks? And Maurice too. Bring him along if you like."

"Maurice was sent back to the minors, in Saskatchewan. At twenty-seven he's a bit old for a minor leaguer. He's thinking of giving up hockey, going into the chimney repair business with his brother. I don't expect I'll be seeing much more of him."

"I'm sorry."

"It was only sexual compatibility that we had, really. After he told me about the chimney repair business even that deteriorated. It's horrible of me, I know, but sex with a chimney repairman is not what it was with a hockey player."

"And I'm the one who falls in love with ideas?"

"The difference is, Walter, I never pretended Maurice was anything but an idea." She sighed into the phone, sounding as she had as a child when Walter had asked something she considered foolish. "But there is another man, Boris Steimlich—a German who owns a string of beauty salons in Manhattan. He's a bit older than me and not really sexually attractive—an overabundance of body hair, too flabby in the midsection—but we do exciting things together. Anyway, it's in the preliminary stages."

"So bring him if you like."

"Thanks, but I think I'll come alone, Walter. But I will come—hopefully sometime this month. I'm so glad you want me."

"Of course I want you. You may have to sleep on the floor and help with the groceries, but what are sisters for?"

"Next time, Walter, you call me. Even if you have to reverse the charges."

"Thanks, Kate. You're something good."

"We're both good, Walter. Tell Father I said hello—and let me know if he dies or anything."

From down the hallway, Walter was greeted with commemorative noises—unrehearsed voices joined together in song, a muffled hip-hip-hooray, the alarmed honk from someone's party horn. The sounds merged gently in the corridor, altering appearances there with the subtle effect of cosmetics. They were not raucous sounds, not even overly loud. Amid the stolid confines of Convalescent they danced briefly, never lingering, as if constantly searching for an avenue of escape.

Along the corridor, the doors to several rooms were open, the occupants in various poses. A man with a carrot-shaped tumor spiraling skyward from the center of his forehead rested on his back in room 209, mouth open, eyes agape, both feet tapping rhythmically against the metal railing of his bed. Walter couldn't tell whether the man was tapping in time to the music or in response to some nervous condition.

Next door, a tiny lady who sat knitting in front of a muted television set smiled and nodded at Walter. The needles in her hands clicked slowly, like the hands on a dying clock. At her feet lay a bag nearly empty of yarn.

Two rooms down, Jacob Johnson was sitting upright in his bed, smoking his pipe, appearing regal. He wore a cardboard crown, held in place by a rubber band looped beneath his chin. Five other people were in the room—Doris Hunchhammer, a nurse from the day shift, two residents from across the hall, and Victor—all wearing crowns as well. Sitting on a table at the base of the Old Man's bed, a record player played big band music.

Next to the record player was a double-layer chocolate cake with vanilla frosting. The commemorative words had been written in purple icing. Pieces cut from the cake's center had all but obliterated the words HAPPY and BIRTHDAY, leaving intact only the guest of honor's name.

The Old Man's crown was askew. Angling off to one side of his head, it resembled a wind-blown tent; beneath it, Victor's face was placid, his lips gently parted in what might or might not have been a smile. Feeling a vague sense of shame, Walter realized that his father was the guest of honor. It was his birthday, and Walter had forgotten.

Nurse Hunchhammer, looking trim and slightly tanned, as if recently returned from Florida or a session beneath a sun lamp, led the partygoers in song. A whisper of makeup circled her eyes. Dancing in the air, her long fingers articulated the highs and lows in Victor's musical tribute. When the song ended, she leaned down and kissed the Old Man gently on the forehead. Then, turning to the others, she offered up a crisp smile and simple words of cheer. "Seventy," she said, "is a good round number."

"Round maybe, but not all that big." Claude Barrow, who had the room directly across the hall, snorted. A frequent visitor of Jacob Johnson's, Claude suffered from a ruptured disk, a sagging stomach, and a bad heart. Folds of skin lay like scales on his face.

"How old are you, Claude?"

"Eighty-one. It ain't round maybe, but so long as it keeps gettin' bigger you won't hear me complain none."

"I'm eighty-seven and look younger than either of you," said Lily Baines. Lily was a great walker. She liked to stroll up and down the aisles, head down, oblivious to objects in her path, a Walkman filling her ears with soft rock. "It's because I take regular exercise," she told Claude Barrow, "eat right, and read books that make me think."

"Them's got nothing to do with it," scoffed Claude. "You've lived so long on account of good genes and a soft life."

"Soft life? Teaching school for forty years to ignorant, red-necked cow farmers like you used to be?"

"Try yankin' them tits for a lifetime, missy! Yankin' them tits is what ruined my back and it weren't long 'fore the rest of me went."

"Cow plop, Claude Barrow. Extra helpings of raw-milk ice cream, washed down with home-brewed beer is what caused your problems!" Lily swished her tiny hips, wiped frosting from her chin. "Look at you, still with a stomach the size of an udder. Best thing you could do is start walking with me!"

Doris Hunchhammer fluffed up Victor's pillow, wiped cake crumbs from the bedspread. Her smile drooped slightly. "Let's not forget this is a party," she said. "If you two can't contain your bickering, I'm going to have to insist that you leave."

Standing just outside the doorway, Walter had not yet been seen. He thought briefly of slinking off, coming back later when the guests had departed, but then it was too late. Turning to blow smoke upward, toward the air vent, Jacob Johnson was the first to spot him.

"Ah, Walter," he said. "You did remember your father's birthday. We thought perhaps you'd forgotten."

"Well, actually . . ."

"Don't feel bad." Tapping his pipe into his hand, Jacob dropped the ashes into the wastebasket. "Just yesterday Nurse Hunchhammer happened to notice the date when reviewing Victor's chart. An impromptu celebration is all."

Walter shuffled his feet, nervously shifting his weight from one to the other, his sheepish grin telling the world that he had forgotten his father's birthday. He stepped forward, into the room, glancing from his father, to the half-devoured cake, to the varied collection of revelers. He spotted Kate's card, taped to the wall above the Old Man's bed—"You're not getting older," it said, "just riper." Another inappropriate kiss, thought Walter, but at least it was timely.

The others appeared uncomfortable in his presence, as if Walter were intruding at his own father's birthday party. The day nurse was the first to go. After removing her crown and dropping her paper plate into the wastebasket, she smiled quickly at Walter before exiting.

Claude Barrow, standing next to the cake, reached down with his bare hand and picked up a thick slab. Glaring at Lily Baines, he shoved the entire piece into his mouth, frosting smearing his cheeks, bits of cake dropping to the floor. He smiled evilly, then hobbled from the room. Lily shook her head, carefully adjusted her wire-rim spectacles, took a deep breath. She seemed ready to say something, then suddenly changed her mind and spryly followed Claude out the door.

Jacob laughed loudly. His eyes flashed with good humor as he dismantled his pipe and placed the parts back into their accustomed hiding place. Now that he was allowed to smoke, the deception was no longer necessary, but Jacob still stored the pipe behind his son's picture. When you get to be my age, he had explained to Walter, the thought of change—even a change as small as where you store your pipe—is burdensome, even frightening.

His swollen prick had subsided, but not before Jacob had gotten Nurse Hunchhammer to photograph it. The framed picture sat on Jacob's nightstand, next to the one of his son. It was a tasteful photograph, the organ of honor draped in a sheet, its proud owner smiling in a top hat. Except for an occasional flutter, said Jacob, the cock was still. In his newly flaccid state, he appeared to be content.

"It's an argument they always have," he said, nodding in the direction of the recently departed Claude and Lily, "as if the why of something is somehow more important than the what."

"You don't think, then, that there's a secret to a long and healthy life?"

"If there is a secret, we each have our own. Claude Barrow, had he been a Christian Scientist, might have choked to death years ago on a stalk of rhubarb."

"What about attitude? A healthy outlook on life?"

"My older brother, Glen, hated the world and everyone in it. He believed it was a hell imposed by another world. He was convinced he would die a long and painful death. Last year—at the age of ninety-two, never sick a day in his life—he dropped dead after drinking a glass of water."

Nurse Hunchhammer had shut off the record player. She replaced the album in its jacket, then tucked it beneath one arm.

"I wasn't sure what type of music your father liked," she said to Walter. "My mother, who's maybe ten years younger than Victor, loved Benny Goodman, so that's what I brought."

"That was very kind of you, Nurse Hunchhammer. It seems to me that he often spoke fondly of the big band era," said Walter, trying to recall just what sort of music his father had enjoyed. Aside from the National Anthem, which every baseball fan was forced to endure, Walter could not recall the Old Man listening to any music.

"He had another visitor earlier," said Nurse Hunchhammer. "You just missed her."

"Her?"

"An older woman. Well endowed. She didn't say how she knew your father, just that she did. She brought him some brownies, which of course he can't eat, and a snapshot of her and Victor, taken, it appears to me, several years ago." Nurse Hunchhammer held the picture out toward Walter, who took it from her hand. The photograph was perhaps twelve years old. Rita Glenberry and Victor were standing on the front porch of the house Walter had grown up in. They had their arms around each other. Rita looked as Walter remembered her—breasts the size of torpedoes, her face bovine, benignly attractive. Smiling defiantly, the Old Man's face was a series of ill-defined lines. The picture didn't reveal any secrets. The Old Man looked pleased enough. Perhaps he had been.

"Did she say anything else?"

"No. Just that she would try and come back sometime when Victor was awake. She didn't seem to understand about the coma. She seemed to think that your father was only sleeping. She said to make sure that he ate the brownies."

Nurse Hunchhammer twittered about Victor's bed. She removed his crown, placing it carefully on the nightstand next to the picture of Rita Glenberry. She pulled the sheets up to the level of Victor's chin. The Old Man's hands were kept from curling inward by two steel braces attached to his wrists. Nurse Hunchhammer examined the braces to make certain they were not cutting into Victor's skin. When she was done, she moved over to Jacob's bed and hovered there. Jacob waved her off with his hand.

"Go away, Doris," he said as if talking to a child. "Walter wants to be alone with his father, then he and I may talk for a while. If we need you, we'll call."

She leaned close to Jacob Johnson's cheek, pecking at it, her chin bobbing like a sparrow's beak. Rolling his head, Jacob managed to fend off several of the pecks, while others landed, making wet smacking noises. "Why must you always be so cantankerous?" asked Nurse Hunchhammer, getting in a solid peck to the forehead, leaving a smudge of orange lipstick in its wake.

"I could say it's because I'm old, but that wouldn't be true," replied Jacob. He reached up with his hand, removed the smudge with a vigorous wipe. "I've always been cantankerous. And mean too, Doris. When I don't get my way, I'm mean and nasty."

"Oh, but you're not, really." As she talked, she backed away from the bed, shaking her head from side to side, still pecking at the air with tiny little kisses. "You're just a pussycat, a sweet little pussycat with eensy beensy little paws to tickle other little pussycats with."

"I am not a pussycat, Doris. I am a mean old tomcat, with claws that scratch." He curled his aged hand stiffly inward and waved it menacingly toward her face. "Grrrrr," he said.

"Ooooh!" exclaimed Nurse Hunchhammer, charging from the room in short steps, her face flushed red. "Bad pussycat," she muttered at the doorway. But her hands were damp, her voice a sugary tremor. And Jacob wore a sly grin.

"It is good to know," he said, turning back toward Walter, appearing not at all self-conscious, "that she loves more than just my prick."

Walter could not help laughing—kindly, he hoped—at this gentle old man, wrapped in hospital linen, speaking so openly of his sexual weaponry.

"Ah! You laugh," said Jacob. "It is no joke, my friend. All women develop fixations about the men they love—be it a man's prick or his money or even his nose. When I was a teenager, I had a girl who had a fixation on my radio. It was the best radio in the neighborhood. She would come over and we would go upstairs to my bedroom and while listening to the radio we would make love. It didn't matter what we listened to—so long as it was on. She had a real fascination for this radio. She screamed while it played. When we were done screwing, she could repeat everything the announcer had said while we were doing it. And believe me, in the midst of such gyrations, that could not have been an easy task! Anyway, I traded the radio for a camera—a real nice camera too, but she didn't like cameras."

"So what happened?"

"I never screwed her again, I'll tell you that."

"And?"

"I know you think I'm going to say she ended up screwing the boy I traded the radio to, but it's not so. You see, the fixation for the radio was unique to me. For every guy she had a different fixation. The next guy she went out with had big biceps—like bowling balls in his arms. She married him, but made sure that he continued to work out. At sixty he looked like Popeye—but he still had his wife."

"And you thought Nurse Hunchhammer's fixation related to your prick?"

"One never knows," said Jacob, smiling openly now, pinching his chin with the fingers of one hand. "She was certainly impressed, but I have now come to believe that the fixation lies elsewhere."

"Where do you think?"

"Who knows? If one could always tell it would be easy. Do you think I would have traded that radio so quickly had I known?" Jacob was taken up with the subject, appeared to be enjoying himself immensely. He pinched his chin harder, causing a small dent to form. "But it's worth knowing, Walter, and I'll tell you why. Once you know exactly where a woman's fixation lies, then you can rest easy. After that, it doesn't matter what you do—run around on her, call her names, even beat her up—this girl will not leave you. It will be impossible for her to even think badly of you, so long as the fixation stays in place."

Walter looked over at his father. The Old Man moaned, not a painful or happy sound, but simply a sound of living, released like flatulence. His head rocked gently back and forth, in the easy motion of wiper blades in a light rain. The rocking, according to the doctors, was not a reason for excitement or concern. It was nothing more than the ordinary motions of a man in a deep sleep. Walter wondered what the Old Man dreamed about. Or if he dreamed at all.

"My mother had a fixation," Walter said. "Something like your girl with the radio, I guess, something that would allow her to leave the Old Man for a few days, but never for good."

"Something more than a radio, I am sure. Do you know what?"

"God knows . . . and maybe the Old Man, although I hope not. I want to give him that much credit at least."

"Would it have mattered if he had known? What might he have done differently? Remember, Walter, it was her fixation, not his."

"He could have walked away . . . just left, which is something my mother didn't have the strength to do. She let it—this fixation, whatever it was—control her life."

"Could be," remarked Jacob, "that she had more in common with your father than you think."

"Like what?"

"Well, you and your sister for one."

"I remember Kate told me that she heard my parents arguing once. My mother told the Old Man that if it wasn't for us kids she would leave and never come back."

"Did you believe her?"

"No. It didn't sound to me like a good enough excuse. I kept wondering what the real reason was."

"Fixations don't have to be complicated, Walter."

"Huh?"

"Maybe your mother's reason for staying was as simple as love and as old-fashioned as loyalty."

Walter turned away from the Old Man, looked once more into the friendly face of Jacob Johnson. In St. Louis they made sheetmetal workers out of philosophers. Socrates, no doubt, would have been required to bottle beer, Descartes, to shovel the shit of Clydesdales. "Or maybe," Walter said with a shrug, "it was just big arms and a radio."

Accompanying an arrangement of flowers worth more, no doubt, than my mother's casket, a card from Henry Truxton III arrived within a few days of her death. "My sincerest regrets upon Mrs. Innis's passing," it said. "She was a loyal and trusted employee."

Tucked inside of the envelope was a sheaf of clean, crisp one-hundred-dollar bills. Not showing the money to anyone else, I slid it into my wallet, then placed the card with the others, on the mantel.

Alone in my room each night, I laid the bills—twenty of them—in a perfect circle on my bed. I spent hours trying to memorize their serial numbers. What was the money for? I wondered. And why hadn't Henry Truxton III come to my mother's funeral? I went through a month-long period of mental and physical estrangement, as if, in my own home, I was suffering culture shock. Words and gestures seemed to have underlying meanings, known to everyone but me. Although it was late spring and warm, I often felt cold. In the middle of the night, unable to sleep, I would get up, walk over to my bedroom window, look out, and be surprised not to see snow. I dreamt that Henry Truxton III had drowned my mother in his marble bathtub before dumping her body in the lake.

I printed his name onto the front of a large manila envelope and put inside of it my mother's key to his house, her rag for calming the dogs, and the two thousand dollars. I walked with the envelope down to the post office but didn't mail it. At home, I opened the envelope again and, to the other things, added a snapshot of my mother. I lay all that afternoon and night on my bed, the envelope on my chest, trying to see past the age of seventeen. In the morning—two days after my high school graduation—I drove my father's station wagon out to the Truxton estate. I rode with the windows wide open, the radio blaring, wanting something I couldn't name, describe, or remember. Hot and moist from an evening rain, the air smelled like flowers growing on a compost heap. To my left, the lake shimmered like a tin roof.

I pulled the car up next to the compound, got out, and rang the buzzer at the front gate. The dogs, all six of them, yapping and snarling, came charging around one corner of the house, headed straight for me until a voice yelled "Stop!"; as if six invisible leashes had abruptly been jerked, they did. A tall man wearing khakis and a straw hat strolled through a lattice at the back of the house. He was carrying a glass in one hand; with the other, he gently pushed at the dogs while wading smoothly through them toward the gate. Fifty feet from it, he lifted his hand, a half wave, and I knew then—from that easy, graceful motion—it was he. I shoved the envelope through the top of the gate; not waiting for it to land, I turned and walked rapidly back to my father's car. The next day I took a Greyhound bus out of Caulfield and didn't return for twelve years.

CHAPTER 49

At Maurie's office, Walter entered a waiting room empty of people. Even Maurie's secretary—who served also as his receptionist—had left for the day. Classical music played softly in the background. A rack of magazines appeared untouched.

In the years that Walter had been coming to Maurie's office, he had never seen anything new in the rack. The selection reflected Maurie's clientele; dog-eared copies of *The Reader's Digest*, several issues of *Sports Illustrated*—including the bathing suit editions from the last six years, covers smudged and all but obliterated by countless fingerprints—a copy of the March 1979 *National Geographic*, glimmering like new, and the most recent issue of *The Stars*.

His office door half open, Maurie was in conference with a client. Reclining casually, he faced the client across his desk and, through thick glasses, appraised the other man. Spotting Walter in the reception area, Maurie waved him into a chair, then flashed the fingers on his right hand twice to indicate he would be out in ten minutes. The client, his back to Walter, sat rigidly in a cloth recliner, his hands tightly gripping the edges of his seat. Leaning against the chair was a pair of wooden crutches.

Walter pushed the office door shut. He reached into the rack and removed the *National Geographic*, then sat down in one of four vinyl chairs in the waiting room. As he sat down, the seat hissed air, Styrofoam stuffing spilling out from two sides of the cushion. He leafed casually through the magazine, stopping when he came to an article on the exploitation of the tropical rain forest.

Overnight, it seemed, the western world had arrived with its modern technology, digging up valuable mineral deposits, chopping down acre after acre of the forest's timber. Men wearing coconut shells on their heads drove bulldozers through the forest, crashing through villages, demolishing the foliage. In their spare time they dressed in khaki and carried automatic rifles; with black men in tow, acting as pack mules, carrying what seemed like entire houses on their backs, the westerners trudged even farther into the forest, shooting animals for sport. The primitive tribes, most of them unaware of the world beyond their own, retreated deeper and deeper into the shrinking jungle.

A naked tribesman holding a spear was shown standing next to a bulldozer. Staring in awe at the machine, he had the spear poised at his shoulder, ready to thrust the weapon through the dozer's heart. "What is perhaps most frustrating to this warrior," said the caption beneath the picture, "is the incomprehensible shape of his enemy."

Maurie's door opened. The client hobbled out on his crutches, one leg in a cast to his thigh, the other stark white beneath his gym shorts. The man looked to be in his mid-forties, face unshaven, eyes lackluster, dulled either by events or unfortunate genes. He wore a pullover shirt, stained yellow beneath each armpit. He glanced at Walter, as if it were he who had caused him to be on crutches.

"Remember, Carl, you will be deposed on Thursday," said Maurie, holding open the door of his office as the man hopped through it. "It's absolutely essential that you have the facts in order by that time."

"About how fast I was going, you mean?"

"About the things we talked about. I can't tell you about the facts. Only you can testify about those things . . . truthfully, of course." Maurie had moved in front of the client and now held the door of the waiting room open for him. "I can only tell you what the law says."

"Right. That if I was . . . ?"

". . . speeding or under the influence of alcohol at the time of the accident, the driver of the other car cannot be held liable for your injuries."

"So, that's what I shouldn't say . . . that I was speeding or drunk?"

"That's the law, Carl. What you should say is what happened." Maurie was at the outside door now, holding this final obstacle wide open for the man's departure. "The facts."

"Right," said Carl, stepping into the street and hobbling off down the sidewalk. "I'll try to get them straight."

Maurie turned back toward Walter, a large smile creasing his face, his glasses pushed deep into the tangle of hair atop his head. He strolled over to where Walter was now standing and wrapped an arm about his friend's shoulders. "There are days," he said, "when I think it was easier to steal bikes on the east side."

"But not as profitable, I'm sure."

"No, Walter, not as profitable, but sometimes more tasteful."

"These days," answered Walter, "knowing the facts is not always easy."

"And that"—Maurie laughed—"is why a man needs a lawyer. To provide him with the context—also referred to as the law—so that he can remember the facts."

Once inside the office, they had placed themselves—Maurie in his recliner, feet propped up on the desktop, hands neatly folded behind his head; Walter in the chair facing him, trying hard not to grip the arms too tightly. Maurie removed the bottle of Chivas Regal from the bottom drawer of his desk. He poured them each a drink, offering some vague toast before polishing his off. Walter followed suit. Maurie poured them another round and then started to tell Walter about Ed Walling's funeral, about how over two hundred people had been there, friends accumulated over a period of years—some from the slam, some from Walling's days as a union enforcer, others acquaintances from the neighborhood. Ed had been a good neighbor, well liked for his generosity, friendly to the neighborhood children, even being accepted—after many years and several skirmishes—as a Boy Scout leader. He was not big on outdoor activities, but had taken the kids to see the Yankees on several occasions and had held monthly pool tournaments in his cellar where his wife, Myrtle, provided trays of refreshments and Ed demonstrated a variety of trick shots. Once a year the two of them had hosted a wienie roast in the backyard.

Myrtle had been there, dressed in black, a dark veil shadowing her face. She had cried on Maurie's shoulder, cursing Ed for a fool, damning him for abandoning her. "Being in jail makes you crazy," she wailed. "He should have known. More than anyone, he should have known."

Maurie had tried to console her without much luck. The preacher's religion, she said, had been a simple salve to the degradation of prison. Inside, the preacher's message had seemed eternal; on the outside, it was just another scam. Myrtle had dumped him even before Ed had died, but of course Ed hadn't known. "I would have come back," she said.

"Did he forget when he was released? How he went on a five-day toot with that bimbo from Bruno? Did I jump from a cliff? Did I throw away thirty years of marriage?"

She was distraught, missing Ed with a pain that would not soon heal. There was no question in her mind about how he had died or why; she and her husband had shared that sort of relationship. They were aware of each other's motives—at least they always had been, until through the pain of separation, Ed had fatally misread Myrtle's.

Their only son, Fraser—a dark, serious boy of nineteen, well acquainted with the family business, determined not to become too deeply entrenched in it—had helped Myrtle to the car. After closing the passenger-side door, he had walked over to where Maurie was lingering politely.

"I know," he said, "that you and my father were involved in some business ventures together, things I don't want to know nothing about. I helped him out some, without asking questions, like any son would, but that's all. It's not that I disapproved of his profession, it's just that I think there's lots less risky ways to make a living."

"I'm certain," Maurie replied, "that your father always encouraged you to make your own decisions."

"He thought a lot of you," said Fraser, frowning, looking down at his feet. "He told me that you were more than his lawyer, that you were a friend. My mother's gonna be needing both, I think. Would it be possible for you . . . ?"

"I'll see that your father's will is probated as expeditiously as possible," said Maurie. "Whenever I can, I'll drop by and see you and your mother. She'll be all right, as long as she doesn't violate her parole."

"Dad told me once that there was no one you wouldn't represent and that there were damn few you wouldn't have a drink with. He meant it, I think, as a compliment." Maurie chuckled, thinking that that was more than a mouthful for Ed Walling, but the boy didn't even smile.

"He wanted you to have this," said Fraser, handing Maurie a letter-size envelope. "It was in his safe, with his personal effects. I didn't open it."

Before getting into his car, the boy turned back to where Maurie stood, still holding the envelope, tapping it gently into the palm of one hand. Fraser's face was defiant; his eyes sought out Maurie's without wavering. "When he jumped," he said, "was the only time my father ever shamed us."

In the envelope were directions and a key to the box that Ed had used as a drop. The box was located at the Greyhound bus terminal, more of a locker than a box really, a depository for wayward luggage and miscellaneous contraband. Situated against one wall, away from the hubbub of the station, Ed's box was in the midst of hundreds.

Maurie had gone to the station in early evening. The usual hodge-podge of humanity milled about—those waiting for departures or arrivals, bums looking for handouts, prostitutes for business, deviants for kindred spirits. No one seemed overly interested when Maurie had opened Ed's locker and quickly removed its contents.

"What are you saying?" asked Walter. "That Henry Truxton had nothing to do with Ed Walling's death? That Walling really did kill himself?"

"The problem with you, Walter," said Maurie, peering at him over his feet, "is that you have a devious mind. You insist that there are motives behind the real motives, as if, somehow, you are the only person in the world who ever acted on instinct."

"When one is acquainted with the act of self-destruction," Walter answered, "one gets a feel for those capable of it."

"Being acquainted is not enough, Walter! It doesn't make you an expert on motives—no more than being a fight announcer makes you an expert on fighters! Unless you have been in the ring with a man, Walter, you cannot know the first thing about him."

"You don't consider Walling's death at all connected to our recent business dealings with him?"

"There are more coincidences in the world than you might think, Walter." Maurie reached down with one hand and scratched absently at an ankle. "There are also fewer people than you might imagine willing to kill someone over a reel of dirty pictures—especially one twenty-two years old."

Lowering his feet back to the floor, Maurie reached for the Chivas. He poured them each another drink. He glanced at Walter and scowled, his great jowls drooping. His patience was wearing thin, his resolve to step lightly waning. Why couldn't the man go forward, for Christ sake? Every time Walter took a step, it seemed, he tripped over his own sensibilities. Did he think he was the only one with regrets? Did he actually believe no one else had ever wandered into hell and then been jettisoned back to earth?

"So what was in the locker?"

"Just this," said Maurie, tossing a white envelope onto the desk, watching silently as Walter opened it and read the short typewritten message within.

"What's it mean?—'No audition, no dance!'—What the hell does that mean?"

"Just what it says, I presume. The man wants to know if we can play."

"Play! Play what?"

"The tune we promised him."

"Speak English, for Christ sake! Doesn't he believe we have the film?"

"He'd like to be convinced."

"But, Maurie, we can't give him the film!"

"That's correct, Walter, we can't. We can give him very little beyond our memories—as specific as they may be, they apparently are not enough to sway Henry Truxton."

"Goddamn it, Maurie. You said that he'd agreed to our price!"

"No, Walter. I said that he was 'interested' in the complete package at our price. That is what he said—in the note you wouldn't read."

"Son of a bitch, Maurie! He was interested and now he's not?"

"To Henry Truxton, Walter, forty grand is fly shit. Whether we were the Boston Philharmonic or a bad polka band from Paducah, Kentucky, he was willing to pay us, simply to avoid negative publicity in the midst of his campaign. In that sense," said Maurie, sighing, "our terms were acceptable."

"Were?"

"Our terms were changed."

"What? By who?"

"By me."

"By you, Maurie?"

"I take my clients as I find them, Walter. You never wanted money out of this. You suggested money because you felt it was the only way I would go along with it, which in most cases would have been true, and because you didn't really know what the hell it was that you did want." Maurie sighed again; he really was growing weary of his own beneficence. He drained his glass, looked again at Walter, and smirked. "That night at Ruston's, I realized that money from Henry Truxton was the last thing you needed. In your twisted, Christian's conscience, Walter, blood money would have been your final excuse for unraveling—the final clarification, for you, that everything evil must ultimately prevail."

Maurie knew of little in life one had to tolerate; when the benefits of a particular wife, for example, were outweighed by her deficits, it was time to get a new one; when one is poor, there are countless ways to obtain money; when bored, stimulation is cheap; when living became too physically burdensome, then dying would be easy. Still, the world was not altogether free of burdens. There were a few things every man had to bear, chief among them being friends. Friends, like physical deformities—the unsightly birthmark, the bulbous nose, the undescended testicle—a person simply had to live with.

"I then saw what it was that you really wanted, Walter."

"What, Maurie? What did I really want? Tell me, please! Revenge?"

"If revenge is what you wanted, you would have shot the man!"

"What, then?"

"Justice, goddamn it! Simple tit for tat, what's right is right, what's wrong is wrong and the twain shall never meet—justice!"

"So?"

"There is no justice, Walter! There is no right! And there is no wrong! There is only fat—your fat and everybody else's fat! I knew that—I've always known it—but you didn't know it and it cost me twenty thousand dollars to prove it to you!"

"Maurie, what the hell are you talking about?"

"The last letter Ed Walling delivered changed the terms of our offer to Henry Truxton. The letter said that money was no longer acceptable, that it was, in fact, an insult, that if Truxton did not drop out of the senatorial race by Labor Day a résumé of his extracurricular activities—as well as a certain reel of film—would be publicly disseminated." Appearing cooler now, Maurie removed a pipe from the top drawer of his desk and began to fill it with tobacco. "You are holding his answer."

"No money, Maurie? You told Henry Truxton to shove forty thousand dollars up his ass?"

"Aptly put, Walter."

"No shit? You told him it was an insult?"

"To voters everywhere."

"But . . . why, Maurie?"

"You are a friend, Walter. Foolish and unprepared for the world, but a friend nonetheless." Maurie lit the pipe, and a great cloud of smoke billowed up between the two men, separating them, causing each to appear blurred and out of focus to the other. "Also, in my heart of hearts, Walter, I believe the man is a shitheel. And there's enough of them in office already."

Maurie dropped his hands into his lap, patting his vast stomach, moving quickly upward from there as if conducting a self-examination. In the area of his heart, he touched something solid. Reaching into his breast pocket then, he came up with a small crystal figurine. "I could never figure out what exactly this is," he said, flipping it toward Walter, who reached out and snared it easily. "I used to think a penguin, but now I don't know—some poor bastard maybe laced into a straitjacket?"

Walter weighed the thing in his hand, his mind going back twenty-two years, to when he had been seventeen years old and ready to dive on the floor to save whatever it was from breaking. Gazing open-mouthed at Maurie, he said, "You snatched it?"

Maurie shrugged. "I had it appraised once. Guy told me—the way it was cut—it was worth maybe three grand. Do you think Henry Truxton's missed it?"

"After twenty-two years?"

Maurie smiled. "You don't think he'd remember it?"

"Doubtful."

"Turn it over, Walter."

Walter flipped the curio over. Engraved into the underside, he saw 'H.T., 1952.' "What are you thinking, Maurie?"

Maurie wiggled his eyebrows. "We ought to start a dance band, Walter. That's what I think. You and me."

CHAPTER 50

The elements of hitting:

1. Keep your eye on the ball—how can you expect to hit something you can't see? Bad hitters occasionally hit what they aren't looking at; good hitters only hit what they see. (In one second, the rest of the world will still be there, but the ball will be gone!) (W.I.)

2. Play within yourself—it is not humanly possible to kill a baseball, yet thousands insist upon trying, causing themselves endless frustration in the process. It is possible to sting a baseball—even to cause it considerable pain—if one hits it solidly. (That means a nice level swing, Billy. Don't go for the fences!) (W.I.)

3. Practice! Practice! Practice!—no matter how much talent you may have, you will never improve if you don't work at it. (Remember Bobby Burns?)

4. Confidence—you are as good as the pitcher. What is so hard about hitting a baseball? Very little—if you follow the above suggestions, and listen to your coach!

5. Don't worry if you strike out—Mickey Mantle struck out more times than anybody else in the history of baseball!

Walter compiled the list shortly after he took over as the Meat Market coach. He had handed out a copy to each player, making handwritten additions to Billy's list during the course of the season. The list was taped to the wall at the top of Billy's bed. Before going to bed each night, Billy read the list, visualizing the various steps within his mind. He knew every word by heart—even Walter's penciled-in comments. He thought of the list every time it was his turn to bat.

But it was Walter who had taught Billy how to hit—the list was just a reminder of all they had talked about. It was Walter who had shown him how to dig in with his back foot at the plate, how to step into the ball instead of away from it, how—using a wiener for a bat—to take a level swing at the ball. It was Walter who made Billy believe that he could hit, encouraging him even after he would strike out. "So?" he might say. "You're still two thousand short of the Mick." Without Walter, the list would have been only words on a piece of paper.

Billy was a great fan of statistics. He knew the batting averages of almost every active major league player by heart. He knew the obscure facts as well—the name of the pitcher who had thrown the pitch that led to Babe Ruth's first home run, the lowest career batting average for a player with over five thousand major league at-bats, who had hit the first ball out of Fenway Park. He knew also that Reggie Jackson—along with four or five other players—had broken Mickey Mantle's record for career strikeouts, a record that was being added to almost every day.

Billy didn't tell Walter that Mickey Mantle's strikeout record had been eclipsed; the knowledge, he thought, might have disheartened Walter, perhaps even have caused him to revise his Elements of Hitting. Billy couldn't imagine Walter saying "You're only two thousand short of Reggie Jackson"; he wasn't even certain that Walter had heard of Reggie Jackson. The way Walter spoke, you'd think the game of baseball had ended with the retirement of Mickey Mantle.

"It's a different game today," Walter was fond of saying. The way he said it—shaking his head in a bewildered manner, the corners of his mouth angling downward—made it clear that he thought the "old game" was better than the new one. One time Billy and Walter had been watching television at Billy's house when a famous player appeared on the screen in his underwear; he stood on the mound in Jockey briefs, winding up and throwing a fastball by another player who was fully clothed. "Now they're selling underwear," Walter said disgustedly, "and posing naked in girls' magazines. The game certainly has changed."

"How has it changed?" Billy summoned up the courage to ask. "Are the rules different?"

"It's not how they play that's different," Walter had answered. "It's the way that they play."

Billy was not sure he understood the distinction between "how" and "way." There were still three outs to an inning, weren't there? If a pitcher appeared on television in his underwear, did that mean he would pitch less effectively? Maybe the players just looked different today. The pictures that Billy had seen of Babe Ruth made him appear fat and out of shape; he didn't imagine that the Babe would look too appealing in his underwear or that many people would care to purchase the underwear he had worn.

"When I was growing up," said Walter, "the very best players didn't make half the money that utility players make today. And none of them would be seen wearing their underpants in public."

"But why does it matter," wondered Billy, "so long as they wear more than that when they're playing?"

"That's not the point," said Walter. "Don't you see, Billy, that what you do off the field carries over to what you do on the field? These guys today are always looking at ways to sell the fact that they're ballplayers, as if that's more important than actually being one. They make as much money selling beer as they do playing ball."

"And it used to be different, huh?"

"You bet," said Walter.

"You had to learn how to hit just like me, didn't ya?"

"Sure. Hitting won't ever change much."

"And ya still had to run the bases?"

"Just like you."

"Well," Billy said quietly—almost under his breath because he didn't like to disagree with Walter, "if you ask me, as long as the rules are the same, it's still baseball."

Walter had smiled then and ruffled Billy's hair. "If you look at it that way," he said, "I guess rules will always be rules."

And now the Elements of Hitting had become even more important to Billy. Now that he and Walter rarely talked, the list was all that Billy had left to remind him of what he had learned. And he had learned a lot. He had learned that he could be good at something, that he could hit a baseball as well or maybe even better than the next guy. And now that Billy had learned how to hit, he never wanted to forget. He wanted to become better and better, to someday maybe even be the best hitter in Caulfield. What he didn't want was ever again to be the pathetic, anemic-hitting third baseman he had been at the beginning of the season.

His mother thought that Billy was mad at Walter. Walter probably thought the same thing—Billy could tell by the look Walter often had, the look he would get when Billy told him that he had homework to do after practice, that he would have to go straight home instead of waiting around for Walter to give him a ride. But they were wrong, both Walter and his mother. Billy was not mad at Walter. He loved Walter—although he would never tell him that, it was simply not the kind of thing one man said to another, unless he was your father and even then—at least if he was Billy's father—you didn't say it very often or very loud. That was the way that Billy felt about Walter nonetheless. But no one else would ever know, especially not Walter or Billy's mother.

Billy wished that he didn't love Walter. He hoped that if he continued to ignore him, in time Walter would not mean so much to him. He hoped that what he felt for Walter would simply disappear, evaporate like water left overnight in a glass. Billy did not want to love Walter because he thought that Walter was not a good person to love. He believed he knew something about Walter that his mother did not. He believed that Walter did not want to be loved, that Walter was one of those people who talk all the while about what they would do if they won a million dollars. And when they finally do win, they give it all away like that man in New Jersey—the one in the newspaper. He gave it away, he said, because he wouldn't know what to do with that much money.

Walter, thought Billy, was like that man. If he wasn't, why had he walked away from Billy and his mother? Billy could have understood if Walter was more like the other men who had been interested in his mother, like the man who had offered Billy five dollars to "get lost," just so he could be alone with her. Those men had not cared about Billy or his mother. They had been after one thing; Walter had been after something entirely different.

Billy didn't know a lot of things, but he knew happiness when he saw it, and Walter, Billy knew, had been happy with Billy and his mother. And they had been happy with him. And then Walter had given it all away—like the man in New Jersey—and that's what had made Billy wish that he didn't love Walter. That's when Billy had decided that he wouldn't spend any more time than was necessary with Walter—not because he didn't want to (there was nobody he enjoyed spending time with more), but because he didn't think it was a good idea, because he believed that once the baseball season was over he would never see Walter again and Billy was tired of learning to love someone and then never seeing that person again.

Neither Walter nor Billy's mother had bothered to tell Billy that something had changed between them. One day, things that Billy had begun to take for granted simply stopped happening; Walter stopped coming by the house and Billy's mother stopped coming to the Meat Market games. Both tried to pretend that there was nothing significant in these changes—as if the changes were nothing more than subtle shifts in the wind, blowing them temporarily in different directions. Instead of calling each other on the phone, they asked Billy about one another. It hadn't taken Billy long to figure out that the degree of change between Walter and his mother was much more significant than either had indicated.

Around the house, his mother was a flurry of activity—cleaning things that had just been cleaned, rearranging furniture that had not been rearranged since her husband's death. She was filled with false optimism—brimming suddenly with "fun things" for her and Billy to do when she got home from work each day. "How about picking strawberries this afternoon, Billy? Wouldn't that be a fun thing to do?" So Billy had gone berry picking even though he didn't think it was a fun thing to do at all, even though the only time in her life his mother had eaten strawberries she had broken out in hives, her entire face becoming one giant strawberry. And halfway down a row, with less than a bucket of berries between them, she had suddenly dumped the bucket in a thicket and made a beeline for the station wagon. "Let's go swimming," she said. "Wouldn't that be a fun thing to do?"

At the town pool, his mother had suddenly remembered that she had never learned how to swim, so, dressed in shorts and a tank top, she had tiptoed tentatively into the shallow end, getting in up to her waist finally. She had splashed water gently over her shoulders and neck, goose bumps erupting like spring buds on her skin, her pale legs shimmying. Slapping awkwardly at the water, she had caught Billy in the spray, then ambled to the steps, reminding Billy of a camel at a watering hole. Five minutes later they were both wrapped in beach towels, shivering in the front seat of the car. "Wasn't that fun?" she had asked.

"How's Walter?" she might inquire, feigning disinterest, acting as if the idea had popped unexpectedly into her head. "Fine," Billy would say, shrugging his shoulders, wondering why the hell she didn't go over to practice and ask him herself. The fact that she wouldn't made Billy think that perhaps she too had decided that Walter was like the man from New Jersey.

Then one day Billy had overheard his mother speaking on the telephone to Dr. Florish, the Palumbo family physician. "I think that is highly improbable, Doctor," she had said. "I just don't see how it's possible. I mean, I'm a thirty-seven-year-old widow. This is not news that I would be eagerly anticipating." Billy was hidden from his mother—behind the living room door, his ear pressed flat against it. He could not see her face, but he could hear the rising pitch to her words, could feel that invisible surge of hysteria.

On his mother's side of the door, there was a short silence—a silence in which Billy was suddenly aware that they lived in a neighborhood filled with songbirds, all of which seemed to have gathered outside the living room window. From where he crouched, Billy could see through the window, to where the sunflower feeder sat in the middle of the lawn.

"I've never been good at waiting, Doctor," continued his mother from the kitchen. "Patience is not one of my virtues. Why must I wait for God's will, when it was the will of Procter Gamble that caused my predicament?"

It was chaos. There was no order to the dive-bombing of the feeder; a couple of birds would sit on the edge of the tin tray, pecking what seeds they could, before being chased away by two or three others. Each bird fended for itself and the bunch of them chattered without rules.

"No. I am not Catholic," said Billy's mother, "but I find the question irrelevant."

But they must communicate, Billy realized. Or else why wouldn't they all come at once to the lip of the feeder? Understanding this did not make understanding the birds any easier. Communication without rules, thought Billy, was still chaos.

After hearing his mother hang up the phone, Billy had tiptoed quietly over to the couch. Lying down, he placed an open comic book on his chest, folded his hands behind his head, and did his best to look nonchalant. Once in the living room, his mother had walked quickly across the room and hugged her son. Her body was warm and moist. To Billy it felt like a vast, living bottle of hot water. Tears ran down her cheeks and onto Billy's face. Their faces slid together. "Oh, Billy," she said, "please don't worry, honey. Everything is going to be just fine."

Until then, Billy had not known for sure that there was anything to worry about. He had not seen the pain that his mother had been hiding, nor had he understood that this was not the first time that she had cried or that all of her fun things to do were simply other, secret ways of crying. Billy understood about hiding things, and he understood that secrets—like dreams—could not be told to just anyone. Such were the rules of life. People were not birds, after all. People don't sit on branches telling the world everything they feel. People must find other people— maybe only one person, but at least one if they are lucky—who will care enough to listen to what they are hiding. Billy had had his father, but then he died. Then he had found Walter, but Walter turned out to be like the man from New Jersey.

Holding his mother while she cried, Billy suddenly understood that things did not become easier when a person grew up; there was no pill for order or fairness to swallow upon entering adulthood. The rules applied even to grown-ups. Regardless of age, no one was ever free simply to jump onto a branch and start to sing. He cried then, more for his mother than for himself, knowing somehow that the phone call with Dr. Florish had made his mother wish that, for the moment at least, the rules did not exist.

"Are you sick, Mommy?" he had asked, patting her back. "Will you have to go to the hospital?"

"No, baby." She sobbed, her chest heaving like a great bellows. "I'm not going to the hospital."

"Can Dr. Florish make you better?"

"Better? No. Not better." She raised her head enough to blow her nose into a hankie. "He can help, I suppose."

"Who's Mr. Gamble?" asked Billy, thinking the name sounded familiar, wondering if he had ever met the man.

"Who?"

"Procter Gamble? Is he the one who made you sick?"

"Have you been listening to my phone calls, Billy?"

"Just a little."

She was sitting up now, dabbing at her eyes with the hankie, then at her nose. When she blew, it sounded to Billy like the blast from a ship's horn. Blowing her nose seemed to clear her head. She held Billy by the shoulders.

"I'm not sick, Billy," she said. "Not really."

"But why are you mad at Procter Gamble?"

"I'm not mad."

"Who is he?"

"No one you know."

His mother would have told Walter who Procter Gamble was, thought Billy, if Walter had not turned out to be like the man from New Jersey. Maybe that was why his mother was really crying; not because of Dr. Florish or Procter Gamble, but because Walter wasn't there to ease her mind—because she thought that no one but Billy even cared. If only Walter was here, thought Billy, Dr. Florish's bad news might not matter. Slowly, methodically—like the emerging picture from the pieces of a puzzle—a plan began to take shape in Billy's mind.

"Will you come to the game tomorrow?" he asked. "It's the last game of the season, you know?"

"Oh, I know, honey, but—"

"You never come any more and I really think we might win."

"I have a lot of things to do."

"Walter wants you to come."

"Did he say that?"

"Well, no. Not exactly, but I can tell."

"How can you tell?"

"I just can, that's all. It might help you to forget about Procter Gamble."

She smiled, then laughed, scooping Billy up in her big arms and pinning him beneath her on the couch. She began tickling him in the stomach until the laughter poured from Billy. He managed to hook a leg around her hip, pushing then with the leg, while using his body's weight against her. She was halfway off the couch before she righted herself; with a great heave of her shoulders—her breath sounding like wind through a tunnel—she laid Billy flat on his back once again.

"You're out of your weight class, buster," she said, before coming at him with her poignant fingers. He was helpless against her bulk.

"Will you come?" he asked between giggles.

"Will you stop mentioning Procter Gamble?"

"Okay."

"Promise?"

"I promise."

"Okay, I'll come," she said, stopping the tickling and shifting her weight so that Billy could slither out from beneath her. She gave him a friendly push from behind, helping him to his feet. "It might be a fun thing to do."

Thus the first step in Billy's plan had been accomplished; his mother would be at the Meat Market's season finale. She would take her place behind the Market bench, in the spot now occupied by Rusty Tillman's mother. She would wish Billy good luck, blow him a kiss from the bleachers, perhaps nod curtly to Walter where he stood in the first-base coach's box.

Only the final step remained—the step that Billy, with the help of Walter Innis, had been working toward all year—a Meat Market victory. The players were ready—they had been on the verge of victory on two occasions when, for one reason or another, the team had come unraveled. It was, according to their coach, because they weren't used to winning. Never having won, the team naturally expected to lose, managing subconsciously then to fulfill their expectations.

Once, in the bottom of the ninth inning with the Market up by a run, they had lost when Rusty Tillman had dropped Todd Bailey's throw from shortstop. The ball had gotten into the outfield, two runs had scored, and the game was over. In the other game, a fly ball to right field was mishandled, the ball bouncing off the heel of Timmy Mealus's glove. When Billy had charged out from second base to retrieve the ball, he and Timmy had collided—Timmy landing on the ball, Billy landing on top of Timmy. By the time they had become untangled, the winning run had scored.

But this time it would be different. They had run out of ways to lose. Walter had them believing they could win. It would be a close game. Maybe Billy would even have the winning hit; but if not, that would be all right too—so long as the Market won, so long as Walter and Billy's mother were both there to witness the victory. In celebration of the win, the two of them would hug each other, perhaps even break into a jig right there on home plate. Walter—unlike the man from New Jersey—would have a second chance; this time he would realize his good fortune and take home the fruits of his victory.

"There's this man named Procter Gamble—" Billy's mother would start to say.

"Don't you worry about Procter Gamble," Walter would interrupt. "Dr. Florish has told me all about Mr. Gamble and he isn't anyone to trouble yourself with, believe you me."

In celebration of the victory, they would all go to a restaurant and eat hot dogs and pizza. At home, Billy's mother would make popcorn. Billy would sit on the couch, between Walter and his mother, the three of them eating popcorn and watching *Star Trek* reruns.

displaced person (dis-'plāst), a person left homeless in a foreign country as a result of war; abbreviated D.P.

Walter had no place to go. His house, although still his home, would not be his for much longer. In less than a week—as a result of his own insistence on a quick and merciful resolution—the papers would be final. If he was not gone by then, he would be a holdover tenant in his own house, a squatter subject to eviction. He could feel Marsha there already, as if she had seeped through the soil, through the cracks in the foundation, into his living room, like radon gas. Amongst the cobwebs, she was the triumphant spider on the wall, impatiently pacing on a thousand anxious legs.

In the bedroom, he had packed all of his clothes that he could fit into two suitcases, leaving out his dappled gray sweatsuit and his canvas boxing shoes. After removing his blue denims and Meat Market pullover, he stood naked in the bedroom window, gazing out at the neighborhood he had never known. There on the street was Bob Forrester, out for his afternoon jog, loose tits bouncing as he ran, his head bent toward the ground at a strange angle. Looking up, he spotted Walter in the window, smiled then and waved, oblivious to his neighbor's nakedness. Walter listened for the accompanying fart, waited for its unmuffled rejoinder, turned away as it mingled with the songs of sparrows.

Next door, Bob Sturgeon was on his hands and knees, scratching furiously at the soil of his barren garden. He used a tiny metal rake shaped like a claw. Murderously he thrashed the earth, rocks shrieking at the claw's impact, dirt splattering like blood. In knee-length Bermudas and sun hat, he smiled maniacally. His wife, serene and pretty, sipped lemonade on the porch.

Across the street, the Warnkes' shades were drawn, their front door securely latched. The whole house, caught in shadow, was dead still this afternoon. Both cars—the family station wagon and Mike Warnke's Volvo—were mysteriously present in the driveway. The lawn appeared half mowed, the mower still sitting in it, left there like abandoned artillery.

And what do they say of you, Walter? Here at 1250 Brewster Ave., where the lawn has not been mowed in over three weeks? Where the missus was last seen on a spring morn in early June, stepping into the backseat of a cab, overnight valise and large suit bag in hand? Where the man of the house—apparently without a job and no visible means of support—stumbles from the front door each afternoon, dressed in yellow and black linens, appearing like a pregnant bumblebee?

Walter turned from the window, catching his own reflection in the bureau mirror. A life preserver of flab wrapped gently about his waist, rippling when he leaned forward, magically unfolding as he straightened up. His breasts appeared aged, infirm, like those old men in towels at the Men's Club, who discussed depreciations and mergers while leaking their insides onto the hardwood benches of the sauna. Until Marsha had left, he had worked out regularly, but now it had been close to three months since he had done anything more strenuous than hit fungoes and it looked more like three years. If only a man could fall apart in stages—lose his mind temporarily, his teeth, or fall into physical decline. At different times, each separate loss might be bearable. The man could then fall back onto the dignity of his other assets, maintain something of what he was at least.

The face he recognized. It was him, all right, but a different him than the one who used to reside there. A slight variation in coloring, a downward thrust to the nose, an awkward angle about the eyes, perhaps. Differences he could not pinpoint, the subtle changes of an acquaintance one sees every day, the altered countenance of a man who, flushed suddenly from cover, abashed at his own nakedness, has been forced to reconnoiter.

On the bureau, at the level of Walter's genitals, was a picture of Marsha framed in fool's gold. She was smiling, lips forming a gentle crease, hair oozing like whipped cream down her neck. Next to the picture was a matching set of mugs, purchased in St. Louis before she and Walter were married, before their lives had been snuffed out by living, before subtle differences had become irreconcilable ones. The mugs had been included with a brewery tour. At their hotel room, they had filled their souvenirs with the city's pride—over and over again—ending up smashed, face to face in a keg-shaped bathtub. Toweled off, ready for bed, Marsha had poured the last of the beer over Walter's unscrubbed parts. "I will drink of you," she cooed, "until I am drunk." And she had, then passed out, face down in a pillow, breathing loudly through her mouth. In the morning, freshly lathered, Walter had proposed.

His genitals sagged. Beneath the lip of the mirror, bags of pain. Pliable, ductile by design. Subject to heat-induced expansion, periodic eruptions. Swayed by base motives. Without pride. Ignorant organ. Ignorant as a shark.

He slipped into his sweatsuit and footgear. He jogged through the hallway, downstairs, over a pile of dirty laundry, through the kitchen (careful on that floor, slick with a layer of grease and mud, layered with a fine covering of dust), down the cellar stairs to what had been his gym. Standing in front of the heavy bag, face to face with the zippered front of the former pup tent, Walter carefully laced up his leather boxing gloves.

He dipped his shoulder, feinted with his head. The bag did not move. He shoved the bag; it swayed gently on its rope. He pushed harder with his gloves. He meant to pummel the bag but wished first to give it a sporting chance. He faked once more before taking a swipe. The punch missed, glancing painfully off the edge of the canvas. He swung again, catching the other side of the bag, bruising his hand on a portion of the zipper. The bag rocked, swayed confidently, seemed even to smile. Walter tore into it with both hands. *Thud. Thud. Thud.* Punching until his hands felt numb, until the bag no longer smiled, until Walter in his mind saw the former tent drop to its knees and plead *"No mas! No mas!"*

The sweat felt good. It was warm, cleansing. After picking up a jumprope, Walter counted out a series of ten one hundreds, felt the rebellion of his muscles, continued then at a steadier pace. Beneath him, a puddle of perspiration stained the cement floor black. His skin glistened. Jowls plunging, genitals knocking, ass cheeks flapping like wind-blown flags, his body was unhinged. He finished with a hundred situps.

On tiptoes, he unfastened the rope securing the heavy bag. Unsecured, the bag thudded into the cement, teetering momentarily, then dying lengthwise onto the floor. It was nothing then. A tent stuffed with rags. He wrestled it up the stairs, through the kitchen, and out the front doorway. He managed to get the bag into the Nova, into the backseat, where he secured it with a seat belt.

Back in the house, he showered, urinated without flushing the toilet, and went back to the bedroom. Dressed in clean clothes, he picked up the packed suitcases and left by the front door.

At the funeral home, I had glanced only briefly at my mother's body, lying redone in one of Joe Dorsey's caskets. Dorsey, everyone agreed, was an artist. A mess when pulled from the lake, in her coffin, Susan Innis, they said, was pretty as a picture. Even the work of the crabs had been neatly concealed. Gazing into eyes that did not gaze back—eyes lifeless as those of the moose I would later come face to face with from the bottom of an Adirondack swimming pool—I had felt nothing. Whatever that is, I told myself, it is not my mother.

The funeral itself then had held little significance for me. Others attending would have believed me callous had they known my thoughts.

His dome shining even more intensely in the afternoon sun than from beneath the chapel lights, the Reverend Beemer had raised his arms in supplication, while overhead a hawk patiently circled. From that height, I surmised, the reverend's bald head must resemble a landed mackerel perhaps, or possibly the discarded bones from someone's barbecue. As the Reverend Beemer had plunged into his eulogy, I had eyed the hawk. I watched it biding its time, wondering if and when the bird would gather up the courage to strike. I was still eyeing it long after Theodore Beemer had gassed out a final amen and the first shovelfuls of dirt had been dropped onto my mother's coffin.

Walter drove first to the Mountain View Cemetery. He had not been there since his mother's funeral—not as the result of any intense feelings for or against his mother in life, but only because he did not wish to remember what he had seen of her in death.

He could not recall the exact location of her grave. It was between three large oak trees, he recalled, but upon entering the grounds and gazing around, it seemed to him as if the entire cemetery was filled with oak. There were literally hundreds of the trees, stationed like muscular eunuchs, waving their great arms over a field of sleeping royalty.

A hundred yards or so past the entranceway, for no particular reason, he took a right-hand turn. With the same vague purpose he veered right again, onto a small dirt offshoot, going up a hill, then found himself hopelessly lost.

On the knoll above him, a man was operating a riding lawnmower. Weaving between the graves, the tractor trailed a swath of green clippings. From the Nova, Walter waved both arms at the man, motioning for him to stop, turning his hands palms-up in a show of bewilderment. After stepping from the car, he leaned against the front door and waited as the mower approached.

The driver, a black man, looked to be in his thirties. His hair was done in tiny braids—tight rows running from side to side, trailing down his neck, his entire head a carefully cultivated field. Between the rows, his scalp was the color of untouched earth. A hand-rolled cigarette was lodged behind one ear. The smell of freshly smoked marijuana was evident.

"I'm looking for a grave," said Walter.

"This be yer lucky day," said the driver, shutting off the tractor, listening to the engine's dying belch. "Best selection in town be right here."

"I mean a particular grave."

"Fer yerself," said the man, "or fer yer friend there?"

"Huh?"

"Yer friend," said the man, nodding toward the backseat of the Nova, his eyes resting on the propped-up, inert remains of Walter and Marsha's pup tent.

"No, no," answered Walter. "That's just a punching bag."

"Look like to me," said the driver, "that somebody punch him one too many time."

"Look," said Walter, "he . . . I mean, that . . . was never alive. It's just a bag full of rags. What I'm really looking for is my mother's grave."

Shifting his weight on the tractor's seat, the man leaned forward. His eyes widened, attempting to focus upon Walter through a haze of marijuana smoke.

"Folks all the time be tellin' me, workin' 'round dead white folk, even drivin' over top of 'em like I do, that it be more'n likely I run up against some weirdos, maybe even a psycho like that Bates dude—you know, the dude in that Hitchcock film? The one that done his Old Lady, then dressed up like her and went and done a whole bunch a other folk? Nasty dude, offed some poor chick right in the shower. You know the one?"

"Yeah, sure," said Walter, "I saw the movie. Listen—"

"Ya ever notice," the man interrupted him, "that psychos—I mean real psychos, kind what offs their old ladies—is always white folk?"

"I hadn't thought—"

"I seen some weirdos, all right—got one old broad shows up to every diggin' we got, all dressed up in her Sunday-go-to-meetin' clothes, cartin' flowers and snifflin' though she don't know nothin' 'bout who's gettin' put under—but up till now I ain't come across no psychos, leastwise none that I knows about." The man removed the marijuana cigarette from behind his ear and began rolling it between his fingertips. "Now, mon—you can tell me—you got your motha in that bag?"

"What?"

"How long 'go you off her?" He lit the joint, inhaled deeply, holding the smoke in for several seconds before exhaling. "Today be the day you finally gonna bury her?"

"Jesus Christ," mumbled Walter, turning away from the man, starting back toward the Nova.

"I only mow the lawn, mon. What do I care?" yelled the driver from his tractor seat. "Unburden your soul. . . . She probably deserve it nohow!"

In the Nova, Walter started the engine and drove off quickly, the car's tires spitting up gravel behind him. "No unauthorized dee-posits, mon," he heard the driver say. "They be rules, ya know!" His laughter hung in the air, trailing off finally like the trail of exhaust left by a passing plane.

Stopping the car at the top of the hill, Walter gazed out over the cemetery through the windshield. There were thousands of graves, each marked with its own headstone, each stone etched with particulars relating to the deceased—date of birth, date of death, with perhaps a quaint phrase summing up someone's view of what had occurred in between. The dates were in parenthesis, the phrases in sanserif. Somewhere in these acres of curt eulogies, he had lost his mother.

Three other mowers were at work; they buzzed about between the headstones like enraged bees. Mowing in a cemetery, thought Walter, must be almost constant. Where but on a golf course, after all, was there a greater need for manicured grass? The men operating the machines were all black; from what Walter could see, they all had corn rows. He wondered if they were all Alfred Hitchcock fans or if one among them did not regularly inhale marijuana smoke. Fearing that the cemetery may have engaged a crew of wise-cracking Rastafarians to do its manicuring, Walter gazed about for another source of directions.

To his left, a small gathering of marked graves had been arranged in a circle. Bunched tightly together, with only empty plots between them, the graves resembled a circle of covered wagons. The earth beneath one of the markers had been freshly turned. Several bouquets lay below the modest headstone. Dressed in green coveralls, with his hands clasped behind his back, a man stood next to the grave. A Yankees cap protruded from his hip pocket. Walter couldn't tell whether the man was affiliated with the grave or with the grounds. He hoped that it was the latter but that the man was not like those who mowed the lawns. Taking no chances, he reached into the backseat of the Nova and laid the punching bag lengthwise along the seat, below the level of the windows, before stepping from the car.

"Excuse me," he said. Approaching the man from behind, Walter kept his voice low in respect for the surroundings. "I was wondering, do you work here . . . at the cemetery, I mean?"

At first the man seemed startled, unsure whether Walter was speaking to him. Gazing slowly around, seeing no one else in the area, he turned back toward the grave. "I'm a visitor," he mumbled.

"I apologize for intruding," said Walter, noticing something vaguely familiar about the stranger, "but I seem to be lost."

The other man turned only his head toward Walter. "Nothing unusual about that," he said, shrugging his shoulders. Walter saw in the easy lift of the man's back, the inherited bulk of physical prowess. He saw also that he was not really a man, but only a boy.

"Pardon me?"

"It's not hard to get lost in a cemetery," said the young man. "All the graves look just alike."

"That's true," said Walter. "I can't seem to find my mother's grave."

"When did she die? If she died recently, the grave would be up here somewhere, unless you have a family plot. Down there"—he indicated with a sweep of his hand—"the plots are all reserved."

"Twenty-two years ago."

"What?"

"My mother died twenty-two years ago," said Walter, "and we have a family plot. I just don't know where it is."

The boy looked at Walter strangely, perhaps trying to ascertain whether he was suffering from some brain disorder that had affected his memory. "You've been visiting your mother's grave for over twenty years," he said, "and all of a sudden you can't find it?"

"Actually," said Walter, "I've been out of town."

"For twenty-two years?"

"Thereabouts," said Walter. He wanted to engage the boy in conversation, to hear something of the boy's own loss, for he now felt certain that he must know him. Was it the heft in the young man's shoulders or perhaps his perfect teeth? "You see, I never knew her that well."

Turning completely away from Walter, the boy stared down at the grave, kicking at the fresh dirt there. When he turned back, his face was hard but not angry. "That's too bad."

"Yes . . . well, I know they buried her between three trees," said Walter. "I'm just not sure which ones."

"Maybe if you drive around some," said the boy, obviously losing interest in the whereabouts of Walter's mother, "you'll recognize the spot."

"Yes," said Walter, starting toward the Nova, and then stopping. "I'm sorry to have bothered you."

"No trouble."

"I hope," said Walter, "that yours wasn't a close loss."

"My father and I were very close," said the young man, "until he . . . died . . . killed himself, actually."

"I'm sorry," said Walter. Struck by a fated feeling, he reluctantly turned back to face the boy. Still, he thought, in a cemetery there must be numerous such chance encounters; there was always death, after all, and there were always those left to mourn. "That's tough," he said, "for the survivors. . . ."

"He was a strong man," said the boy, "who—for a moment, at least—forgot about love and faith and family and went and did a dumbass thing. I guess he thought he had good reason, but he never made much of an effort to find out for sure. Now my mother and me are the ones who gotta live with it."

"The guilt, you mean?"

"What guilt? We loved him and that's all anyone can do. It's the loss I'm talking about . . . the loss of my old man. That's what my mother and me gotta live with . . . not having him." The boy turned away from the grave then. On the front of his coveralls, in red yarn, were the words F. WALLING, VIC'S AUTO BODY. His hands, sleeves, and pant legs were covered with grease. He smiled slightly at Walter. "One moment after he died, I figured he musta missed us like we missed him. But what did it matter then? It was too late then."

Fraser Walling was close to twenty years younger than Walter, but seemed so much older and wiser as he spoke of his father's death.

"Do you think," asked Walter, "that there is ever a good reason for someone to choose suicide?"

"Probably lots of 'em. I can think of reasons why I'd do it," said

Fraser, "but ya better be damn sure it's the right reason, is all I'm saying. 'Cause once ya do it, it's done."

If a boy's father was dead, what difference did the reason make to the boy? Of course, realized Walter, reasons ultimately do matter—but not initially, not when a child still stands angry and bewildered over a grave from which grass has not yet begun to sprout. Reasons—like the pit at the center of a peach—are what's left when all else is gone.

"Gotta get back to work," said Fraser. "A cemetery is one hell of a place to spend a lunch break, huh?" He extended his hand toward Walter, offering it self-consciously as if it would have to take the place of further words. Walter took the hand in his own and shook it, feeling the power in the boy's grip, hoping that Fraser's strength was more durable than his father's had been. "I hope you find your mother."

"She couldn't have gone far," said Walter. "In fact, I'll bet she's right where I left her."

Fraser managed a crooked smile, looking down at his feet, then back at Walter once again. "How did she die?" he asked. "Do you know?"

"Oh, yes," said Walter. "It was a boating accident. My mother was an avid fan of water sports. She particularly liked to row out onto the lake in the early morning—when no one else was around—just to enjoy the solitude of the water. She liked to pretend, I think, that she was someplace else. Anyway, one morning—probably while she was daydreaming—she got careless and fell overboard. Of course, no one was there to hear her screams."

"My father was never careless," said the boy, "and he rarely daydreamed. He was a simple man. He used to tell my mother and me that everything he wanted, he had. Then when he thought my mother had left him . . . well, I guess he musta thought there weren't a way to replace her."

"But she hadn't really?"

"No. That's the shame of it. For one second, he didn't have no faith and now here I am and here's my mother sitting home by herself, cooking three-course meals with no one but her and me to eat 'em. He made a mistake, but what good does it do to say it?"

Fraser shrugged his shoulders. A second later, he yanked the cap from his back pocket and pulled it on. Walter watched him amble off down the hill toward a rusted-out Corvair.

.   .   .

Back in the Nova, he drove down the opposite side of the hill. He had about decided to abandon the search for his mother's grave—wondering what had prompted him to undertake it in the first place other than some vague feeling that he would have to visit it sooner or later. It was something he would have to get out of the way before he could do much of anything else, so it might as well be sooner—when he came upon an area that he recognized.

Three oak trees, forming a sort of triangle, surrounded a small clump of graves. The trees were larger than they had been, of course, and there were a few more headstones than he remembered, but Walter was certain he had found the spot where Susan Innis was buried. In the clearing, above the three oaks, was where he had watched the hawk circling, praying that the bird would have enough temerity to put a sudden end to Theodore Beemer's piousness.

At the top point of the triangle was his mother's grave; adjacent to it, just off to the right, was the spot the Old Man would soon occupy. They were not prime spots, explained the proprietor. In the autumn, when the oaks shed their leaves, the graves would be covered temporarily. Also, as the trees grew, the area might encounter problems with expanding roots. But Walter's father had been swayed by the price. "What's a few leaves," he had asked his wife, "when we'll already be covered by a ton of dirt?"

The roots, in fact, had been a problem even sooner than the proprietor had anticipated. When digging Susan Innis's grave, a backhoe had been broken when its scoop became lodged beneath a root as "thick as a python," or so the hoe's operator had claimed. Upon further investigation, the entire area was discovered to contain a network of shallow, fibrous roots just beneath the earth's surface. The workmen, much in the manner of oil speculators, had poked around with shovels until they found a spot between two roots, barely large enough for a coffin. As it turned out, their measurements had been off and the coffin was a bit wider than the space. In the end, the workmen had had to wedge Walter's mother into the ground using crowbars. "At least," Kate had pointed out upon hearing of it, "we won't have to worry about her being stolen."

Now that he had found the grave, Walter was not sure what to do next. He shuffled his feet, kicking some leaves away from the head-stone, clearing the area above where he envisioned his mother's coffin to be. He had brought some flowers—a mixed bouquet, purchased at a shop conveniently located just outside the cemetery's gate. He placed the flowers next to the headstone and sat down next to his mother's grave. His mind was blank. He could summon up neither tears nor laughter. Even his memories of her seemed sparse. It was only a grave. Wherever his mother was, Walter knew, she wasn't here. Even if she were, he didn't guess he had a lot to say to her at this late date. He was alive and he was doing his best. What more would a mother wish to hear?

As he tried to summon up more vivid memories of her, he could not forget the look that he had seen on Fraser Walling's face. The boy had been hurt and confused, as might be expected, and he had been ashamed—ashamed for his father's lack of faith. Fraser would always love his father, but never again would his love be free and clear. There always would be that small touch of shame. That was the price Ed Walling had paid for a quick and merciful death.

And suddenly there was Susan Innis, in all her stately beauty, wearing her Sunday dress and the hat that looked like a bird's nest. Bending low over Walter, she planted a dry, delicate kiss upon his forehead. One eye was blackened. As she leaned over him, Walter saw her grimace from some concealed hurt. "Once you see the whole truth, Walter," he heard her whisper, "through the pain, God willing, there will be . . . love."

A small portion of her grave where the leaves had sat too long was barren of grass. Walter found a fallen twig beneath one of the oak trees and rubbed the soil beneath the leaves until it was only dirt. Using the point of the stick to write with, he scribbled into the ground:

And faith, Susan? How could we have forgotten about faith?

On his way out of the cemetery, he whistled as he drove: "My Bonnie lies over the ocean, my Bonnie lies over the sea. . . ." He hoped he would be able to find a motel with a sauna and maybe even an exercise room. After having worked out for the first time in months, Walter realized how much he had missed it. He needed to get some kind of routine back into his life, make himself lean and mean. He turned on the car radio, playing with the tuner until he located a ball game. The teams did not matter. What mattered was the game.

He was going a bit too fast, perhaps, and maybe wasn't paying enough attention as he rounded the last corner before the exit gate. Suddenly one of the lawnmowers was in the road in front of him. Swerving to miss the mower, Walter headed the Nova off into the grass, barely avoiding a tombstone, before righting the car and getting control once again.

The driver of the mower was not so fortunate. He managed to miss the tombstone he was headed for, but could not right his vehicle. The tractor teetered on two wheels—its driver clinging desperately to the seat, his braided hair bouncing along at ground level—before going over completely, ending up on its side, wheels spinning in wasted effort. The driver was thrown free, losing only some cloth from the knees of his pants and several marijuana cigarettes from his shirt pocket. It was the same man Walter had encountered earlier—the wise-cracking Rastafarian.

"You one crazy motha fuck, mon," he said to Walter, who had sprung from his car to assist him. "You close ta kill me!"

But Walter could see that the man was not overly upset; even from a sitting position in the grass, he managed to maintain the equanimity achieved through a lifetime of dope smoking. Getting slowly to his feet, smiling warily from one side of his mouth, he groped about for his lost weed.

"Now I get what the rush be," he said, gazing toward the Nova and its apparently empty backseat. "You betta say where she be buried now, mon. Didn't I say no unauthorized dee-posits?"

"I didn't bury anyone," said Walter, helping the man to right the mower. "I was just visiting my mother."

"Lookit my trousers, mon. These ain't cemetery issue, ya know? I got to pay for my own."

"I'm sorry," said Walter. He reached into his pocket, fished out a twenty-dollar bill, and handed it to the man. "This should take care of it."

The driver folded the twenty carefully then shoved it into the heel part of one of his work boots. "That'll take care the pants all right," he said, "and anotha jis like it'll take care a everythin' else."

Casting his eyes slowly about the grounds, Walter smiled. The driver and his coworkers had done a magnificent job. The entire cemetery glistened like a giant putting green. The smell of the freshly mown grass reminded Walter of Sunday afternoons on Gardner Street; in the summertime, everyone in the neighborhood mowed their lawns on that day, even the Old Man. He remembered flags flying over every house, his mother in her summer dress waiting with a pitcher of iced tea on the back porch—all four of them sitting there then, drinking iced tea, for one afternoon, at least, a perfect family portrait.

He reached into his pocket, pulled out another twenty, and paid the man. "She's buried up beneath those three oaks," he said, pointing in the direction of his mother's grave. "Make sure she doesn't get covered over with leaves."

"Now you buried her like you s'posed to, mon," said the driver, putting the new twenty in with the other one, "she gonna leave you alone. You see . . . it be right now."

"Maybe," said Walter. After getting back into the Nova, he started the ignition.

"A motha she forgive her son for killin' her," said the driver, "some of 'em maybe even deserves it. But till you give 'em a right burial, no motha never, no way, no fuckin' how, will give this mon a moment's peace."

Walter smiled and waved at the man as he put the Nova in gear. In the rearview mirror, he saw the driver methodically shaking his head, fingering the double row of joints in his shirt pocket as if they were worry beads.

CHAPTER 54

Walter found a room on Salina Street, at a place called the Lake View Inn. Why it was called an inn as opposed to an economy motel he was unable to ascertain. Perhaps by depositing a complimentary packet of instant coffee along with an aged sweet bun at the head of each bed, the management felt justified in giving the establishment a more familiar designation. Or was it that there was an open lounge area, complete with canvas-backed recliners and a coin-operated bowling machine?

The Lake View was located in what Marsha would have called the undesirable part of town, surrounded on one side by a pawnshop, on the other by a cut-rate liquor store. It was hard to imagine that Owasco Lake—or any other body of water—was visible from anywhere on the grounds. This apparent misnomer so bothered Walter that he made reference to it at the front desk, where he was given directions to the roof of the building—the clerk smiling benignly, raising his eyes toward the hallowed spot as if in silent supplication.

Once atop the building, Walter found that by stepping on a piece of plastic patio furniture, while using the roof's railing for ballast, he could indeed spot the southernmost tip of the lake. With binoculars, he might even have been able to make out a few of the buildings that dotted that portion of the shoreline.

The room, however, was not uncomfortable, and the price made it bearable. Walter, much to his chagrin, was becoming acutely aware of the transparent qualities of money; four thousand dollars, when left unnurtured, could disappear in a hurry. The forty dollars he had so nonchalantly doled out to the mower operator at Mountain View, for example, had represented 1 percent of his remaining cash assets. At such a rate, he would soon be without funds; still, the threat of poverty would not seem real until it arrived, until the moment Walter reached into his wallet and came up with nothing but his driver's license. As with the other losses in his life—childhood naïveté, for example, or, more recently, the loss of his wife—until the actual loss occurred, Walter would be aware only of a vague pinch, an unspecific pain easily attributable to innocuous causes, such as an overindulgence on Indonesian food.

It was not then with a sense of urgency that he purchased the afternoon edition of the Caulfield *Banner* and began slowly to make his way through the want ads. Sitting cross-legged on the bed, a cup of coffee in hand, the paper spread open atop his legs, he at least felt useful. Away now from the marital abode, his vision was less clouded by lurking memories of Marsha. For the moment, at least, he felt no animosity toward her; instead, he viewed her as one might the slayer of a long-suffering housepet. Of the two of them, Marsha had simply been the one closest to a gun and with the wherewithal to use it.

Calvin Motors was seeking to bolster its sales staff. "Excellent pay, good benefits," said the ad. "Must be self-motivated." What self-respecting person, wondered Walter, could be motivated to sell the kind of recycled junk that adorned Calvin's trade-in lot? Walter remembered seeing rusted-out fenders stuffed with newspapers, painted over then to make the car's body appear like solid metal; he remembered the wrecks that would be brought into the shop on the back of a truck, frames bent beyond repair, and, a few days later, seeing the same cars—miraculously reincarnated—advertised on the lot as cream puffs. In an impulse born of self-righteousness, he picked up the bedside telephone and dialed the number in the ad, a number he knew by heart. He covered the phone's mouthpiece with a pair of his underwear. The voice that answered was none other than Calvin Junior himself.

"Leonard Calvin?" asked Walter, speaking mostly through his nose, disguising his voice with a heavy downstate accent.

"Bingo! And on your very first try! New or used, my friend, we have got the car you want, at a price you *cannot* refuse."

"Robert Boulais, Mr. Calvin," said Walter, "of the State Attorney General's office."

"Don't tell me, sir! You are looking for something big. Am I right? Like maybe a late-model Lincoln? Low mileage?"

"Consumer and Criminal Affairs Division?"

"Ah-hah! Something more inconspicuous then? Something safe on a stakeout? Like maybe a simple beige Duster? Or how about a Volaré?

Nobody would ever think of looking for a cop behind the wheel of a Volaré. . . ."

"I'm not looking for a car, Mr. Calvin."

"Of course not! You sound like the kind of man who drives a truck! Am I right?"

"Didn't you get our summons?"

"Summons?" Calvin's voice became a whisper, sales puffery disappearing like a rabbit from beneath a magician's hat. "What summons?"

"It was sent by mail. When possible we try to avoid the embarrassment of personal service at someone's place of business. However, when we don't get a response—"

"What summons? I never got any summons."

"I will be blunt with you, Mr. Calvin—although I would have preferred to explain this to you in my office." Walter cleared his throat, coughing lightly before continuing. "You are under investigation for deceptive business practices."

"What?"

"Specifically, we will be looking into allegations that you have regularly turned back the speedometers of used automobiles during the preceding five years. A criminal offense, as I am sure you are aware."

"Who says we have! Jesus"—his tone now a pathetic whisper—"a criminal offense?"

"There is no need to alarm yourself prematurely," said Walter, lowering his voice slightly, as he had often heard Maurie do when speaking to a particularly irate client. "The investigation will be explained to you in detail when you arrive at my office."

"Your office? What do you mean, your office?"

"It was all in the summons, Mr. Calvin. If you would like, I can have someone come over now and personally serve you . . . perhaps even a sheriff's deputy?"

"No! No! No!" said Leonard Calvin, his words bubbling and popping over the line. "That won't be necessary! Of course we'll be glad to cooperate, Mr. . . . ah, Boulais . . . sir. Obviously a mistake has occurred. Something that the two of us—"

"The summons directs you to appear here at my office tomorrow morning at nine o'clock. You are to bring all of your records from the preceding five business years. You know where our local office is located? On Vine Street?"

"Records? My father—Calvin Senior—is the actual owner of the business. Maybe you should talk to him? I . . . Jesus . . . a criminal offense?"

"You have operated the business for the past five years?"

"Well, yes. . . ."

"That's the period of time that we're interested in."

"But . . . I'm not sure I can locate all of our records. I mean, that quickly."

"Perhaps a subpoena would help?"

"They're not exactly in order."

"Just buff 'em and puff 'em, Leonard," said Walter. "The rest will be up to us."

"Who is this?"

"Tomorrow morning at nine o'clock, Mr. Calvin. I hope it won't be necessary to send someone out to assist you," said Walter, before hanging up the phone, fearing at any moment that his accent would give way to laughter. It would take Calvin hours before he bothered to call and check on Mr. Boulais's credentials, even longer than that to think to call his own lawyer. At the moment, he was no doubt scurrying around, frantically trying to doctor the company's records for the last five years. It would be a difficult task—Walter had seen cars come onto the lot with over a hundred thousand miles on their speedometers and go back out with less than half that amount.

Curled into a ball of mirthful bliss, shivers of hilarity shaking his body, Walter laughed out loud. He was instantly energized, his sense of balance momentarily restored. If Jacob Johnson could only see him now. Walter's conversation with Leonard Calvin had been the type of gag that would have made the old sheetmetal worker proud. Seriousness, perchance, was not fatal after all; like the skin of a snake, perhaps a man could shed its morose trappings over time. One day, Walter's eyes— like Jacob Johnson's—might sparkle brazenly out at the world.

Unfurling his arms and legs, Walter came up again to a sitting position on the bed. He picked up the newspaper, spreading the want ads section across his outstretched legs. The print was clear and concise, with opportunities that suddenly seemed abundant. Walter's future was in no one's hands but his own. His finger flowed down the page, in a gentle current of its own making.

It passed by several opportunities to do what Walter had already done—to sell refrigerators and take a commission, to sell water beds and take both a commission and a salary, to peddle vacuum cleaners door to door or insurance premiums in his own house. There was nothing wrong with buying or selling—it just seemed to Walter that for his entire life he had done nothing but that.

Halfway down the page was an advertisement for coaches for the coming school year. Included among the openings was a coach for the varsity baseball team at Caulfield Junior Senior High. Walter dialed the number given and asked for Ronald Spankly, the school's athletic director.

"Innis, eh?" Mr. Spankly said. "Any relation to Victor Innis?"

"He was my father."

"Was?"

"Is."

"I thought so. I read about him just recently in the Sunday paper. It was a nice piece, I thought. He seemed quite proud of you." When Walter didn't answer, Mr. Spankly continued. "My own father graduated a year behind Victor, still remembers when he used to play. In those days—when your father was pitching—they would fill the bleachers, not like today when we can barely get enough money for uniforms. Course there aren't many players around like your father either—a sure major leaguer, I guess, if he didn't get injured. A real shame."

"Yes," said Walter, "it was a tragedy."

"How about you? You play at all?"

"Some."

"And you're coaching now, according to the article?"

"Yes."

"Well, we're always looking for coaches," said Mr. Spankly. "It doesn't pay much, I'm afraid, and the schedule is quite demanding. Do you work during the day?"

"My hours are flexible," said Walter.

"I see. What do you know about girls' lacrosse?"

"Not much," said Walter. "I guess they use sticks, huh?"

"Right."

"Why?"

"Well, when possible we like to get folks who will coach more than one sport," said Mr. Spankly. "You see, baseball doesn't start until the spring and . . . well, we need somebody for girls' lacrosse in the fall."

"I guess you've probably got a rule book I could borrow?"

"No problem. If you read it, you'll know more than half the coaches in the league."

"I guess coaching is coaching."

"And kids are kids," added Mr. Spankly. "Why don't you stop by my office in the next week or so and we'll have a chat. If we can accommodate your schedule, I'm sure you would be an asset to our program."

"Fair enough," said Walter, "I'll stop in sometime next week."

Walter got up from the bed and went over to his suitcase. He removed a yellow pad and pencil, then sat down at a three-legged desk in the corner of the room. The desk was actually a bureau covered with cheap varnish, its top a collage of assorted stains and rings left by countless coffee cups. Walter placed his own half-empty cup on top of the bureau.

He spent the next half hour making out his line-up card for the Meat Market season finale. Wally Seymour would pitch, of course. In his last couple of starts, Wally's control had shown signs of improving. Walter had convinced him to take something off his fastball—even at that there were few hitters in the league who could touch it—and now Wally was getting at least one of every four pitches, as opposed to one of every six or seven, in the strike zone. The problem was, sometime during the course of each game Wally would unravel completely. Then he'd no longer be able to throw the ball into the ocean if he were standing next to it. When that point arrived, Walter would have to bring in another pitcher, and so far he had no one else able to get the ball consistently to the plate, much less across it.

Walter decided to move Billy Palumbo to the lead-off spot in the batting order. Billy had brought his average up close to the three hundred mark, and when he couldn't get a hit he would look for other ways to get on base. He'd turned into an aggressive base runner as well, never afraid to go for the extra base, always sliding into the bag spikes first. Walter smiled when he thought back to the shy Billy at the beginning of the season—how he had stood in the shadows of the batting cage tying and untying the knots in his glove. Then Walter frowned as he recalled that Billy no longer talked to him, not on account of the kid's own shyness but as a matter of choice.

Rusty Tillman was Walter's clean-up hitter. Rusty was connecting more often than he had in the beginning of the season, and now he waited until he had safely reached base before breaking into his uncontrollable fits of laughter. Rusty's complexion, however, had not improved; new pimples appeared on his face with the frequency of summer bugs on a windshield. Concerned with the effect that all of these pimples might have on Rusty's confidence—and noticing that the boy never seemed to be without a candy bar or Hostess cupcake—Walter finally made up his mind to speak to Mrs. Tillman about her son's diet. Following the team's most recent loss, he had leaned into the bleachers where Mrs. Tillman, finishing a postgame beer, occupied nearly half of the bottom row of seats. "Does it seem to you," he had asked, "that Rusty eats an awful lot of candy?"

"No more than other kids," replied Mrs. Tillman, sloshing beer onto her skirt, her moon face turning the color of her son's hair. "No more than me or my husband."

"Perhaps if he were to eat a more balanced diet," suggested Walter, "his pimples would disappear."

"Would it make him a better hitter?"

"Probably not."

"Well," she had said, then belched, "since it's your job to coach 'im and my job to feed 'im, what's it to ya?"

"Without the pimples, Rusty might not be so self-conscious."

"It ain't pimples that bother Rusty," Mrs. Tillman had replied, "it's all the time losin'. Pimples ain't nothing next to losin'." Walter did not have an answer for Mrs. Tillman. He could not argue with her logic. Her son had pimples and one day he might be as big as his mother but—unless the Meat Market fortunes changed for the better—the most lasting stigma from that summer would be the team's hapless record.

But Walter had done all he could. It might not be apparent in the team's record, but the Market was a much better ball club than it had been at the beginning of the season. Walter had seen improvement in nearly every player. Skills, no matter how limited, had been honed;

confidences, if only slightly, had been bolstered. Despite appearances to the contrary, it had not been a wasted summer. Over the winter, the players would dwell on small victories—a raised batting average, a perfect day in the field—and dream of larger ones. Next year, thought Walter, we might win the championship.

Sitting there, looking at the names on the Market roster, putting a face with each name, he was aware of some intruder moving rapidly within him; like a diver out of air, it rushed upward and was suddenly upon him. Walter was embarrassed to feel tears well up in his eyes without apparent reason. People—men, Walter specifically—did not cry over baseball teams. He did not recognize this emotion, so foreign did it feel, so out of sync with anything he had felt.

He leaned back, closed his eyes, and pressed his thumbs against the lids. He had not cried when Marsha had left him or when his mother had died or even on that terrible day at the Truxton estate. He had not cried, in fact, since the day he had thrown his baseball mitt into a trash barrel and he and Maurie Winthrop had sworn never to cry again. Yet he was crying now. And about what? The fortunes of a Little League baseball team? The irony made him laugh, but still the tears did not stop.

He quit laughing, felt a slight calming, and opened his eyes. Tears rolled like wet, soothing tracers down his cheeks and still he did not understand why. With the Market he had made an effort, done his absolute best to be a successful coach. Yet if success was measured in wins and losses, then he had failed. But that, he knew, was not why he was crying. Was it that he was proud? Could it be that simple? That he had done his best at something and the only ones who counted—himself and the Market players—were the better for it?

Christ! How he hated people who needed to define everything they felt, as if it didn't mean anything unless they did. When someone starts to cry, he told himself, he should ask but one question: Do I feel good or do I feel bad? Walter had to admit that, despite everything, at the moment at least, he did not feel bad—although for the life of him, he could not figure out why and, goddamn it, he was not going to try. He didn't want to tinker with the feeling or ask too much, but, still, to win a ball game would be a fine coup de grâce.

Wiping his eyes, he got up from the desk, tore off the sheet of paper containing the line-up, folded it into quarters, carried it over to the closet, and stuck it into the pocket of his Meat Market uniform. Then he changed into his sweatsuit and walked over to where the heavy bag slumped over a lounge chair. After lugging it over to the center of the room, he climbed onto the bed and hung the bag from the overhead lamp support. Anyone looking through the window would likely believe that there had been a murder or suicide at the inn.

It would be a light workout—after all, he had exercised that morning for the first time in almost three months. Still, Walter felt a need to become deeply entrenched in his reborn obsession. By doing this one thing each day—by pummeling a senseless bag—he hoped never again to reach the point of total alienation. If the whole world became suddenly strange, if the words of friends became like those of strangers, he would still have the bag. Its senselessness, to Walter, was its greatest virtue; being of dense origins, the bag would never change. Even a dog could turn mean or run away, but a tent full of rags could be nothing but consistent.

After finishing his workout, he unhooked the bag and tossed it back onto the easy chair. Glancing into the mirror before taking his shower, Walter imagined that he appeared leaner, more fit for whatever came next. By the time he had finished showering and had changed into a clean pair of clothes, it was dark out and time for dinner.

On Salina Street, two blocks down from the Lake View, he found a take-out Italian restaurant, Mama Nina's, where he ordered a meatball submarine sandwich, along with two cans of light beer and a quart of potato salad, all of which he brought back to the inn.

In the lounge, before going upstairs, he drank one of the beers and bowled a game on the bowling machine with the night clerk. When it looked like the clerk was going to try to engage him in conversation, Walter excused himself and went up to his room. Propped up on the bed, he spread the food out between his outstretched legs, opened the second beer, and placed it on the nightstand. The Yankees were playing the Red Sox on television. The game was close. If he knew how, Walter would have frozen the moment, singed it indelibly into one corner of his mind, as a constant reminder that, after everything was said and done, what was best in life was rudimentary.

A light breeze blew through the open window, a chattering, befuddled wind that belonged neither to summer nor fall. This confused air, Walter knew, was nothing more than a premonition, fair warning to those carefree souls who believed that summer would never end. Outside the window, Walter heard the customers at the cut-rate liquor store as they came and went, the glass door jangling on its hinges, the customers' cars idling and then roaring into the night. Exiting the store, two men chose a spot just beneath Walter's window to discuss what the night held in store.

He fell asleep in the top of the ninth inning with the Yankees up by a score of four to one. He awoke, still in the dark, to the sound of the eleven o'clock news: ". . . the sudden and unexpected withdrawal by the Caulfield millionaire and former front-runner evidently came as a surprise even to those closest to his campaign. In a short, prepared statement, Henry Truxton III, citing a desire to spend more time with his family, apologized to his many supporters . . ."

There was a night one summer when the noise of my parents drove me from the house. The Old Man had arrived home before my mother and sat down to watch a retrospective broadcast on the McCarthy hearings. He would comment occasionally upon the proceedings. The comments were not insightful, but boozy editorials on imagined improprieties— the swarthy youth of McCarthy's counsel, the hushed tones of the television narrator. The witch hunts were a blot in history, their progenitor dead of alcoholism. My father's fervor had long since subsided. His marine uniform, shed forever, had been laid to rest in mothballs. He was then but a casual observer, a man who'd drunk too many beers while waiting for his wife to come home.

She had gone to the Truxton estate to help out with a Friday night bash and did not arrive home until several hours later. The accusations and rebuttals, the threats and reprisals, had started immediately. They had moved through the house below me, stalking each other like bored cats in a zoo runway. I had not waited for the final confrontation, that moment just beyond sputtered words, when frothy, rabid rage was all too predictable. Without being seen, I went downstairs via the back stairway, moving quickly through the kitchen and safely onto the back porch.

In the backyard, the stars were close, bright, like a million friendly eyes that would watch but never tell. After the sounds inside, the night noises were calm and soothing. I moved to the back portion of the yard, just beyond the pitching mound, where the grass met the woods bordering the next house. Spreading my jacket on the moist grass, I lay down and gazed upward, pretending I was someplace far away.

Something Bill Hurley had once told me came back to me then. "Walter," he had said, "there ain't nobody that thinks more of your old man than I do, but I got to tell ya, the way he went and ruined his whole future on account of some goddamned five-spot bet is one of the worst tragedies I ever seen."

Thinking about it that night, what Bill had said gnawed at me. It got into my head and started rattling about, stirring up questions that must have been there all along, only not until that moment had I known about them. Questions that I was not sure I wanted to know the answers to. Since, for example, Kate and I—and my mother, for that matter—had all come along after the Old Man had injured his arm, did that make us a part of his future? And if my father had ruined his future like Bill Hurley had said, where did that leave the rest of us?

And there, lying on the wet grass of the backyard, I closed my eyes and thought backward. Later I would swear I had not been dreaming at all but had simply traveled back by some power of my own concentration to a place I had once been. But I could never be absolutely certain that that was the case, for when I awoke several hours later it was as if from a dream. My trousers were damp from the grass, the darkness had lifted, and I was sure of what I had seen.

Snugly tucked within my mother's abdomen, I was no larger than a spool of thread. I was upside down, of course, gazing up, peering at where the sky should have been. Confined within such narrow quarters, there was no place to hide, no escaping the fact of my own vulnerability. Sounds reached me, voices, incessant like the hammering of woodpeckers, nearby rumblings that seemed to be the sounds of my own creation.

Discussions without words—for I did not possess the power of language, only a primeval knowledge of unspoken gestures—jostled my fragile cradle of fluid and jelly. The vibrations were sometimes gentle—warm and comforting, like a mother's soft push upon her baby's cradle—and then I would reach out with a tiny arm, fingers not yet formed, to touch its source. Other times, the sounds were harsh and frightening, their touch like shivers of cold steel, and I would shrink from them, panicked that I had no place to hide, dreading the day I would have to leave even these thin walls of protection.

I had attempted then to go back even farther, to see what I had been before they had got hold of me, before they began to mold me with their own sweet confections of love and misery. Blackness, not like that which comes with the setting of the sun, but an expulsion of all earthly light, enveloped me. I heard a noise like the wind makes when whistling through a half-open window. Yet I could not ascertain from where exactly the sound was coming. Try as I would, I could not transcend the blackness. I could not get back any farther, yet there was no end in sight. Something was there, but it was not of this world.

When I awoke I felt better than I had. I felt I knew something more about the world than did Bill Hurley. The world—the wet, green grass of which was soaking through my pants, the same world in which heroes became drunks and bomb shelters were turned into pitching mounds—had its limits. Bill Hurley, in short, was full of shit. Nobody lives, dies, gets rich, or fucks up their arm other than within those limits. If the Old Man had destroyed his future, it had happened while I was in another world, beyond the limits of his steel vibrations. My own future was still up for grabs. I was thirteen years old then, and never again had I gone back to listen to Bill Hurley speak of my father. A short time later I met Maurie Winthrop and threw my baseball mitt into a trash can in the junior high school corridor.

CHAPTER 56

"How would you feel," asked Walter, lifting the beak of his cap, scratching at the sparseness beneath it, "about the idea of expanding?"

"Expanding?"

"The Meat Market. Well, not really expanding, but—you know—taking on a partner?"

"Why would I want a partner?"

"It might lessen your workload, maybe at the same time increase the profits."

"Whose profits? Mine or my partner's?"

"Both. I mean, having a partner might mean a new infusion of ideas—it might enable you to move the business into a bigger building, perhaps do more advertising."

Walter and Jeannie were sitting on the bleachers behind the ballfield at Yendes's Park. Game time was still an hour away, but Walter had asked his players to arrive early for the last game of the season. He had wanted to be sure that they were not caught unawares by the condition of the field, it still being somewhat mangled from the previous weekend's moto cart races. In agreeing to schedule the races, the park supervisor had apparently decided that a few tire ruts in the infield would not adversely affect a team that was 0 and 24.

The players were divided into groups of twos and threes, engaged in games of pepper and hot potato on the outfield grass; a couple of them, with rakes, were working to smooth out the infield. Billy Palumbo was throwing a ball against a mesh backstop, anticipating where the ball would bounce, scurrying to the spot and lowering his glove a moment before it arrived. He had come with his mother in the family station wagon, the car trailing a cloud of dust as it pulled in next to Walter's Nova.

A brief discussion had followed within the wagon—Jeannie talking animatedly from behind the wheel, Billy listening without apparent comment—before the two had stepped from opposite sides of the car. Waving nonchalantly at Walter, Billy had pulled at the crotch of his Market trousers and trudged off doggedly toward the backstop. His mother—large and loyal in a yellow and black pants suit that matched the Market uniforms—smiled shyly and took her old spot in the bleachers.

"The worst mistake that a successful business can make, Walter, is to overexpand. There's a tendency to become flushed with one's own success, to think that the market is infinite, the profits never-ending. You move into a new building, take on a giant monthly mortgage, only to find out that nobody cares, that the community has only so many meat eaters—most of whom you already sell to. Next thing you know you're struggling just to make the overhead."

"So, forget expansion," said Walter, lowering the bill of his cap and tugging on it firmly. "Wouldn't you like a little more free time?"

"What for? To watch soap operas?"

It wasn't as if Walter had awakened from sleep at the Lake View and seen clearly the course he must take. His was the mind of a schemer, a mind that mulls and homogenizes various particles of truth, hoping then to eventually arrive at some pure blend of happiness. He missed Jeannie—that is, he preferred life with her as opposed to without her. He missed Billy as well. And even Spatula. It's true that he often believed that the three of them were acting in concert to trap him, to bring him irrevocably into the family fold. He feared that they might so smother him with family intrigue and pancakes that he would never again be his own man. Yet even these fears seemed no longer to matter; after all, if a man wishes to be caught and finally is, he can hardly blame those who have set the trap.

Did all of this mean that he was in love? Walter did not know nor did he much care. The fact was, he had not much trusted the word nor his own judgment on what the word might possibly mean ever since Marsha had left.

Even after all of their actions began to speak otherwise, Marsha and Walter had continued to tell each other that they loved one another, as if the word were a life preserver to which they both desperately clung. Very early in their marriage, Marsha concluded that Walter had permanently stagnated, that he would never rise beyond being a used car salesman, that, married to Walter, she would never rise beyond being a used car salesman's wife. Along with the knowledge of Walter's limitations came misery for Marsha; only the thought of being alone was worse and, finally, even that had seemed more bearable. Somehow, all this misery had been Walter's fault—at least in Walter's mind it had become his fault—and all because he had told Marsha that he loved her.

No. He could not trust definitions. He could not believe words, even his own words, for someone was sure to misinterpret them. So what remained? For Walter, after all was said and done, there was only stimuli—and a vague desire for partnership.

"What are you saying, Walter? That you know someone who's looking to get into the meat business?"

"Maybe," said Walter, "although this person doesn't have much cash."

"Does he have any expertise?"

"He can walk and chew gum at the same time. I have heard he is an experienced lover."

"Is he a butcher?"

"No."

"Does he know anything at all about the meat business?"

"Not a lot—although he is a quick study."

"What about customers? Are there any new customers that he might persuade to patronize the market?"

"None, other than himself."

"What can he offer me, Walter?"

"Well . . ."

"Why should I make him a partner? Is he looking for a free ride?"

"He just wants," said Walter, "to invest in something. To be part of a growing concern."

"Invest, Walter . . . or dabble?"

Billy Palumbo had turned the backstop far back on its hinges, so that when a ball was tossed against the net it would pop straight up into the air. Walter watched as Billy slammed one into the netting and then drifted backward, waiting for it to drop lazily into his glove. Walter was too far away to hear the pop the ball made as it settled into Billy's mitt.

"No. He's not a speculator, if that's what you mean. He's looking to make a solid investment, to put all that he's got into something."

"What's he expect to get out of it?"

"Something . . . that's real, that will last for a while."

"An honest day's pay for an honest day's work?"

A great invention, thought Walter, the one-man backstop. How many idle hours he could have filled if he had had access to a backstop as a child—throwing the ball and then catching it, not needing a playmate, not even needing a father really. All he had had was the side of a garage and then—once the paint had started to chip and the noise of the ball thudding into the wood had begun to disturb other families in the neighborhood—not even that. If only Victor had purchased a backstop for his son. Perhaps then, thought Walter, neither of them would have felt so much guilt in the other's absence.

"Yes, an honest effort . . . his best effort. That he would guarantee."

"That's all?"

"Results are tough to foresee, of course. I mean, life is fraught with so many uncertainties. . . ."

"Particularly in the meat business," said Jeannie. "So much in the meat business is uncertain. Who knows, for example, when there will be a shortage of beef or lamb or when a popular cut will suddenly become unpopular?"

"This fellow I'm thinking of has an adaptable nature. He tries always to stay abreast of the times and is not inflexible in his approach to business."

"In the meat business, the latest trend can wipe you out. Every day it seems people are giving up on meat entirely and becoming vegetarians—for the rest of their lives saying that they will never again eat something that isn't grown in dirt."

"With a partner," said Walter, "one would think it might become easier to weather those times . . . to see them through, until the pendulum swings the other way. I don't know—I never considered myself much of an optimist—but I think we are basically a society of meat eaters."

"You do?"

"Yes. I mean, I was a vegetarian for a while, that is, I told myself that's what I was. I ate nothing but fruits and vegetables. I lost weight—people said I looked good—but I started to feel weak, everything tasted the same. You know, no matter how you season or blend vegetables, they're all quite bland."

"And they don't stick to your ribs."

"Right. Not once during that period did I have a solid bowel movement."

"I could never live with a vegetarian."

"Nor I. I mean, they're such finicky people, twittering from zucchini to summer squash to lima beans to chickpeas to tofu. They never seem able to settle on one vegetable, whereas I could eat a steak every night."

"Every night? Surely you're exaggerating?"

"No. Well, different cuts perhaps—"

She placed her hand over Walter's mouth, cutting him off in midsentence. The hand rested on his lips for a moment and then she dropped it back into her lap. A second later, she picked the hand up again and dropped it like a stone into Walter's lap. She found his hand and wound her fingers into his.

They gazed out together at the field, an inch or two of painted wood dividing them at the hips. Walter listened as Jeannie breathed—each breath slow and deliberate, as if breathing for her was an acquired discipline and not an involuntary act. She swallowed once and it seemed to disconcert her. Closing her eyes, she began taking in oxygen again with a loud, sucking noise.

Unmasked by clouds, the sun landed on the field like a spotlight from heaven. The breeze was gentle, with a subtle hint of fall. Baseballs plopped softly into cowhide mitts. Voices rose, sharp and echoless, in the unfettered air. Overhead, an early V of geese got a jump on winter, the noise of their southward honking sounding like polite laughter.

On the pitching mound, Wally Seymour lay on his back, casually tossing a ball into the air and catching it as it came back down. The pitching rubber served as Wally's pillow; he dreamed, perchance, of how humble he would remain, even after he had made it to the big leagues and had tossed a no-hitter in the seventh game of the World Series. Rusty Tillman was hitting fungoes to a group of players in the outfield—his mind, no doubt, dwelling upon a mountain of junk food. Three or four other team members were doing cartwheels between second and third base.

"When I called the other day," said Jeannie, not turning to look at Walter, but still gazing in earnest at the activity in the field, "there was something I wanted to bring up but couldn't. It seemed, suddenly, so out of context."

"Out of context?"

"And silly—I mean, I am thirty-seven years old."

"Of course," said Walter. "Why was it out of context?"

"Well, maybe it isn't now. I don't know. But I want you to know that it doesn't have to have anything to do with you or me—at least in relation to the future. It's just that I thought you should know."

"Know what?"

A boy jumped down from the right-field fence. He was dressed not in a Market uniform, but in blue denim from head to foot. In such attire—against the bright Market colors—he somehow looked forbidding. He began walking toward a group of players in center field.

"We must decide whether or not to have this child."

"What child?"

"Your child. Apparently there was an ill-timed blowout, something I never told you about, a manufacturer's defect in my diaphragm— something we may or may not wish to explore with Maurie Winthrop."

"Mother of God."

"Having it or not is something I thought I should discuss with you."

Play had suddenly stopped. Everyone but Billy Palumbo was gathered in the outfield. The players were bunched in a circle, as if watching some activity within its center. Even Wally Seymour, rising from the mound, had ambled out to see what was happening.

"But they are each individually tested . . . hermetically sealed. . . ."

"What?"

"Diaphragms. Each one is tested on a machine, blasted by jets of water from a fire hydrant."

"By who, Walter? Not by me they aren't! Jesus! Who in their right mind has a fire hydrant in their bedroom?"

"They're bombarded with ball bearings, bounced on like trampolines."

"What's the point in analyzing things that have already happened? What will you change, Walter? It happened, that's all! Sometimes—in the real world—things just happen!"

"Yes, of course. I'm sorry."

In the outfield, the circle of boys was moving back and forth as if trying to escape a writhing snake. Loud shouts came from the center of the circle. Timmy Mealus, the smallest of the Market players, was running toward the bleachers, yelling for Walter, in his hysteria mispronouncing Walter's name. "Mr. Inny! Mr. Inny! Come quick! Come quick!"

"I have no moral reservations about abortion," said Jeannie. "God knows, there are enough unloved children in this world. I'm not one of those people who believes that abortion is murder. On the other hand, it seems pointless, if the prospects for love are good."

They both got to their feet, standing on the bottom row of bleachers, waiting for Timmy Mealus to scamper across the infield. Timmy's cap blew off and was caught by the wind. His tiny arms pumped furiously as he ran.

"Think about it, Walter. You know a little something about love," said Jeannie, stepping from the bleachers down to the ground. "We'll talk about prospects after the ball game."

CHAPTER 57

Timmy Mealus would have run right through Walter and Jeannie and into the bleachers if Jeannie had not grabbed one arm and Walter the other. His momentum carried the little right fielder completely off the ground. Squirming between Jeannie and Walter, he pedaled his legs in the air, pedaling nearly out of his uniform. At first he was too unhinged to get his message out. Walter and Jeannie placed him back onto the field, Walter pulling Timmy's trousers back above his waist, Jeannie kneeling down and tucking in his shirt.

"What is it, Timmy?" she asked. "What's the matter?"

"It's Bobby Burns!"

"Who?"

"Bobby Burns! He hit Rusty in the privates!"

"Who," asked Jeannie, "is Bobby Burns?"

"Jesus!" said Walter. "He was your clean-up hitter!"

"Now I remember," she said, running to keep up with Walter and Timmy as they began to sprint toward the outfield. "The boy you threw off the team. The one who threatened to castrate you!"

"Right," said Walter.

"He showed up when we were playin' pepper," said Timmy, "and started makin' fun of Rusty's pimples!"

"Son of a bitch!" said Walter.

"He did have a filthy mouth," said Jeannie, "as I remember."

"He's always hittin' below the belt," said Timmy. "He thinks it's funny!"

As they approached the ring of Market players, the shouting increased. Some yelled for Walter to hurry. Others appeared to be yelling at the two boys who were in the center of the ring. Some of the players stood quietly to one side, hands on hips, gazing at their own feet.

Walter plunged into the middle of the circle, making a path through the crowd. Rusty lay on his back, attempting to cover his face with his hands, as Bobby Burns, sitting on his chest, flailed away at him with his fists. Blood oozed through the spaces between Rusty's fingers; the front of his uniform was ripped open, so that his stomach showed through. Even here—on the white skin on Rusty's belly—were pimples.

"What's going on here?" shouted Walter. He reached down and snagged Bobby Burns by the back of the neck. The former clean-up hitter looked up, snarling, lashing out at Walter with his right hand. Grabbing the hand, Walter twisted it behind Bobby's back and held it that way while looking around the circle of players.

"Jesus!" he shouted. "How could you just stand there and let somebody beat on another player like that?"

Rusty was sputtering and crying through a stream of blood, most of which seemed to come from his nose and mouth. Breaking through the circle of players, Jeannie knelt down next to Rusty. Cradling his head in her lap, she wet her handkerchief with saliva and dabbed gently at the bruised spots, cooing all the while like the gentlest of doves.

"He's your teammate, for Christ sake!"

"It was a fair fight," mumbled a boy in the back.

"It wasn't fair!" shouted Walter. "Rusty's not a fighter! He's a first baseman!"

"Bobby Burns is a bully," said another boy in a small, pathetic voice. "We was afraid he might hurt us."

"There is only one of him!" screamed Walter, shaking Bobby Burns with one hand, gesticulating madly with the other. "You're a team! Haven't I taught you anything?"

"Why don't ya yell at him?" asked Todd Bailey, pointing to where Bobby Burns squirmed at the end of Walter's arm. "He's the one that beat Rusty up."

Walter only waved in disgust and did not answer. He shoved Bobby Burns away then, telling him to go home, warning him never to set foot on Yendes or any other ball field again. Bobby Burns blew loudly through his nostrils, opening holes of anger, as he sulked off. Once safely out of reach, he stopped and looked back, his tiny eyes darting and moving, never resting, like fish that must swim forever or die.

"You're all a bunch of losers," he hissed. "Sissies and losers! You won't never win a game!"

Walter had hoped for so much more from this team. If nothing else, he had wanted them to gather from the season some sense of team spirit. He was dismayed to find that, even in the face of twenty-four defeats, they could not summon up more courage. And yet they had gained something, some intangible thing that, even if the players themselves could not yet see, Bobby Burns had seen. Why else, after all, had he bothered to come back and taunt his old teammates?

Walter remembered when he himself had been rescued from the wrath of two boys much larger than he; he recalled the sick, helpless fear that had enveloped him as he lay on the ground and the gratitude he had felt afterward toward his savior. Maurie Winthrop had not withered at the sight of Stanley Ball and Cleeve Seward; he had not cowered at the specter of Henry Truxton. Maurie would have been a great ballplayer—a natural, thought Walter, one of those rare souls who was born with an unobscured vision of team loyalty.

"If you have learned nothing about loyalty," said Walter, "then the season has been a waste!"

Around the circle, several players' heads were bowed in shame. Some rubbed their chins or kicked dejectedly at the dirt, others tiptoed up to where Rusty Tillman lay with his head in Jeannie Weatherrup's lap. She had wiped away most of the blood and was running her hand gently over Rusty's forehead. Trying to smile, Rusty dabbed at his eyes with a shirt sleeve. Near the left-field wall, Bobby Burns lingered. In right field, Billy Palumbo tossed a ball against the mesh backstop and hurried after it.

But we are not all so lucky as Maurie, realized Walter. At birth, most of us do not have such a clear vision of where our loyalties will lie. For most, youth is a more cluttered path than that, one dotted with bloodied friends and losing seasons, where occasional acts of cowardice are offset by equal portions of strength. Youth is where corners are not wholly turned, but sniffed at and backed out of several times over; it is a time for, if nothing else, learning about life's prospects. Yes, Walter, a coach must always be on the lookout for prospects.

"Anything broken, Rusty?"

"No, sir."

"Anything hurt so bad that a Hostess Twinkie won't cure it?"

"No, sir."

"Well, let's get you over to the bleachers and let you lie down for a while."

"Mr. Innis?"

"What is it, Rusty?" The pimples glowed in his cheeks, so that—lying faceup in Jeannie's lap—he appeared to have bloomed there. Strangely, the boy had never seemed so animated; as he spoke, Walter could detect barely a trace of his customary giggles.

"I don't want to miss the game."

"Today?"

"Yes, sir. You see, I told my mother we were going to win today. She already baked a double-layer chocolate cake with vanilla frosting and M and Ms on top—that's how sure I was we would win. But if we won and I wasn't playing . . ."

"There'll be other games."

"Not like this one. We were going to have a party. She bought three half gallons of Heavenly Hash."

"Let's see how you feel at game time," said Walter. "If you feel all right and your mother doesn't mind, you can be sure I'll let you play. How well do you think we would do without our clean-up hitter?"

Walter and Jeannie helped Rusty to his feet. The wounds were mostly superficial. Once Rusty's nose and mouth stopped bleeding, it was apparent that his teeth were all intact; they worked perfectly when he smiled. Bobby Burns, he said, had hit him only once below the belt, enough to take Rusty's breath away and to prevent him from offering any kind of a defense.

Each taking an arm, Jeannie and Walter assisted Rusty to the sidelines. They found a cool spot beneath the bleachers where he could rest and watch practice, without having to worry about being hit by a baseball. He lay down on a blanket, a wet washcloth pressed to his head and with two Milky Way bars for sustenance. He seemed quite comfortable, chewing on a candy bar, using one of Jeannie Weatherrup's thighs as a headrest.

Walter left them there and walked over to where he had parked the Nova. In the car's trunk, along with his golf clubs, an old leather basketball, and his fishing rod, was where Walter stored the Market's equipment between games. With only a half hour left before the start of the game, he still had not removed the bats and bases from the trunk, equipment he would need in order to run infield practice. Walter preferred to take his team through pregame drills before the other team arrived, so that he could make suggestions and offer gentle criticisms without causing the players embarrassment in front of the opposition.

As he searched through the debris of the Nova, Walter worried about how the team would respond to the afternoon's excitement. He hoped that he had not been too hard on the players and that the incident involving Rusty Tillman would inspire the team rather than demoralize it. Don't you see, he had wanted to shout at them, that Bobby Burns is afraid? Afraid that you may have gained while he has lost? But in shouting out such a thing, he sensed that he would only cause the message to be irretrievably lost.

Gazing out toward right field, he saw Billy Palumbo slowly making his way in from the outfield. Beneath one arm he carried the collapsible backstop; over the opposite shoulder he balanced a bat. Watching Billy trudge along in his slow but determined gait, Walter realized again—as he had on the previous evening, while lying on his bed at the Lake View Inn—how basic were the ingredients to happiness. Sincere and simple things—like a solid single to left field that a man has seen a thousand times but still applauds, a pat on the ass for love or effort—were all that it took to make boys of any age happy. On a team that was 0 and 24, Billy was a winner. Walter wondered if Billy was able to see that for himself. Right after the game—win or lose—they would talk and Walter would tell him so.

Standing there, Walter had a vision of the future. He imagined how nice it would be when they were all under one roof, a family of four— Walter and Billy and Jeannie and the Unborn One. Of course Jeannie would give birth to her and Walter's child; and of course Walter would be there when she did. Theirs would not be a static child, but a kicking, screaming, male or female, complete with accessories. Unlike Jeannie, Walter would not delude himself with thoughts of other options.

Walter knew something about options. He had once traveled backward and seen just where options begin and end. After the void of darkness, he remembered, there was a small cavern of vulnerability where the smallest children slept; there, in that cavern without options, even a harsh word could send shivers through a child's spine. What might more serious talk cause? What might mumbled threats of termination do to one so young?

After all is said and done, thought Walter, this must be what life comes down to—painting oneself into a corner until, with no place left to go, the little patch one is left standing on becomes one's home. How long after that, he wondered, before everything beyond simply disappears? Ah well, he thought, better a small, warm patch than no patch at all.

Billy Palumbo had quickened his gait. Having dropped the backstop, he appeared now to be running. He waved at Walter. Walter waved back, smiling. Billy began then to wave more frantically—not as a form of greeting this time but with both hands, as if being attacked by a swarm of bees. He yelled something to Walter that Walter didn't catch. Walter cupped a hand to one ear, at the same time becoming aware of a rustling noise directly behind him. Then Billy shouted again and this time Walter heard what he said. "Look behind you!"

Walter turned around then and saw Bobby Burns with a bat in his hands. Bobby's eyes—empty of prospects, full only of hate—grew big as baseballs. Walter was aware of the bat coming forward with tremendous velocity and of his own hands going up to protect his face.

Hearing the bat connect with his skull, Walter recalled what a fine hitter Bobby Burns could have been. The boy had been blessed with natural talent and let it go to waste. If only he had developed self-discipline and had not had such a fixation on male genitalia.

As he fell gracefully backward—feeling himself land gentle as a badminton birdie in the grass—Walter saw Jeannie leap on top of Bobby Burns, preventing Bobby from taking another swing. He heard other players join the fray. And as his vision went dusty and he slipped rather than fell into blackness, Walter thought how quickly Jeannie moved for a woman of her size and how lucky he was to have such a combination of speed and strength in his corner. Then, he thought, in her condition, Jeannie really should not be exerting herself unduly.

ABOUT THE AUTHOR

Matthew F. Jones was born in Boston and grew up in upstate New York. He attended Hartwick College, Boston University, and the Syracuse University School of Law, from which he graduated magna cum laude. He was an attorney, for twelve years in both the private and public sector. He currently resides in Charlottesville, Virginia, with his wife and son.